A Naxal Story...

A Naxal Story...

Diptendra Raychaudhuri

Vitasta

Vitasta Publishing Pvt. Ltd.
New Delhi

Published by
Renu Kaul Verma for
Vitasta Publishing Pvt. Ltd.
2/15, Ansari Road, Daryaganj,
New Delhi - 110 002

ISBN   978-81-89766-31-3
© Diptendra Raychaudhuri 2010
Reprint 2010

Cover Design and Layout by Vitasta Publishing Pvt. Ltd.
Printed by Repro India Ltd., Mumbai

A Note from the Author

The dividing wall between fact and fiction is a thin one and often it wavers in a way that fact becomes fiction and fiction becomes fact. This is more so if the land itself lies in myths, believes in magic, and is often shrouded in mysteries. It is not strange that in such a land the nature or even hue of an ideology changes and acquires a particular twang so different from what it is conceived as elsewhere!

The book follows closely the genesis and developments of the Maoist movement of the last century, from the days of Charu Mazumdar (late 60s) to the time when big groups started merging (end of the century). Some renowned personalities, as well a few real incidents are mentioned in the book, but they have only referential presence. Many other incidents, killings by the police or the landlords' army or by the Maoists, kidnapping of high government officers and so on appear in the book with names of place and characters changed. This was necessary to fit those in with the main story line. The organizations named here, or many of the characters (the Maoists as well as police officers, landlords or politicians) may have varying degree of resemblance with the reality, but the matter ends there. The rest is pure fiction.

The main story (portions with the sub-heading 'The Present Continuous') starts in 1981 and ends in 1996, but to comprehend the reality, the book goes back (Glimpses of the Past) to 1940–80 and comes forward (Glimpses of the Future) to 1999–2000.

Indebtedness

Shri Biplab Chakrabarty
Late Harinarayan Adhikari
Late G V Nayar
Comrade Rabi-da
Bisakha De Sarkar
Ditro, my son who insisted that the protagonist should have a son, and
Those comrades and police officers,
Whom I cannot name.

PART I
Waiting for the Doom

1

The Present Continuous (1982)...

SILHOUETTED AGAINST the fading light of dusk at a remote hamlet, the man is often seen standing like a statue, creating an impression that he has arisen after his funeral by disowning the dilemmas and desperations, worries and expectations that pass for life.

The man, tall and dark with sharp slit brown eyes, sports a set of dusty, darned olive green uniform that seems to pride itself on his dirty, dog-eared shoes. A beret with a big hole near the temple perfectly matches the double-barrel gun with a bandaged butt hanging from his shoulder, as though to buttress the point that he is a poor imitation of a professional soldier.

He comes to the hamlet that lies between a range of bald hillocks and a rivulet without notice, sometimes alone and sometimes accompanied by a few comrades in uniform, spends a day or two, converses with the locals, takes a secret meeting with a chosen few, reads out booklets, or settle accounts. And then he slinks off through the hills and jungles like a cheetah.

The locals look at him with awe, except a few women, in whose enamoured eyes flash a bizarre fit of passion. The women, either aborigine tribeswomen or Hindu Harijans, do not hide it, for they have not learnt to hide the colours of passion, be it love or hate. But the elders—the men and women who have lived the stories of many upheavals, of the droughts that burnt their fortunes, the epidemics that killed their souls, or the money-lenders who robbed them of everything they had—warn them with a grim foreboding: "Don't try to litter him with your ugly bodies; he is our messiah... the only hope for us!"

In this land of hundreds of gods and god-men, he seems to be a strange sort of messiah. He talks of overthrowing the system, of creating 'free zones' and 'guerrilla squads', of annihilating the moneylenders and the police officers as the 'class enemy'. The villagers believe this 'messiah', who is neither young nor old, will never fail, though they know nothing about him, except that he is a Naxalite called Mahendra, by caste a Chamar, an Untouchable. That his head carries a bounty of thousands of rupees is as irrelevant to them as the opulence of the big cities.

The villagers cannot recall exactly how many years ago the messiah came here, for they cannot count. Yet, they can tell anyone the exact timing in their own way: "He came to Kalipura during the year when the drought was so severe that even the skies burned, the earth became stone and the mighty rivers turned dry. When our souls too were smouldering, he came to lead us to our own kingdom." This is something anyone in the proximity of the Magadh-Bhojpur region of Bihar can easily follow.

The villagers vividly remember how on that day he was looking desultorily at them, as though he was a *mussafir*, though a beret-wearing one with a gun, the butt of which was not bandaged then. It was late afternoon and the harassing sun was going down towards the horizon, nonchalantly promising another fiery spell the next day. He approached through the fields filled with pebbles and shrubs, and then he stopped, scratched his spiky week-old stubble and looked steadfastly at the ramshackle huts and hovels where men and women walked in skeletons.

The villagers were scared, for their eyes were glued to the gun hanging from his shoulder. The women, their hair uncombed, skin giving off dry dirt, shoddy saris tattered, went hurriedly back to their cottages dragging along with them the children suffering from a spleen disease that made them pot-bellied, and the hens that laid precious eggs. The men, their bare bodies showing purulent abscesses and scabies, wore a grim contrite expression, though they had not done anything wrong. They were scared, but curious. They had seen men with guns before, but those were forward caste men before whom they cowered. But this man, despite his remarkable height, looked downtrodden; must be an Untouchable or a Backward caste man.

They waited tentatively without daring to disturb the tense equilibrium. The tall man took the gun off his shoulder, an act that made the villagers flinch, and then asked, "Where is Baguna Oraon?"

Baguna came running down within a few minutes and exclaimed, "Hey, Comrade, you have really come!"

The villagers were relieved. Since that moment, they too started calling him '*Comret*' with a degree of respect and love that remained unaffected even after knowing that he was a Naxalite, an outlaw. But a few months later, when he tried to galvanize a rebellion that he believed was dormant within their souls, when he spoke of their rights over the land and the jungle, when he made efforts to make them remember their link with the past that had become tenuous, they got confused. They convened the *panchayat* that was held on a night of no moon with clouds hiding the stars and a stormy wind whistling in their midst.

"He has come to lead us to a new life," a short dark man with stubby nose claimed. He was a Munda tribesman named Bhola. As the others kept looking, he explained, "There will be a revolution. No one will be able to dupe us, bully us, or play with the honour of our women, if we follow him."

Then Baguna came forward: "It has happened in many countries. In China."

"Where is China?" someone asked.

"Far away. Across the Himalayas," explained Sunder Besra, a Maoist belonging to the Santhal tribe.

That was too far to inspire the common aborigines, and after a long silence someone asked, "Will he succeed?"

"Why not? Haven't you heard our tales that talk of a liberator who will lead us to our own kingdom?" Bhola tried to be decisive.

Still, not everybody was convinced. "Will Indira Gandhi support it?" asked Kailash who years back had attended a rally addressed by the then Prime Minister and had since developed the habit of dropping her name whenever and wherever a remote chance appeared. However, to this, Mahendra retorted with a smile: "Indira Gandhi? No. But President Nixon may. He loves China."

No one had anything to say to that as they had not heard of any Nixon.

Yet, there were questions and feigned thoughtfulness, forcing the head of the village to postpone the meeting till the next evening to seek unanimity. The villagers then lined up and moved their body in time to the wild beats of the drums. An hour later, they attended the community feast that always followed a *panchayat*, ate the meat of a deer hunted by the youngsters, and drank as much rice-beer as they could.

Several hours later, at the fag end of the night, a dream, an overwhelming and lingering dream descended over every roof, penetrating the sombre sleep of all the locals, keeping them awestruck for a long while and then waking them up slowly with hope and bewilderment. It was an exception after the endless nights of nightmares that made them look run-down.

The wives got up, looked at the husbands and asked, "Have you seen what I have seen?"

The husbands nodded, looked outside, and like driven by some inexplicable spirit, walked slowly out of their huts, only to find the others appearing in the open.

Just then the cocks crowed, and the first refractions of light from a primordial fireball brightened up the peak of the highest hill known as the 'abode of the spirits'. The villagers looked at the brightened peak and their hearts started throbbing, for they recollected an old adage: 'a dream at the end of the night is bound to be true'.

A while later, squatting at the centre of the hamlet they looked at each other, but said nothing, while Mangu the drumbeater took up his *dhamsa* and started beating it.

"Someday it will be our rule, and we will have land... we will own land... that's what I saw in my dream, and that's what the drum is telling us now," the first man opened up apprehensively.

"True," the next man said.

Another man declared, "I saw... the jungles would be ours again."

It was the day of Sarhul, the day of worshipping the Sal tree, and the ceremony started. The *pahan*, an Oraon tribesman, built human figures with mud at the foot of the tallest Sal tree, offered it flowers, sweets and incensed green powder. The women, almost each one of them in a shoddy red-bordered white sari, sat in a circle about the *pahan*, their hearts content with the dream still haunting them. After completing the puja, the *pahan* asked a young woman in Oraon language, "*Chikan bana mai batda, hurum sukhu biure tan* (What have you brought that attracts the honeybees)?"

It was a part of the ritual held every year, and the woman was supposed to say, 'Sal flowers'; but that year, the woman answered, "A dream in the form of Sal flowers."

Many hours later, when the sun sank behind the hillocks and the shadows fell, the villagers came back to settle the question hanging on their heads. But there was nothing to decide anymore, as there was no dissenting voice, no question, no confusion; the dream had settled it for once and for all, enabling everybody to extrapolate the imminent victory. In the *panchayat,* they just dedicated their bodies and souls to the '*Comret*', who would lead them to their own kingdom.

"Nobody will arrest us for taking anything from the jungle," stated a villager.

"And we will be paid proper wages, won't we?" another one, whose emaciated face looked like a skeleton, asked.

"Sure. Who wouldn't pay? We will fix the wage."

"Then fix it at five rupees per day."

Now Mahendra intervened: "The minimum statutory wage for eight hours of work is Rs 25, cash and kind combined."

The villagers were awestruck, and they tried to imagine how much money they would then earn in a month if they get work for 15 days. It was an intricate multiplication, so Mahendra came forward and uttered the figure. The sum humbled the villagers, who sat quietly and contemplated what they could buy with that much of money, an amount that they had never seen. After a few minutes, someone said, "Soon enough there will be money to buy a bicycle."

The villagers were excited as they took that as the first step towards liberation. "When we worked in the road project last year, the contractor did not give us any money. Only one and a half kilo of wheat for one man and one kilo for a woman," sighed someone.

"It will change," Mahendra intervened. "But, be cautious. A dream is a dream; to translate it into reality one has to dedicate one's mind, one's life and, at times, even the dream itself."

His audience heard him with confusion, cut quick glances at each other, and decided to sit silently in silhouettes like faceless entities.

Mahendra waited for an inquisitive one to come up with a question, but when none risked it, he said, "Nothing changes overnight. It takes time. Many years, perhaps. You will have to be bold and will have to fight." He made efforts to prepare them for a long-drawn battle, explained to them how any drastic step could be dangerous, as well as despicable, and reminded them of their actual condition in his characteristic style, "*Hamar to aage kuan piche khain* (We are caught between the well and the gorge)." At the end, he added, his face still taut, "Someday we will win. Just remember that we are fighting for our freedom and honour."

That was too luring for the Dusadhs or Chamars, both known as Harijan or Untouchables, or tribesmen like Santhals, Mundas, Oraons and Kurmis, who often rued their lost glory as depicted in their age-old myths. Mahendra also lent them a slogan to assimilate them to what he described as the ongoing rebellion: "Power flows from the barrel of the gun."

Though the villagers knew it by their conventional wisdom—one who wields the stick takes away the buffaloes—it was now reinforced as they found men with guns among them.

That night, Baguna asked Mahendra, "Comrade, are you a magician? Otherwise…"

Before he could proceed further, Mahendra posed a question to him, "Did you see the dream that the others saw?" As Baguna shook his head, Mahendra explained, "You didn't because you are with us for a couple of years now. For them, it all came like a big jolt. The dream was always in their subconscious mind… it surfaced in their sleep."

"But they feel you are a god who can send dreams…"

"Explain to them later," Mahendra whispered. "Maybe after a year."

Over time, the dream began to spread, from one village to another, from one region to the other, making people believe that once the dream turned into reality, they would have a plateful of meal twice a day, would have cure for diseases and a steady means of livelihood.

Now, after a few years since he arrived at Kalipura, Mahendra goes about a much larger area, and tries to ignite the hearts of the people of those lands so that the dream overwhelms them too. In the invincible dark of the lingering nights, he conveys the same message to faraway places, to the tribesmen, to the Harijans and the Backwards. Often he addresses a small gathering even in the daytime, but only in a remote area. "This land, the rivers and the forests… all belong to you," he tells his audience. "You will pluck *kendu* leaves from the jungles, defy the contractors and the government… make and sell bidi… and make *kattha* from the catechu tree whenever you wish. Acquire anything from the forest. All these belong to you, and to no one else's father. And in the bazaar, we will fix the price of our products. The middlemen pay you less than even one-tenth of the price at which they sell it to the shopkeepers. Now you should fix the price. No one has the right to stop you. You till the land and no one can evict you."

They chant at the end "Long live Charu Majumdar" without knowing who they are referring to, probably mistaking him for a god. Someone among them, an inquisitive type, may dare to ask, "Who is this Charu Majumdar?"

"He was the first great leader of Indian Maoists," Mahendra replies.

"*Mar chuka ka* (Is he dead)?"

As Mahendra nods, someone else asks, "And what is that Maoist thing?"

"Mao Tse Tung was a great leader of China who taught us how to fight against the oppressors. He taught us how we can overpower the big cities by surrounding them from the villages. We follow him and call ourselves Maoists."

With time, a few young persons are selected as '*comrets*' for the armed squad and a handful, mostly aged, for the political wing. Mahendra strains to explain that the political wing is more important; but the younger lot looks unimpressed as for them guns and uniforms are the most sought-after things, the magical objects standing for pride and power.

For the comrades, Mahendra remains an enigma, showing up suddenly for a day, holding secret meetings, redistributing responsibilities, reading a newspaper that says 'Prince Charles has married Lady Diana', and then vanishing again. But, once in a while, in an odd dark night, a daring young man comes and sits beside Mahendra with a question: "Comrade, how long will it take for the conflagration?"

Fixing his gaze at the stars, Mahendra smiles indifferently, and chants in Sanskrit: "*Karmanye vadhikaraste, ma phaleshu kadachana.*"

The comrade does not understand a word and gapes at the leader.

"That was what Krishna, the God, told Arjuna," explains Mahendra. "You have right to work only, but no right to its outcome. We don't believe in God, but the concept is applicable to us... Have you read the *Mahabharata*? Do you know reading and writing?"

The comrade shakes his head slowly.

Mahendra seems worried. "You must learn it. I will arrange for that."

If the same question comes from a close associate, like Comrade Karma, the man whom Mahendra has given independent charge of the Garwa region, he answers, "Actually, it will be many, many decades before we reach a meaningful stage. I hope our impact will be felt two decades from now, in the new millennium. By then, we will probably be able to rule a large chunk of rural area, but only during the night. Even that will come after the loss of many more innocent lives, many more tragedies…"

For a moment, Mahendra seems upset, and he intently looks towards the dark horizon. But soon he recovers to carry on. "When I address the ordinary men, I never tell them how far the revolution is. I do it deliberately, for I know if you believe you are weak, you will cower before all those you feel are strong. But if you believe you are strong and capable, you will fight." He breaks into a pause to formulate a thesis, and avers, "You are what you believe you are."

Comrade Karma too looks at the dark horizon, as though the thoughts have wings and they come down from there, and asks, "You said we are what we believe we are?"

"Yes," nods Mahendra. "People believe in God. At a very young age, I heard someone telling me that God has created castes and human beings cannot overrule them. She told me that being born as an Untouchable Chamar, I would have to cower before the highborn lot for the whole of my life." He looks at the sky where thousands of stars have formed a canopy of light in a moonless night, sighs deeply and continues, "I decided to defy God… It may take a hundred years or even more. Maybe centuries. The gods will retaliate repeatedly. But we are sure to defeat the gods who have created castes, poverty and inequality. For that you have to have faith in yourself. That is why I say, you are what you believe you are."

Karma ponders for a while and then asks, "But if really we are what we believe we are, why can't we overthrow the system now?"

Mahendra again looks at the skies, and mutters, "Nothing happens before time. The sun cannot rise in the midnight or set at noon." He sounds distant and lonely, dwelling in a different world where others' efforts, thoughts, beliefs, or imaginations cannot reach him. He then sits silently, his eyes riveted at the sky from where a distant voice comes back to haunt him: "You have a long way to go. You will challenge the gods and the gods will retaliate... and at the end, you will be able to see through the stones." He does not know what is meant by seeing through the stones; but he knows well that the gods have already retaliated.

LOOKING STEADFASTLY at the distant hills and jungles, the abode of snakes and snails along with gods and demons, Sister Lillian feels she has changed a lot. The magic of the surroundings has cast a spell on her and has smoothed the rough edges of her mind away, curing her of an old hurt.

The world is ruled by magic. That is what the tribesmen living around her in this land of hills and jungles believe. The belief is sneaking into her mind, and as belief is something that cannot be wiped out by reason, she has drawn her own conclusion: reality is often tweaked by many such absurdities, making life simpler to live.

Beyond the jungle, a range of hills fades as a distinct reality as grey clouds envelope them. Looking at that dark horizon from the roof of a school building, the nun feels her whole life has remained under different spells of magic; brutal to begin with, smoother but austere later, soothing and placid now. What next, she does not know.

After darkness, according to the locals, the jungle goes under the control of the ghosts and the bandits. Lillian is not sure of the existence of ghosts, but she knows for sure that in this land, the bandits are a rare species for there is nothing they can loot from the locals.

She thinks of herself, and soon her thoughts digress to the significance of the word 'magic'. Many of the locals believe everything—words, looks or clothes—manifests itself through magic that attracts, distracts, enrages, pacifies, and prompts to love or hate or even kill. "And that is not a thesis to be ruled out," she tells herself and goes on weaving her thoughts. "Maybe the world is actually ruled by magic, a fact that those who left the jungles hundreds and thousands of years ago have forgotten; and these people will also forget decades later, as they are winkled out from the forests everywhere."

She has reasons to believe in it.

There was a time when, broken by an experience that had crippled her mind and soul at a tender age, she rabidly hated men. Her hatred was so strong that it bothered her even as a schoolteacher in Calcutta, where she had to mingle with the parents of the wards, her colleagues and the authority, at least half of whom were always men. She could never overcome her suspicion that those men were actually wearing a mask which hid Joseph the elder's face. She feared that the mask would suddenly fall off and Joseph would reappear with his 'weapon'. She was only 14 when Joseph, the physical training teacher in a school in Panaji, made her a regular victim of his weapon, a long, dark, erect rod hidden inside his trousers, a horrendous and hideous spike that hurt her and bled her severely. Each time after his cruelty, he would threaten her that if she revealed it to anybody, she would not only face expulsion from the school, but also ex-communication of her entire family.

There was no escape from him until Jesus answered her prayers and Joseph the elder was found lying on the beach—the famous Calangute beach—with his neck broken. He had drunk beer to his heart's content and then gone into the sea, and a big wave that Lillian believed God sent to save her did the rest. He died, but left behind a bitter memory in the mind of a young girl who was slender, green-eyed, beautiful and fair like the Europeans, for she had in her European blood. Her father, Pedro Gonzalez, was a Portuguese who had left India just before the Indians drove them away from Goa, where he had lived for 20 years and had married a local woman. Lillian was born in Panaji, and was the third among the three daughters of the couple. Her father never came back, forcing her mother to move into a cheap accommodation in a semi-rural area and fend for herself, expecting till the last day of her life that her husband would come back. Her two elder daughters were dark like Konkanis and inherited nothing of their father except the title Gonzalez; but the third, Lillian, took after her father. Her mother was always extra careful about her—aware as she was of the hankering of Indian males for white skin—but she never knew that a man nearing 40 had already 'doomed' her.

After Joseph's death, Lillian became deeply pious as she believed God had liberated her from the demon. She decided that she would never marry, be a nun, and would dispense her life for the service of God who was so gracious to her. Her mother died a few years later. By that time, Lillian's hatred towards men was becoming explicit. Young men with good youthful intentions were making advances, which were normal and expected, but every such gesture infuriated her. However, a year later—when she landed in Calcutta as a nun—her attire prompted the boys of the city to keep a safe distance from her. She was a student of Loreto College which was exclusively for women, and there she met Agnes Murmu, a Santhal tribal girl orphaned in her childhood, and the duo made a perfect match in contrast: Lillian was fair, tall, timid, urban and an introvert, while Agnes was dark, short, bold, rustic and an extrovert. The only thing common between them was English, which was their medium of education and in which only they could converse with each other.

Agnes was a daring girl, who lost her temper with all sorts of injustice, and this added a trait of bellicosity in her character. Once, when Lillian and Agnes were in a Delhi hotel, a drunken young man burst into their room all of a sudden. Lillian was scared, but Agnes immediately took up a knife and growled, "Just get lost. Otherwise, I will chop off your thing, dry it and will keep it hanging on my door along with a lemon and chilli."

They burst into laughter when the intruder fled, holding his thing tight over his trouser. "What is this lemon and chilli you talked of?" asked Lillian.

"Haven't you seen those in North Indian houses… dried up lemons and green chillies hanging from the door-tops? Those are for scaring away evil forces."

"I see. But I never knew you are so fluent in Hindi."

"I was brought up by Sister Vimla who was a North Indian," Agnes replied casually.

After passing out from Loreto College, and then from the University of Calcutta, Lillian was directed to join a school as a teacher, while Agnes, who was not a nun, joined a welfare organization linked with the Church. For the first few years, Agnes worked in Calcutta. Then she took to going out for short periods. Then the period of her disappearance increased and often she was out for a few weeks together. After one such period of what Lillian described as 'underground life', she appeared in the teacher's hostel with a definite purpose, to persuade Lillian to join a school which was coming up in the district of Hazaribagh in the neighbouring state of Bihar.

It was a rough evening. A severe *kalbaisakhi* that had hit the city in the afternoon uprooted some tall trees, damaged old houses, and the ensuing rain inundated the roads through which buses, taxis and trams could hardly move ahead, allowing only hand-pulled rickshaws some degree of manoeuvrability. Agnes came braving such odds, was drenched but buoyant as she talked about the school. "It will be run by the Church. So, you can easily join it. It's in a remote village. Within 10 kilometres, there is no town, no hospital or doctor, no electricity, and you won't find a road that leads to that village."

"It's so remote!" Lillian was apprehensive.

Without bothering to counter her apprehension, Agnes carried on, "That's not all. Listen. No girl in the locality has ever gone to a school, can you imagine? We will have our school there. Isn't it fascinating?"

"You will be there?" Lillian asked hesitantly.

Agnes took a couple of steps to stand in front of a mirror and nodded, her eyes on her image. She gave Lillian a week's time to decide. "Otherwise someone else will take charge and you will lose the opportunity," she presented it like it was a coveted job. The next moment, she asked for a sari, pointing out that if she did not change, she would be an object to watch on the road. "Even my nipples are showing," she commented, shockingly direct as ever.

Now Lillian was in a dilemma. She had never been to such a remote place, out of the reach of electricity, which was to her, like most urban Indians, synonymous with civilization. She had been to a village in Goa after her father deserted them, but in no sense could that be called remote. Later, for more than a decade, she was in Calcutta where power cuts often continued for hours, but people lived those dark hours with a definite hope of getting light back. What Agnes proposed was, contrarily, a place where a night would be a night in all its pristine form, allowing insects and scorpions or even snakes to hide in any corner of the very room she would be in. She was not a coward, but the uncertainties bogged her down while the enthusiasm shown by Agnes beckoned her. Her Principal Sister came to her aid and advised her to read books about the place before she decided on her future course. "That's the thumb rule," she declared. "Read and note down the major points."

Lillian started her search for relevant books and soon got hold of a dozen. And only then a new horizon opened up before her eyes, a different world about which she was not aware of. The millions of tribal men and women who inhabit that world amidst the jungles and plateaus and hills called it Jharkhand. It was not the name of any actual state or region; it was a dreamland of the tribes living in a large contagious area consisting of three districts of Bengal, entire south Bihar, the Chhattisgarh region of Madhya Pradesh, and parts of Orissa in the south, altogether a large chunk of central-eastern part of India. The tribes demanded a separate state in this land, but the demand was turned down soon after Independence as they did not have a common language.

They could not have a common language, as the tribes only from Bihar were so many: Munda, Oraon, Parhaiya, Santhal, Savar, Banjara, Asur, Baiga, Bedia, Bhumij, Birhor, Chero, Gond, Ho, Kharia, Lohra, Karwar, Khond and so on. The number was much more in Madhya

Pradesh, which was not far from Hazaribagh district, where the school Agnes had talked about was located.

When Agnes came back a week later, the first question Lillian asked was whether the school would be surrounded by the tribesmen.

"Of course yes," Agnes sounded a bit amazed. "Why?"

Lillian's mind was bubbling with questions, and she chose the most obvious one, "Do they still practise black magic?"

Agnes looked at her curiously and retorted, "Do you know I am also a tribal girl, a Santhal?"

"Yes. Yes." Lillian was uncomfortable for a moment, but soon found the point to counter, "But you are a Christian."

"True, but all the tribes believe in what you call black magic. They practise it… of course."

Mousumi, a Hindu Bengali teacher sitting with them, was amazed and shocked, "Black magic! Oh my God. Have you seen it, Agnes?" She expected some weird stories.

"I don't give importance to these things," Agnes said, sounding a bit rude. "But this is no secret. Haven't you seen Hindu Bengali mothers marking the forehead of their children with a black dot so that no one can caste an evil eye on them… *najor na lage jaate*. Don't you do that Mousumi to your daughter?"

"Yes," Mousumi nodded casually, without understanding the relation between her question and this simple practice.

Agnes struck just then, "Doesn't that also belong to the category of black magic? I have also seen mothers biting the small finger of their little kids to protect them from *najor*. Isn't that black magic?"

While Mousumi sat dumbfounded, Lillian said, "Yes. Yes. I have seen the writing at the back of the trucks. *Buri najorwale tera muh kale* (whosoever casts an evil eye would lose his face). It shows the concept of *najor* is everywhere in India."

A month later, Lillian landed in Ranchi, and after staying the night in the office-cum-hostel of their organization on Jail Road, she left for the school with Agnes in a jeep early next morning. They passed through the highway that for sometime went through the plains with thin jungles, then allowed the distant hills to come closer, and again sent them away, and finally jumped up to climb the hills to expose vast valleys before human eyes. After Ramgarh, she felt sleepy and dozed off until they reached Kuju, where she realized the jeep was moving through the jungles, which again cleared up just before Hazaribagh, a big sprawling town. Here they stopped near St. Columbus College for their breakfast. Then they again proceeded towards the school through the jungles, going past the occasional villages that appeared by the side of the road. The jeep finally crossed Padma Gate, where a signboard announced the existence of a training school for the police, and a while later, it left the highway to roll through a narrow road, which soon turned just into a track, on which the jeep barely managed to move through the fields and thin jungles.

"A few kilometres from here and there is a colliery in almost every direction and the Tilaiya barrage is not far away," said Agnes, pointing to the soil, which was reddish in colour, and occasionally ashen.

The school was a two-storey cemented building with six rooms on each floor, a colossal structure by local standard. The dense jungles were at least a kilometre away from the building. Lillian surveyed it from all sides and asked, "Are snakes expected to travel this distance from the jungle?"

Agnes smiled mockingly, "It's nothing. They can travel much more. But don't panic. We have enough carbolic acid."

In the next few hours, many people came to meet her, including the village head, referred to as the *hatu-munda*, and all of them said a lot of things that sounded strange to her ears. A more perplexing statement came a few hours later, in the evening, from Michael the cook, who came and sat at her feet and addressed her as *Memsaab*. "For years I was worried, and the worries gradually took the shape of a hill. But now, as you have come, I am relieved," he mumbled in Hindi.

"How?" Lillian was confused.

"Aren't the mines coming up nearer day by day?" the man sounded bitter. "Someday it will take away everything from us. There will be no land, no jungle... only mines and ashes. Now you have come, you will be able to save Mother Earth." And then, as a veil of mystery shrouded his eyes, he started again, "You save us, *Memsaab*. The mine has an insatiable hunger. It will come and grab everything. Nothing will be saved... Not Barhi, not Chatra, not even this Taslibazar. I try to convince everybody. But nobody listens to me."

From a different culture and a different milieu, still fresh from the city, not comfortable in Hindi, Lillian could not comprehend the man, who seemed fascinatingly elusive. Then Agnes explained it to her, "He is from the mine area near Koderma. His family was evicted from the village where they had lived for God knows how many years. Coal was discovered underground. He settled somewhere else where again coal was discovered. Since then, he has become a psychological case. He believes coal will be found everywhere and everything will be lost."

"But why do they all feel I can do something?"

"Probably because you can."

"What can I do?" Lillian was utterly confused.

"I don't know," Agnes turned enigmatic.

"Come on Agnes. It's you who can. You have a fighting spirit. You have zeal. I lack those qualities and... you know better."

Agnes came closer, put her hand on Lillian's shoulder and whispered, "I was brought up by Sister Vimla. She used to say that those who are quiet, thoughtful and determined, only they can change the world."

Lillian thought for a while and said, "To change the world, one has to understand the world. I cannot understand the world; it is so good and so bad at the same time."

Lillian still remembers her confusion and uneasiness in those initial days, her conversation with Agnes about changing the world, and the horrid impression the first few nights made on her mind. With innumerable bright stars huddled all over, the sky appeared too close, as though preparing to pounce upon the earth. But after spending many months in this locality, she now knows that stars only seem bigger and brighter and are seen in much more number in this place where no artificial lamp distorts the pristine darkness. She has inured herself to the situation in which she has to run a school where pupils walk down five or six kilometres to reach it, and disappear whenever scope of any employment arises. She has realized that one's heart rebels and goads one to leave the new and unpleasant place until the brain sends it a definite instruction that it has to be where it is. And then, slowly, one's heart adjusts and develops a sort of love for the place.

And the magic that the locals believe rules the world is now casting a colourful spell on her. But she still has a lot many problems to solve. She had earlier taught in Calcutta where even children coming to the school at the age of four or five knew English words such as 'good morning', 'thank you,' 'father', 'mother', 'aunty' or 'my name is…'. But here she has not come across any adult who knows these words. An urban child starts from a point where these local children may not reach even after years of schooling, and the gap will only increase with more years in the school. Even the adults here cannot read or write, do not know why the sky is blue, or what is the freezing point of water, forget about what is photosynthesis. Lillian does not know how to bring these children at par with those who are culturally far, far ahead; but she is trying hard to find the answer.

"This is probably the beginning of your understanding of the world," Agnes told her a few days ago when she had broached the topic with her. "I have also seen what you have seen here, but that particular question never came to my mind. But this is an obvious question: how to bring these children at par with those in the cities?"

"But what is the answer? What do you feel?" Lillian asked rather impatiently.

Agnes shook her head. "When you have the question in your mind, someday you will find the answer. I don't think I can help…

I thought we must build a school and teach the local children." She uttered every word thoughtfully, as though a wrong word would make the whole thesis come clattering down. "So I insisted that you come here. My initiative ended there. I don't know how to bridge the gap you are talking of. Opening schools is a step towards that. But what do we do after that? You have a vision. You will get the answer. That will help all of us."

But Lillian does not feel she has any vision, for she always remains confused, like she has been left alone in a dark dense jungle and does not know where to go, how to trudge along the path, or how to get out of it. Unmindfully, she turns to the other side, and leaning on the four feet high wall on the roof, she notices Michael the cook. He is going somewhere with Padma, a tribal woman who grudges her old age, as otherwise she could have earned much more by providing 'company' to the middlemen, or the contractors, or their debauched sons. Lillian's eyes follow the duo while she wonders where they are heading to when it looks like it is going to rain heavily. As she looks back to see the rain clouds spread almost overhead, another thought crosses her mind, a thought that does not concern the world, the surroundings, or the pervasiveness of magic, but only her own self. She feels she too has the right to live a normal life, away from the haunting shadow of Joseph the elder. For that, she needed a place where she was insulated from her past. She feels she has found the place; it is Taslibazar, which has helped her change, maybe for the local males here do not evoke in her mind the hatred she once had towards all men.

"I have already learnt to live like the others, learnt to live a normal life," she tells herself. A while later, as the birds perched in the nearby trees fall silent, as a streak of lightning accentuates the darkness, as pure magic takes over the world, she decides to go downstairs.

AT TIMES, when he puts his feet up and ruminates, Ashok Sharma enjoys the sobriquet 'Romantic Cobra' coined for him by his colleagues.

In Hazaribagh, the district where he is on his second posting as Superintendent of Police, Sharma has so ruthlessly contained the criminals and has come down so heavily on corrupt elements that he has turned into a terror for those on the wrong side of the fence. He enjoys that. And now, after spending three years in the district, he has enough time to carry on his old habit of writing poetry in Hindi, many of which have found place in leading magazines of Patna and Allahabad.

He knows people in his profession envy his courage, fear his honesty, and that has earned him his nickname; they call him 'romantic' because he is a poet and 'cobra' because he is swift in his operations and unwavering before imminent danger.

Today, as he reclines on an easy chair in the lawn of his bungalow and looks up at the evening sky, his mind meanders through another side, the flip side of his life. Courage, his mantra of life, brought him and his wife together, but has not been able to keep them together.

He met her in Calcutta, the city from where he had done his Bachelors and Masters and had appeared for the administrative service examination. He clearly remembers that bright sunny morning when he was travelling to Barrackpore through BT Road. The road was dusty, damaged and narrowed down to half with the rest encroached upon from both sides by garages, shops and hovels for dwelling; but vehicles managed to move on in the absence of much traffic in those days. However, at a place near Barrackpore, the traffic came to a sudden halt. As he peeked through the window, he saw a policeman beating up someone whose shrill cry sounded like a woman's wailing. He could not see the victim because of a crowd of silent and apparently indifferent spectators. Ashok got down from the bus and found a police officer beating a woman, a poor rice seller, by holding her hair in one hand, slapping her on the face, and even twisting her breast, not so much for sexual pleasure as to inflict pain. The woman shrieked and then started crying loudly.

For a moment, he felt so bewildered that he gaped on, while a woman, young and beautiful, certainly from the upper middle class, protested loudly, all alone. Ashok went to join her, but the police team showed no interest in them, like they were adolescents prone to be affected by the disease of fighting injustice. Just then, a middle-aged officer jumped down from an Army truck, went straight to the police officer and kicked him from behind so badly that he fell straight on his nose. The police officer, a hefty man with bushy moustache, recovered quickly and with a filthy abuse that came out from his mouth like a thunder looked back with fire in his eyes. But the fire got somewhat tempered as he saw the man in uniform. His look changed, his eyes reflected bewilderment that gradually turned into fear; though he tried to hold his fort and barked angrily, this time in a language that apparently seemed English, "What is this? What are you?"

"Apologize to her," the Army officer ordered, his voice calm and low. Thereafter, he actually forced the policeman to do so by touching the rice seller's feet while the audience watched the scene in silence, their faces betraying elation.

The Army officer then thanked the two who had protested, and advised them to hire a cab to proceed to Barrackpore.

In the taxi, for the first time, they talked to each other, and he, then a young trainee IPS officer, came to know that the bold and beautiful woman's name was Rani, literally Queen, and her title was Bannerjee, and that she had just joined the Medical College. That was 1966. They got married six years later when she completed her MBBS, but the marriage did not go down well with his conservative Maithili Brahmin family that owned a huge tract of land in the Darbhanga district of eastern Bihar. They thought he had betrayed them by choosing a bride who was neither Hindi-speaking nor prepared to be confined to their home like all other *bahus* of the family. He walked out of the family house, but even his own small family is trifurcated now; he is in Hazaribagh, she is in Patna and their daughter, only nine years old, is in a residential school in a hill-city in northernmost Bengal called Kalimpong, where his father-in-law also resides these days.

"Saab," an orderly who has appeared by his side calls him from a little distance.

The Romantic Cobra misses it as he remains engrossed in his thoughts. He would have liked his daughter to be with him, but is prepared to accept that she has to be in a boarding school in the neighbouring state for the sake of academics, as the education system in Bihar is in shambles. But his wife, Dr Mrs Rani Sharma, could have come along with him and joined the local government hospital, but Rani never sought a transfer from Patna. She runs a TB camp on her off days at a place about 20 kilometres from the city and is not inclined to accept any transfer either.

"Saab," the orderly is louder this time.

As the Romantic Cobra turns to him, he says, "Someone wants to meet you," and hands him a card that reads 'Hari Pratap Singh, Managing Director, Puraina Haveli group of industries'. He nods to the orderly and wonders why an MD would like to meet him.

A while later, as he sees someone coming straight towards him, he gets up from the easy-chair, but lingers at the same spot. The stranger, who is in his 40s, introduces himself as Harry Singh, instead of Hari Pratap Singh. It makes his name sound like a fusion, for Harry is an English name while Singh is an Indian title used by a huge spectrum of people, Sikhs as well as Hindu Rajputs and many other castes.

"How can I help you?" Ashok asks courteously as he looks at the man in an expensive suit, his tie almost constricting his neck and his shoes shinning even in the fading light of the afternoon.

Harry Singh composes himself and then says in a fervent tone in English, "I have come to request you to perform your duty."

Taken aback, the SP shows him in to his bungalow, and after being seated in the couch, asks, "What duties you are talking about?"

"That's why I have come here," Harry Singh says confidently in English. "This is what I am preaching to all your officers. I am knocking at their doors for years… for justice."

"Justice? But that's a court's job," Ashok Sharma too switches to English.

"Only when you nab a culprit. You have failed so far to do so." Harry turns his gaze away from the SP and looks at the carpet on the floor intently. "I am an industrialist," he announces a while later. "Not a very big one. But I have several factories with a few thousand workers. I know some big shots, leaders and officers. Of no good…"

Is he going to request for something related to an industrial problem, like a strike, Ashok wonders.

"Coming to the point," Harry Singh continues without shifting his gaze from the carpet, "I want justice for some ghastly killings… of my father, my uncle, my two elder brothers, and my eldest brother's son who was barely 16-year old. Seven years back… this is January 1982, and that was December 1975… they were killed in Puraina, our native village."

"I know," Ashok nods. He was the DSP of a distant district in those days and it was the time of 'internal emergency' in the country, a critical time that prompted the police department to underplay the incident and show it as a feud over land between the landlord and low castes.

"But why did they kill them?" Ashok asks. "The motive remained a mystery."

The other man retorts grimly, "Not at all. They were killed only because they belonged to an upper caste landlord family."

"That's all?" Ashok tries to clear the air of confusion. "We have seen Naxalites killing the upper castes elsewhere, but those are direct fallouts of land dispute or retaliatory killings."

"No such things happened in Puraina," Harry's voice sounds shrill. "Two or three Naxalites were killed a couple of months before that, but our family was not involved."

"No involvement at all?"

"Not at all," Harry says in a resolute tone. "I know, because I belong to that family. We had no enmity with those who struck at us. The killers, belonging to the Naxalite gang of Mahendra Chamar, are yet to be brought before the court."

"But, as far I know, three of them were arrested and the trial is still…"

"Small fries," Harry thunders brusquely, and then looking at Ashok Sharma, he explains, "They are landless labourers, some disgruntled elements who had joined them. Of course, they too should be hanged." He waves his hand and adds, now in Hindi, "But the real devil, the Chamar, is still at large."

Ashok leans back on his couch, looks at the expansive lawn lit by lamps on the boundary wall, and speaks softly, "I understand why you have come to me. This gang is active... in Gaya and Hazaribagh districts."

"And also in Palamu and Garwa."

Ashok thinks for a while, a frown appears on his face, and he shakes his head. "Right. Probably Palamu is also under the Red Salute group of Comrade Mahendra."

"Mahendra Chamar," Harry snorts exasperatedly to correct the cop. "Even that is repugnant. A low born Chamar's name cannot be Mahendra, which literally means Indra the great, you know. Indra is the king of the gods and a Chamar cannot be named after him."

"As for Palamu," Ashok decides to carry on ignoring the venom the other man has spewed. "Comrade Karma and Dipak... maybe a separate group, maybe same group. Whatever, none of these gangs is potentially dangerous. But of course, we are trying to finish them off, particularly Mahendra. They had killed policemen and looted arms..."

"I want justice," Harry sounds like a haunted man repeating a same set of words. Then he looks at his watch and says, "I had just 10 minutes, and I utilized the opportunity to meet you. I heard your colleagues describe you as a Romantic Cobra. I want to see whether this cobra is real. Goodbye."

As Harry leaves, Ashok Sharma wonders whether this man, who is outlandish but sombre, has actually challenged him and his mantra of life. A moment later, he feels that having lost so many dear ones, the man must be very lonely. As minutes pass by, the feeling of loneliness turns into an invisible bond between them, and Ashok Sharma mutters to himself, "I will show you that the cobra is real."

2

Glimpses of the Future (1999–2000)

HAPPY TO be still alive, Karma wakes up in a clammy room with a corner of its floor glistening with intruding sun rays slithering down from a hole in the roof.

It is a regular drill for him; to go to bed with the dread that he will be condemned to darkness forever, and waking up the next morning with a sense of relief. He hates to die in the dark, in a dingy room where a bullet will not penetrate his body, where the comrades will not utter their 'red salute' to his dead ears, where he will have no claim to 'martyrdom'.

"It has been many months since a comrade came to see me," he thinks as he looks on at the broken ceiling from where a small chunk of tile has fallen off. Then he remembers that today is the last day of 1999. That was what Lillian told him last night. "So, it is six months since Comrade Raul visited me," he mutters to himself, "but to me it seems years."

A sparrow enters the room through the window and approaches a spot not far from his bed for a few tiny crumbs of *roti*. As it gleans those, swiftly turning its whole body right and left, he watches it while wondering why the room has turned so clammy. Suddenly, the streak of sunbeam sneaking in from the roof disappears, bringing to his mind the fact that it was drizzling the night before. "A drizzle in the winter," he thinks to himself, "means the fields will be juicy, but the cold will be severe."

"Wake up and wash your mouth," says Lillian as she enters the room with *roti* and tea. "A young woman will come to meet you today."

"Meet me!… Who?" He asks as he gets up.

"A young writer," Lillian puts down the aluminium plate and two steel cups. "She is planning to write a book on the Maoists who she believes are shadows in the jungles. I told her that she could meet at least one such shadow."

He comes out of the room, brushes his teeth with a twig of neem tree and washes his face as he thinks about Lillian, the former nun, a middle-aged demure person who looks like a European.

Lillian and he had lived their lives separately, he among the Maoists and Lillian among the priests and priestesses and teachers. But when he felt rejected by the world soon after a doctor told him that he was suffering from an incurable disease that would kill him slowly, he left the hospital to come to Lillian. He knew she had left the Church and was living here.

The young doctor treating him in the government hospital had said, "Your disease is akin to something that we call myalgic encephalomyelitis. But it is not exactly that. You will not recover from this, and as days will pass, you will feel tired and exhausted. The lungs also seem to be affected and that has complicated the whole thing." His voice was grim and face sodden with sadness, a clear sign of resignation that prompted Karma to ask, "Do you think I will die soon? Tell me the truth. That's very important for me."

The doctor shook his head and whispered, "May not be so soon. You may still live a few years if you take the medicine."

The next day, Karma walked out of the hospital with the prescription in his hand, without any formalities like a discharge certificate, and nobody bothered, as disappearance of patients is quite common in government hospitals.

But even after walking out of the hospital, he did not know where he would go. He boarded a train from Gaya, a passenger train that stops at every station, and when it halted at Pusauli, he got down. From there, he could have headed for his base, but with his exhausted body and shattered mind, he decided to go towards Ghosi. From there, he reached this village on a tractor that ferried passengers.

"I have decided to die here," he told Lillian, without realizing how shocking it was for her who did not even know about his illness.

She has never shown any sign of annoyance for such an intrusion by him in her life, but has looked after him like any other ordinary woman of Hindustan, loyal to the core, even hampering her own work.

"I did not know that I would trouble you so much, Lillian," he utters in contrition as he enters the room, imagining Lillian is inside. But she is not there, and his words are lost in vacuum like seeds spilled on barren land. When she returns a while later, and sits down with him to eat, he does not repeat his words.

Later, left alone in the room, he sits beside the window quietly. Gradually, the present begins to evanesce from his eyes and he starts his journey with Comrade Rudra, a Maoist from Nepal who took him across the border from West Bengal, across a river called Mechi, to a village near Pathri. He knows what he is watching is a repeat of something that happened more than a year ago, but it unfolds in a way like it is happening again in the present. "Why do the past and present get mingled up like tea and sugar in my head," he asks himself. He has asked himself the same question for innumerable times. Being unable to find an answer, he has already assumed that time does not only flow in one and the known direction, from past to present. At times, it also goes in reverse, like the tide and ebb in a river near the sea.

He finds himself looking again at the Bhedetar hill. Up there, the royal soldiers are pacing up and down in a bright and beautiful morning, and he shudders to see them there, for the hill is hardly a couple of kilometres away. "It's so close, and Comrade, your armed squads are here," he cringes. "I feel they can easily target you."

He went to Nepal to see how the 'people's war' declared by the Nepali Maoists was advancing during its third year, and after reaching the village near Pathri and spending the night in a hut—it was cold even in the spring—they went westward, often trekking through the hilly jungles, crossing streams and brooks on foot, and sometimes forcing a lift from a four-wheeler. They stopped in the evening in a remote village, and pointing to the silhouette of a hill that did not seem to him to be far off, Comrade Rudra said, "That's the Bhedetar hill. They have camps there, so we avoid it. But someday, we will capture the hill for there is a telecom tower there."

A few comrades appeared in the night and introduced themselves as workers of the Kirat Party, a frontal organization of the Nepalese Maoists. Comrade Rudra explained, "They are either Rais or Limboos… warrior tribes. Earlier, they were with the parliamentary communists, who call themselves Marxist-Leninist party."

"In India, you call yourself Marxist-Leninist. But here, in Nepal, the Marxist-Leninist party is a bourgeois outfit. They had a prime minister also. They did nothing for us," someone else said.

Comrade Rudra started laughing while scratching his head. "See, how militant our comrades are. Now Comrade Laxman Bahadur Thapa has taken control of this region. He is a real militant comrade. Isn't that so, Comrade Birat?'

Birat nodded. Though his name was Birat, literally huge, he was short and lean, just like those men who work in India in tea gardens or elsewhere. Karma was about to say something when an armed squad comprising seven boys and three girls, all aged between fifteen and twenty-five, arrived. The gathering dispersed as the local comrades got busy attending to the squad members.

In the morning, and it was a bright and beautiful morning, Karma shuddered to see that the Bhedetar hill was hardly a couple of kilometres away. "It's so close by and Comrade, your armed squads are here," he cringed. "I feel they can easily target you."

And now, on rewind, as he mutters the same words, he shivers lightly and listens to the answer Comrade Rudra gave him.

"Yes," Rudra acknowledged in a plain voice. "They see us everyday, and we see them everyday. That's all. We have not attacked them yet. And they, well, they will not dare to come down on us. At least not here. They mostly kill our unarmed comrades, just as the police do in India. Here we are prepared to welcome them."

Leaving the higher regions behind, later on that day, they trekked towards the highway named after the late King Mahendra. With the Bhedetar hill still dominating his mind, he asked, "How is that they know your strength, but allow you to stay so close by?'

"They too don't have much strength," Rudra answered casually. "That's why we feel they will call the Indian army. India is the biggest imperialist power in this region, and we will have to fight Indians like the LTTE. They fought and defeated them in Sri Lanka. But, you know, what is our biggest strength? People in Kathmandu are not aware of our might. They think that we are no great threat, that we are a force on the periphery, far-away ghosts.... It helps us. We are spreading very fast. Everybody will realize our strength within a couple of years from now."

"Comrade Karma."

Still absorbed in the thought, seeing that beautiful hilly land with wretched people and dilapidated shanties before his eyes, he wonders who calls him and why.

"Isn't the highway dangerous?" he asks softly, keeping in mind, his experiences in India, to which his comrade answers that the highway has actually helped them to spread their ideology.

"Comrade Karma."

He hears a woman's voice that seemingly emerges from the rocks surrounding him, but he wants to ignore it, he wants to tell Rudra that they have progressed much more in Nepal than the Indian Maoists have in the last one decade.

"Comrade Karma."

A female voice. Who is she? Women always remained a distant entity from him, and though he was always charmed by their eyes, by their fragrance or by their voice, the charm always remained at an abstract level, away from the real harsh and mundane life he lived, except for that one night when bizarre coincidences took place.

"Comrade Karma."

He wakes up to the reality of the present continuous form, turns his eyes from the window, and notices a young face, neither fair nor dark, bespectacled, curly hair with central parting, her glowing eyes looking at him.

"*Namaste*, I am Nidhi," the young woman introduces herself. "I think Lillian*ji* has told you about me."

Now he vaguely remembers what Lillian had told him, but fails to respond for a while as he has not settled down into the present that is still unfolding in a village in Bihar, far away from the Himalayas in Nepal.

"I think Lillian*ji* has told you that I am working with an NGO that gave me a chance to see the immense poverty in our rural areas… particularly in Bihar. And then I decided to write a sort of novel on the Maoists. That's why I have come to you."

"Yes," he responds. "Lillian told me about you."

He takes more time to settle in this different, dull reality. He pulls up a shoddy blanket and again looks through the window, still lost in better, glorious days. Many years ago, his mentor Comrade Mahendra had advised him to avoid publicity. He has followed that like a devout disciple, never discussed anything with anyone who was not concerned. He still does not think it is right to divulge something to someone who is going to write about it. However, since Lillian has let the girl in, she must have some reason.

"Comrade…"

"Why do you want to write a book on us?" he asks, without moving his head, or betraying his feelings.

Nidhi flounders for a while and then says thoughtfully, "Thousands of men and women have been killed… comrades, police and ordinary men… due to this movement since '67. I want to understand the logic behind so many killings. There have been so many mass killings in Bihar in recent times. The Naxalites killing 20 and the Ranjoy Sena, the landlord's army, killing 30 and so on and on…"

"Earlier also upper caste lords killed people. Police killed 36 of our unarmed comrades in Dharwal 12 years ago, in 1987," he says in a tone that is not genial.

"But I think earlier only the upper caste men killed the lower caste men," replies Nidhi. "Now the lower castes are also retaliating and the situation is taking a dangerous turn. It may start a civil war!"

The answer irritates Karma. "If you feel the earlier system, where the upper castes enjoyed the monopoly of inflicting death, pain and misfortune was more desirable, I don't think I have anything to tell you."

"I am sorry," Nidhi says after a while. "I didn't mean it. Or, maybe I meant so, because I had never thought in this way. You are right."

Without moving his head, Karma utters, "When status quo means injustice, one has to fight."

"And the phrase you used… monopoly to inflict death, pain and misfortune… has opened my eyes," she says softly, desperately hoping to flatter him.

"It was an expression Comrade Mahendra used so often…" he whispers.

"Comrade Mahendra! May I meet him too?" Nidhi asks.

"He had fallen out from the movement more than a decade back," Karma says as his voice turns deep, "He was expelled by our top leaders."

3

The Present Continuous (1982)...

THE ROOMS on the first floor of the *haveli* are cavernous and connected with each other by innumerable heavy teak doors, many of which now open with a screech. The white walls that once upon a time glowed with a fresh wash of lime every year now give off plaster at places and look gloomy with huge damp marks; big paintings that added to the glow of the walls now hang dusty, faded, corners peeling off; hefty and luxurious furniture like beds, secretariat tables and sofas now lie with frayed cushions and ripped covers in locked rooms where cobwebs grow bigger and bigger and cockroaches run about fearlessly.

"Everything was in order, was thriving, bouncing, and blooming only seven years ago till the last night of 1975," Chhote Thakur, the youngest of the senior generation of the landlord family of Puraina, mutters to himself. He looks through the window placing his hand on the thick wide frame, but instead of the vast irrigated wheat fields lying before his eyes, he sees the ravages of time; the diminishing role of the rural elites after independence that came as a challenge to the *haveli*, the attraction for the big cities that weakened the *haveli*, and the ultimate deadly blow served by a bastard Chamar who virtually demolished the *haveli* by killing five male members of the family. They were his two brothers, two of their sons and a grandson.

But that is not all. Deep inside his mind, in some dark cells, some other thought creeps in, buttressed by a deep sense of sin, and he has no escape from it. Why was it that seven years ago, on a wintry night, Mahendra Chamar and his team of red bandits wreaked havoc on the *haveli*, killing innocents and plundering the pride with which the *haveli* stood for more than hundred years?... Why? He knows his family had no role in killing of those three Naxalites who were trying to impress upon the villagers to fight the system, and even he, who believed in maximum bellicosity, never felt that those have assumed as much importance as deserving to be killed. But they were killed. And then a gigantic symbol of wealth and pride, a heritage of exclusivity and vivacity, a tribute to a grand old tradition was ravaged, ruined and reduced to utmost insignificance. Why?

Even that was not all. As though to rub salt into the wound, the attackers did not steal anything from the *haveli*, did not touch the women, but just killed five men and went away. What a grave insult!

Standing against the backdrop of a colossal void, Chhote Thakur seems to have turned into the symbol of the *haveli* that, with each passing day, faces the harder stare of the inevitable doom. He often stands like this and wonders about the past, the present and the future, with a futile desire to wish off everything that had happened seven years ago. It inevitably leads him to think of his sin and to identify himself as the sole culprit for whatever has happened. These seven years of his life were preceded by 62 years of colour and pride. But time is a relative concept qualified by proximity, compactness, and state of mind, and that is why Chhote Thakur feels these seven years have surpassed those 62 years in magnitude.

As he sees two men on horseback, the last two of the guards who were once a big force, his mind starts reflecting on the secret acts of his sins that he can neither share with anyone, nor forget for a day. And now, there is no way to forget it, for the jingle of the anklets chases him every day, just at noon, just when he committed the gravest sin for which even hell will not open up before him to live his next life.

All through the first phase of his life, those 62 years, he lived almost a secluded life in this palatial house, without caring for the family or the sentiment of the elders. He had a passion for women, and he found his first woman inside the *haveli*, and even the second one, with whom he had a long-standing aberrant relation. He slept with her umpteen times while the seed of sin germinated, grew and bloomed, but the last time he shared the bed with her was about 10 months before the birth of her third son. She was almost of his age—elders said two years younger to him—and when she came as a bride at the age of eight, he became her only friend. Another eight years later, on one humid afternoon, he had her. He saw her lying on her bed casually with a part of her breast bare—women of the *haveli* in those days did not wear blouses—and got overwhelmed by her big pinkish brown aureole and pink nipples. She tried to cover her breast with her sari as she saw him, but he could not resist himself from getting closer, from touching her gently and from getting excited. She stared straight at his face, but her green eyes were not reprimanding; what her face reflected was genuine astonishment. He apprehended resistance, but she stroked his head gently and asked him to shut the door.

She was the wife of his eldest brother, Badhe Thakur, who was about 10 years elder to him. When they were done, she whispered, "You are a real man. Have you done it before?"

"Yes," he murmured, "a few times."

He saw a sudden flash of disappointment in those bright green eyes. "With whom?" she asked in a timid, tired tone.

"Lachhmi, the maid… But she is ugly. You are a fairy."

In the next few years, when she gave birth to her first and second sons, he slept with her innumerable times. But after she gave birth to her third child, a girl, for some unknown reason, she lost interest in making love. But he burned in desire, particularly in late mornings when the women spent time lazily in the *jenana mahal*, the back portion of the first floor of the *haveli* where adult male outsiders had no entry. At times, he almost forced her to satisfy him and when he did so for the first time, she said, "It is high time you get married."

"I won't. I want you only."

"That's absurd," she averred firmly. "It's a sin."

"Sin? This seems a sudden realization! But I will sleep with you anyhow."

"You have changed so much," she said in a glum tone.

In fact, he changed even faster as days passed when he pledged his life to find another Kaushalya, his sister-in-law, who was no more allowing him to sleep with her. But nobody had that grace, that elegance, or the physical traits, a fact that compelled him to go after more women, one after another, almost every day. Two years later, when he rather raped her for the last time, she slapped him hard to free herself from his aggressive teeth and nail, and muttered darkly the same set of words time and again: "Beasts... all of you are beasts... all... all are beasts. You will pay dearly..."

That was the first time a woman resisted him so violently, and he neither approached her till her last day, nor spoke to her, though he knew that the son she gave birth to after the last meeting was actually his son, for during that period his elder brother was not in the village. He knew it for certain that Hari Pratap Singh, also known as Harry Singh, was actually his son.

The second time he faced resistance was from a local low-born girl, who kicked him in his balls as he tried to pin her down. To avenge the act, he let loose 15 men on her. She fainted after five or six of them performed their acts, but the rest also performed it inside the dark cell at the back of the *haveli*, and then strangled to death her unconscious and profusely bleeding body.

He had 62 years for all that; enjoying the women without a sense of sin. He went to places for getting different women every night, women who could give him such pleasure that he would be content, and then for another high, he would take opium or some other hallucinogenic drug, and would float in the light air; but very rarely could a woman satiate his desire. He turned old, his organs turned weak, failed to respond at the minutes of his need. It turned him dependent solely on opium and Phulmotia, a maid in the *haveli* and a nymphomaniac in her mid-30s, quite elderly by village standard.

He still has Phulmotia, now above 40, her breasts turning huge and sagging, hair getting thin, but her desire and capability still intact. But even she cannot inflame his body with active desire. He is sure she has some other man, or maybe men, but he does not care as long she sleeps with him every night, tries to titillate him and even after his abysmal failures does not leave him. That is enough. Only she knows that in the last few years—to be precise for the last six years and nine months—he has never succeeded. And that is important. Seven years ago, the *haveli* was ravaged, but the cauldron of his sin spilled over two months later, and since then, the house seems haunted to him with a pair of anklets chasing him every forenoon.

Seven years ago, he was not in the *haveli* on that fateful night. Someone told him that some drugs were available in the market— hormone injections—that could bring back his lost vigour. He went to Patna and was supposed to return in the evening to attend the birthday celebration of his eldest brother's grandson, but could not wake up after having an overdose of *ganja* at forenoon. He came back the next morning when the world had changed forever. The men and women of Puraina were traumatized, their faces either glum or expressionless, their eyes still trying to cope with the unimaginable. From the spot where the iron gate opened, he saw five bodies lying in the courtyard, neatly covered with white sheets to hide the corpses that were riddled with bullets. The women of the family, who never came out in the open, were yelling, bawling, fainting, rolling on the grass and tearing their hairs as hundreds, some inside the iron gate and some outside, watched them on. He felt the commoners were actually observing the fair ladies, their sari not in place, their blouses unbuttoned, some of their legs bare even above the knee. Even he had never seen them like this, without the veil. And then, as fate would have it, he saw that his second nephew's wife Kokila had fainted on the lap of a maid, not far away from her husband's body. What alerted him was not her state, but her bare left bosom that exposed a big pinkish brown aureole. As he saw her, he suddenly remembered Kaushalya, who had died years ago, and felt his somewhat-lost vigour was being resuscitated. With desperate efforts, he could ultimately turn his eyes away from her, but the scene got imprinted in what he himself now sees as his perverted mind!

As the place was slowly cleared off, as the local police officers came and started their futile exercises, he wondered what was wrong with him, for he still had no overwhelming sense of grief choking him. What he felt simmering in him was outrage, a desire to mete out retribution, and he told one of the police officers, "I want revenge."

"We shall find them out, be sure. But... pardon me... we will have to take the bodies and return them after postmortem."

Hours later arrived Harry, known in the family as Hari Pratap. As Chhote Thakur saw his shattered face, his defeated eyes, as Harry knelt down before him and putting his arms about his waist started weeping like a child, he felt the corners of his eyes were turning wet. Chhote Thakur knew the reason: Harry was his son.

After a fortnight, he, the Chhote Thakur, saw the whole family shifting to Allahabad from where his ancestors came to this village more than hundred years ago, just after the mutiny of 1857. The brides of the family, who had never thought they would step out of the iron gate alive, crossed the boundary and along with their daughters got into three Mahindra jeeps, escorted by the private guards who were caught napping when the Naxalites attacked the *haveli*. As he saw the tradition being broken, Chhote Thakur felt it was the end of the *haveli* that thrived for more than a century only on tradition, and in his mind, he considered himself the villain who had maligned the high standard of the *haveli* by sleeping with his sister-in-law.

A couple of months later, Kokila returned to the *haveli*, as though only to provoke him, to make the pot of his sin spill over. From the moment she entered the *haveli*, she turned into a constant temptation for Chhote Thakur. Had he not seen her on that morning, had he not known that Kokila had breasts like Kaushalya, it would have been different; had she not come back, it would have been different. But with her so close, Chhote Thakur could hardly resist himself. After so many years, he had a chance to see Kaushalya again, and he could not afford to let it go.

The next morning, after a sleepless night, he walked towards Kokila's room and found the door ajar. He stood silently, still confused, the beast in him slowly getting better of him. She was looking for something in a huge trunk and had not heard his footsteps. He coughed to make her alert. She turned back from her squatting posture and looked at his face as her eyes reflected astonishment in its most fascinating form, reminding him of the eyes of the other woman of the *haveli*. He still remembers the confusion, the agony and the panic in her eyes as he went close and then held her tightly, as he tore apart her blouse and dragged her to the bed. "I am your son's wife," she repeatedly said, as though that was a mantra. He did not care, for he was having Kaushalya after many, many years, for her bare breasts resuscitated his old passion, a new dose of excitement making him increasingly strong and feral. Then he heard her weeping and saying, "You have defiled your son's wife."

"My son?" he was confused.

"Yes," she slurred and wept. "Our father-in-law had no ability. All the children of your eldest brother are actually yours. But you are all beasts. Only I knew that you are our father-in-law. I heard it from my mother-in-law. I had come back to look after you, in your old and lonely age. But you... You will have to pay dearly. You have to..."

The last words unnerved him; they had been uttered by another woman so many years ago, and was being repeated by the other who had a strong similarity to her. He felt like being thrown off the top of a hill. He realized that he was a real rogue. Unsure of what to do, he looked into her eyes and shuddered to see a terrible combination of tear and fire in them. An hour later, she committed suicide—that went down as an expression of her grief after being widowed—and took away with her the power of his organ. Since then, for last six years and nine months—that was '76 February and this is '82—he has survived on opium and *ganja* and on the futile service of Phulmotia, whose heavy breasts and hefty buttocks lit up a prospect every night, but like some buds that never bloom, nothing happens ultimately.

But the nights, though futile, are still tolerable. Intolerable is the late morning, from eight to nine, exactly the time when he raped the *majhli bahu*. He tries to spend that period in the open, for if he is inside, he hears the jingle of a pair of anklets. Such anklets were worn by all the women of the family. Chhote Thakur feels panicky; his heart throbs faster and faster as the sound chases him from one room to another, yet to another, until it drives him out to the lawn.

Looking through the window, Chhote Thakur wonders what will happen to him if he falls sick some day. Surely, the jingle will catch him up and then... then? A shriek comes out from his throat inadvertently.

But he cannot leave the *haveli* either, for he cannot live anywhere else.

He stands at the window and thinks of Harry, and suddenly feels that it is high time to marry off Harry with a suitable girl. "It is very important, for he is the only son of the family living, and if the spirits of all the ancestors are to get water in future, Harry should have a son," he tells himself and decides to consult Giridhar Swami, the family astrologer living in Banaras.

THE HEAT has not let up inside the small barn even in the night, making it difficult to sleep as sweat wets the sheet placed on the string cot and creates a wet discomfort, even in early winter. The region has turned humid and rather warm suddenly as air from the north, from the Himalayas, has stopped blowing in, allowing warm air from Bay of Bengal to have its sway over the land. But in a while Ranjan has got inured to it, for sleep is such an irresistible love for him that he has slept anywhere and everywhere and in every condition, be in the jungle, on the fields, in shivering cold, or sweltering heat.

He was already dozing when he smelt burning gunpowder, heard the sounds of footsteps, muffled voices, coughs, and sensed a problem. But his brain has started interpreting all these in its own way. "Elephants have come out again tonight," he mutters, doubtful whether he can sleep anymore. He knows the comrades will come and wake him up and he will have to go out, be with the villagers for the whole night, light up the gunpowder torches to ward off the elephants, and if there is a bull with long tusks, it may create a lot of problems, as it did last year.

In his dreams, Ranjan not only interprets sounds and smells, he also compares the locality with his village; in the jungles and hills, life is different, altogether different from the villages of the plains, like his village that lies in between the River Poonpoon and a quagmire where, at times, ghosts light up a glow in the dark. The thought of the glow puzzles him for a while, keeps him busy in analysing its source while the smell of gunpowder grows stronger. And then his head stops thinking, it turns off all the sensory switches to plunge into much-coveted placidity.

Ranjan has not slept for a couple of days, and now his body and his brain, maybe his soul too, need unhindered rest to reinvent life within him. The heat or the sweat no more disturbs him, though it is true that the sleep would have been much sounder had he stayed in the hut instead of inside a closed barn.

But, a while later, Ranjan's brain starts functioning again, under duress, for the sounds are no more muffled, the danger is no more ignorable. Rather, it seems some people are close by, some shouting and abusing others, and a dull thud is heard that Ranjan cannot interpret. He wants to wake up, but his body fails him and his eyelids remain glued. He senses danger and sees, through his mind's eye, the bull, the big black one with white tusks which can be seen even in the dark, rushing to charge him.

After another couple of minutes, as Ranjan wonders whether the herd of the elephants has come closer, something hits him hard on his back, from the right side. "Hey *baba*!" Ranjan shouts in fear as he feels the elephant has kicked him. His head hits against the poles of the cot and he almost falls to the floor.

"*Shala Dusadh*… an Untouchable wants to be a hero… hit him harder."

Ranjan hears a voice that annoys him. Why should the elephant abuse him for his low caste before killing him? Why should even the animals behave like the upper castes?

And then he is compelled to face the reality as someone hits him with a rod, as a whip comes down on his body like a serpent, as someone else comes up to the cot, holds him by his shaggy hair and starts dragging him towards the door. Ranjan recalls now that he is not in the hamlet that is in the hills; he had come to his native village to see his ailing mother a few hours ago. He reached the village when it had turned dark and came to know that his mother had died and was cremated the previous day. Then and then, he thought of leaving the village, but he was too drained and decided to sleep for a few hours.

He had two brothers and three sisters when three years ago he left the village to join the Naxalites who freed his father, a bonded labour whose debt—amounting to five hundred rupees—to the moneyed landowner was considered 'not repaid' even after working for 12 hours daily for the man for years together. In lieu of liberating him, they demanded one of his sons to join them, and Ranjan agreed to do so, for he knew food would be assured out there with the Naxalites who camped in the jungles and fought for the poor. When he left, he had no worries about his mother, but one after another, his father and two elder brothers and a sister died in the last two years. His other two sisters were married off, but one of them, after being deserted by her husband, disappeared. For the last few months, his old ailing mother was left alone, trying to survive with the help of the meagre money he sent through some acquaintances or by begging from the villagers.

As he is dragged outside, as he sees through the corner of his eyes how the barn he was sleeping in is being put on fire by the attackers, Ranjan now realizes the gravity of the mistake he made by deciding to spend the night in the village. Sleep, his irresistible love, has brought in his doom.

The attackers savagely drag him out; his body down the waist bleeds, and his head aches severely. He has no power to resist them, and he starts hating himself for such a meek surrender. The attackers tie him up to a bamboo poll posted on the ground; one of them kicks him; another hits him on his head with a stick, and yet another stabs at his arm. About 20 men, their faces shining in savage pleasure, surround him with swords gleaming in the light of the fire that has engulfed the hut. One of them shouts bitterly, "Where is Mahendra Chamar? Where is that son of a pig Sunder Besra? They thought they would take away our land! Where are those devils? Tell us."

As he bleeds, as his stomach churns and his body aches severely, Ranjan thinks his last thoughts: he has seen 20 summers in his life; he is sure he will not see the 21st, but he will not yield. "I don't know," he shouts like a mad man.

"Don't know!" one of the men impales a spear in his chest about an inch deep, pulls it out and then watches blood spilling out. "Bring salt," he thunders.

"Tell us bastard, tell us everything," another one growls. "Otherwise, we will cut you into pieces."

Ranjan does not know who is saying what, for he cannot see them anymore as blood has gone in his eyes, blinding him. But pulling all his nerves together, he prepares himself for the last and the ugliest moments of his life. His head is bursting apart in severe pain; his whole body is burning, throbbing wildly. Still he tries hard not to groan; but when he realizes that he can no more control the scream coming out from deep within, he surrenders to his instinct.

He hears someone saying, "If you want to live many more years... and what is your age... think of your future. What's the point dying now? Tell us where those two are. We will let you go. We want Sunder Besra and Mahendra."

Someone rubs salt into his wound on the chest and Ranjan's body writhes uncontrollably. He knows there is much more in store for him, and soon he will lose his ability to speak, and the lights will go out from his eyes forever. "This is the last chance," he tells himself. He has surrendered meekly, for he was sleeping, but now he assembles all his strength, overcoming the savage torture to utter, "Comrade Mahendra told me... if the hatred... is pure... you can never... surrender to the devils... who call themselves highborn... but are actually dogs."

It pours oil in the fire and brings out, from shapes of human beings, the deadliest demons that have ruled over the world. For the next few minutes, the attackers start hitting him all over his body. Ranjan knows he is dying, but he has a deep sense of satisfaction as he has hit them back with words. A Dusadh, an Untouchable, has called them dogs! What more does one desire to achieve in this life? The last words appear repeatedly in Ranjan's mind, and then his brain stops functioning forever.

Someone chops off his right hand; someone presses a just-burnt-out torch against his penis, someone scoops out his eyes and cuts off his tongue. But Ranjan does not feel further pain, for his whole existence has crossed the line of the severest of pain any human being can bear. He is now only a bundle of shrieks and groans, the last sounds of resistance of the body, of the flesh and blood; his brain has saved him by sinking into the unconscious.

Another 10 minutes later, the upper caste army gets going, leaving Ranjan in a pool of blood.

The Dusadhs, Ranjan's castemen, now come out from their huts and from a distance watch the boy dying. They are grateful to the God for the fire has not caught their huts after burning down the barn. They have seen the upper caste men leaving after urinating on the body of the Naxalite, who promised to fight for all of them, but died the loneliest death. They decide not to touch the body, neither to cremate it nor float it in the River Poonpoon as they have done for ages to wash off the sins of the lords. They abandon it as it is for the vultures.

WHEN HE wakes up in his bed of hay spread on the floor, a bed that keeps one somewhat warm even in the winter, the first thing that comes to his mind is the image of a three-year old, loquacious, bubbly, naughty girl who was with him minutes before. He heaves a heavy sigh as he thinks of the dream he just had, a recurrent dream that he had seen innumerable times, in which the three-year old always abandons him at the end.

It always starts suddenly and the first scene remains the same: his little daughter lying on his hairy chest, cajoling him not to go out to work, promising to share with him some new stories that the 'granny' of the locality has told her.

"But I have something very urgent to do. A fight is going on and I have to go today," he tries to convince her.

The thought of fighting excites the girl, "*Ka tum tir leke larhte ho bapua*? (Do you fight with arrows, Papa?)"

He laughs. "I think we need arrows."

"But whom do you fight Bapua?"

"The landlord."

"Landlord! What a funny name! Hee hee." She giggles, and becomes thoughtful.

After a while, she says, "Don't fight. You will lose. You don't have guns. To fight one needs guns, you know Bapua, like that policemen who guard the tition (station)… You don't know anything."

That statement distracts him so much that even in his sleep he searches for his gun, his only solace like the walking stick of a blind man, but even that is not to be found anywhere. And then everything changes, the ambience, the surroundings, the characters, as it happens every now and then in a dream. Now he gets his gun in a new place where he is surrounded by different people who are writing slogans with red on Bengali newspapers: "One is not a Communist if one's hands are not coloured by the blood of the class enemy."

Now someone asks him, "Do you enjoy killing the class enemies? Do you feel a savage joy when you slit the throats of the enemies?"

The scene changes again, placing him between the foot of a craggy hill and a lake in which he finds his daughter again, but in deep transparent waters, where she plays with fishes, swims farther and farther away from him. He tries to call her back, but no sound comes out of his debilitated vocal chord, except a sort of moaning, reflecting his misfortune and vulnerability.

Like today, each time Mahendra wakes up at this point, and for a while ruminates the older times when he lived, according to him, an ignominious life, initially in a village called Puraina under the rigorous rules of castemen led by the landlord, and then in a town called Katihar, as a slave of the Communist Party. Thereafter, one Charu Majumdar gave a call for an armed rebellion, as though to play with his destiny, and he decided to join him, to follow the dream wherever it led to, leaving his wife and daughter to their fate. He went back to meet his daughter three years later—by then his wife had died of pneumonia—but it was too late, and she was lost in this vast world.

Mahendra wraps about his body the shoddy woollen sheet that he used in the night as a blanket. It rained a couple of days back and the late nights, as well as the mornings, have turned cold. For a second, he wonders about his daughter: if she is alive, she is now 15 years old, though in his mind she still is three years old, as she was when the 'spring thunder' started. "It is strange that the age of those who are lost remain static while the world moves forward," Mahendra mutters to himself. With this thought haunting him, he gets up and comes to the threshold of the hut to look at the jungle beyond the almost dry stream by the side of the hamlet called Kalipura.

Out in the open, Mahendra breaks a small branch of neem tree, starts chewing one side of it to soften it so that he may use it like a toothbrush, and tries to recollect his day's schedule. But before he could proceed, he sees a shadow through the corner of his eyes and turns back fast, only to see Baguna, a comrade, approaching him with an aluminium kettle, blackened by direct contact with fire, and two earthen cups. Mahendra has missed the sound of Baguna's footsteps. Though those were feeble and soft, for Baguna is trudging with a bandaged foot smashed by a chunk of stone that fell on it, still it leaves the comrade worrying. As he washes his face while the morning breeze brings in the message of a long bitter winter, he realizes he has also missed the wake-up calls from the red-crested cocks in the dawn and slept on, something that never happened earlier. Mahendra realizes that his reflexes are turning slow, his body is getting worn-out and his mind is losing the alertness it always had. According to his calculations, he was possibly born in 1940 or thereabouts. So he is now, as the villagers count, two twenties and two or three or four. That makes someone in these remote villages an old man, maybe not old enough to die, but people do not care even if they pass away.

"Comrade Sunder has come back," Baguna says while pouring tea in earthen cups.

Mahendra listens carefully, wondering again how he forgot about the operations undertaken by Sunder, particularly when he knew that Sunder was supposed to be back by last night.

"They have killed Haria and the other three. He is sure all of them were hard core elements of the Emancipation group," Baguna says while handing over a *kulhad* to Mahendra.

Sunder was sent for a certain mission they referred to as the 'annihilation of enemies', without the prefix 'class' before 'enemies' in this case. Keeping that in mind, Baguna comments lightly, "But I don't understand why we have to fight them. They also claim to be Maoists. Then why do they attack us?"

Mahendra shivers for a second, wraps the warm sheet more tightly about his body and sips his tea, holding the *kulhad* between his palms to make them warm, but does not say anything. Baguna knows that his leader, who tries relentlessly to unite all Maoist groups, is pained. For a while, the two comrades sit quietly, absorbed in their different shards of thoughts, until Baguna says abruptly, "Sonari's son died last night."

Mahendra turns his head towards Baguna, and his jaws tighten for a moment, for he knows what is implicit in this message: doomsday is not far away. The villagers believe it has come dangerously close, and the ordinary Maoists agree, but together they have failed to convince Mahendra.

They are sure of the impending doom, for the bamboo trees have flowered!

The bamboo trees flowered many years ago and the story had it that famine and epidemic and disaster had followed. They had flowered many times even before that, the villagers know from their collective memory, and each time disaster struck them soon after like a wild fire. They are sure it will happen again, they will have to leave the village for uncertain destinations, may have to huddle in some slums in Jamshedpur, and many of them will perish.

And now within a week, five children have died.

Regular illness and deaths of children, who suffer from malnutrition or diseases, or of some adults, or even occasional epidemics are not unusual in the villages of such remote areas, not even the death of five children in a week; but now everything is getting an additional dimension since it is a different time, a difficult and tiring time, as the bamboo trees have flowered.

Mahendra has argued repeatedly with the villagers that it is in no way related to any disaster in human lives; his audience heard it attentively, but were not convinced, not even his comrades. He knows Baguna is now trying to bring home his point that the inevitable is unfolding. At such times, Mahendra feels dejected and forlorn, for he does not know how to counter closed minds, how to break the barrier of superstition, how to impart a scientific temperament among the wretched unfortunate lot.

Baguna apprehends a reprimand from Mahendra and waits a while, but as he is answered by a stunning silence, he says, "We have to shift our base."

"Right," Mahendra responds now. "We have to, not because the bamboo trees have flowered… because the road is being constructed dangerously close to this village."

Baguna looks at the face of his comrade vacuously, and remembers the day when the question of the road was discussed in a secret meeting. Comrade Shankar, another leader of their organization, proposed that the road should not be allowed to be built, only to be overruled by Mahendra. Baguna takes time to understand the contradiction in Mahendra's attitude, and then asks, "Then why did you allow the contractors to build the road? We could have shooed them off."

Mahendra shakes his head. "The villagers would be benefitted. They have got work in the project. They will be able to travel further for work when the project is completed."

"But what about us?"

"We will leave."

"Why? Comrade Shankar said the organization is supreme as it serves the people," Baguna turns argumentative.

Looking intently at the distance, Mahendra says, with his commanding voice that often settles a debate, "Our interest should always be subservient to the greater interest of the people. Comrade Shankar was wrong. We are not here to serve the interest of an organization that itself is an end. Our end is to serve the people. If a measure by the government... we know that a government only serves the rich... but still, if they do something that helps the people a little, we shall not stall that."

Baguna falls silent for the time being, for he has heard the basic premise, just explained to him now, earlier too.

"Sometimes we make mistakes," Mahendra explains again. "Our southern comrades who have formed the PRG think that liquor should be available to the poor toilers at a cheap price. They think it is essential for those who work hard. They have started forcing the dealers to sell country-made liquor at a cheaper price. I have told them that this conception is utterly rubbish..."

"But when will the trident come again?" Baguna asks lightly. "Won't we have to inform the southern comrades about shifting our base?" By trident, he refers to the three comrades from the south-central India—Nagjyothi, Sainath aka 'the protruding nose' and Rambabu—who always come to this village together to discuss matters with Comrade Mahendra.

"We should. They insist that we should also join the Unity group in which all the eastern groups except the non-Naxalite Maoists are joining. But I have failed to convince Comrade Shankar."

"MCO is not a Naxalite group?" Baguna asks suddenly.

"No, Naxalites are those who were with Charu Majumdar. MCO, earlier Uttardesh, didn't join Charu *babu*. They always remained a separate Maoist organization."

For quite some time, both of them sit quietly in the sunny morning while from a nearby branch a raven goes on cawing like an angry soul.

"It wants to tell us something," Mahendra comments a while later, looking at the raven. "But we don't understand its language."

Suddenly Baguna starts laughing. "We often do not understand what you say. The upper-caste dogs killed Comrade Ranjan most savagely. We should have avenged Ranjan's killing by killing all those who were involved, but you have ordered to kill only three of them. Why? We don't understand you and often it seems that you live within a shell that can't be broken."

Mahendra smiles sadly, but does not come up with a reply.

A couple of hours later, he walks slowly down the slope towards the lowland which is full of gravels and orchids, towards a place where Bijuriya, literally the lightning, waits for him. She is the most attractive woman of the village and the wife of a villager called Shyamlal, and is the only woman who has succeeded in seducing the tall dark man, whose beret covers a three inches long scar on his temple. She has asked him several times how he got the caterpillar there, but apart from making the man more enigmatic, has never succeeded to extract an answer.

SISTER LILLIAN can hardly conceal her laugh as she watches Samru Baiga running and dancing about within a small imaginary circle in his traditional attire, a skirt-like cloth without a top and a helmet of varicoloured feathers. He has a spear in his hand, which he is moving about in different directions while chanting unknown words, his wobbling belly creating a perfect synchronization. Despite being bare-bodied, he is sweating even in the month of December.

The locals have called him to ward off a leopard that has been roaming in the Taslibazar area for the last three months. It has, apart from killing goats and cows at will, mauled two boys to death and injured several others. The locals are sure that the leopard is not a common one, but a wicked spirit, for it appears from and vanishes into thin air and most often does not devour its prey. To combat such a spirit, rotted away by unfulfilled desires, one needs to call a magician from the Baiga community, known as the kings of the jungles with their stunning command over all ferocious animals!

But why Samru, the magician Baiga, chose to perform in front of the school building is a mystery. He felt the school was the centre of attraction of the wicked soul, and the commoners had to agree, though some of them felt he actually wanted to impress the teachers of the school, the outsiders who never cared to believe in magical powers of the Baigas.

Lillian watches his dance, realizes how serious he is, but can hardly conceal her laugh. Though she has accepted the axiom that the world is ruled by magic, she has no faith in such sort of sorcery, but she does not intend to impose her opinion on others, and has even arranged for food for the magician.

After he is through with his rituals—a session lasting for three hours—the magician comes inside the building, sits down on the floor and waits for the promised food and gift. With a smile that she cannot hide despite her best efforts, Lillian asks him, "Now the leopard will be scared, won't it?" She has come down to watch whether Samru the magician is being treated well for his great performance that he undertook for only five rupees and a meal.

"I have tried my best. Had my grandfather been alive he could have forced it to go far... far away. His mantra was very powerful," Samru Baiga says rather apologetically before adding, "Once he was travelling with a *bilayti* hunter who came from the other side of the ocean. The hunter was red and tall, a he-man. But when he faced the tiger... it was the biggest animal in the jungle... he could not fire a single shot from his gun. Then my grandfather stared straight into the tiger's burning and hypnotizing eyes... and chanted his mantra. The tiger went away hurriedly with its tail between its legs."

"They are simple men with simple faith," Lillian reprimands herself for her intention to tease the man, and concludes, "This so-called civilization has taken away this simplicity from our lives."

"Even before that," Samru Baiga continues, "many years ago… all the animals of the world used to be under our control. But the white men stopped us from hunting and forced us to plough the land. Since then, we have lost almost all our powers."

Now, Lillian becomes inquisitive. She has heard different stories from different tribes, stories that juxtapose their agonies of the present with the glory of the past, and now Samru is hinting at some administrative decision that he believed had ushered in their misery. It may be a myth, a misconception, or superstition, but it is backed by the strength inherent in these people who have survived against all odds for thousands of years.

"Eh eh Samru," someone says from a distance, "don't bother the Sister with your stories."

"No. I want to know. Tell me," Lillian insists.

Samru looks about him to make sure that there is no one there to mock him and thereby smudge the great tradition of the Baigas. Then he says, "You know when the earth was created, it was neither solid enough, nor stable. The Creator asked Pawan, the god of the air, to fix it. But as he was blind, Pawan could not do so. The Creator then asked Bhima to make the world stable. But Bhima was hefty and… a drunkard. He failed. Then came Nanga Baiga, who emerged out of the womb of the earth, the forefather of all the Baigas. He made the earth stable by posting four poles at its four corners. He was the son of Mother Earth." Samru now seems proud as a descendent of the Nanga Baiga and adds, "We never ploughed the earth. How could we plough our mother? But one day, the government stopped us from hunting in the jungle." Samru sighs. He stares at the food brought by the cook, chapati, *daal* and vegetables, but sees nothing.

"Then?" Lillian asks like an inquisitive child.

"Then they said we cannot hunt in the jungle, and cannot keep the animals under our spell. So, we were forced to take up cultivation. We began to plough the land, to plough our own mother! So many of us have died since then, so many have gone mad, so many have become rogues." Samru is still looking at his food, but seeing a different vision, as evident from his words that come out like a sob. "Nanga Baiga used to come and help whenever the Baigas faced any big problem. He came so many times. But he will not come again. We have defiled his mother. We have sinned. He will not come."

Lillian looks on, over the head of the Baiga, towards the sprawling lawn where the grass has been mowed recently, and even beyond, towards the wooded hills. She wonders why these people were forced to cultivate land, and asks softly, "When did the government stop you from hunting?"

Samru Baiga faces a difficult question—how does one measure time that is infinite—and comes up with a vague answer. "When my grandfather's grandfather was there."

Lillian tries to do her arithmetic. Samru Baiga is a hefty dark man, aged somewhere between 35 and 50. The tribesmen marry early, but as they do not have any custom of child marriage like the Hindus, they allow adult boys to marry adult girls only. One becomes a father by the age of 20 plus something and often one has six or seven children. So adding up 20 to 30 years for each generation, the order was probably delivered by the British India government at least more than a hundred years ago; maybe one hundred fifty years ago. But why independent India did not reverse it? She wonders and then she remembers what Agnes says: "For the Harijans and more so for the tribal population, the colonial rule has not ended. For development... and this development is for the richer, urban and upper castes... the tribesmen and Harijans were, are and will be evicted from their land, kept in wretchedness. They will remain half-fed, will die, and India will prosper."

After Samru leaves, she stands silently with a heavy heart, for she is easily moved by the small woos of these simple men and women who are trapped in a world that could have been beautiful for them, but was not to be so. It is late afternoon with the shadows of everything, of the trees, of the building and even of human figures growing tall, as though to remind the inhabitants of earth that their space is elastic. Lillian looks at the distance and gradually drifts away towards a different thought that concerns the future of the school.

Initially, she thought she should turn the school into a residential one to salvage the whole idea of establishing a school from turning into a big disappointment. The local students come from about a diameter of five to seven kilometres, and are so irregular that the whole purpose of bringing them to school is lost. She had discussed the plan with Agnes a month ago, and then Agnes followed it up by going about the hamlets from where the students come. The feedback was a mixed one: some of the parents liked the idea if no costs were involved, but others wanted the children back at home for slogging it out with them in difficult times. This led Agnes to come up with a novel suggestion: pay the children scholarships so that the parents also look at it as a source of earning. Lillian does not know how to get that kind of money, but she is preparing a report for the church authorities to decide on it. She ponders over it deeply as the reddish glow on the earth fades slowly, quietly into darkness, making the nocturnal creatures happy. The first of them appears in sight now, a titmouse that flies in a constant zigzag way like being chased by invisible enemies.

Lillian climbs up the dark stairs, still lost in her thoughts, and stands in front of her room that she shares with Agnes when she stays in Taslibazar.

Suddenly, she hears footsteps approaching her, and as she turns, she finds Agnes with a stranger.

"This one is Bhola," Agnes tells Lillian. "A Naxalite."

Creases on Lilian's forehead become evident as she looks at the man in the light of the lamp that Agnes has brought, her eyes reflecting the degree of odium the church keeps in store for the Communists.

"He went to commit suicide by hanging himself from a tree," Agnes divulges. "The locals saw him and have brought him here. He says he wants to confess something, but only before you... He is not a Christian, but..."

Now Bhola looks at Lillian in her white gown, and says, "You save me Sister *memsaab*... I want to confess something... to you."

When Bhola is left alone with Lillian, he breaks into a sob, and a little while later says, "I am a sinner. I have betrayed all of them. And for me a leader will be killed, along with the others."

"Leader? Who?" Lillian is a bit confused, as she had never seen a political leader visiting these jungles and hills.

"Comrade Mahendra," Bhola labours hard to utter the name.

Lillian has heard the name from the locals, who often describe him as a messiah who has come to liberate them. Lillian asks, "Who will kill him?"

"I informed the police about his whereabouts. Soon they will encircle the village and kill them."

"Why did you do it?" Lillian asks, out of curiosity.

Bhola, the short, dark man with a stubby nose, starts howling. "Greed. This is greed. And jealousy. At one time, I was closest to Comrade Mahendra. But he ignored me. He made me a 'comrade' all right... but did not discuss the secrets with me. That made me jealous. And you know jealousy is like an abscess. It grows and grows..."

Despite her strong disapproval for the non-believers, Lillian feels this man has sinned by betraying his friends and his leader. She sees in him a reflection of Judas, and though she argues with herself that the parallel is wrong, she cannot set aside the thought, and asks wryly, "If you are repented, then contact them and tell them about it. Maybe, still there is a chance..."

"If they come to know that I have informed the police, they will kill me. Comrade Mahendra may plead for pardoning me... I know that... but others will not listen to him." The man breaks down and starts sobbing.

Lillian ponders for a while and as she suddenly remembers something, she asks, "Why do you confess this before me? You are not a Christian."

"They say if you confess before a Father you are absolved of your sin."

Lillian sees Agnes coming back. After she takes away the man, Lillian wonders whether the man is really repentant or playing a trick.

She heard about the Naxalites many years ago in Calcutta, and those were mostly educated young boys hated by her acquaintances, the rich or higher middle class people. That was in 1970–71. About a decade later, after reaching this place, she has found the Naxalites have not gone extinct, but are working rather silently in the jungles and hills of the Chotanagpur plateau, and the locals hail them as friends. Lillian walks along the balcony and reaches the stairs, but just after descending a few steps, she stops as she hears someone reciting the *Hanuman Chalisa* (the eulogy of Hanuman, the monkey-god) in a room on the ground floor.

Bhoot pisacha nikata nahi aabe, Mahabir jab nam sunabe. (The mere name of the great warrior keeps away ghosts and ghouls.)

Nase rog hare sab pira, japat nirantar Hanumat bira. (If one relentlessly chants the name of great Hanuman, all diseases and grief will be overcome.)

Lillian decides to go back, for the locals will end the session if they notice her, as they know Lillian is a *kerestan* who does not worship Ram or Hanuman. She knows the person who is reciting is a Backward, but among the listeners, surely some are tribesmen, who along with the Bongas, their traditional gods, also worship the Hindu gods and goddesses. The tribals believe the victor's gods are more powerful than those of the vanquished like them, and they have no qualms with Jishua *Baba*, that is Jesus, either.

Lillian climbs the stairs and walks slowly into her room which has plunged into darkness, sits on her bed and allows a chain of thoughts to overtake her. A while later, Agnes comes back with a lantern and asks in English, "May I share the thought that you are lost in?" Whenever left alone, they talk in English, at times in Bengali also, but not in Hindi as Lillian is still not fluent in Hindi, though she understands it.

Lillian articulates her thought in the form of a simple question, "Has that man done something wrong?"

"Who... that Bhola?" Agnes asks and answers, "Definitely."

"But hasn't he informed the police about a criminal?"

"In this land, the poor have to fight for the right guaranteed to them by the constitution of the country," Agnes proceeds carefully. "Whatever money the government allots for the poor is siphoned off by the government officials, the contractors and the politicians. Right to life, which includes providing work so that they earn money for food and shelter... otherwise how one will survive... is a sham. Those people, the Naxalites, fight to ensure the people are not deprived, that they get justice. And you know that too. Otherwise, tell me, why do you ask if he has done something wrong?"

Lillian sits silently for a while in the room dimly lit by a lantern, and then says, "I found in him the shadow of Judas. But I am not a radical like you. For me, it is becoming grey. I can't see any more in terms of black and white."

"I am not a radical," Agnes says. "But if... if liberating a large section of population from their sub-human level calls for a radical, if radicalism denotes movement for freedom from hunger, malnutrition, avoidable deaths... even fighting against the state that deprives a huge number of people from their basic rights to food, shelter and medicine... I am prepared to be a radical. As far as you are concerned, you won't be able to serve God without looking at it. Law is not sacrosanct, for it was the law of the land that crucified Jesus. Judas was on the side of the law, wasn't he?... I got this idea from you just now."

A while later, Lillian says, "I don't understand. I always remain confused."

Agnes sits down on the other end of the bed and says softly, "Those who are not confused cannot achieve anything. Confusion leads to truth, if the confusion is genuine and sincere."

"I only pray to Him. May God lead me to the truth," Lillian murmurs and touches the cross hanging from her locket.

4

Glimpses of the Future (1999–2000)...

KARMA, WHO is one of the most wanted Maoists in Bihar, looks straight at Nidhi and asks, "You want to know about our movement?"

"Yes."

Karma clears his throat, "What are your questions?"

Nidhi spells out her queries while switching on a slick voice recorder and laying it on the cot. "You adhere to an outdated ideology. Why? And why do you take recourse to violence? Why don't you use democratic methods?"

"Water," he says almost after a minute when he sees Lillian entering the room. Lillian moves towards a pitcher in a corner, pours water in an aluminium glass and hands it to Karma.

"Outdated!" he repeats the Hindi word uttered by Nidhi after drinking water, his voice sounding rigid and solid, as though the once-upon-a-time galvanic rustic orator has made a reappearance in the body that turned weird and old. "What is the date today?"

"This is the last day of the millennium. Today is 31 December 1999."

"I may not live to see the next year, or the year after. Does that mean whatever we discuss today will be outdated by then?" His voice turns even more intense as he goes on. "About ideology... well... I am not learned enough... but this is the only ideology we have that inspires us to work for changing the society where some people—why some—where many people earn Rs 50,000, forget richer people like the professionals, managers and capitalists who earn how much I do not know... and on the other side, surely millions and millions of families cannot earn even a thousand rupees per month... and there are people who die of malnutrition." He breathes deeply, as though he has not breathed for long, coughs and starts again, "Someone told me that according to World Bank, those who earn less than a dollar per head are below poverty line... and if adhered to that, more than two-third of India's population live below the poverty line."

"Yes, Comrade Karma, I came to this region, and saw those poor people," Nidhi concedes in a conciliatory note, as though to repair the damage she has done.

Ignoring her, the comrade continues, "You will understand the significance of this outdated ideology after a decade..."

Nidhi can feel the intensity of his voice, which even touches her heart, but she also thinks desperately of ways to come out of the trap that she has laid for herself. What Karma has said so far is not interesting material but repetition of the same hackneyed words that even the parliamentary communists say so often. She wants to know about interesting characters, those who fight from the jungles like Robin Hood, some thrilling incidents and bizarre anecdotes that can help develop her theme with real stories and conjectures.

"The problem is that the rich in this country are callously ignorant of poverty in villages and more so about remote areas," she says in a supportive tone.

He shakes his head. "That is not the problem. The problem is... the poor of this country do not know how much wealth is being amassed by a few. Even politicians, who are parasites, have tens of millions of rupees."

"But Sir," Nidhi gets irritated and retorts, "your people also extort money from contractors and businessmen."

He turns his head towards her. "You are surprised?" he smirks. "It shows your bourgeois proclivities. Do you think an organization can be run… food, clothes, shoes, and yes, arms, can be bought… in exchange of air?"

Nidhi feels uncomfortable and wonders whether this man still carries a revolver, a thought that distracts her as she tries to counter in a soft voice, "No. But you can raise money from your sympathizers."

"Sympathizers! Those wretched lots who are unsure of what they would get to eat the next day?" He smiles, his face showing the stress of a smile that is sad and mocking. Then he asks, "Why do you raise the question of extortion only when you think about the Maoists? Why don't you write about the extortion of the police… from all poor people… that runs into billions of rupees?"

Nidhi does not know what to say next, for she does not understand how she can stop this man who is still talking like a militant ideologue despite being seriously ill. Her friend Madhu, a young doctor and the daughter of a former journalist Dinkar*ji*, who had reported on many Naxal-related incidents, gave her the impression that the man had turned vegetable and might divulge everything he knew. "Absolutely wrong," she tells herself and wonders whether her two-hour long journey from Patna to Jehanabad—a 50-kilometre stretch speckled with small villages among fields full of tiny saplings of wheat and blooming yellow mustard, dilapidated bridges and potholed roads—is going to be a waste of time.

Comrade Karma looks at the distance through the open window, and then says, "In reality, we take levy from all the rich who come under our purview. We are an alternative state, and as the state raises tax, we collect levy… And be sure, we will always do that."

Neither of them says anything till Lillian enters and comes close to them with a smile that reassures Nidhi. "Comrade," she tells Karma, "This is a young woman, almost a girl, who has come to you to hear your stories. I don't think she is a class enemy. So why are you angry with her?"

Nidhi watches the reaction of the comrade who sits quietly till Lillian smilingly turns away and leaves the room. Then he asks, "How did you reach this place?"

She reveals that she started from Patna at sunrise and before reaching this village, she went to meet Madhu who stays on PG Road, the main road of the Jehanabad town. "She told me how to reach here," she concludes.

"It's a long journey," Karma nods. "I don't want to disappoint you. But if you want to write something, you have to understand it. You asked me about violence. Do you know we are working in Punjab and Rajasthan? That is, I have heard, 1,200 kilometre from here. The state government does not know, so it does not unleash terror, and we do not have to take up arms to counter them. We do not believe in violence. We believe in counter-violence. We know the state will come up against us to eliminate us in various forms. We must be prepared to fight the police, the army, the private militia as you see in Bihar now, and will see in other states in future..."

Lillian comes back again, but without paying any attention to them, takes the pitcher and goes out of the hut, to fetch water. Suddenly, a thought appears in Nidhi's mind: Why has this woman sheltered this Naxalite? Is there any relation between them?

The sun comes out tearing the cloud and the room brightens up with its water-soaked walls and damp floor, allowing Nidhi to see the features of Karma's face more clearly: a square face with broken chin, nothing special in appearance that fits in with his image of an irate, violent man. "I am sorry Sir, I didn't want to hurt you," Nidhi says in English.

Lillian has kept the pitcher somewhere else and has come back to clean up the water from the floor, and as she hears Nidhi speaking in English, she turns back to translate it into Hindi for Karma.

"Doesn't matter even if you hurt me," he replies. "My mentor used to say that the people of the cities, or generally the richer men, who mostly belong to higher castes... live in a separate world. We may live in neighbourhood, but the gap between your time and our time is huge, maybe centuries. But what do you want to hear from me?"

"People do not know much about you," Nidhi has found a ray of hope, and she tries to utilize it to the hilt. "They think you are criminals. I want to know about your lives so that I can portray how extraordinary you people are."

"Extraordinary?" he sounds confused. "Okay. Then listen. I will tell you about a comrade... who was like a saint... who himself was an enigma."

"Is he dead?"

"Yes. Maybe. No one knows. But probably yes. Long before that, he left us to see through the stones."

"See through the stones? What does that mean?"

"I don't know. You also don't understand. I doubt whether anybody will understand it ever."

"What was his name?"

"Comrade Mahendra."

"Is he... is he the same person you referred to at the beginning? The person who was expelled you said?"

Karma nods uncertainly, trying hard to remember whether he had referred to Comrade Mahendra to this girl earlier. Then he again looks at the outside where time creates, nurtures and then destroys everything that it brings to life.

5

The Present Continuous (1982–83)...

BY NINE in the evening, Kalipura sinks into a serene sleep, allowing the bats to screech and fly over the sky, and the jackals to take over the fields fearlessly. The jackals have reasons to be fearless as the last of their enemies, a couple of hungry dogs, have left with the families deserting the to-be-doomed village. Some 15 families are still there, for they belong to the '*comrets*', all of whom have decided to stay until the base is abandoned by Comrade Mahendra. The only exception is Shyamlal, whose wife Bijuriya, the lightning, insists that they will go along with the rest, and though everybody understands what she means by 'the rest', no one pokes fun at her, for the time is too difficult, too disturbing.

This afternoon, Mahendra held a meeting and decided that from the next morning they would start shifting the base to a village in the neighbouring district of Hazaribagh. The others attending the meeting felt their leader was disturbed, but no one dared to ask him why, nor did he reveal that he had got the distressing news that Comrade *babu*, his mentor, died last night. He had no reason to tell them either, as for them Comrade *babu* was an unknown entity. Soon after the meeting dispersed, Karma and Raul, two comrades who had come from different regions, left the village with a young comrade who was to guide them through the fields and hillocks to another village, nearly 10 kilometre away.

Now, about three hours later, the comrades arrange for the night. Baguna and another one go to a nearby hillock to keep a watch so that the team and their treasures remain safe; the Maoists have six rifles, five revolvers and more than hundred cartridges stored in the huts, and those are very, very precious possession for them.

"Where is Bhola?" Mahendra suddenly asks Sunder.

"I don't know," Sunder yawns. "Not here."

"That's unusual," comments Mahendra. Bhola is a nosy fellow, and even when not invited he often breezes in during a secret meeting. Seconds later, Mahendra tries to suppress a feeling of uneasiness haunting him, and says, "Let's sleep. Tomorrow we shall pack up our arms and ammunition."

Sunder agrees, and after lying down on the floor, covers his body with a shoddy blanket and within five minutes sinks into a deep sleep, which is the only entertainment in the lives of comrades like him.

Mahendra remains awake and tries to imagine where Bhola can be by collating the facts he knows and remembers, but before reaching to a conclusion, his eyes start to droop. As he floats in a region between sleep and wakefulness, he sees Comrade *babu*, the parliamentary communist leader, who almost compelled him to be a Communist, chanting the hymn: *Karmanye vadhikaraste, ma phaleshu kadachana.* You have right to work, but no right to its outcome. Mahendra smiles in his dream and mutters, "I tell you Comrade *babu*, whatever you chant, you are a coward. You shudder to think of an armed rebellion. I could never tell you this earlier when you were alive. But it is true." While Comrade *babu* retorts and jabbers on and jackals howl in a distance, Mahendra sinks deeper into a region of void, where sounds and sights cannot penetrate.

A while later, he again floats up towards alertness and hears the howl of the jackals. He realizes something is wrong but fails to wake up as he hears Comrade *babu* say, "I heard you said you would come back and demolish the *haveli* at Puraina."

"I will," Mahendra mutters, though his tone lacks its usual firmness.

"But this is not the time," Comrade *babu* argues with his characteristic calm and confidence. "You cannot demolish the *haveli* till the subjective and objective situations match…"

The jackals howl again and Mahendra realizes that their cry is not normal, that the animals sound scared and are actually retreating. He jumps up, comes out of the hut and sniffs something that prompts him to run towards the edge of the land to look over the slope. It is past midnight, the crescent moon has set and the stars are twinkling as though to convey a message of eternity to the ugly world of Kalipura, besmirched by hunger, bamboo flowers and gunpowder. The bats and the fireflies are reigning in the dark, through which Mahendra notices certain silhouettes in the distance. He crouches on his hands to have a better look, to see if the intruders are armed, though he knows very well that they are. Just then, Baguna and Lakhan, who had fallen asleep on the hillock, come running to him and announce, "We are surrounded."

"Why didn't you notice it earlier?" Mahendra reacts routinely.

In the next five minutes, there is a flurry of activity; all the comrades are called into action; two of them go to wake the villagers; another two put bullets in the guns while Mahendra keeps a watch on the force that seems to be static at the distance, beyond the range of the Naxalite guns.

A while later, using a loudspeaker that blares distorted sound all over the fields, the police asks the villagers to surrender and move down the slope. One of the comrades asks Mahendra, "Should we surrender? No point in fighting the police. They are fairly large in number."

Sunder, who along with the others is loading the guns, reacts sharply, "Why did you come to join us, you scared ghost?"

Turning his head towards Sunder in the dark, Mahendra says, "We have no choice, but Sunder and Baguna will surrender."

Sunder is so shocked that he flinches but cannot utter a single word. Baguna reacts, "It's impossible."

"Possible. Both of you are from this village. You have your wives and children. You surrender with our political workers. Even the police will not suspect. You will be there to carry on the fight in future." Mahendra coughs, probably due to stress, and continues, "Baguna, you shall tell Comrade Raul and Comrade Shankar that Sunder and Karma must be included in our core committee in my place. You should tell them that it was my last wish."

"No," Sunder now reacts vehemently, his voice cracked. "You will surrender with my wife as her husband."

"That's useless," Mahendra argues in a tender voice. "You can persuade your wife, but your children will reveal the truth. And ultimately, I will be identified. You too maybe identified and killed. But I want to take a chance."

Both Sunder and Baguna keep on insisting, but Mahendra sounds firm. "It is much more difficult to live on with a dream in a hopeless situation than dying for it. No one knows it better than me. Now, you have to perform that difficult task. This is an order from your commander." And then, for a second, Mahendra looks over his shoulder towards the other comrades and says, "Always remember, hundreds and hundreds have died to realize the dream that we all share. Be true to that dream till the end comes."

As others fall silent, he asks the young man who wanted to surrender a while ago, whether he really wants to surrender. "If they identify you, they will kill you. But, it's possible that you may escape and not be identified."

"I will fight," the young man says, in a determined voice. "I must fight."

After half an hour, the distorted announcement begins again on the loudspeaker, this time with the threat that the force will open fire if the villagers do not surrender. "Don't listen to... ghrrrr Naxalites... they are not bnoooo... bnooooo," the announcer tries to entice the villagers. "Those who surrenderhhhh will be safe and we will provide them goats and bnoooo... bnoooo... ood and clothes."

"What happens if we don't surrender?" asks Shyamlal, the husband of Bijuriya. He had never supported the Naxalites, but at this moment of gravest crisis, he shows concern.

"They are beasts, Comrade. They will kill many of you and will show everybody as Naxalites," Mahendra is brusque, but convincing.

As the villagers line up to surrender, Shyamlal notices Sunder in the queue. He asks, "You are coming with us? What about *Comret* Mahendra?"

"He would fight. He would die. He told me to surrender."

Bijuriya too hears it, looks back for a moment and then starts moving with tears in her eyes.

The queue moves slowly down the slope, like a long serpent, but suddenly, it stops altogether as policemen switch on spotlights at a distance, targeting the hamlet and the queue. The villagers had never seen the backyard of their homes to brighten up like this in the night, a few of them panic and start running back, only to be followed by all others.

The lights are put off and the loudspeakers again booms with distorted words. "Bnooo... bnoooo... rghhhh... friends, don't panic, we are friends... these lights to see whether anyone bnooo... You come... nothing to fear."

Crouching down at the top of the slope, Mahendra tells them, "Go, comrades. Don't panic. Go back, or else those dogs will open fire."

As they again move down the slope, as the spotlights again illuminate the harsh callous land, Mahendra divides his team in three rows: two near the edges of the village, and one in the middle. Then he gives his instructions, "Try to carry on fighting as long as you can. When day breaks, they will become easy targets. Then we win. But avoid the spotlights, remain in the dark. If you die, you will become a martyr."

As the last of the villagers goes down the slope, the Maoists take position. Mahendra is about to fire, targeting a spotlight when he hears the shrill cry of a child from a nearby hut, as though the little soul is protesting his being left out.

"Oh god," Mahendra mutters and jumps up to find the child. As he takes him in his arms—it is a boy of about a year, a small thin dark animal that clings to his shoulder and stops crying—Mahendra remembers his daughter, who was of this age many years ago. A couple of seconds later, he takes the baby out of the hut, moves towards the passage through where the villagers have gone down the slope, and hesitantly pinches the buttock of the baby. It cries out hoarsely, and as the sound travels the distance, a woman enters the lighted zone, running frenziedly towards the hamlet.

Mahendra waits for her, his eyeballs moving to and fro to watch any sudden movement behind the woman. The woman comes close. Handing the child to her, Mahendra whispers, "Go back fast, very fast."

But Mahendra has missed the movement at his extreme right, where a pair of policemen, swaddled in the bushes, has crawled up a hillock stealthily. The moment the woman turns away, they start firing and a bullet pierces through the back of the baby and reaches the heart of the mother, felling them both. The baby does not cry, he is still; the mother twitches and vomits blood.

"Beasts," Mahendra mutters and stands up with his gun, his body exposed to the light as well as the firing from the policemen on the hillock. He fires back targeting the duo.

One of his comrades cries out, "Sit down... Comrade, sit down."

It falls on flat ears and the comrades witness, some of them for the first time, the bravado and the nerve of their leader, the legendary Comrade Mahendra. While the constables fire again, Mahendra walks up towards them in a way as though their bullets are nothing but imaginary dreads, and shoots at both of them in turn, making them roll down the slopes of the hillock.

Mahendra sits down and crawls back to his earlier position. No one shoots at him from the other side. Mahendra and his comrades also wait as they see the focus of the lights shifting to show how the police are arranging the villagers at the front of them, undoubtedly to use the locals as human shields.

Mahendra assembles his men again in one place. "The dogs should wear bangles," he screams.

"How do we fire on them, Comrade?" croaks someone.

"We have to push through the other side. We can't fight from here, nor can we wait for the morning. Let's fight them abreast and see what happens."

Mahendra orders his men to prepare for a frontal clash with the police at the rear, who are not yet covered by the human shield. He is sure that the number of policemen at the rear is much more, for now they have actually compelled him to run into the trap they have laid down so meticulously. He looks at his comrades, three of them still in their teens, and says, "We will die, but for a great cause. Isn't it worth dying?"

His comrades were not prepared for such a question, but before anyone else can utter anything, Shibu, a teenager, answers, "Of course, Comrade. And... we are sure to go to the heaven, aren't we?"

Mahendra looks at the boy and smiles in a way that exposes his vulnerability. Probably he had forgotten to tell this boy that there is no heaven, that there is only hell and that is in this world, the other name of innumerable villages like Kalipura scattered all over the globe. Now that it is too late, he feels a lie may be worth a young life that will wilt soon. After all, truths and lies are qualified by time, and as time ends with death, truths and lies become irrelevant. With the thought taking him over, Mahendra whispers, "Yes, Comrade, be sure."

A minute later, Mahendra runs down towards the rear of the village and stops under the shade of a tree. He scrutinizes the surroundings, and as he finds no trace of any human being up to the dried up brook, he crawls further and comes close to the fields, keeping in mind that men from the other side are probably hiding in the fields, lying scattered in between the knee-high bushes.

A while later, Mahendra hears the sounds of shots from his own side; probably the comrades have located some policemen, or else they have started shooting the air out of nervousness.

The cops retaliate immediately.

With both sides using firearms, the surroundings reverberate in fury. The smell of gunpowder fills the air and panicked birds start flying blindly, protesting the brutality that human beings infuse into the world. Mahendra moves forward and takes shelter behind a tree, wondering why he cannot locate a single cop. He sits up in a kneel-down position and looks about him.

Suddenly a piece of burning metal impales his chest, from a point just adjacent to the armpit; the gun slips down from his hand, numbness engrosses his body, vision starts fading from his eyes. He tries to hold the trunk and get him behind the tree, but he fails and falls on the ground. For a few seconds, he remains fully conscious. Will he die? Maybe. He thinks quickly. No regrets as such, only two unfinished works: he is leaving the world before he can find Chini, his daughter, and without avenging the death of Munni, who was killed nearly three decades ago. A moment later, Mahendra feels he is being engulfed by dense darkness that is slowly taking the shape of a tunnel, a whirling, eerie and unpleasantly cold tunnel taking him down... down... down...

ASHOK SHARMA, the Romantic Cobra, stands near the pyre of his colleague and looks on at the flames dancing in joy of devouring a human being. He is not a philosopher, but as he sees the avarice of the fire and the opacity of the thin cloud of smoke, as he hears the crackle of woods and the whine of the mourners, he remembers the last words of his colleague and inadvertently wonders whether courage emanates from fearlessness, or from goodness.

As the superintendent of police of Hazaribagh district, Ashok is the person who led the operation against the Naxalites holed up in Kalipura. His meticulous planning had left six Naxalites dead and one injured. From his side, five were injured, two gravely, and one was killed. The man who got killed was DSP Suraj Singh Munda, now being consigned to ashes.

"We have enough time," the DSP said minutes before being shot at. "We have to finish the operation before dawn. And that's two or three hours away."

As he remembers his interactions with the DSP, Ashok stands in inattention, his hair whipped by a wind that is getting stronger every minute with the spread of the fire over the pyre.

Suraj was not a bold or a dynamic man, and he never aspired to be seen as one. But being a tribesman, and thereby disadvantaged, he walked his way up the ladder quietly and laboriously. Ten years ago, when he worked directly under Ashok, he told him about his past; he was the eldest son of poor parents who could not pay for his studies and he could continue with his studies because the Fathers of the missionary school he was in did not charge money from him. They even paid his examination fees for matriculation. A Father helped him personally during his college days, and wanted him to study further, to do his master's degree. But he joined the police service—that was few years after Independence when reservation for Untouchables and tribes had just been introduced through a schedule of the nation's constitution— to look after his parents and younger brothers and sisters.

He was not very efficient, not bold, not even enough bold to be corrupt. Ashok knows that from a sub-inspector, he walked up the ladder conscientiously, without harming anyone, without ever retaliating for the angry or jocular abuses he heard regularly for being a tribesman. He was scared to be part of the operation which he felt would be a dangerous one, but when he found an injured Naxalite aiming his revolver at Ashok, he threw his body in front of him to guard his superior. And when he was shot at, when he fell down, when he writhed in pain, it was evident from his face that he was not repenting. Taking him in his arms, Ashok asked him, "Why did you do this?"

A smile flickered across his face as he uttered, "You are too young to die."

Then he gasped and said something which Ashok heard with an effort, "My insurance policies are in my drawer... and post office passbook... and..."

He could not complete the sentence.

"You were not courageous," Ashok mutters to himself looking at the pyre, "but your ingrained goodness turned you into the most courageous man at a critical moment."

The police department suddenly woke up to the danger of the Naxalite when they came to know that the rebels were making strong bases in places like Kalipura. Ashok felt proud when the home commissioner asked him to lead the hurriedly planned operation, code named Flush Out, which was actually a joint operation by the police of Hazaribagh and Gaya districts and the Special Force. Kalipura is in Gaya district, though not far from the boundary of Hazaribagh, the district under his charge. He planned the whole mission meticulously to keep the damage on his side at the minimum, and never imagined that he would lose such a colleague with whom he had a bond that was thin but not tenuous.

Ashok might have done the same thing that the DSP did, yet that would have been not out of love so much as was the case with the DSP.

Someone beats the corpse burning on the pyre with a bamboo poll as the dry and gutted flesh contracts the body, enticing it to sit up for the last time. The scene hurts the Romantic Cobra and he turns his eyes towards the river flowing close by.

This morning, he was asked to address the Press in Gaya, and again the order came from the home commissioner, but he was reluctant, because he felt the SP of Gaya was the person who should do it.

"Doesn't matter," the home commissioner said casually. "Within a couple of months, you will get your next promotion. You will be made a DIG, and of Magadh Range. Gaya SP will be reporting to you. He knows it, he won't mind."

While briefing the correspondents, Ashok harped on one and his most favourite theme: the unparallel courage of the force during Operation Flush Out. "The Naxalites were holed up deep inside..." "Our men have shown that they can take on any challenge..." "Our men died, but did not budge." Within 15 minutes, the Press conference was over, for the local correspondents who work at district level do not come up with disturbing questions.

Half an hour later came Dinkar, who is actually Mishra, a Brahmin, but does not use his second name denoting his caste, for he believes in socialist ideology. He works as the state correspondent of a national daily published from Delhi, but has no sympathy for his profession that he feels is increasingly being dominated by corrupt men and women. Even before he sat down, he hurled a question like an arrow that struck bang on its target. "Do you think the courage of your force outweighs the courage of those men who fought and embraced death?" And then, after being seated, he continued his tirade, "After all, you were about a hundred men... they were only seven."

Ashok had no obligation to answer, but avoiding a question from an intellectual who thought about social mores and class positions did not behove a courageous man. So he tried to justify his action. "Well, they were hiding and we had to capture them. You can't dispute the fact that the one who is hiding has the advantage."

"You had trained men with better weapons. They fought till the end."

Ashok did not reply, for he had no point to retort with, and to distract Dinkar, he enquired whether he had already filed his report. The middle-aged journalist shook his head and said, "I'll send a small despatch. Who is interested in Delhi about the poor? Everybody is busy with the Asian Games."

A while later, tired of standing near the pyre, Ashok moves away from the site towards the river, and gazing at the water lights a cigarette. The sun has turned soft as it has sunk westward, allowing the breeze to continue its reign of cold that would be more and more severe with time and will make the land shiver in the dead of the night. He looks on rather blankly, trying to cool his mind, and suddenly a bizarre thought strikes him, "Does the pyre relish devouring a human body more if it contains goodness?"

"I understand your state of mind," someone says from behind, forcing Ashok to look back. Abu Fazal, the District Collector, smiles with a semblance of sympathy in his eyes. "But you should set out now."

"Yes," Ashok nods. "Please look after the family of Suraj Singh. Ensure that they get all their dues."

"Sure, Mr Sharma," Fazal assures him.

"What about Mahendra Chamar? Will he survive?" Ashok asks casually.

"I don't know. I heard the doctors in Gaya are clueless."

Inside the car, Ashok suddenly remembers the man who came to him about a year back seeking justice and almost challenged him to prove that the cobra, as he is nicknamed, is real. He thinks hard for a while, and as the car starts rolling, he remembers the name that seemed like a fusion to him: Harry Singh.

He decides to contact the man to ask him whether he now admits that he is a real cobra that lunges with a speed that even dreaded scorpions cannot escape.

EVERY TIME the plane is about to land at the Patna airport, Dr Mrs Rani Sharma holds her breath: will the huge bird miss the target and bump into the buildings near the airfield, turning everything into a huge ruinous fireball?

That was the case with her this time also, but nothing happens. The plane lands smoothly and after collecting her hand luggage, she heads toward the aircraft door. Suddenly, a hefty man stands up, blocking the passage. She is sure the man is on his way to Calcutta, but is standing there so that he can get the feel of her body, her bosoms, or at least her buttocks as she goes past him.

"Excuse me," she says, and the man moves away in haste.

She knows that there is something in her voice, she does not know what, but something that compels others to obey her. Her husband, the Romantic Cobra, indulgingly says it happens because she is a 'Rani', a queen.

She hails a cab, and on her way home wonders who the patient is for whom she has been summoned from Delhi by the medical superintendent of the hospital. She was in Delhi to attend a seminar on tuberculosis, to voice her concern about the growing number of poor people who are not completing the full course of the treatment and are thus fanning the spread of a drug-resistant version of TB. She told the audience that the statistics she had used in her speech to show how many poor patients disappear every month without completing treatment were actually collected from her own centre in rural Bihar. She started the centre because Mohan Lal, a retired principal of the Patna Medical College, had urged her to do so, and had arranged for it to be set up at a place 20 kilometres from Patna. He made her the director, for he himself was too old to run it. "The disease will come back as an epidemic in the next century, if steps are not taken now," she concluded in her speech in the seminar.

Rani reaches her Patna home on time, sleeps for a while, and then wakes up to find the light outside has died and her head is aching mildly. She wonders if a small dose of brandy will do her any good. Just then, the phone starts ringing. She answers it. A known voice says to her, "Hey, Queen, we have put up a patient, very critical one in your hospital and particularly for you."

"Why for me?" Rani asks casually.

Ashok Sharma, her husband, replies, "I asked your Super to provide for maximum care for the man. A while ago, he told me that you would be in charge from tomorrow. Is that true?"

"Yes. That's why I came back today."

"How was your seminar?"

"Good. But who is this patient?"

"A deadly Naxalite called Mahendra Chamar."

The Queen is amazed, for she knew about Naxalites, her cousin Badal was one, in the 60s and the early 70s, and that too in Bengal. Then, for a while, the Naxalites had surfaced in Bhojpur in Bihar, but even that movement was, as far as she knew, snuffed out during Emergency when Indira Gandhi gave the authorities an absolute power to muzzle all fundamental rights. She had no idea that among the Naxalites still operating there could be an apparition who has to be delineated as a 'deadly' one, and that too by her extremely courageous husband.

The next morning, she enters the small cabin where the patient is kept, and shudders to see him chained. His legs are tied to the railings of the cot and arms hitched to the iron bar of the window. She storms out of the room—assailed by a sense of repugnance—and asks the policemen guarding him to remove his chains. The cops look baffled, and an elderly man comes up to tell her politely that dreaded criminals are always chained like this. "Then tell your superiors that I will not treat him. I can't treat a man in shackles," she thunders and stomps out of the ward.

For some time, the hospital sees a flurry of activities; the stunned policemen call their superiors who come, loiter through the corridor, and then call up their superiors, a process that continues till the SP of Patna comes and after meeting the superintendent, orders the chains to be removed.

Rani attends the patient and goes through the report. He had a serious bullet injury for which he was operated upon earlier in Gaya, but the cause of concern now is a clot in the brain that has sent him to semi-comatose stage. "Such a patient needs a surgery that is better done in the US," the doctor attending him so far remarks casually.

"It will be done here someday, I think…" Rani stops suddenly as she sees the face of the patient. Though emaciated, it is the same face with the long scar at the forehead that she knew long back. She continues to look at him, creasing her forehead, for as far as she knew, the person now lying before her had died a decade ago. She realizes the man identified as Mahendra Chamar is actually Comrade Mohan. She first met him with Badal, her cousin, who had turned into a Naxalite while studying in the elite Presidency College in Calcutta. She once asked the duo why they could not stop fighting and spend their lives in peace like the others.

Badal had answered, "We want to change this society. Many people do not have food and shelter. Haven't you seen those people who throng Calcutta after a flood or draught every year to beg for the starch of rice? We want a society where people would not have to leave their home and hearth for a fistful of food. There will be no rich and no poor. All will be equal."

While Badal said all this, like he had taken up a mission to regale his sister with difficult thoughts, Mohan kept on smiling like an affectionate elder brother.

After more than a decade, those days seem unreal. Many of those firebrand activists like Badal are away in the US, or have established themselves in life, earning good salaries and living well. As for Badal, he surrendered and Rani's father, a well-known doctor with important connections, rescued him and got him settled in the US, where he is now with a multi-national company. Once, when he came to India, Rani asked him how he felt working for one of those companies that he used to describe fervently as the 'pillar of imperialism'. Badal tried to shrug off the question, but as she insisted, he replied, "The world is changing too fast you know. You can't sit pretty holding on to an outdated ideology. Can you?"

Rani agreed at once.

As Rani remembers those days, she becomes confused and looks on at the face of the patient lying in semi-comatose stage.

At night, her husband calls her up, "I could not get through for long. STD is a real hassle. Congratulations. They said you had led a revolution."

"Revolution? I don't know, but I couldn't treat a patient who was chained up."

"You still have that revolutionary zeal. Good," Ashok Sharma says with a sigh.

"Have you lost it?" the question from the Queen breaks into the receiver like a splinter.

The Romantic Cobra sounds sceptical, "I don't know. They called me up and asked me to persuade you. I told them… that's impossible. But about me? How can you have revolutionary zeal when you are in the police?"

"I thought we had discussed and settled that a long time ago. The police can be the common man's friend, and it would be a revolutionary attempt for someone who works for that principle in a country where the police is the largest organized criminal gang."

"True. But I don't know what a solitary individual can do."

"Are you losing out?" Rani's voice turns concerned.

"I don't know. My friends…"

"Don't bother about them. But I have something serious to tell you. The man whom you call Mahendra Chamar is actually Comrade Mohan. I saw him with Badal."

"What do you mean?" Ashok sounds astounded. "With Badal? In 1970–71? More than a decade back? In Bengal? What was his title?"

"I don't remember, or probably I never knew it. They used to call him Comrade Mohan. They said he was extremely militant. When the police surrounded our locality in Bali, he escaped through the marshy land towards the rail line. But he was a nice man… cool, sympathetic, not at all like an extremist. I heard later that he had died in an encounter in '72 or '73. But obviously that's not true."

"Are you sure that he is the same person?"

"Two hundred per cent."

"Strange… very strange," Ashok Sharma mutters thoughtfully.

Rani hangs up after a while. She stands at the window, combing her hair and trying to solve a problem riddled with bizarre questions. First, how can a man declared dead appear again, as though conjured up by a rowdy magician who wants to upset God? The second question is even more intriguing. Badal had told her that Charu Majumdar's call for revolution was a bad dream, the height of immaturity and a thing of the past. Then why someone is still pursuing that nightmare, that thing of the past, risking his life and threatening the system? She stands intrigued, her eyes set on the railings of a park where some poor people, casual workers and household helps, have made makeshift arrangements for shelter, and her mind boggling with the final question: why do perceptions vary so much so to make the world contradictory, confronting, or even clashing?

BHOLA WALKS as fast as he can through the rugged fields between the hillocks, and at times breaks into a run so that he can cover the distance before the sun rises too high. He is not scared of the late morning heat, for the sun is not unpleasant in January; he is scared that time itself may turn against him if he is late.

A small hamlet comes up to the right, and he bends his way further left so that he can slink past it, like he is a leopard winding its way home after daybreak. He starts running towards the east, for he knows not farther ahead is the highway, his passport to the coveted unknown world away from the clutches of the Naxalites.

From the highway, he boards a jeep which already has about 15 passengers, and he has to travel standing on one leg, the right foot on the foothold and the left without any support. He does not mind it, for he wants to be away from this land where he grew up and spent so many years of his life. A few hours later, he reaches Hazaribagh and from there boards a bus that takes him to Ranchi, a very big town with cobbled roads and big buildings. But he is still not safe. Since yesterday, he has been carrying Rs 25,000 in his cotton side bag without arousing any suspicion; but now he feels nervous, as he understands that he is in a 'foreign' land, by which he, like all other locals, means a land unknown to them.

Actually he was supposed to get Rs 50,000 for informing the police about Comrade Mahendra, but they said they would give him a cheque, which was an absurd proposition for he never had, and would never dare to have, a bank account. But, as luck would have it, a gentleman came to his help and told him that if he gave his thumb impression on the voucher made for Rs 50,000, he could get half the amount by cash. "That's the rule," he said, "if you don't accept a cheque, you get half the sum." Bhola felt so indebted to him that he saluted him again and again when he got his Rs 25,000, something that he never imagined even in his wildest dream to possess. Bhola was happy and content; happy because he thought this much money was enough for the rest of his life, though it was actually about a month's salary of a high executive of any big private concern; he was content because he felt the sin that he committed by his betrayal had been washed away after his confession to a Sister. But the policemen ruined his life after giving him the money, for they took him to identify the Naxalites from the villagers detained since the force swooped on Kalipura. There he trembled in fear as he saw Sunder Besra, the aggressive and adamant commander of the red army, along with Baguna, the quiet but thoughtful secretary of the revolutionary committee. But he had no choice then, for they had already seen him as they stood in chains with fire in their eyes that marked their difference from the others whose faces were glum and eyes still clouded in fear.

Since then, the scene keeps invading his mind: Sunder spitting on the floor before shouting, "*Saala kutta*, our men will cut you into pieces."

Bhola pointed his finger to those two, uttered their names and explained what they did. When the officer asked him who else were associated closely with them, he scrutinized the faces and apart from identifying the headman of the traditional panchayat, pointed his finger to Shyamlal. He had a definite reason for doing so: Shyamlal had slapped him a couple of months ago when he informed him that he had seen Bijuriya, his wife, naked in the jungle with Mahendra.

"She had gone with him on her own volition, but why did you creep up on her?" Shyamlal asked him after slapping.

Bhola sits under the shadow of a tree and recounts everything that has happened in the past few days, and though his eyes turn heavy, he remains awake and alert to keep a watch on his side bag. He wonders how he amassed so much courage to do all this when even those few who felt what the Naxalites were doing was a crime against God also remained tight-lipped. He has plans to go to Jamshedpur, where his cousin works as a gardener in an officer's government bungalow. The officer also has a private house, a very big one, on the verge of the Dalma forest from where elephants occasionally come and pass by in their own rhythm. His cousin wants Bhola as a caretaker for the big house which has two rooms lying vacant in the servant's quarter. Naxalites have no hold there, for it is a huge town, maybe the biggest in the world, his cousin has told him.

As Bhola's thoughts meander through varied shades and tinges, he suddenly remembers Damni, Comrade Mahendra's wife. He had met her several times, for he was the link between her and Mahendra after their marriage, and on every occasion when he was next to her, he was attracted by her charm and felt amorous, for which she had reprimanded him on occasions. But she never complained to her husband; otherwise Mahendra would not have sent him again and again to her, with money, Rs 15 or 20, or a strip of tablets, or sometimes a message. "What if I elope with her?" Bhola thinks. It is a daring thought, but it allures Bhola to turn it into reality, to take her to Jamshedpur with him and then live with her. Bhola was never a brave man, but now he has realized that it is taking the first bold step that is difficult. Once you cross that threshold, you really turn into a fearless man.

But then, there is no reason why she should agree. "No, she won't," he tells himself. But the magic of her body is so enticing that neither can he let the chance go. He sits down under a tree and wonders how he can trick her to agree to come with him.

6

Glimpses of the Future (1999–2000)

NIDHI FEELS perplexed by the bizarre statement made by Karma a while back that Comrade Mahendra was one who turned into a saint. But a saint is someone who preaches love, the antonym of violence, and who can see through the most intriguing facts of life. Then why should a Maoist, everybody knows they are atheists, dub someone a saint? She waits for Sister Lillian who has come to give a medicine to Karma to leave, and then she asks, "Why do you call him a saint?"

Without attaching any importance to her question, Karma says in a sad voice, "Comrade Mahendra came like a meteor, and though he was among us for years, none of us knew who he was, or where he came from."

"You never asked him?" Nidhi seems surprised.

"We asked him, he didn't answer. We only know he was in Bengal earlier." Karma takes a break as his eyes meet a sparrow that has appeared on the window frame. He then picks up a small tin box from the corner of his cot, takes out a few peas, and put those on the ledge. Though his hand goes close to its body, the sparrow does not fly away, but starts eating the peas.

Karma says apologetically, "What everybody discussed about him was that he was as fast as a cheetah, that he could see through the night like an owl, that he could hit like a tiger… sudden and swift. Our comrades knew him from the early '70s when he came to work with Master*ji*, who started the movement in Bhojpur. After Master*ji's* assassination, he worked with Comrade Manik, who came from Bengal. After Comrade Manik's assassination, he worked with the third secretary of the Emancipation, Anand Mishra, for some time. But when they circulated a document that said class struggle must be the basis of the movement… and it also called for being prepared for all tactical manoeuvrability… he saw a trap."

"Just a second," Nidhi interrupts. "Wasn't your movement based on class theory before that?"

Karma looks up and says, "90 per cent of Harijans and tribal population are oppressed and poor. Among Muslims, it's the same. Among the Backwards, more than half are poor. So, if you rally people through caste movements, you are actually reaching to a particular class which is two-thirds of this country's population."

"Right," Nidhi nods as she sees the sparrow flying away.

"Let that be," Karma says uncomfortably. "Anyway, he had differences with Emancipation as they were preparing to contest election. They too disapproved of our action in Puraina where we killed four… no… five members of a landlord family."

"Why did you kill them?"

Karma notices a lonely vulture coming down to land, and the sighting prompts him to search for something which has died somewhere and is being devoured by crows or ravens or other birds. While his eyes scour the fields, he says, "Because they killed our comrades. Our comrades were just carrying on with their campaign, and they didn't have arms. Our unarmed political workers were killed by them."

"I see. But why then did Emancipation object?"

"They thought it was on caste line. Later, the MCO, those non-Naxalite Maoists, carried on the practice of killing people from a particular house or a particular caste… the genocides you mentioned. But we did not undertake any such operation."

"I never knew that. Why didn't you?"

Karma cannot see a cadaver, and concludes that the vulture is merely thirsty. "Comrade Mahendra urged us to retaliate against those who have committed a crime, not against other members of the offender's family. And he was against involving common men in large numbers, as the MCO does, for they cannot be protected later. This was also the view of the Unity group or the PRG, the southern Naxalites of Andhra and neighbouring states."

"Your organization joined Unity and now Unity has merged with the PRG, right?"

Karma nods. The vulture does not come down to the fields, neither does it show any interest in the pond, but flutters its wings as it tries to settle on the branch of a mango tree.

"But, then, why did you kill five people in Puraina if all five were not involved?"

To this, Karma shakes his head, keeping his gaze fixed on the vulture. "I don't know. Even Comrade Raul didn't know. Someone proposed that action, and Shankar, who later joined the MCO, was enthusiastic. And that was the only time Comrade Mahendra allowed us to kill all male members of a family. We don't know why only once in his life he consented."

Karma stops suddenly as he sees the vulture repeatedly slipping from the branch while trying to settle on it, and mutters, "But this is also interesting."

"What?" Nidhi sounds confused.

Karma looks at Nidhi and points to the tree, "That vulture. It's probably sick."

Nidhi gets up and looks at the vulture which slips again and falls on the ground. It flutters its wings in futile attempts to go back to the blue canopy overhead that it has known so dearly for all its life, but fails to take off.

"Oh, my goodness," Nidhi exclaims. "Another victim of pesticide."

"*Matlab*?" Karma sounds confused.

"It's dying. It's called the drooping neck disease. It's finishing off the Indian vultures. This is the result of their systems getting polluted due to the pesticide that enters them through all that they devour."

"But they don't eat vegetables," Karma is surprised.

"We eat it and it gets stored in our bodies and when they eat our cadavers, it goes into their bodies."

Karma finds a similarity between him and the vulture. "Surely it knows it's dying," he thinks, "but it's fighting till the last moment." He sits still, feels a bit uneasy, as though the restlessness of the vulture is getting into his body, and wonders whether for everyone the end comes like this.

"Comrade Karma," Nidhi asks after being seated.

Karma snaps out of his thoughts, and tells her about Mahendra. He goes up to the point of time when he ignored others' advice and did not stop the construction of a road that came close to Kalipura and brought in his doom.

Nidhi asks, "Then?"

"He survived after being in a semi-comatose condition for a few months, but he never recovered fully. You know one of our comrades betrayed us and informed the police, and... then Comrade Mahendra's wife eloped with him. We killed both of them."

"She eloped with the betrayer because of whom Mahendra was doomed?" Nidhi almost shudders.

Karma nods, and his face shows he is pondering about something.

Nidhi tries to get him back to her topic, "What happened to Comrade Mahendra?"

"We smuggled him out of the hospital. And some years later, he saved a police officer from our mines somewhere near Raipur. He himself wrote a letter and intimated us about this. The leaders of Unity of Bihar and People's Revolution of Andhra and everybody associated with us decided to expel him from our movement."

"But why did he do that?"

"Nobody knows. But, he must have had some reasons."

A while later Nidhi asks, "From what you said, it appears that you started working in this area almost three decades ago... from about 1970. Can you tell me, in concrete terms, what has changed in these three decades that saw so many killings, so many, particularly in the last few years when in Bihar we have seen one genocide after another on caste lines by MCO and Ranjoy Sena?"

"I can tell you," someone rings out from behind them, and turning her head, Nidhi sees Lillian entering with utensils carrying their lunch, some chapattis and a vegetable curry.

Lillian wipes her hands and says, "Three decades ago, any so-called high caste man could rape or kill a low caste woman with impunity. But now they can't. People will compel the police to act. But if they take bribe and start dilly-dallying... then the Maoists will take action. This is surely a great change."

Nidhi nods tentatively, still trying to realize the significance of the achievement and wondering whether so much bloodshed was worth it.

Just then Lillian announces, "It's time for lunch. Come."

7

The Present Continuous (1983)...

"WE HAVE to ensure that those two are hanged," Harry tells Chhote Thakur looking at the greenish white lion atop the gate of the *haveli* at Puraina.

"Not two, we have nothing to give or take with that Santhal… Sunder Besra," Chhote Thakur avers in Hindi, leaning forward from his couch. "I read his name in the paper. Let him go to hell. He was not in the team that attacked us. We have to ensure that the Chamar is brought to book."

Harry notices the lion has lost a chunk of its mane, and it looks like a tonsured king. He nods to respond to his uncle, but the lion sets off a chain of thoughts in his mind, prompting him to think of his family. Badhe Thakur, his father, was not an ordinary landlord; he thought big and tried to translate those thoughts into deeds. Majhle Thakur, the other brother of his father, was a rebel of sorts, for he went back to their ancestral house in Allahabad and devoted himself to business, a profession that was looked down upon by the landlords and in which he was moderately successful till Harry joined him. But Chhote Thakur, the youngest brother, stayed back in the village even after five members of the family were murdered, and by his deeds proved that he was really a courageous man, a true Thakur, though in the family he was always rated as 'good for nothing'.

"We have to ensure that... that Chamar is brought to book," Chhote Thakur says again and allows his body to slump on the couch.

"I had a talk with the superintendent of that hospital," Harry whispers. "He says that man has lost his senses, has become vegetable."

"That is unfortunate... that may spare him."

Harry nods and wonders why his uncle has built an outhouse with only one big room, which turns hot even in early March. Sitting in that room, close by the door from where the iron gate is seen sideways, they drink fruit juice while discussing various concerns. Harry looks on at the tonsured king, and suddenly he feels a hair-line crack has developed on the hind leg of the lion. The locals describe it as the lion king, but with that insidious crack, it now runs the danger of becoming a maimed king. "We must do something about that lion," he mutters spontaneously.

"Lion? Which lion?" his uncle's voice betrays utter confusion.

"I mean the lion at the top of our gate," Harry quickly explains.

Chhote Thakur leans forward from his couch, and resting his hands on the walking stick with its silver plated handle, looks at the lion. "Are you talking about the chunk of its mane?"

"Yes, and it has a crack on its hind leg."

Chhote Thakur shakes his head in despair, and says, "Can't do anything. It is one-piece stonework. More than a hundred years old."

Harry looks at his uncle, then again at the lion, and sips from his glass of juice. "It's a pity," he comments in English.

"There are a lot of things in life, Hari Pratap, which cannot be repaired if damage; glory, pride and prestige, for example." Chhote Thakur turns cynical.

A cuckoo, a bird not easily seen as it hides itself in the thickness of leaves, is cooing from a nearby tree. With its mellifluous sound filling the air, both Chhote Thakur and Harry sit quietly, as though they are there only to listen to the dark bird.

After a long pause that becomes increasingly unbearable, Chhote Thakur breaks the silence. "I have called you here in the village with a definite purpose. I have something to tell you. But before that I must know whether your heart is strong enough."

"Heart!" Harry croaks in amazement. "I think it's okay."

Chhote Thakur looks about him and finishes his juice.

Harry turns sceptical, for he can imagine that some awkward turn in the story is in store, something that may upset him.

"Then listen, you will have to marry your cousin's widow," Chhote Thakur says in a plain voice.

"What, are you joking?" Harry feels intrigued. "Why?"

"There's no other way," Chhote Thakur's voice turns grim.

"What do you mean? It is impossible. Never, never and never. People will laugh at me."

"There's no other way," Chhote Thakur repeats with the same degree of grimness.

As Harry realizes that for some reason his uncle has turned too serious, he asks, "No other way for what?"

"To keep our family going... to have male descendents. You know how important it is for us Hindus. Our forefathers would not get water and their spirits will burn in thirst."

"Okay," Harry nods. "For that I have to marry. I will do that. But why Sanjua's wife? Why my dead cousin's widow?"

"There's no other way," Chhote Thakur repeats like he is stuck in a time warp.

"I don't get it," Harry sounds irritated. "Please explain what you mean."

"I can tell you," Chhote Thakur suddenly sounds angry, "but if you hear it, you will never die a natural death. You will die an accidental death."

"Why?"

"It involves our family secrets and whoever from our family hears it will die an abnormal and pitiful death," Chhote Thakur says grimly.

Harry thinks for a while and decides that he still needs to know.

Chhote Thakur stands up from the couch and starts pacing up and down. Then he stands still, like a statue, and takes a plunge into the recent past when he met Giridhar Swami, the family astrologer. He remembers that while describing his problems, for the first time in life, he broke down and revealed to the astrologer-priest his each and every sin, from Kaushalya to Kokila.

Giridhar—roughly of Chhote Thakur's age—was not surprised. "I think the time has come for you to know the truth about your family," Giridhar said calmly. "It's necessary. But tell me before that, whether you are prepared for a bitter death?"

"Why?"

"Anyone in your family who hears this would die a bitter, accidental death. But you are already condemned. So…"

Chhote Thakur smiled a sad smile and said, "Tell me."

"For more than 200 years, the secret was confined to us, the eldest sons of each generation of our family. Now it should be revealed because the time has come when a fire has engulfed you and you will have to live each day by fighting the fire."

"What does that mean?"

"I don't know," Giridhar smiled wryly. "It's written in your astrological family book that was passed on to me by my father."

"What does it say?" Chhote Thakur asked mechanically.

"Some 250 years ago, or slightly more than that, something happened that was bizarre and unbelievable. Ganga Pratap, your ancestor, had no son. As his family was going to be extinct, Ganga Pratap's father employed a *tantrik*, who was the priest of an ancient temple in Kashmir, to have a grandson. After he conjugated with the wife of Ganga Pratap, the *tantrik*-priest said that she would give birth to twins. While Ganga Pratap could keep one of them, he would take away the other."

Giridhar paused, scratched his body with his sacred thread, and started again, "Ganga Pratap did not know about these things. He was not supposed to know either, as his father arranged for it secretly. But he heard the conversation and in a rage abused the *tantrik* before leaving home forever. The *tantrik*-priest too was enraged and cursed your family by saying that the women entering as wives in the family would not be able to give birth to a real male child. He was a *tantrik*, who learnt *tantra* sitting in front of a corpse. So imagine the extent of his power and..."

Chhote Thakur comes back to his couch and after sitting comfortably, closes his eyes, as though to see what happened the day when he met Giridhar. He starts telling Harry about it, echoing Giridhar Swami, slowly proceeding towards the curse that has supposedly guided their lives since then.

"Then Ganga Pratap's father started weeping like a small boy, asking for mercy," continued Giridhar Swami. "The *tantrik* also felt compassion for him and said, he could not wish away his curse, but could only add something to it. Earlier he had said the women entering as wives in the family would not be able to give birth to a real male child. Then he added... 'by their husbands'. Thus, the curse remained with the provision of an exception. A *bahu* could give birth to a real male child, that is one who is not impotent, but not by her husband."

"What happened then?" Chhote Thakur asked like a fool.

"When the twins were born, one remained with your family... your ancestor Sadhu Pratap. The *tantrik* took away the other. We are descendents of the other who was named Ratneshwar Swami. According to the book, thrice our forefathers had donated their semen to the mothers of your family."

Chhote Thakur thought for a while and then asked, "Then who was my father?"

"I don't know. Your family left Allahabad after the 1857 mutiny. For the next few years, your forefathers apprised us about everything. But there is nothing about what happened in the last almost hundred years."

As Chhote Thakur reproduces the conversation before Harry, he gets up from his couch and says, "I don't believe this. A curse doesn't work. So many people curse Indira Gandhi everyday. What happens?"

Chhote Thakur opens his eyes and says, "But in our case, it must be working."

"How?" Harry shifts into a querulous mode.

"In our generation only, I had the semen that gave birth to real male boys," he utters uncomfortably and again closes his eyes and reclines on the couch.

A few seconds later, Harry sits down slackly and asks, his tone betraying rare degree of nervousness, "What does that mean?"

"You three brothers are my sons," Chhote Thakur whispers.

Harry sits in stunning silence, allowing the old man to recall the most important part of his conversation with Giridhar Swami.

"Now you must see the danger," the astrologer said.

"What's that?" Chhote Thakur asked in discernible anxiety.

"You are the father of all the children of your eldest brother. But your second brother also had a son. I don't know whether you…"

"No," Chhote Thakur shook his head vehemently.

"That boy has died without an issue, hasn't he?"

"Yes," Chhote Thakur nodded, and muttered, "You mean Sanjua was impotent."

"Yes. Now you have to think of Hari Pratap. You want to marry him so that your family gets a descendent. But he will not be able to present a son to his wife. Wives of the family will never get a real male child by their husbands…"

Chhote Thakur scratched his head and nodded in despair.

"And you won't get any help from my family," said Giridhar. "I am too old and have no brother, no son. So no more can you borrow the seed…"

Chhote Thakur had not even thought of borrowing seed as his forefathers had done, but the situation was really intriguing. "Our family tree will die?" he asked.

"There's only one way. You must compel your nephew, who is your son, to marry the widow of your middle brother's son."

"Then what happens?"

"She is, according to Hindu scriptures, the wife of her late husband. From that man she could not get a son. Neither was she supposed to. But from Harry, she will. A widow's marriage is not accepted in our religion. So according to religion, Harry will not be her husband, and she can have a son by him. If you can do this your family… or I may say the family of that *tantrik* who was our ancestor… will carry on and will achieve something for which he fathered the twin sons."

"What achievement are you talking of?"

"That's not written in the book. It only says that the great *tantrik* donated his seed so that one of his successors would be able to protect dharma. It was not explained."

Chhote Thakur looks back at Harry, finds him sitting like a limpet, without having moved an inch, and says, "So you have to marry Sanjua's widow."

Harry looks askance, and makes a last desperate attempt to save himself from disgrace, "Anyone I marry will have children. I know that for sure."

His uncle looks at him for a while and whispers, "You mean you are already a father, is that it?"

As Harry nods, he asks, "But what is the guarantee that your formal wife will give birth to a son? We can't take risk. We can't challenge our destiny."

"Why will she agree?" Harry slurs.

"She has agreed after I revealed everything. I had to do that. Yes. I am a servant of destiny, waiting to see the unavoidable raising its head everyday in this *haveli*, and I am working according to the wish of that all-powerful destiny."

Harry stands up, slowly walks out of the room, and stands in the open, looking at the lion that may soon turn into a maimed king, maybe after the monsoon. His uncle comes to stand next to him and says, "Don't resist destiny, Hari Pratap. Your father did that, and we paid so dearly."

"What did he do?"

"Many years ago, one Chamar, Mohan Ram, threw a stone at the gate of our *haveli*. He did the unimaginable. We should have cut him into pieces and set ablaze the Chamar-*tola*. But your father handed him over to the police and pardoned the Chamars. Had he done what he was destined to do, the Socialists or the Naxalites couldn't have dared to challenge us."

"I will not resist, though I don't believe this cock and bull story narrated by the astrologer. I will marry her if she is willing. But I will change the destiny when time comes." Harry mutters grimly looking at the lion atop the gate, and decides to save it from becoming a maimed king.

A FEW months after a bullet went into his chest, he wakes up in a calm and quiet night breaking the opacity that was troubling him so terribly for so long.

As he wakes up, looks about him and finds by his side a saline tube and an iron table on which different ampoules of drugs are lying, he realizes that he has won. He turns his neck towards the right and what catches his eyes in the faint light is the silhouette of a human being lying on a raised platform. He looks on for a while as he realizes his vision is slowly clearing up, and then he understands what he sees: a woman in a white sari sleeping on a bench. He moves his gaze slowly from the woman to the wall, to the door kept ajar and the dimly lit corridor, and then to the shafts of the cot he is lying on.

He feels relieved, being convinced that he has won. He fought the opaque tunnel about him with the firm belief that it was impalpable and needed only one big effort to make it vanish in thin air. He failed repeatedly, but did not lose that faint ray of hope. He closes his eyes and thinks hard for a few minutes, trying to relate the scene he has just seen with the knowledge acquired before the walls of vagueness imprisoned him, but fails to reach a conclusion, and like a wise philosopher, he tells himself, "I need some more time to understand this world." He feels worn out and breathes deeply, trying to relax as he hears a muffled sound of rain that, to him, sounds like the chime of a stream.

He opens his eyes again, this time with passionate fervour, as though to be sure that he has finally come out of the daunting, irritating vagueness that clung to him. He turns his head again and as he sees the same scenes, a woman lying on a bench, the door, the corridor, he feels assured.

After a while, a question comes to his mind, a relevant and fundamental question: who is he?

With no answer in his mind, he feels restless. He wants to be seated and raises his head from the pillow, but the world starts reeling before his eyes and his head falls on the pillow again, making him gasp for air.

A while later, he realizes he is sinking into sleep again in which, he fears, the tunnel is waiting for him.

But, in his sleep, or a state of half-sleep, the tunnel fails to reappear. Instead, he sees a vast and seemingly endless field of a village, smells ripe golden wheat, and remembers the mangy dogs in the *tola* of the Backwards and a few healthy dogs roaming in the Rajput-*tola*, the upper caste colony.

"Dogs are very important," he mutters, starting a monologue. "But less important than the lion that stands atop the gate of the *haveli*; it's the king."

But why does Chamar-*tola*, the colony of the untouchables, not have a dog, he wonders. The answer appears in his mind a while later: Badhe Thakur had sermonized long back that the Untouchables could not rear a male dog for it might mate with the bitches of upper caste area and desecrate them! The Chamars are allowed to have only bitches. For a bitch raised by the Chamars, it is an honour to mate with a male dog from the village, just like that of a Chamarni who should feel proud if any upper caste man pours his semen into her. But while the Chamarnis can rear their sons, the bitches cannot, according to the writ, and so the Chamars chase away all the dogs from their *tola*.

"*Hei* brother, why do you listen to that Badhe Thakur? Don't you know all the animals in the world, even a lion king, are scared of wild dogs," he wants to ask the people of the Chamar-*tola*, and tries to laugh in disdain; but that only invites a severe pain in his ribs. For some time, he tries to cope with the pain, and when it ebbs, he remembers, without doubt, he is Mohan Ram, son of Birju Ram, of village Puraina, district Rohtas.

He wakes up again and as he remembers his childhood, he feels happy and content, and after a while, lying still on the bed, he continues his monologue without any emotion. "The lion at the gate of the *haveli* should be demolished," he mutters.

Now his thoughts start flowing; he sees Munni lying naked on the floor of a thatched hut, her small breasts illuminated in a strip of light straight from the moon beaming on her through a hole at the roof. He can almost smell her, a curious mix of manure and perspiration.

What comes next to his mind is a little girl hugging him with all her might and talking like a parrot, "*Ka tum tir leke larhte ho bapua?* (Do you fight with arrows, Papa?)"

"I think we need arrows."

"But whom do you fight bapua?"

"The landlord."

"Landlord! What a funny name! Hee hee." She giggles, and becomes thoughtful.

Just at this point, he gets a severe jolt, and his memory bursts into his mind like a flooding river: he was born Mohan Ram, but later became Mahendra Chamar. He was a Naxalite and the little girl was his daughter. She was with him years ago, in another part of Bihar called Katihar, Mahendra remembers and feels restless.

"What has happened to this half-dead; why does it groan?" the attendant woman grumbles, waking up from her sleep, and looks at the half-dead patient for a while, but as the patient remains calm, she falls asleep again.

Now fully conscious, Mahendra looks about to discover that he is in a hospital, in a room that smells of rain, and remembers the last battle he fought at Kalipura. What happened after that? He does not remember. He tries to get up again but his head reels, and the bed pulls him back. Lying quietly, he feels he was happier when the opacity surrounded him, for he forgot about his daughter who got lost in this vast world because he had not cared for her, had left her and her mother for a dream that, like the horizon, had slipped back further and further as he approached it. Now, he has no option but again to live a life where he has to perform his duties, but where the chances of finding Chini seem bleak, so bleak that one may relegate them to the level of impossibility.

He now yearns for the opacity that lies beyond the futile clamour of a revolution, the buzz of memory, or the myth of life.

After a while, comes a clear voice that recites a hymn he knows very well, "*Karmanye vadhikaraste ma phaleshu kadachana.*"

"No, Comrade *babu*, no." He again resorts to monologue: "There cannot be any work without expectation. Lord Krishna was a great philosopher, the greatest philosopher the world has ever seen. That is why he could think of such lofty ideals. But we are ordinary mortals. We can't shed our expectations... Comrade *babu*, are you there?"

"I am here. The question is, aren't you drifting away from your belief? You believed in it."

Mahendra thinks for a long time, and then the answer comes to his mind. "I had no belief Comrade *babu*. I was a directionless boat. But a sadhu told me that he had read strange things on my forehead... that I would challenge the gods and they would retaliate, and then... what was that? Yes, I will see through the stones. I asked him what it meant. He said time would tell me and ordered me to follow life as it appears before me. Follow your destiny, he said. I was doing only that."

"I never knew that," Comrade *babu* says grudgingly.

"Then I came across you... and you said you stood for blowing up the *havelis*. So, I became a Communist. But you never meant what you said. So I had to leave you. I didn't know that I was leaving you only for that... to see through the stones. I didn't know, but the gods knew it. They retaliated, snatched away my wife and my daughter. But I cannot see through the stones. I still don't know what it means... seeing through the stones? Do you know?"

He waits for Comrade *babu* to say something, but he hears nothing. "Comrade *babu*, are you there?" he asks again.

As no one answers, no comrade *babu* comes forward to explain the thoughts of either the *Bhagavad Gita* or of Karl Marx, he feels tired and slips back into the dark tunnel of sleep, hoping that he will not rise again. Or, if he does, he should emerge as Mohan, the untouchable, and not as Comrade Mahendra.

PART II
The Doom

8

Glimpses of the Past (1940–1980)

MOHAN RAM was born from the womb of a severely anaemic mother who had died in a dilapidated hut in a colony of the Untouchables some 15 minutes before his birth.

The Chamars and the Dusadhs, both Untouchable castes, turned edgy at the suggestion that a child had been born after its mother's death; but the midwife, an old corpulent Chamar woman of Puraina, insisted that it was not aberrant. She was positive about it and nobody dared to dispute her, for her hands had given birth to innumerable children—the highborn and the lowborn alike. "The mother was dead before the big child came fully out of the womb," she shuddered as she puffed hard at her bidi. "I looked at the trident atop the Valmiki temple and tried to enlarge the passage. Come out, I said. This is actually a wonder, but it's always possible if the *dai* is deft."

The elders of the Chamar-*tola*, silhouetted across a *nullah* in their ever dishevelled outfit of tattered dhoti, the upper part of the body as well as the feet uncovered, pondered over the disturbing fact. It was early morning at the onset of summer, neither hot nor cold, an ideal time to wonder about and comment on anything and everything in the world, which was small and restricted for them.

No one bothered to enquire why the mother had died, but that was not something unusual, for it was a time when diseases and poverty reigned over the majority of the people of India, and more so in the *tola* or ghettos of the Untouchables, aborigines, Backwards or Muslims. After sitting quietly for some time, their blank faces feigning thoughtfulness, the Chamars and Dusadhs walked away one by one. The sun had risen and they had to go in search of the day's livelihood. Budha Chamar, the newborn's grandfather, too got up and walked slowly up the way with his walking stick, a bamboo poll five feet long but small in girth. He crossed the dry and stinking *nullah* through a bamboo bridge to dodder towards the village, the abode of caste Hindus, both upper and lower castes. The Chamars, like all Harijans, had to live outside the village as they were treated as outcastes, untouchables.

Budha Chamar went up to the *haveli*, the palace of the Badhe Thakur, the landlord, and squatted outside the iron gate, holding the poll with both his hands as a prop. He knew it would be an indefinite wait as the sun was still not ripe. The iron gate of the *haveli* was embedded with the severest of might the villagers could imagine. The Thakurs were Rajputs, the warrior caste in the traditional sense, and in the upper caste *tola*, they lived with the Bhumihars, the mighty agriculturists who clamoured for the status of Brahmins. After the Bhumihars came the Kurmis, earlier known as a tribe but elevated to the status of 'Backwards' from the beginning of the century. They owned large amount of land, but straggled in status.

More than half a century ago, the then Badhe Thakur gave his sermon: "The sun shines only for the Rajputs, Brahmins, Bhumihars, Kayasthas and Banias, all upper caste men. The lower castes, the Backward, the Untouchables or the Tribals have no entitlement to anything!" The sermon came because the Dusadhs, an Untouchable caste who did not consider themselves Untouchable or inferior, claimed a portion of land across the *nullah*, close by the village. They had to leave the village soon thereafter, as they were crushed, brutalized and excommunicated, and with them went the *Barahazari* Cheros, a tribal population who claimed to be the descendents of kings of older times.

In later days, a few Dusadh families settled in the Chamar-*tola* again, but they were not from the rebels who had left the village, though like the earlier lot they too belonged to the Bairagi sect and had separate deities. The Chamars worshipped Hindu deities, though they were not allowed to enter any temple or recite the *Ramayana*. It did not matter to them; even without the ban, no Untouchable could read the holy book as they were illiterate, and as for worshipping a god, they had built the temple of the author of the *Ramayana*, Valmiki, whom the caste Hindus did not worship as such.

Budha Chamar, the grandfather of the newborn, always preached total loyalty to the lords and virtual gods of Puraina, the Thakurs of the *haveli*, since he had known rebellion meant death while loyalty paid. He sat like a frog and putting his right palm over his wrinkled eyes, noticed all those who entered or came out of the *haveli*. He could not see the faces well for light was gradually dying from his eyes, but could make out who was who by the figure and the style of walking.

After three hours, Badhe Thakur, literally the eldest Thakur, came out with Sampat Singh, a Congress leader, and stood just beneath the greenish white lion atop the gate.

"*Parnam malik. Jai ho, jai ho.* (Hail the Master! The Master be victorious!)" Budha Chamar shouted at the top of his voice as he grovelled on the ground with folded hands, his nose rubbing the soil.

The Thakur turned to him, his eyes showing no reaction, and after a while wondered aloud, "Why! Is it not the old Chamar?"

"Yes," one of the guards of the Thakur replied, and went up to the Chamar to tell him, "Get up Budha. Tell us what the matter is."

If they came across an upper caste man, the Untouchables were supposed to bend their head to the height of the waist, and fold their hands from a distance before getting off from the path; but when they cowered more, there had to be some reason.

Budha Chamar got up as fast as he could and said, his hands folded, "My son's second wife has given birth to a son. Now I feel confident that my family tree will be saved."

"Why, don't you have another grandson?" Badhe Thakur asked.

"I have another grandson from the first wife of my son Birjua. But one is uncertain. If he dies, it would be a closed story."

The Thakur nodded, called someone by indicating his finger, and asked the Chamar, "How is the mother?"

"The mother? She is dead," said the Chamar indifferently.

"Dead?... That's sad," the Thakur commented and asked the man he had called to hand over a rupee to the Chamar.

As the Thakur was about to turn away, the Chamar said again, "Master, I fear harm to the newborn!"

"Why?" the landlord looked amused.

"For no particular reason. But... would you allow me to say something?"

As the Thakur nodded again, the old Chamar pleaded, his hands folded across the bamboo poll, to suggest a name for his grandson, a name that would protect him from the evil eyes.

The Thakur thought for a while and said, "Mohan. Name him Mohan. Do you know whose name it is?"

"Master?"

"It is another name of Lord Krishna, the god. He had 108 names. It is one of those."

"Master!"

"And it is also the name of Gandhi *baba*. His name is Mohandas Gandhi."

"Hail the Master." The Chamar again touched the ground before him, this time with his hand, and left for his *tola*. But even before he had taken a couple of steps, he heard Sampat laughing, "A Harijan named Mohan! Mahatma Gandhi has renamed the Untouchables as Harijan. That much is okay. But this is too much."

His purpose served, the old Chamar doddered out of the upper caste colony as fast as he could, gasping heavily, but not wasting a moment. No Chamar, for that matter not even the Backwards, could ever imagine talking to the Badhe Thakur, the lord of the village, but Budha Chamar, who had served the *haveli* for many years, had the courage to approach him, and the feudal relationship had finally paid him, as he had extracted an upper caste name for his grandson!

He knew well that the noble lord would not recall a suitable Chamar name and would suggest some 'good name'. He knew very well that Mohan was the name of Krishna, but he did not reveal that as he wanted to pass on the full credit to the landlord for naming his grandson. His subterfuge had paid him, and now nobody would be able to prevent him from calling his grandson 'Mohan'. Otherwise, the Chamars, or any other Untouchables, were not allowed to name their sons or daughters after the names of gods or anything that tangentially related to a god or a noble characters except Ram, which many of them used as a surname.

And thus, from a dead mother's womb, a soul came out in a society bearing the dead weight of time, and was named Mohan Ram.

IT WAS a time when the 'red-faced' *bilaiti* soldiers, who were travelling by trains towards Gaya, and from there to farther east—maybe to Calcutta, maybe somewhere else—got down at stations, walked to and fro near their compartments and sometimes shouted at each other in English. If, by chance, any Indian went near them, they abused him by calling him a 'dirty nigger', but nobody took exception to those incomprehensible abuses from the superior white men, for the abusers often threw a packet of biscuit or chocolates towards the children who stared steadfastly at them from a distance. Chocolate was hitherto unknown to those rustic famished children, who picked those up without gratitude and at once ran away lest those had to be returned.

"Look, they have wealth, but they have no peace. The white people are fighting a big war among them. One man called Hitler has dragged them all into a war," said a strongly built man in the village called Puraina, which was a bit away from the rail track. He was a railway man and a Socialist, Hukum Lal Yadav, who always wore a worried look on his face and never used the caste name 'Yadav'. The Socialists, in those days, were part of the Congress, the party synonymous with Mahatma Gandhi. Of course, Hukum Lal—respected in the village for his knowledge of the outside world—was repeating what he had heard from his union leaders.

That was the age of Gandhi *baba*, whom Puraina knew more as a saint, despite the fact that the village had a few persons linked with politics, mostly the upper caste men, and one or two Backwards. The Untouchables of Puraina, whose *tola* was not even considered a part of the village by the upper castes or the Backwards, were still secluded from the world outside the village; neither the ripples of the Second World War, nor the tremors of freedom movement could penetrate their wall of ignorance. They did not even know about Jagjivan *babu* who in those days was organizing a miniscule section of the Untouchables in the Bhojpur region itself. But, unlike them, the leading section of the Backwards were making efforts to assert themselves politically. They had earlier formed Triveni Sangh, an organization of the Yadav-Koiri-Kurmi combination, to challenge the upper-caste-led Congress. They were routed in the polls, and though some of them joined the Congress, an overwhelmingly larger section saw a new dimension in the burgeoning force called the Socialists.

When Puraina was thus being connected with the mainstream of politics, came the news of Gandhi's clarion call: *Aangrezo, Bharat Choro* (Britishers, Quit India). Roshan Lal, a Backward who had left the village earlier to be with Gandhi Maharaj, came back with news from Patna that students came in thousands and hoisted the national tricolour on the eastern gate of the Secretariat, while seven of them died in police firing. While spreading the news, Roshan Lal urged the villagers to rise against the British and to take out a procession in the village. "*Hatheli pe dahi nehi jamta* (curd cannot be set on the palm of the hand)", he told them, and added, "If you don't fight, you will never be free."

But the local Congress leader, Sampat Singh, an upper caste Rajput, was reluctant. "Badhe Thakur does not want any trouble in the village," he told his close aides, and the words spread in whispers permeated the whole village, compelling the villagers to ignore the call of Gandhi. But provoking and prodding news poured in regularly: 'In Muzaffarpur district, people have disarmed the police and taken possession of a police station'; 'a national government has been established in the northern part of Bhagalpur'; 'Siaram Singh has established a parallel administration in Sultanpur'. The steady flow of news refused to stop, as though it was a wild fire and would burn down everything. It came from everywhere: Deoghar, Sarwan, Paharpur, Ranchi, Dalbhum, Jamshedpur, Rupauli, Bikram…

And finally, some young boys decided to leave the village with Roshan Lal, the Congress volunteer, for some unknown place in the Tarai of Nepal where Jayaprakash Narayan, Kartik Prasad, Shri Krishna Singh, Anugrah Narayan Singh, and some others had set up a centre for training the Azad Dastas, the soldiers of independence. Before leaving, they took out a small procession only to chant the mantra: *Bande Mataram*. Hail thee Mother. This happened despite the definite disinclination of the Badhe Thakur, and thus was something revolutionary, something the people discussed for days and weeks and even years. It was irrelevant that the procession avoided the vicinity of the *haveli* and even Roshan Lal did not insist.

But the resonant mantra gradually died down as the movement of 1942 evaporated suddenly like camphor. However, that was not the end of news. From Netaji Subhash Chandra Bose, who had escaped from India and was in a far away land called Japan, came the clarion call that people would cherish for long years: "Give me blood, I will give you freedom." His desperation that brought him to the door of the Axis power threatened the establishments in India; the Congress criticized him severely, while the Communists dubbed him as Tozo's dog. During those days, Puraina saw further emergence of Hukum Lal the Socialist, the first person among the Backwards keeping his hair oiled and combed despite persistent frowns of the upper castes. On every Wednesday night, he came back to his village with scintillating stories, and on one such night, he revealed dramatically, "Pandit Nehru is bristling lest Netaji Bose comes back, and is asking the British to fortify the Red Fort."

The vast majority of the listeners had no idea where this Red Fort was, but ignoring the point they asked, "Pandit Nehru has become a friend of the white men?"

Hukum Lal laughed wryly and answered, "Ah ha ha, he was always like that. He wants to become the Prime Minister. He is not Ram Manohar Lohia."

The listeners asked who this Lohia was and Hukum Lal explained that he was an exceptional leader whom the Congress would not allow to rise, for given a chance he would outshine Nehru.

Bose became a myth in the vast fields of innumerable villages like Puraina when he disappeared all of a sudden, leaving behind the incredible news of his death in an air crash at Taihoku, an incident shrouded in mystery. Many dismissed the air crash as a fabrication, and believed Bose would be back.

In Puraina, Hukum Lal got going; he would propagate his message on his off day when the young and interested Backward men huddled themselves in his one-storey tile-roofed house. "Independence is imminent," he said confidently. "But what does it mean if you do not get two square meals a day, if you remain neck-deep in loans and bow before the upper castes? Be prepared for a long drawn battle against the landlords and the money lenders." This message, directed against the *haveli*, was spread secretly only among the Backwards, and though there were few takers, some of those Backward boys who had left the village with Roshan Lal in '42, heard it respectfully. Hukum Lal would go back to Gaya early Friday, only to come back to Puraina the following Wednesday with a new story: "Mahatma Gandhi and Pandit Nehru have fallen apart. Mahatma wants to give the reins of the country to Mohammad Ali Jinnah to avoid the partition of this country, but Nehru, a greedy man, won't agree."

Suddenly someone from the listeners, one Mahadev Chaudhary, an outsider visiting Puraina regularly in those days, burst into a loud protest: "Why should Jinnah be given prominence... so that the bastard can butcher the Hindus? Gandhi has gone mad." The sheer pitch of his voice stunned the others, and he utilized the opportunity to spit venom against those Muslims who were clamouring for the partition of the country. It was not something strange in those days. Hindu chauvinists were preaching hatred against the Muslims, while even a greater number of Muslim fundamentalists were preparing for 'direct action' against the Hindus.

India, which survived centuries of invasion and plunder, foreign rule and strife for freedom, thus saw the darkest clouds hovering over its soul. A blinding dust storm brewed over the western province of Punjab and the eastern province of Bengal and surrounding areas... A call for Direct Action by the Muslim League with the direct fallout in the form of riots... The retaliatory Great Calcutta killings... An all-pervasive communal frenzy brutalized the message of coexistence propagated by the Sufis, by the Bhakti proponents, and by Gandhi *baba*. Thousands were murdered, trainloads of corpses reached their final destination, thousands were raped, tortured, vandalized and millions were pauperized.

As Gandhi's voice got muffled, on the fields of Puraina and other adjacent villages emerged Mahadev Chaudhary. Openly he preached, "Kill the Muslims to take revenge of the killing of your Hindu brethren in Bengal. Don't listen to Gandhi, he is not *Mahatma* (the great soul), he is a *Duratma* (the wicked soul)."

The poison tree was growing fast.

Then the inevitable happened. After centuries of strife and fraternity, the majority of Muslims decided to part ways with the majority of Hindus, and two new free nations, India and Pakistan, were born in mid-August 1947, over the bodies of its own people. The country was divided on the basis of religion, but millions of Muslims, who had no means of migration, or who had decided to stay on in India, were left to fend for themselves by their own leaders. A significant number, though much less in proportion, of Hindus stayed back in Pakistan, mainly in the eastern part of it, which was two thousand kilometres away from the western part.

Now it was time for restoring peace within the countries; the Congress under Nehru and the League under Jinnah started the process in their respective shards of land. Mahadev Chaudhary, the propagator of hate, was arrested near Gaya a few days after the British withdrew from India, and in protest, the Hindu Mahasabha arranged a *dharna*, but without much success.

Puraina gradually came back close to its old and eternal self, but not without exceptions. One such exception was the growing aspiration of the upper castes who hankered for more facilities, more wealth and more power, as they considered the new regime after Independence also their monopoly. Hukum Lal too came back with his old message, and turned more intrepid when the Socialists planned to sever links with the Congress. Socialists under Lohia declared that they would not only strive for a classless society, but also a casteless society, and that enthused Hukum Singh like anything.

Days later, Gandhi fell to the bullets of Nathuram Godse, a man suspected to be linked with the RSS, a Hindu chauvinist organization.

The Congress volunteer Roshan Lal, who by then was known to Rajendra *babu*, the most prominent leader of the party in Bihar, asked everybody to go on a fast for a day, and even those living across the *nullah* observed 'no cooking', something which was neither occasional nor significant to them. Roshan Lal left the village a few days later, this time to join Vinoba Bhave, a Gandhiite who was about to start his movement to urge people to donate land.

On his next off day, Hukum Lal the Socialist briefed the villagers, "For all his life, *Mohatmaji* preached non-violence. But his body was carried for cremation on an Army cart. This is what Nehru has done. Lohiaji is hurt." Gradually the villagers, particularly the Backwards, who were almost half the population of the village, started accepting Lohia as another great man and as an answer to Pandit Nehru, the Prime Minister who was too westernized, too distant.

After Independence, different dimensions were also being added to the quiet life of rural India. "Gandak Project is initiated by Rajendra *babu* who has become the Union Agriculture and Food Minister," the upper castes and a few Backward Kurmis who also owned land at Puraina started discussing in their private conversation. "Saran, Champaran, Muzaffarpur would now get canal water. But, what about us? What about our area?"

Expectation was running high among the well-off men, who were solidly with the Congress. Another section was also with the Congress; the section untouched by the Independence, planning or democracy—the 'Untouchables'. They were now going to be known by another nickname—SC, i.e., Scheduled Castes—as all Untouchable groups, along with all tribes, were being mentioned in a schedule of the new Constitution to give them reservation in employment and in legislatures. They were, however, not allowed to go near the polling booth by the forward castes during the first general elections, for they did not treat them as equal citizens. But if they were allowed, ironically, most of the Untouchables would have voted for the Congress!

MOHAN RAM did not grow up much in the first eight years of his life, though he appeared lanky and taller than all other Chamar boys of his age, but destiny took charge of the winding path of his life thereafter.

He started working as a drover from the age of eight, tending the pigs of a Dusadh, the richest in the colony known as the Chamar-*tola* whose family never starved. Other boys of his age also worked in the fields, or anywhere else, as drovers or servants or labourers, and sometimes they huddled together in the evening to share their experiences. "I heard strange sounds while I was shitting near the pond," a boy of 12 said. "Then I raised my head and found a kid being dragged into the water by a three-headed snake." Mohan Ram, sitting in one corner, thought of the three-headed snake—or could it be a monster—and wondered why he saw only normal animals, neither monsters nor ghosts.

One morning, his grandfather Budha Chamar, who had by then become so old that he had started talking to the trees, walked across the bamboo bridge over the canal that was full to the brim in mid-August.

He reached the gravelled road through which the carts managed to roll on, ambled aimlessly for some time and then crouched down on one side of the road, casting his long shadow on it. And, as fate would have it, Badhe Thakur and Sampat Singh were just then passing by on a cart run by two horses to attend a function in the city to celebrate the second anniversary of Independence Day. Pullu Yadav, the head of the guards of the Thakur, waved his hand furiously, indicating to the Chamar to get off the road—the shadow of an Untouchable was polluting—but his attempts failed, for the Chamar could neither see nor hear well. So, Pullu had to shove him off the road.

The Old Chamar rolled down the slope to the field and tried to get up for the last time by keeping his palms on the ground, like any other dying animal, but failed. It was Hukum Lal, the Socialist, who saw the incident and with the help of some other Backwards took the old man to Chamar-*tola*. The Chamars were baffled as they saw Hukum Lal in their *tola*, for no Backward had ever crossed the canal before. It stoked up a furore in the *tola*.

A furore was nothing unusual in the Chamar-*tola*, as almost every other day there was a burst of an ugly brawl among the women, who often attacked each other and fought severely, often with the sari off from the upper part of their bodies, as though their survival depended on the outcome of that particular fight. It was a scene that was occasionally witnessed in the colony of the Backwards also, but never in the colony of the upper castes. The arrival of the body of the oldest Chamar of the colony, however, gave rise to a furore of a different tone.

Hukum Lal narrated what had happened, and tried to rouse the Chamars to lodge a complaint with the police. "Be brave," he said, but other Backwards accompanying him did not approve of such bravery. The Chamars turned their faces glum, and later decided to go to the *haveli* and beg money to cremate the old man.

Mohan was stuck with the words: "Be brave." For days, he wondered about its meaning. Though the answer eluded him, he began to get out of his old shrunken world, and suddenly grew up.

The second time Mohan leaped forward was a few months later when he saw Mangu Chamar striking his old mother on her head with a bamboo pole and heard the sound of her head cracking like a coconut. Those were the days of severe vagaries of nature, causing an epidemic of hunger that engulfed village after village, the whole of the Rohtas district and beyond. Mangu Chamar's mother was a nagging woman who whinged the entire morning with her allegation that her son and daughter-in-law and their children were eating good stuff, even rice, but not giving her any food. Mangu tried to convince her that there was no food even for the children in the hovel, forget about rice, which they had eaten occasionally in better days. But she was not convinced, and started crying loudly, inciting the skeleton called Mangu to lose his cool and kill his mother. Within minutes, the menfolk gathered about her body, and the women came up to cry in accordance with the tradition that called for loud grieving.

But Birju, Mohan's father, shut all the mourners up, asked the elders to consider where the money for the cremation would come from, and came up with his proposition: "The Thakurs are unlikely to pay anything as they have already paid for three cremations in our *tola*. But if we fail to cremate the body, they may punish us… The only way out is to pull her body to the bank of the Son and let it float away." By then, Birju was accepted as the traditional headman of the colony, as he was cunning and sharp like his father, the Budha Chamar, and after hearing him, the Chamars and the Dusadhs turned worried.

The body was pulled away from the open and kept under a bush about half a kilometre away. Late at night, some young men put it on three supple bamboo polls, dragged it towards the west until they reached the bank of the Son, lit a stick, touched it on the mouth of the old woman and then, going down further into the river, pushed it into the water without any sense of grief, as though the river had taken that away too.

The whole incident had an unlikely observer, beyond anyone's imagination, a young Mohan Ram. While all those who carried the body were so scared that they ran back to their colony, Mohan sat along the bank and looked on towards the mighty Son.

A few months later, in the field where he grazed pigs, Mohan Ram met Dilshad Singh, a man from a distant land, who came across the Son to hide in the jungles as the police was after him. He told Mohan something that he had not heard before, and failed to comprehend even when he heard the words: *Yeh azadi jhuti hai; desh ki janta bhukhi hai* (This freedom is a sham; the people of the land are hungry). He also talked of an armed struggle and raised questions, "Why should you work at your age instead of going to school? Why should people remain unfed, without clothes? Why?"

And then young Mohan Ram added another question, "Why should we be treated as Untouchables?"

"True. Gandhi asked people to abolish untouchability and renamed you as Harijan. It has changed nothing. But we shall have to fight for our rights."

"If we Untouchables fight, would we be able to live with all others... inside the proper village, instead of at the outskirts?" Mohan asked.

Dilshad nodded uncertainly and muttered, "We have never thought of that. But that should be a part of real freedom."

"We would be allowed to keep a pet dog too?" Mohan was excited.

It befuddled the Communist, who did not know that the Untouchables there were not allowed to keep a male dog. He was there, hiding in the woods for a couple of days, and then he disappeared; but, by then, Mohan had become different from the others, though no one, not even he himself, knew it.

Mohan, however, really grew up one night. It was a time when the canal was overflowing, inundating the Chamar-*tola* where ankle-deep water remained logged for weeks during the monsoon. It had no scope of overflowing to the other side—known as the 'village'—as that was on higher ground. Mohan created a stir by slapping a Thakur boy of his age, who playfully slung a mud-ball on his face when Mohan was passing by the place where he was sitting.

Mohan turned towards him and asked, "Why did you do this?"

It irritated the upper caste boy, who came up to teach the Chamar a lesson, but Mohan slapped him on his face tightly and then shoved him aside so hard that he fell down and sprained his leg.

Within hours, the incident reverberated through Puraina and reached the Chamar-*tola*, which winced at the dastardly act of their boy, scared that it might bring in tragedy for all of them. Badhe Thakur, however, pronounced a bizarre punishment, "The boy should be tied up to the oldest banyan tree of the village throughout the night, and if the gods do not kill him, he shall be freed the next morning."

It rained that night. And in the middle of it, a jackal came up close to him, its white fangs showing, but suddenly a dog fed by the *haveli* came running down, and the animal made a hasty retreat.

Mohan was brought back home the next morning half-conscious, running a high fever.

When he was convalescing, one day he asked Munni, his sister-in-law, "What was my father and the others were doing that night?"

Munni got a start, stared at him with her melancholic eyes, but said nothing, for she had nothing to say. She knew that her brother-in-law, who was still shorter than her in height, was turning into a dangerous rebel; a fact that even Mohan did not know. She embraced him to cajole the rebel, and said, "You suffered too much. Don't fight them. They are much more powerful. They will chase you everywhere. They are highborn and powerful people."

Mohan felt her breasts, soft small lumps of flesh touch his back, and for the first time in his life, he felt a bit uneasy with such touch. But ignoring that, he asked, "Who has decided that they are highborn?"

"God. It's God's design and you cannot alter it."

"I shall alter it."

Munni flinched in a way like she was singed. "Never say that again. They will kill you Mohanowa. They will kill you."

"They won't get me. I'll leave this village."

Munni withdrew her hand from his body, sat beside him, and after a long time whispered in his ears, "That's better. Leave."

And Mohan really left the village a few days later with the Mushahars, a group of Untouchables who reared male calves only to sell those for meat. For pursuing such an 'unholy' profession, they were barred from entering even the Chamar-*tola* of Puraina. When the Chamars heard the news of their boy going with them, they were so shocked that they cursed Mohan with choicest abuses.

From Puraina, the Mushahars went northwards along the mighty River Son and reached a place where the rail tracks crossed the river and big boats waited for ferrying passengers. The leader of the Mushahars said, "Ten miles ahead the Son conjoins the Ganga."

"And what happens to the Son then?" Mohan Ram seemed puzzled.

"You won't find it anymore," the Mushahar replied, sounding indifferent.

An incredulous Mohan Ram jostled in his mind with what the old man had said, for it was beyond even his fevered imagination that there could be some place in the world where the Son did not exist! Then he realized that even those who looked mighty could cease to exist after a certain point.

9

The Present Continuous (1983)...

MORE THAN a couple of weeks after regaining his senses, one night he manages to get down from the bed, and staggers a few steps using the wall as a prop to have a look outside through the door. He notes down the facts in his mind: the attendant woman is not nearby... the passage outside is dimly lit... two constables guarding him are asleep.

Seconds later, his head starts reeling, sending a clear signal that he may fall at any moment. That will certainly invite frenetic efforts to cure him and much stronger vigilance, he knows. Assembling all his strength, he shambles back to his bed and allows his body to slump onto it. A few minutes later, gasping and trembling under the strain of getting up, he manages to look about the room, and realizes his effort has gone unnoticed. The fact gives him so much satisfaction that he starts chalking out a plan of escape. He realizes he cannot just walk out of the hospital; he requires a back-up system for which he needs to contact his comrades.

He keeps waiting for days and weeks, like a lizard waiting for its prey to come close, not betraying any sign of his regained senses. Without opening his eyes, he watches or feels everything about him; the humid heat of the end-monsoon which is often soothed by a shower, the footsteps of a lady doctor who visits him regularly and makes his body turn to avoid bed-sores, the odour of spirit that indicates the attendant is going to give him one more injection…

Suddenly, one day he hears the doctor asking a nurse whether the patient has stopped opening his eyes, and he realizes that earlier he used to open them. He decides to do that again.

Days pass by. At times, he understands everything perfectly, but often his senses turn weak, he cannot open his eyes and remains stagnant in a twilight zone from where he can hear, smell or realize certain things, but cannot respond to anything. He realizes that the lady doctor must have known him for years, for often she calls him softly, as though trying to wake him up, by using the name 'Mohan *dada*'. The voice is familiar, but Mahendra cannot remember where he could have heard it. Next time, he opens his eyes to see the doctor, and she too recognizes the difference in his look. "Mohan *dada, aami Rani, chinte parcho* (I am Rani, can you recognize me)?" she asks in Bengali, for she knew Comrade Mohan as a Bengali.

Mahendra now asks, "Badal's sister?"

For a few seconds, Rani is stilled, absolutely rattled, for she had never imagined that the patient would come out of his coma so magically, as though he was just kidding with the doctors all these months. "You have got your senses back?" she struggles to mutter as she regains herself, staring at Mahendra in disbelief.

"This is Magadh Hospital?" he utters the words with difficulty.

"No. This is Patna," she whispers, still unable to overcome the shock.

"How many days have I been here?" his voice is still feeble.

"Days? You have been here for months. This is June 1983. You are here from January."

Mahendra, who had noted that there was nobody else in the room before he spoke, now asks for a favour, "Rani *didi*, can you keep it a secret that I am now better?"

The air outside is heavy, indicative of a shower, while in the room, an old fan screeches along, as though to create an ambience of uncertainty.

"But, why?" Rani asks.

Mahendra has already seen a ray of hope at the end of the long, ruthless tunnel in the form of Dr Rani Sharma, whom he knows as Rani Bannerjee. He mumbles, "If they do not know that I have come round, they will not guard me properly. That is my only chance of fleeing."

"Fleeing? Are you mad? You are too weak… you will not even be able to climb the stairs." Rani strikes the proper note of caution. "And even if you escape, you will die very soon, for you need medication and special care yet for many, many months."

"It doesn't matter if I die; what matters is whether I have tried till the end," he says while keeping his eyes on the door.

Rani too looks about her to ensure no one is watching them from outside. "You are still like what you were in those days," she comments. "But Badal, who was your comrade, is a rich man in America now. All those middle class men and women… they are all in the rat race again, working as lecturers, journalists, intellectuals and what not, using their angry image to the hilt for material benefit. Why are you still fighting?"

The answer comes after a long pause. "They came to fight for the others. That's great, salutary… but that gave them freedom to leave. I fight for myself. I can't leave me." He spoke in Hindi, though Rani was speaking in Bengali.

A second later, Mahendra closes his eyes in a way as though he has nothing to add anymore.

Rani becomes so obsessed with his words that she does not report the development to anyone. But the incident unnerves her, unsettling her beliefs and convictions. When Rani had gone to the USA a couple of years after the Naxalbari days, she found Badal a hero among the Indians in Dallas for his struggle against the system in his previous avatar. Rani felt disgusted when another woman told her that they admired Badle (that was how the Americans pronounced Badal and, how funny, the Indians were imitating them!) for his courage and conviction. "Conviction of what?" Rani could not resist herself from asking.

"Conviction of fighting, of course."

"Fighting? Does he fight here?" Rani asked the swooning crowd.

The women were disheartened, but one of them still insisted, "He broke a jail in India... that is no small thing."

Rani was shocked, for she knew Badal never broke any jail. She understood Badal had fabricated stories before those idiotic lots who were devotees of everything American. She later narrated the story to Ashok Sharma, her husband, and insisted for a reaction from him. Ashok came up with a strange thesis. "Badal has transformed to Badle, and by that, from an outlaw he has become a safe hero. Who is a safe hero? We, the middle class people, worship heroes who don't bite anymore, whose stings are broken. They can be safely eulogized. Like Che Guevara. Too distant. So a hero. But if their deeds affect us, we abuse them. If they are around till the time they can bite, have stings, they are considered rogues."

Rani believed that all of those who had decried and challenged the system during those 'Naxalbari days' had turned into safe heroes; she had no idea that some of them were still fighting, were moving about the jungles and hills, were being hit by police bullets, were dying. With all this at the back of her mind, and the emaciated body of Mohan alias Mahendra in front of her eyes, she asks again a few days later, "Why are you still fighting the mighty state when the result is known?"

"What would the result be?" Mahendra Chamar asks.

"The state will crush you like a piece of paper," she replies without any doubt.

"*Nahi Rani didi, nahi*," Mahendra's voice is feeble but unwavering. "Have you seen those concrete platforms where women place their earthen pitchers to get water from tube wells? After a few years, because of friction with those pitchers, the concrete platforms begin to soften up... and after a decade, you have to remake that place as it turns into a big hole. You won't believe it now, but... this is which year?"

"1983."

"See how things shape up by the year, say, 2003."

The doctor is sure that the state of India will never wear out like those concrete platforms, but that is a question of perception. And despite all her efforts to overcome her emotion, from the deepest core of her heart she cannot but salute the man for his courage and conviction.

A day later, Mahendra's condition starts deteriorating, his body turns feeble, thoughts get all tangled up and his memory fails. But again he improves, and one day, a name suddenly strikes him. He remembers Phalguram, a comrade's brother who worked in the hospital. The next time Mahendra finds Dr Rani alone in his room, he asks her, "Is there a ward boy called Phalguram?"

Rani thinks for a moment and nods. "But why?" she asks.

"Do me a favour. Arrange his duty here," Mahendra says as dispassionately as possible.

Rani looks at him for a while and then goes out without committing anything.

HARRY FEELS that he has stepped onto a trap laid by his uncle. Now, at times, he even wonders whether his uncle fabricated a bizarre story to lure him to marry Maya, literally the illusion, so that she may compel him to behave like a warlord. But the unfortunate part is that some things once done cannot be undone.

He knows his thoughts are evil, for casting such an aspersion on his uncle, or branding his marriage as a mistake is unholy, but he cannot suppress the feelings that come from the core of his heart. His wife Maya has astounded him to such an extent that he cannot escape the disturbing thought. He married his cousin's wife soon after his uncle asked him not to resist his destiny. And then, as though to validate the story he was told, Maya revealed to him that she never had any physical relationship with his cousin. "He avoided me in the nights," she told him.

Harry took Maya to foreign lands and wanted to stun her with his resources, but to his dismay, he found her ability to be excited limited. It amazed him and finally he asked her the reason one day when they were in the lap of the Rocky Mountains in Colorado state.

They stepped out of Denver airport and the glace-topped Rocky Mountains at about a distance of a hundred kilometres dazzled in magnificence, but her eyes did not sparkle. When they drove to the Rocky Mountain National Park with the River Thompson rising and falling along the road, Harry started telling her, "Those tops are the Tundra region of the glacial peaks that you must have read about in geography books; and the trees on the slopes are aspen, fir, spruce and... and... and ponderosas. Isn't all this exciting?"

"Yes," she replied in one word and that was all from her side.

Even the Trail Ridge Road through the park, the 'overlooks' from where both sides can be viewed, the valley, or spotting of elk, nothing could cast a magical spell on her. As Harry walked the Copeland Falls trail and reached a point from where the sound of waterfall could be heard, he told her, "I feel like staying here for the rest of my life, in this serenity of nature and cool breeze."

She did not respond.

A thundershower hit the area in the afternoon, and the locals said it was a regular feature. And Harry was more excited then.

At the end of the day's trip, after gifting her a $5,000 diamond necklace, Harry asked her why she was not excited.

"I was in the hills in my childhood, and the Himalayas are much higher and richer in every aspect than these ranges," she said confidently in her plumy tone that attracted Harry even when she was not his wife.

In a bid to lighten the atmosphere, Harry said, "So you don't like the idea of settling down here."

"Never," she shook her head slowly. "I agreed to marry you because uncle said you would avenge the killings of so many members of our family. He said a man without a wife remains a raw force, for 'woman' means 'power'. He wanted me to guide you towards your destiny."

A while later, after realizing her true intentions for the first time, Harry asked, "So what do you want?"

"You must take out that man from hospital and kill him in your village… in full view of the locals."

"Come on, we are no more the landlords of the old times. What do we gain from this?"

"That should not be your lookout. You should do your karma, you must do what you are supposed to do. You need not ponder over the outcome."

For a while, Harry could hardly say anything. He was astonished to see that she was seemingly prepared to sacrifice love, pleasure, money, comfort and everything for which ordinary women yearn for, only to achieve something absurd representing a dead and decayed time.

Coming back from the United States, Maya went straight to the village and decided to stay on in the *haveli* at Puraina, and not in Allahabad. Harry was initially shocked to know of her decision, but later he felt relieved, as the burden of a missionary wife had become too much for him in less than a month of their marriage.

He came back to the *haveli* after a gap of a month, vaguely hoping that his long absence could have turned her missionary wife into a real spouse, but nothing like that happened. His wife along with his uncle called him on the first night to discuss something urgent, and there his wife announced, "You should arrange for killing the man."

Harry thought for a while, and as he saw a flicker of hope, he said, "That won't be difficult. I will hire someone who will sneak into the hospital and will kill the…"

"No," the illusory Maya was brusque. "You should bring the man here, tie him to a tree and cut him into pieces in full view of the people."

 "Then you will mete out justice in the same way as your forefathers did in this village," his uncle added and Maya nodded in agreement.

Since then, the thought is doing rounds in his head. It creates a discomfort in his body too as he remembers everything while sitting in a jeep that has developed a snag just in the front of the *haveli*. He has made a mistake by marrying Maya; but probably his marriage was part of a conspiracy hatched by his uncle Chhote Thakur, who is actually his father.

Suddenly, Harry's eyes zero in on the lion king atop the gate, and as he sees it with its part fallen out, he gets a severe jolt. He keeps looking at it intently till the driver returns to the jeep, having sorted out the mechanical problem. "I failed to save the lion king because I forgot all about it," he tells himself. "I have failed to challenge my destiny and now I have no escape from it."

SHYAMLAL, WHOM Bhola identified before the police as an associate of Sunder Besra, earns freedom after spending more than six months in jail.

He reaches Kalipura at dusk, when the horizon is painted with an abundance of red that will soon turn into orange and then gradually fade into darkness. But he gets confounded by the appearance of the hamlet—the hens and roosters are not running about to get into the shelters, the children are not crying, the elders are not axing the dry woods to put those into earthen ovens. All the sounds and sights he was acquainted with in this village from his birth have died out, as though a *dano* has devoured all the elements there, leaving the terrain, the hills, and the brook to long for the lost verve.

Then he understands it all: the village is absolutely deserted!

Shyamlal sits for hours on the threshold of what once-upon-a-time was his home, at a loss with his present continuous form, wondering how the people have disappeared. At least, 15 families were there, he remembers, and though some people were talking about leaving this place, nothing was finalized. Then where have they gone?

After spending the night in his dilapidated hut, hungry and thirsty, victim of a recurrent nightmare in which he found himself caught in a quicksand and drowning, he sets out in the early morning to find his wife Bijuriya, the lightning, who must have gone somewhere with the others along with her sons. He begins his long journey towards civilization, eastwards towards Barhi, the place where the villagers used to go whenever they faced trouble. As the road by the side of the village still lies incomplete, he walks for an hour to reach the highway and takes a jeep from there. He reaches Barhi another hour later, for the jeep cannot cover more than 20 kilometres an hour, as its old and over-roaring engine has to be cooled every now and then. The engine seems even more burdened as the jeep is heavily crowded on a highway that needs immediate repairing.

At Barhi, Shyamlal gets his first clue about the missing folks. Gitram, a local *mukhia*, who seems to be quite a responsible man, informs him that several months ago 'some 15 or 20 families from a village in the west' came to Barhi carrying all their belongings with them— aluminium utensils, earthen ovens, cheap mirrors, shoddy clothes and broken hearts—like refugees. But as Barhi had no chance to provide for them, they spent the wintry night in the open, and the next morning left for Koderma in two trucks that were going to haul coal.

Pursuing the trail, Shyamlal reaches Koderma, the township bordering the collieries, where, after one and a half day's effort, he meets some of his old neighbours, a few of whom are working in the mines or in a construction project, and another few, mostly women, in households. But his wife Bijuriya and their two sons are not there. Jhumru, an aged man, tells him sadly, "She was here for a month waiting for you. But then a local constable noticed her and along with two other men, he came in the night. They demanded money from us. As we told them we have no money, they demanded they should spend the night with Bijuriya."

"Why Bijuriya?"

Jhumru hangs his head in shame, crosses his hands and reveals, "They did not know her name. They said they wanted the bitch who was taller than the others and who had buttocks like a horse and bosoms like ripe mangoes. We tried to dissuade them. But they threatened they would evict us from here. So we had no choice."

Shyamlal knew his wife was flamboyant, not having a very clean character, but in this case, she was not at fault.

"If it were Kalipura, we would have called the red forces and got those policemen beaten black and blue," mumbles Jhumru.

"What happened after that?"

"She has gone to Bokaro. Some of our people have gone there also. Not much job left here. So…"

"Why didn't you tell me that you were leaving Kalipura?"

Jhumru looks amazed, "We were too scared to go to meet you. They could have arrested us if we went to the jail to…"

Shyamlal starts his journey again, and reaches Bokaro, which is too big for the locals to know about all the happenings in the city, a fact that amazes Shyamlal. After a long search lasting for several days, he finds a few people from Kalipura who tell him that she might have gone to Dhanbad. A worn out Shyamlal reaches Dhanbad, which is an even bigger city, full of people with whom he does not even dare to converse, for they look at the likes of Shyamlal with a frown. The roads seem abnormally broad, buildings and offices are overwhelming and even the railway station is perplexing with many platforms and rails like a fisherman's net. Then finally, a man comes to his help and after knowing of his mission, he asks, "You know the address? Otherwise, you won't be able to find anyone."

Shyamlal stands puzzled. His address was, Village Kalipura, district Gaya. So now, Bijuriya's address is Village… not village… City Dhanbad, district… district he does not know, but that should not matter, for he is already in Dhanbad.

"You don't know?" the man says compassionately and adds, "Then where will you search for them?"

"I never knew this place is so big," Shyamlal mutters in a sad tone.

"This place is not that big," the man replies. "There are cities like Calcutta which are 10 or maybe 20 or 30 times bigger than this."

Suddenly, Shyamlal gives in to the weight of depression and bursts into tears; if Bijuriya has gone to those cities with her sons, he will never find them in his life, as he is too scared to go to any bigger place. He is now certain that if he ever reaches any of those places, he will not even find himself, and the world itself will be lost to him!

The man looks on sympathetically at him. Then he advises him to search for his dear ones in the adjacent tribal villages and leaves.

A day later, his search brings him on to a quicksand created by a deserted mine. All of a sudden, it begins to collapse as he walks on the ground, giving him no time to recover. He just caves in... whhrrrrr...shrrrrrrrrr...whrrrrr... The more he struggles to bring his body out, the more he invites further erosion in the loose ground that blocks even a part of the hole above him. He shouts at the top of his voice, but it invites no one except a mild shower of a mix of coal dust and sand, only to settle him deep inside that is dimly lighted by a ray of light coming from the mouth of the hole at about one-twenty degree on his right.

Shyamlal sits quietly, gasping and terrified, and after quite a while, starts dozing.

He wakes up amidst total darkness, and wonders whether he is dead, for such darkness, which has absolutely no element of life, where one cannot see anything even after opening one's eyes, cannot be mundane. Either he is dead, or he is fully covered by the earth, in which case he will die sooner rather than later, concludes Shyamlal and resigns himself to fate that has been playing tricks with him for months. With no expectation from either life or death, he tries to sleep again, but fails as his belly crumbles in ache, his muscles pain, and his legs buried under the earth goes numb. If he is already dead, then death is sheer agony, he tells himself and wonders how long this period of remaining dead is supposed to continue. Months? Years? That will be terrible. "I won't be able to survive it," he mutters to himself, without knowing what the options are before a dead man if he cannot survive the 'afterlife'.

Some minutes pass and the pit becomes faintly lit, and a while later, a streak of sunray sneaks into it. Shyamlal realizes he is alive, which means he has hope of another lease of time, of getting out, of seeing the world that is cruel, but still loveable, like the unchaste woman called Bijuriya. He again tries to get up and get out, but it only sends him another foot deeper and makes him understand the futility of his efforts. Suddenly, he breaks out into a yell, as loud as possible, a shrill ha-ha-ha-ha that rends the air, and apart from causing further erosion, brings back into the pit a faint babble of human voices along with the echo of footsteps gradually fading away.

"Oh god," thinks Shyamlal, "There were people who must have thought I am a *dano* and rushed away."

With his last chance gone, Shyamlal is now more exasperated than exhausted; he starts shouting in filthy language in a way as though his adrenalin has started working in an immoral way, as though he has turned into an altogether different entity, a human ghost. When he had lost all hopes amidst the darkness, he was prepared for a nasty death under the ground from where even his soul would not be able to escape. But after seeing the sunlight, after hearing human voices, after feeling the vibration of footsteps, he is now doubly eager to live. His irate uttering, however, makes him more exhausted, and all the more irascible. He abuses Mahendra Chamar for all his misfortune, for had that man not come to their village, he would not have lost his family, would not have had to embark on a journey through the corners of the world and fall in a ditch.

After a while, he stops abusing anyone and almost faints.

The next time when he wakes up, he hears a clear loud voice, "*Bhitar kono admi hain?* (Is there anyone inside?)"

And now, gathering all his strength for the last time, Shyamlal shouts, "*Bacha lo... hame bacha lo.*"

His voice chokes suddenly after that and he remains uncertain whether anyone has heard him.

But a while later, he hears the sound of a flurry of activities; of shouting, digging, dredging and of abusing, a definite sign of a rescue team working above, on the ground. It continues for a long time, till a man appears close to him, throws a lasso and asks him to put it around his body. Then the rescuer goes up, slowly and cautiously, occasionally slipping a bit, but somehow managing to be steady while dragging Shyamlal by the rope. Shyamlal now sees a vista of the blue sky above his head as the walls on the two sides begin to crumble down on him; but he clings to the rope with all his might and faints as he comes out in the open.

After he regains consciousness, he says, "I'll go back to Koderma."

"Yes. Of course. Do you live there?"

Without knowing who is talking to him, Shyamlal nods. He does not know why he lies.

"I also live in Koderma. My village is lost. So now I live in that town," the other man says again.

Shyamlal turns his head and sees an unknown face. "Where was your village?" he asks as he tries to get up.

"Don't try to get up, your legs are numb," the stranger cautions him and adds, "It will take two to three days to heal. And... about my village... I don't know. It was near a hill that rose up towards the sky in the shape of a bird's head. Just like a bird's head... even with a crest. I had heard about it when I was young. Then those people who told me about it were lost. I don't know where that village is."

"I have also lost my family," Shyamlal says, writhing in pain.

A week later, Shyamlal goes to Koderma with Stephen Munda who was born in the village near the hill shaped like a bird's head. On the way back, sitting together in a crowded bus in which people crouched even on the gangway, Stephen whispers into his ears, "At the root of all our problems are the outsiders. We have to get freedom from those *dikus*. You went to Jamshedpur, that big city. They call it Jamshedpur from the name of the person who established the steel plant there. But where are those tribal men and women, who lived there earlier? Where are they?"

"Where are they?" Shyamlal asks nervously, left without any hint.

"They have turned into beggars, or if fortunate, coolies. That is why we want our own state, a tribal state. We want Jharkhand."

"Are you a Naxalite?" Shyamlal asks as he finds a similarity between what Comrade Mahendra used to speak of and what Stephen now says.

"Naxalite?" Stephen frowns, "No. We are Jharkhandis, who want to make the dreamland of the tribal people a reality."

And then, after a long pause, during which the bus stops and quite a few get down, he says, "The Naxalites are no force. They are in some pockets and that too in the hills and jungles of the western parts of the state. They have different groups who abuse each other. But…"

Stephen lights a bidi and after exhaling a lot of smoke, says, "I mean all non-tribals are not outsiders. The poor Harijans, or some Bengalis who live here for generations and teach in the schools or work in the post offices… we do not treat them as outsiders. But those who are holding all those big jobs in Jamshedpur, in Damodar Valley Corporation, the Bengali and Bihari officers, the rich Muslim money lenders, the landlords, all those who take away our resources, coal, iron, manganese and everything else, denude our forests, they are outsiders. They are our enemies."

"Even some tribal men are notorious," Shyamlal mutters. "I was put in jail because Bhola Munda identified me as a Naxal, though I was never with them."

AS HE waits for a criminal who will show him light, Harry wonders whether this maybe called an irony of fate; he stayed away from the fiefdom for most of his life and became a capitalist under the guidance of his uncle who was killed along with his father, but the past has caught up with him and is prodding him to behave like a brazen feudal lord!

He is standing on the banks of the Ganga, at Dashashwamedh Ghat in the holy city of Banaras, and on his right, under the cool shadow of an umbrella, someone is reciting from the *Ramcharitmanas* by Tulsidas, though no one is listening to him. A few yards away, a man is doing sit-ups, beyond which a priest is performing a ceremony, and the sacred Ganga, carrying industrial waste and human sins, is still shimmering in the afternoon sun. Harry looks on, but does not drink in the veritable sights and sounds about him. He does not even see anything, for he is absorbed in thoughts circling about his wife Maya, the illusion, who has started prodding him towards his dharma.

He does not know why he should try to avenge the killing himself, when there is the police, or the paramilitary force and even the army. But he has no option.

He contacted a man few months ago for the job ordered by his wife, but the man demanded Rs 500,000, and Harry aborted the idea. Maya was furious when she heard this and declared, "I can't stay with a man who cannot avenge the killing of his father and other family members. I will divorce you if you cannot gift me a tuft of hair from the killer's head within a year."

Badly shaken, for he had never heard the word 'divorce' being uttered in the *haveli*, Harry came out of the room, took the steps and a minute later was on the terrace. His ears emitted heat as he tried to imagine himself as a man who had been divorced by his wife! He paced up and down from one end of the roof to the other and fumed in insult and hatred. In Delhi, or in Allahabad, he took on his extreme irritation by watching TV, which in India, unlike in the West, showed only the government channel known as Doordarshan; but in Puraina, the box offered only a few blurred lines due to lack of a clear signal. A few minutes later, as he saw a servant coming up the stairs, he ordered, "Bring a woman who can sleep with me now."

A while later, a woman came up and sat beside him. "You have asked for a woman?' she asked plainly, as though this were a routine affair.

Harry looked at her for a while to see her in the darkness. "Middle-aged, unattractive, but big boobs," he told himself, and next moment, he asked the woman to work on him. She started immediately.

But just when the hurricane within his body was ravaging the woman, he found that she was fighting to make an escape, and it added to his excitement. But she managed to free herself and ran away.

"She was scared of something," Harry concluded and looked behind to see what it could be, only to find another woman standing near the stairs. It took him a few seconds to realize that the woman was Maya! He remained static for a while, and then he pulled up his pyjama and tried to work out a sort of reaction for the moment.

"I came to ask whether you are willing to pay the amount for which that man will bring that Chamar here," she said in cold indifference.

"Oh… oh, *haan*, yes," Harry spluttered, still groping in the dark about the reality of the moment. "I will finalize it tomorrow."

She turned back, towards the stairs, but after taking a couple of steps, stopped to say, "I don't have any objection if you enjoy other women. But try to know something about the women before making love." She paused, probably to give time to Harry so that he could comprehend what he was being told, and then added, "The woman you just enjoyed… Phulmotia… is your uncle's kept woman. The woman thus becomes equivalent to a mother."

"Hello sir," someone greets him from behind.

With a start, Harry comes back to the present and realizes the man is Sher Singh as he spots the negotiator standing at a distance.

"It's a dangerous job." Sher, literally a tiger, breaks his knuckles and adds only a few words, "It will require a lot of money."

"How much?" Harry asks without looking at him.

"Ten lakh rupees."

"Well, but why so much?"

"It's risky. I don't know who you are. Pratap Singh or something. If we are caught while smuggling out that man… Mahendra Chamar… from the hospital, we will not even be able to tell them who ordered us."

"That's why I have contacted you."

"That's why I claim that much."

As they fall silent—the deal is yet to be finalized—Harry lowers his gaze at some women bathing at a distance, and through the wet sari of one woman, aged maybe about 45 or even more, he sees her heavy conch-shaped breasts. "What is the colour of her nipples?" he wonders unmindfully as the woman brings to his mind the woman whom Maya described as equivalent to his mother.

As he is ageing—he is above 40—the desire for sex in him is just growing; 10 years ago, he is sure, he would have just shifted his gaze from such a woman. "But now I take interest in women of any age, and I am getting kinky," he rebukes himself.

Sher Singh says suddenly, "I don't have much time."

"You are demanding too much. Another one demanded half the amount, but unfortunately he was arrested for some other case before he could do anything and is in jail now."

"It's the minimum," Sher Singh says in his laconic style.

"I will pay you." Harry feels excitement in his body, a slow process reaching its crescendo as he looks on at the woman.

"The whole amount in advance."

"Why?" Harry looks back at the man.

"Where shall I find you afterwards?"

"You must. You have to."

"Why?" Sher Singh seems intrigued.

"Because you will have to hand over that man... alive... to me."

"Alive to you?... okay. Then half the amount as advance. But it would have been better if we killed him and handed over the body to you."

"No," Harry is so loud that the man reading Tulsidas glances at him. Harry lowers his pitch. "You must give that bastard to me alive."

"That's risky," the Tiger looks straight at his face. "Police will be on the prowl, and you say he is terminally ill," he utters thoughtfully, trying to imagine the scenario and weighing the possibilities.

"Whatever, if you don't hand him over to me, there's no deal."

"Well, if you insist, that would be done. But pay us half the amount and then get the man. Okay?"

Harry nods and, turns his gaze at the steps leading to the water, but the woman he was leering at a minute ago was nowhere to be found.

WHEN BIPLAB is through with his briefing about a daring plan before his comrades, he breathes deeply, as though he is out of stamina at the moment. "You must have a dry run first," he asserts.

"Is that absolutely necessary?" Karma asks tentatively. "I mean," he explains his point, "if somehow it arouses suspicion, the whole plan will be over."

"That is why it is absolutely necessary. You must know whether at any stage it can arouse suspicion. Otherwise, when you will be taking out Comrade Mahendra... if then something happens, it's over forever. Right? Who will be leading the operation?"

"Comrade Raju, for he has the advantage of knowing everything from his brother who works there as a ward boy."

"It's so great that Comrade Mahendra has come round and nobody knows that. He has planned his escape. We must not fail him," Biplab, literally 'Revolution', says in an emotionally loaded voice. He then heaves a sigh and gets up. A minute later, he hits the road, walking fast towards Lohardaga station from where he will take a train to Ranchi, where tonight he will meet the leaders of Lok Manch, a frontal organization of the Unity Group. They held a people's court last night at a remote place and thwarted the possibility of a riot breaking out between the Hindus and the Muslims of the local area; he is interested in knowing the details from them.

He is keen to continue the distinction between the hit-and-run guerrilla squads and the frontal organizations, which have to work in the open, carry on a struggle for genuine demands of the people, arrange *dharna,* or call for strikes. He feels the leadership of the party should come mostly from those frontal organizations, where people deal with issues politically, and the armed squads should play only subservient roles, similar to the roles of the army in a democratic country, be it bourgeois or socialist. He knows, though he is not prepared to acknowledge it openly, that Charu Majumdar mixed up the two, and since the movement has not clearly demarcated politics and arms.

He boards the wooden train that runs between Lohardaga and Ranchi through the narrow gauge line and opens a Bengali novel by Samaresh Basu, his favourite author, though many of the leftists criticize him as vulgar. As the train moves slowly through the jungle, between the hillocks, as the black soot from the smoke emitted by the engine fly in, Biplab wonders whether human beings can be one-dimensional. "No," he mutters to himself, "even a revolutionary can be attracted towards many women, exposing the many layers of his heart where zeal, love, affection, and sex coexist." He has heard that Mahendra Chamar was also attracted to many women. "He is a character who perfectly matches with this land of jungle and hills and myths," Biplab mutters to himself and wonders why such a man's wife eloped with the traitor called Bhola.

Some days ago, the comrades killed both Bhola and that woman. He knows because they sought permission from him as Mahendra's group has merged with his Unity group.

Biplab feels tired after going through a few pages. At times, he feels tired of his long years in hiding, as a corollary to which he has to do so many other things, remembering his assumed names, travelling on endlessly, and most disgustingly of all, continuously be on alert. He knows that refreshment for him is a debate on the Marxist ideology, a discussion on the life of Che Guevara or the writing of Frantz Fanon, but his underground life limits the scope of such refreshment.

He looks at the world outside that is moving with a slow but steady rhythm, but he does not see anything, for now Frantz Fanon has occupied his mind. He mutters to himself the lines that moved him years ago: "… violence is a cleansing force. It frees the native from his inferiority complex and from his despair and inaction; it makes him fearless and restores his self-respect." He looks at the reddish brick-dust platform the train has stopped at. Maybe Nagjua, or Tangarbasli, or Irgaon, he thinks unmindfully, and wonders how Comrade Mahendra could echo Fanon when he had not read either Fanon, or even Mao. He met Mahendra for the first time in Bengal and then, after a gap of a few years, in Bihar, when the comrade seemed to be a changed person. As they conversed on various topics, Mahendra said, "Arms are necessary not only to fight the enemy, but to imbue confidence among the masses that they can fight and win against the upper castes, the landlords, money lenders and the police."

Biplab looked at him in surprise and then, as though to settle his confusion, asked, "Have you read Frantz Fanon?"

"Who's he?" Mahendra turned his eyes on him for a moment, then again fixed it on some distant object he was gazing at earlier, and without any hesitation, without being defensive, he added, "I don't know. I am not a learned man."

"But how did you reach your conclusion that arms instill confidence among the masses?"

"From my life," Mahendra said impassively. "The lower castes in this country cannot revolt against the system, only because they are scared of arms in the possession of upper castes in the form of landlords, police, and whatever else. From the collective memory, the lower castes or the tribal people know whenever they rebelled, they were crushed by arms that they did not possess."

Biplab could understand him clearly, for he was well acquainted with the history of hundreds of rebellions in India, and he asked, "But why do you talk in terms of castes only? I understand the lower castes are 99 per cent proletariat. But why do you exclude upper caste proletariats?"

Mahendra answered routinely, without much interest, "A poor Brahmin has his pride, his education and caste-culture. Even if he has not gone to the school… he would surely inherit these from the family. And ultimately, he does not remain jobless. He can perform puja and earn something. He is acceptable to all. He lives in a world so far away from the world of the Untouchables!"

As Biplab looks outside and finds two young tribal women laughing merrily, their white teeth glowing, he feels he needs Comrade Mahendra by his side, not as an active soldier, but as a guide.

10

Glimpses of the Past (1940–1980)

DESPITE BEING the third son of his father, Harry was considered as the fourth one in the family, for brothers those days included all the cousins. For Harry, that identity of being the 'fourth' was more important, as under the scheme of things in his family, as conceived by his father, no major role was left for the fourth.

In those days, when he lived in the *haveli* at Puraina, he was of course not Harry, the similar-sounding anglicized version of his name, but Hari Pratap, power of Hari or Narayan. In his generation, all the boys in the family were named after Narayan, a supreme god, who had 108 names—the eldest was Krishna Pratap, the second was Narayan Pratap, and the third was Madhav Pratap. The earlier generation too had Pratap suffixed to their names—the Badhe Thakur was Ravi Pratap, his second brother or Majhle Thakur was Surya Pratap and the third, Chhote Thakur, was Diwakar Pratap, and their names carried the same meaning, the power of the sun.

Harry's father, Badhe Thakur, devoted most of his attention to the first three boys and planned the future meticulously out for them; the eldest would look after the estate, the second would run a school at Puraina and get involved in local politics, and the third—the son of Majhle Thakur—would be in state-level politics. Harry, the fourth son in the family, had no place in this futuristic projection charted out by his father, but he was the favourite of his uncle, Majhle Thakur, who had started his own business defying his elder brother's silent frown. Badhe Thakur was a landlord, a puritan landlord, and he looked down upon the profit-motive that drove an industrialist.

The family was, however, in a transitional phase in those days. While the attraction of the big cities and big money was creeping in, the future of fiefdom itself was under strain. The lord of Puraina was more concerned about the fief, for he knew that after Independence, pressure was growing on the government to abolish fiefs and kingdoms. Nehru, the Prime Minister, was a Socialist in disguise in the Congress Party, up against the kings and zamindars, believed Badhe Thakur, like many other feudal lords.

The immensely powerful family of the lords of Puraina, however, did not possess that kind of land that the lords in eastern Bihar owned. But the family was rich and had houses in various cities, apart from the *haveli* at Puraina. Badhe Thakur was so concerned about the glory of the family that he had started looking for a pawn, someone who would be in politics and stand by him in bad times. But there was no one who could play the role in his family. While his second brother was after making money, his youngest brother, Chhote Thakur, was good for nothing, always after women or opium, and could not be counted upon.

That was when Sampat Singh, the Congress leader from Puraina, was contemplating leaving politics. He felt slighted by the party which had not given him the post of the head of bloc Congress.

When Badhe Thakur came to know it, he decided to visit his house and took Harry, still known as Hari Pratap, with him. Sampat's house was about a hundred metres away, but Badhe Thakur and Harry boarded the horse cart to reach there. Sampat was already at the door and as Badhe Thakur entered, a few children poured flowers at his feet and women hidden inside the house blew conch shells.

"I heard that man Jamaluddin is leaving for Pakistan? Is it true?" Badhe Thakur asked nonchalantly, while being seated in the drawing room.

"Yes. But how do you know him?" Sampat was a bit surprised.

Suddenly Badhe Thakur started laughing like a child. His rosy lips quivered, his fair face turned red, and the look in his eyes turned elusive. After a few seconds, still laughing, Badhe Thakur said, "I know so many things. Do you know Sardar Patel… the Home Minister of the country, the iron man… is an invalid who hardly goes to office?"

Sampat just smiled as he knew the Thakur was a man of inside knowledge and bizarre actions. About 20 years ago, just after taking over the mantle of the Badhe Thakur at a young age, he banned *nanga naach* in his *Khas Taluka* comprising the villages of Puraina, Mohanpur, Koshi and Dakshingaon, going against the sentiment of the people who had considered nude dances a part of their entertainment package. A Bhumihar family in the village of Dakhsingaon violated his writ, organized one episode and was excommunicated by the Badhe Thakur, after which they had to leave the village.

A little later, the landlord started telling Sampat about the importance of being in politics. But the other Thakur was so miffed with the nomination of another man as bloc Congress president, that he countered, "What good would that be? If I have to remain under that Kayastha, why should I be in politics?"

Badhe Thakur, now no longer laughing, answered, "The times are changing. The old leadership of the Congress would be replaced by people who are constructive in their approach. Agitation is something different and those who have led it will find it difficult to be in place. Now you have to rule a country. The party will become less and less important now."

"What do you mean?"

"In Britain, who are the party leaders? It is the government that is important. And the opposition leader with his shadow cabinet. After the election, the party leaders in India will gradually become less and less important. So, you have to concentrate on becoming a legislator and then a minister. You must acquire power. I will see that you contest from Puraina in the coming election. I have already spoken to Anugrah Narayan."

After lunch, Harry came out of the house with his father, and was surprised to see him handing over a one rupee coin to the Congressman, and the latter accepting it gratefully. "Why did you give him money?" Harry asked his father in the cart on their way back home.

"We are lords," Badhe Thakur said nonchalantly. "We only donate, we only give away. We cannot accept anything. So I paid for the lunch, though it was only symbolic."

Soon after, Harry left the village again for Allahabad, where his uncle tried to inculcate in him a different set of values; the values of capitalism. But still, in his mind, his father's charisma won over his uncle's rather vague justification of a new system yet to unfold in the country.

Harry was in St Joseph, the school run by the Germans, and it was during his school days that Harry became interested in girls—it all started with those who studied in St Mary's, just a wall apart—but that was purely romantic. His uncle had brought a big bungalow in Civil Lines after the owner—the area was for whites only before Independence—had left for his country. As he grew up, Harry cycled round the city along with his friends, past the clock tower into old Allahabad for having some good dishes from Loknath, or to Muirabad, the Anglo-Indian colony. By the time he was about to pass out from St. Joseph's, he was in love with Allahabad, and also with a lanky girl with green eyes who studied in St Mary, though they never conversed.

Allahabad was full of fun and fantasy, where people often discussed the impossible, from an impending third world war to the wolf boy. An astrologer predicted that the third world war was only six months away, and people began to store rice, wheat and such other essentials. The weird speculation probably had a seed in reality in the Korean crisis, and the astrologer used it to stake claim on irreversible fame.

The wolf boy, an injured boy of six or seven found among a pack of wolves, however, was sheer entertainment for the locals. After spending many years with the wolves, the boy considered it as one of them and ate only raw meat or fruits and growled like the canines.

He was treated in Balrampur hospital where people thronged to get a glimpse of the boy, and a fortnight later, the story took another turn when a couple from the Khatik community identified him as their son lost in his childhood by birthmarks over his forehead and right thigh. As people read this, they folded their hands in reverence and said, "*Ja ko rakhe Saiyaan, maar sake koi* (If God protects who can kill)?"

Harry was about to finish his school and was all set to join the Allahabad University where his elder brothers went earlier. He hoped that he would meet the lanky girl with green eyes—he still did not know her name—in the university. His uncle, however, announced a different plan for him, that he would go to Calcutta for higher studies. "Bengal and Bombay are the two states where industry is the mantra," said Surya Pratap and asked, "Do you know who the chief minister of Bengal is?"

As Harry looked on blankly, his uncle said, "Dr BC Roy. And Bombay? You must know these names. Mr Morarji Desai."

During those days, the whole city was shaken as a disaster had struck the biggest holy congregation known as *Kumbhmela*, where hundreds were found lying dead after a stampede that started while a procession of *naga sadhus*, a sect whose members remain naked, was passing below the bund on the day of *Mauni Amavasya*, the main bathing day. But now, Harry had to leave all these, the charms or the shock of Allahabad, and to board a train to Calcutta to join the Scottish Church College.

In the train, Harry's companion was a letter from his father that his uncle handed him minutes before the train was whistled off. It started with greeting and blessings for him for the start of a new chapter in his life, but dealt with some other issues too. "Professor Julian Huxley, biologist and author, recently delivered a lecture in a gathering of university students and teachers in Patna. The subject was 'Evolution and modern thought'. He said that the need for the humanity in the present age was to make efforts to understand the new picture of the universe and apply it to the problems of human life to help man realize his destiny. He referred to Marxism too. He said while it was based on scientific thoughts, at the same time it was dogmatic."

Harry alighted from the train at Howrah, with the letter in his hand. He had been told that from the station, he had to reach Calcutta by crossing the Ganga, locally also known as the Hooghly River.

Calcutta was too big, too complicated a city after the cosy, quiet and easy life of Allahabad. To begin with, Harry was depressed by the impersonal appearance of the huge city that had trams rolling on the rails, massive Gothic structures in its central part and old oriental constructions in the north. People ran all the while, either to catch buses or trams, or to attend their offices, or else to buy commodities. Still the men who did the maximum running were the rickshaw-pullers, almost all from Bihar. But the most striking feature was the city's inability to understand Hindi; the locals referred to the Hindi-speaking population as 'Hindustani'. Harry found that surprising, for India or Bharat was also called Hindustan, which meant that all Indians were Hindustanis. But Bengalis had not only kept the term earmarked for the Hindi speaking population, they also had resentment against them. "They have divided Bengal into two so that no Bengali can become prime minister; otherwise, Subhash Bose would have come back and taken over," people said confidently, dismissing the news that Bose had died in an air crash at Taihoku.

The term Hindustani, as used by the Bengalis, was still better as it was value-neutral, but the locals had other derogatory terms in store for Harry. "Are you a *Khotta*?" asked his college friend in English.

A few students could speak in English and Harry could only converse with them, for almost no one knew Hindi. "What's that?" asked Harry.

"That's the term, a bit derogatory one, used for Biharis," his friend Manoj replied. "But I am not insulting you, I am just asking."

Harry took the Bengalis as a toffee-nosed supercilious population, who used such derogatory terms for other communities like the Oriyas, Sikhs and Marwaris.

Manoj, the son of a barrister who was looking forward to going to England to do a bar-at-law, changed Harry's name. He told him that his name, Hari Pratap, gave the impression that he was a haggard old man.

Hari Pratap winced, for he had never imagined he would hear such a comment from anyone. "It's a God's name. Hari means Vishnu, Krishna," he muttered.

"Forget those names. You must be modern. You are rich, have a car and a house in Bagbazar. Man, be modern."

A demoralized Hari Pratap almost cringed. "How?"

Manoj thought for a while and then suggested, "Make it Harry. You don't need to change the spelling; just tell everybody you're Harry. People call me Harry, that's how you should present yourself."

It was a suggestion upon Hari's heart, and thus by denouncing his own name, and by anglicizing it, Hari became Harry.

Harry still dreamt of the lanky girl with green eyes in the night, but he never told anyone in Calcutta about her, for she was the symbol of Allahabad that flourished in its grandeur of homeliness, totally in contrast with Calcutta, which in those days appeared to him as a jungle of concrete. Manoj often took Harry with him to his Sukias Street residence, an old three-storey house with massive pillars. It was considerably bigger than Harry's house in Bagbazar that his uncle had bought a decade ago. Manoj had a separate room on the first floor, near another room where his father would sit with his friends on Sundays or other holidays.

On his very first day there, while Harry sat with Manoj, he heard a loud voice come in from the next room, "The Chinese army has killed 150 odd members of the Tibetan Peoples Party in eastern Tibet. The reason? They opposed the policy of sovietizing their country. What has the government of India done? Tell me."

Harry heard the loud voice and looked warily at Manoj, as in Harry's family shouting was prohibited, and was treated as an expression of crudity.

"It's nothing," Manoj assured him. "My father and most of his friends are with the Jan Sangh. But others, who come to chat with them, are Congress supporters. They argue among themselves."

"Oh," Harry nodded.

A while later he asked, "But what has happened in Tibet?"

"Damn Tibet!" Manoj did not have any interest in politics. He was two years older than Harry, but had wasted academic years because he had been bedridden for months after a bout of typhoid in his childhood.

Harry went to Allahabad a few months later, only to get a bad news, "Your heartthrob, the lanky girl with green eyes, is a Muslim. Her name is Reshma," said one of his friends. A Muslim girl could not be loved, for Hindus and Muslims belonged to two different worlds segregated by mutual mistrust, and there was not even a remotest chance of a change in attitude.

Back in Calcutta, he took his studies very seriously—he was always a topper in his school—and made efforts to forget everything else. But just when he was settling down, Manoj opened up another vista of life, which was puzzling, repulsive and nauseating in the beginning, but gradually turned out to be enchanting, attractive and overwhelming, for it involved nude women. Manoj took him to Free School Street where in those days Anglo-Indian women were prepared to sleep with the 'blackies'; they were much, much more expensive compared to the Indians, but affordable for Harry and Manoj.

Harry passed out from University of Calcutta as a postgraduate in Economics, and soon after he came to know that he had become the 'uncle' of a boy, as his eldest brother's wife had given birth to a son, leading to much festivity in Puraina. Had she given birth to a female child—she already had two daughters—it would have been a quiet affair, though daughters were not unwelcome in their family, unlike many others.

Harry's uncle told him over the phone that the newborn would be named Chandra Pratap, the power of the moon, and all male children of this generation would be named after moon.

And then, his uncle Surya Pratap, bent upon making him an industrialist, asked him to manage a paper mill he had bought at the northern suburb of Calcutta. Within months, Harry realized he was drifting away from his previous world, from his friend Manoj who had suddenly found an interest in politics and was studying law, and even from his father, who treated commerce and industry as the refuge of the Banias.

Harry was no more interested in the Hindu Code Bill or the Chinese occupation of Tibet, or what Jillian Huxley said; he realized it best when Manoj came to his house in the early summer of 1960 and began to brief him on how Union Defence Minister VK Krishna Menon had argued in the Lower House against a private member's resolution for withdrawing the Kashmir question from the United Nations.

Harry, reclined cosily on a big teak wood armchair as though firmly entrenched in a different world, said, "You people remain too busy with politics. The only way to compel the world to listen to you is by empowering yourself economically. Dollar diplomacy may be countered by Rupee diplomacy, not by the non-aligned movement of Nehru, neither by *Akhand Bharat*… as your Jan Sangh leaders dream…"

Harry was thus all set to sail on a world that would be created by him, a soothing world marked by a hot pursuit of money that is power, a risky world where barriers are to be broken to survive.

11

The Present Continuous (1983)...

PASCAL FERNANDEZ reaches the hotel in Patna exactly at 7.30 and finds BV, the chief of the state detective department, waiting for him in the posh lounge.

"The meeting is at eight," BV says casually. "But no need to hurry."

Pascal goes to his room, takes a quick bath and dons a white pyjama and a white kurta with a black jacket. He arranges his notes, but just when he is about to leave for the dining hall—where he will brief others about the problem of Naxalism—BV enters his room. "Wait. I want your help. It's a small matter for you."

Pascal looks at him, surprised why BV should sound so formal and diffident when they both belong to the same batch.

"One of my relative is in the US," BV says sheepishly. "He took a maid from here few months ago. She has committed suicide there. You know these nasty girls. Now the authority there has found that she was pregnant. My relatives are in a fix in that country, you know. You are an IB officer posted in Delhi and if you ask someone…"

"It's very difficult. The US doesn't care for Indian Intelligence officers. She was either raped or willingly slept with someone in the house."

"True," BV's voice suddenly imploded in irritation. "How does it matter? She was a dhobi, washerwoman, by caste. Are they very important people?"

For a moment, Pascal feels like slapping the man hard. But he closes his eyes for a second, regains his cool and mutters, "The way Indians have started taking servants and maids… soon the West will discover our secret."

Now BV is forced to ask, "What's that? Something secret you said?"

"That we still have slaves in this country, in the form of servants and maids for 24 hours. The whole world will shudder when they will come to know this." Pascal smiles and looking at the jaded face of his colleague, adds, "I will try to save your relative."

Half an hour later, Pascal starts his briefing at the dinner-meeting, attended, apart from BV, by Ashok Sharma, the DIG, Special Branch and two other DIGs who are in charge of Magadh and Ranchi ranges, police superintendent of Patna and Rohtas. And there is one empty chair. At the onset he says, "I have come to discuss the problem informally, keeping in view that someday it may take a disastrous dimension. It may… or may not. But the problem is very simple. It started as a flutter, and that was when I went to Bengal and studied the problem. In fact, I did a comparative study of Bengal and Andhra… two most affected states in the late 60s and early 70s. Bengal was an expression of intellectual anger against inequality, unemployment, opportunism and whatever the middle class youth perceived as injustice. The downtrodden joined them, but the leaders were, with a few exceptions like Jangal Santhal or Leba Tudu, all middle class. It was a romantic outburst that was easily crushed. But…"

As a waiter comes and stands near the table, BV orders drinks for everybody except one, and then points to the exceptional one and says, "Hey, Romantic Cobra, you would like some milk, I suppose."

The others dissolved into a laughter.

"A fruit beer," the Romantic Cobra answers smartly.

"These Cola drinks are awful. Since they have kicked out Coke, I don't touch these Indian products." DIG Magadh comments, ruing the decision of the Janata Party government to ask Coke to wind up its business in India.

Pascal's experienced eyes convey to his head that except the man whom BV has introduced as Ashok Sharma, nicknamed the Romantic Cobra, no one in the gathering is much interested in his briefing. With his eyes fixed on Sharma, Pascal says, "But Andhra was different. The intellectual element was there, but the strength came from mainly Harijans and Girijans, the hill tribes. When three months ago, I was asked to study the problem again after a gap of more than a decade, I was reluctant. But I can tell you the movement that you see now… or better to say you don't see now, for it is just bourgeoning… is very different from the earlier movement. Still middle class people are leading it, but the base seems to consist of the most wretched section of the people, whom we don't treat as human beings. Chamars, Dusadhs, Malis… Dhobis."

Pascal does not intend it, but his eyes go to BV's face where no reaction can be seen. "In this form," Pascal says again, "it is much more dangerous. Potentially dangerous. More than half the population are theoretically… potentially… sympathetic to the cause for which they are fighting. The movement may fizzle out… or it may become a major threat." He stops as he sees a tall handsome man approaching them.

"It's breezy outside, but you can't feel it here," the man remarks in English and takes the empty chair.

"Sorry for being late, sir," he tells Pascal and stretching his hand towards him, says, "I am Srivastava, the DIG."

"Nice meeting you. We have just started." Pascal tries to be pleasant and shakes his hand, but he is irritated. He looks at the man's hand and realizes that all the rings on his fingers together cost more than hundred thousand rupees. "From where does an IPS officer manage so much money?" he wonders.

"My other car has almost packed up. My wife has taken that today, and that worries me," says Srivastava, though no one has asked anything about him or his wife.

None cares either. BV calls the attendant to ask for Vodka for the newly arrived guest, and also gives the order for food. Pascal prefers a simple menu: butter naan and a preparation of chicken with salad.

A while later, by then Srivastava has been served his drink, Pascal starts again, "I will tell you the brief history of these Maoists."

Someone asks, "Naxalites and Maoists are basically the same?"

"Yes. Basically, for us they are armed guerrillas who want to overthrow the system," says BV.

Pascal starts again, "Anyhow, the whole thing was the brainchild of one Charu Majumdar... you probably know that. He was arrested and died in the central lockup in Calcutta. That was in early 70s. He was a heart patient. I think that explains his hurry. He gave a call for revolution without any preparation. And the movement degenerated into antisocial activities. It culminated in hooliganism. It became a blood-thirsty movement."

"That is the true colour of the Communists," remarks Srivastava in English.

"Of course there is another explanation," Pascal says. "They found a photo of goddess Kali from his residence. At that point, the explanation that was doing the round was that Charu *babu* was a *tantrik*, a worshipper of the dead, and so he initiated these killings in the name of a theory of annihilation."

"A wacky creature indeed; but it explains a lot." Srivastava comments again, in English; he is imbibing his glass of vodka too fast.

Pascal switches to Hindi, and continues, "But I don't agree. He was too radical a Communist... but I believe he never fired a shot from a gun. It was rather a type of romanticism. It all started from the tea gardens and surrounding areas of north Bengal. The labourers in the tea gardens were poorly paid and had no job security. The land system was even worse."

"A leader of the guerrillas who cannot fire a shot! Hah," Srivastava comments again while stroking the table with his fingers.

Pascal looks at a child in another corner who pops three balloons in a row by pricking a pin into them, and continues, "At that stage, our top officials tried to make a deal. The second man among the Maoists in those days, Kanu Sanyal, was agreeable. The condition was an honourable settlement of land disputes and some land reform. Jangal Santhal and others would have accepted it. But Charu Majumdar, the top leader, sabotaged it and came out with the call of a revolutionary armed struggle. That was 1967. Still, this was contained within a few months. But it took a larger dimension with the participation of students and youths of Calcutta who spread out to the rural areas—1969 to 71 was the pick... by 1972, thousands were in jail or killed. Again it surfaced in Bhojpur of Bihar, but that too was crushed during the Emergency."

Suddenly Srivastava becomes vocal, "Yes, Emergency. That was a nice time. Sanjay Gandhi was great. I don't care if he was a sort of extra-constitutional authority. It worked. You know this Patna station... you came out of it and that was hell. Thanks to Sanjay Gandhi, everything was cleared up... with bulldozers, you know. And that was a fantastic time. The forces got their freedom. How can you run the country if the force is not given a free hand? Courts and all this bullshit. And then..." He stops suddenly and it seems he has forgotten his point.

Pascal cuts a quick glance at BV who winks at Pascal and says, "But some groups again emerged and have been active since then in certain belts."

"And they work silently," Romantic Cobra joins in. "Except a few sporadic events, they don't surface at all. I feel now that their base is fairly widespread in Bhojpur, Rohtas and further south. Emancipation, the group that started it, is becoming a part of the system, and may participate in elections soon. But others are more dangerous."

The DSP of Magadh range asks, "Do they have any foreign connections as they had earlier?"

"None of these groups have any foreign connection," Pascal clarifies. "Even in '70–71, when China openly supported them... yes that was a fact I forgot to mention, the Chinese Party hailed them, but even then we did not come across any evidence of China supplying arms or money to them. Rather, those other insurgent groups of the north-east get it."

Pascal now takes out a chit from his pocket and staring at it continues, "But for us, the important point is that even after emergency period of 1975–77, the Naxalite violence is continuing and increasing. In 1981, 325 incidents were reported and 92 people were killed. It is much less than the mid-70s to mid-71 figure when about 4,000 incidents were reported and... and the death toll was, as far I remember, some 560 or... maybe 65... not sure."

The discussion continued till midnight, mainly on exchange of information and maintaining records so that the problem, if it ever took a serious dimension, could be effectively tackled.

Some hours later, at 6.30 am, the telephone rings incessantly in Pascal's room, and as he picks it up, from the other end the Romantic Cobra says, "Good morning, sir. But actually, the morning is not so good for us. We have bad news."

"What's that?"

"That man Mahendra Chamar was taken away from the hospital last night," says the DIG, his voice crisp, though he has not slept for more than four hours.

"My goodness! I heard he was in a bad shape."

"Right, sir. That's why I said he has been taken out... rather smuggled out from the hospital. I don't know whether the constables guarding him just fell asleep... that's what they have said... or they connived."

"Where are you?"

"At the reception of the hospital, sir," the Romantic Cobra says plainly.

After hanging up, Pascal gets up, and pulls the curtains to see the break of a densely clouded day. And he looks on rather blankly.

12

Glimpses of the Past (1940–1980)

MOHAN RAM entered the world of adults on a magical night when a bear transformed itself into a woman, as though to allure him towards the trap destiny had laid for him.

He left the eternally mobile Mushahars to join a group of masons, who had no objection to include an Untouchable in their team as a construction helper. They were another sort of nomads who worked in distant lands, totally cut off from their families, whom they could visit only once in the year during *Chhat*, the festival of the Sun God. With them, Mohan began another journey, this time to Jamshedpur, for which he had to board a train that emitted smoke like an angry demon and chugged on creating a bizarre rhythm, as though to convey some unintelligible mantra in the ears of the passengers. "What does this rail cab say?" he asked.

Dayal, the head of the team, took a few seconds to understand the question, and then he came up with his answer, "*Nachoi na abe anganwa terh* (One who cannot dance blames the stage)."

Mohan was at a complete loss when he saw the city; it was studded with big houses and from some of those houses blurted out a confounding contraption called radio; it had roads where an occasional car appeared all of a sudden and then honked like a trumpet; more disturbingly, here the lights glowed in the steel plant like imitation suns in the night, and the men and the women were like from another planet. But Mohan never contemplated fleeing the city; rather, he tried to adopt the life of a construction worker with his food and shelter assured. A few months later, when the group decided to move further east to another state called Bengal, to be more precise to a burgeoning town called Durgapur, Mohan decided to go with them. The contractor offered him a little more money to work in Durgapur, and they all agreed.

Durgapur was a different place altogether with people speaking a completely different language called Bengali. In that town, when the nascent nation was dreaming of a giant leap forward after the just concluded first general elections, Mohan saw a procession ranting a strange mantra, "*Lal jhanda kare pookar, Inquilab Zindabad.*"

"Who are they?" asked Mohan Ram.

"The Communists," a middle-class Bengali man told him.

Communists! He knew the word. Mohan raked through his memory cells until he remembered Dilshad Singh, the man who hid in the jungles near Puraina. "What are they saying?" he asked.

"They are shouting slogans. It means, the clarion call of the red flag is long live the revolution."

"What is this revolution?" Mohan Ram wondered aloud.

"A total change where there will be no rich, no poor… where everybody will be equal."

"No poor?" Mohan Ram was sceptical, but as the middle-class man nodded, he asked curiously, "Then who will build houses for the *babus*?"

That afternoon, as the small procession passed him by, Mohan got no answer.

A few months later, Kanai joined the group along with his wife Moina, a tall and slender woman, who could carry 12 bricks on her head while going up a ladder made of bamboo, compelling others to appreciate her courage and deftness. The team worked the whole day, and in the evening, when the women cooked food, the men drank cheap *desi* liquor, picked up a brawl and often beat the wives or children. Mohan did not like the smell of liquor, and he stayed away from them and slept at some different place.

One night, Mohan was lying on the first floor of a house under construction, beneath the open sky. In his sleep, he was in Puraina where a jackal wore the mask of the Badhe Thakur to intimidate him.

But Mohan refused to be scared and chanted a mantra, *Inquilab Zindabad.*

And just then, the jackal turned into a bear he saw in Jamshedpur and began to hug him; it scared him so much that he tried to rouse himself and kick the bear away.

"It's me, Moina," a female voice purred. She held him tightly with one hand, and started playing with his organ with the other.

Mohan woke up with a squeal, "*hei baba*," and tried to get away. He fought with the bear that had turned into Moina, but she hooked his body with her legs and was soon almost on top of him. Within seconds, his body began to undergo a metamorphosis with heat emitting from his cheeks and ears, and he surrendered to her game that turned out to be a mixture of pain and pleasure, though for the whole period he remained worried about himself.

The next morning, when he stood face to face with Moina, to hand her over the bricks, she did not take any cognizance of his presence and shouted, "*Aare jaldi karo* (Act fast)." Mohan had expected a smile from her, but got a rude shock, and her behaviour left a bitter taste in his mouth. However, it was all washed away in the dead of the night when Moina came again. But, the next morning, she again behaved in the same way, and again in the night she came; what was peculiar about her was that she seldom talked to him—either in the day or at night.

The construction was over in a few weeks and the contractor split the group, separating Mohan from Moina. Now that he had no woman, Mohan felt sad and uneasy in the nights. On one such night, he went back to Puraina where Moina was waiting for him, and more amazingly, talking to him, that too in Bhojpuri! Then, as the scene changed, he found Moina standing by the River Son calling his name repeatedly. Suddenly he realized the truth: it was not Moina, it was Munni, his sister-in-law, who was calling him... *Mohonowa... eh Mohonowa...* a call that reverberated in the dense dark space of time as though it would not stop till Mohan answered.

"I am coming," muttered Mohan as he woke up, and decided to visit Puraina.

Mohan entered the Chamar-*tola* after a gap of about five years, wearing a pair of old trousers and a Hawaii shirt donated by a Bengali gentleman, and with slippers bought from a cheap store at Durgapur.

His trousers and slippers amused the Backwards, enraged the upper castes, and terrified Munni, who was now living alone in a separate hut, as after becoming a widow she was thrown out by the third wife of Birju Chamar, Mohan's father. Munni's husband had died after being run over by a lorry near Sasaram, where he had gone in search of work.

Birju was not happy to see his son, and the deep creases on his forehead indicated that he was fearing trouble. He asked him to leave the Chamar-*tola*, which was being renamed as Harijan-*tola*, as soon as he could.

Munni took him to her hut and pleaded with him, "Mohanowa, don't put on *chappal* and pants in the village, for God's sake."

That night, Mohan approached Munni and pulled her body close to him. She shuddered for a second, and then became still. When she finally surrendered like a felled bamboo tree, a tangy smell of manure and earth filled his nose. Mohan anticipated some resistance from her, but it appeared to him that she was searching for solace, and security, in his body and mind.

That same night, Mohan came to know of a bitter truth. When Munni worked in the fields of the priest's son, he often forced her to sleep with him under the threat that he would not employ her if she did not yield. He stopped her from working in the fields and promised to feed her. "We will later move to the city," he said, and to earn money for the contemplated shifting he decided to leave the village for a few weeks. "I will come back, we will marry here and then leave," he announced.

Marrying an elder brother's widow was common among the lower castes.

Before leaving, Mohan murmured to Munni, "Meanwhile, if the priest's son, that bastard, tries to molest you, just kick his balls."

She did exactly that during Mohan's absence, though the man after her was not the priest's son; it was the landlord's youngest brother, Chhote Thakur. He groaned in acute pain and asked his men to take Munni to the 'black cell' at the back of the *haveli*, where 15 men took turns to rape her before they strangled her bleeding body to death.

The malefolk of Harijan-*tola* blamed Munni for her fate. "She kicked the Thakur! What sin!"

"*Jaisan karni, waisan bharni* (You reap as you sow)," the women commented, though sadly.

A week later, on a cloudy afternoon—when kites suddenly swooped on the trees and the breeze stopped swaying the leaves—Mohan Ram heard the story and rushed towards the *haveli* like a deranged spirit, seeking revenge. "You have killed her, you beasts," he shouted, picked up a chunk of stone, and chucked it with all his might at the iron gate, the symbol of secluded supremacy. The metallic sound... and its reverberations... like a shot in the endless frame of time... became such a terrible myth in the land of myths of Puraina that even decades later, when the *haveli* would outlive its shine, people would still say grimly, "A long time back, a Chamar, Mohan Ram, threw a stone at the gate of the *haveli*. The time began to change from that day..."

But on that cloudy afternoon, the private soldiers of the *haveli* came rushing out and started beating the 'sinner'. They bludgeoned him with a stick, cracking his forehead from where blood oozed out, and continued to beat him like they would not stop till the last drop of blood plopped out of the Chamar's frail body. Pullu Yadav, the head of the guards, with his small eyes spitting fire, did most of the beating. Mohan Ram saw the jaws of death plunging into him with light fading from his eyes. Just at that moment, Badhe Thakur intervened and asked them to take the boy to the police station and lodge a complaint against him. Pullu and others rued the decision, for traditionally the *haveli* played the role of both the police and judiciary in the locality, and killed anybody who showed a rebellious spirit; but they had to obey the lord. Chhote Thakur, who was inside his room, also heard the order that could not be overruled, loitered about in his room, and muttered several times, "It's a mistake... a mistake."

The ruffians dragged an almost unconscious and profusely bleeding Mohan Ram from the *haveli* through the ground, bruising him even more, to a distance of about half a kilometre where a tarred road was being built. He was dumped into a jeep that Badhe Thakur had bought few weeks ago. The upper castes enjoyed the scene, the Backwards saw it in dumb silence from safe and distant corners, and the Untouchables silently prayed for the soul of the boy, for they were sure he would die. Even Hukum Lal, the Socialist, commented, "If you trample on a snake's body, it would bite for sure." He knew that even if he had lodged a complaint, the raped woman's body would not be found anywhere in the *haveli,* for it had either been dumped in the River Son, or in a ditch even further away, and even the Chamars would not come forward as a witness against the Thakurs.

When the jeep carrying Mohan Ram started rolling down, the severest dust storm in recent memory hit the Rohtas district, and the locals shivered in unknown fear as trees got uprooted, thatched roofs blew off and bullock carts swirled over the fields.

That night, Badhe Thakur announced his writ, "The Chamars would not be permitted to cut bamboo trees and use it for their huts for free anymore. They would have to atone for the sinner."

The next morning, the Chamars went to the *haveli* to announce that they had decided to excommunicate Mohan Ram. Mohan's father, the headman of the Chamars, went on abusing him with all the others joining the chorus. Though they were squatting a little bit away from the *haveli* and the loud conversation was exclusively among them, they knew it would reach the ears of Badhe Thakur; they were relieved again after a few hours, when Pullu Yadav came to them to announce that Badhe Thakur had pardoned them and had permitted them to cut the bamboo trees.

Just then, Mohan Ram was lying in the hospital at Sahar where he had to stay for days with almost all part of his body bandaged. Doctors, however, were concerned about the injury to his temple, a three inches long cut that bled for hours before being sewn ineffectively and was still bleeding through several points.

Later, he was sentenced to two year's rigorous imprisonment, but it hardly mattered to him, as the jail was a place where work and food were ensured. What really bothered him was the image of the *haveli* that appeared before his eyes suddenly to arouse an overwhelming but futile desire to demolish it.

Inside the jail in Sasaram, Raghuram, an under-trial everybody dreaded, a criminal with multiple charges against him including rape and murder, told Mohan, "You will someday become a seasoned killer. Be with me. I will train you."

Someone else asked, "How do you know that?"

The man replied, "Look at his eyes. You will also understand."

Since the night he was tied to a tree, Mohan Ram had started avoiding looking at anyone's eyes, and his stare had turned so burning that it compelled others to avoid looking at his eyes.

Raghubir was a terror inside the jail, and whatever he ordered had to be executed by the others, for even a frown invited his wrath and got translated into action, into physical torture meted out by his followers. But it all changed when Keshrinath Ojha, a Hindu activist, sentenced to 12 years' rigorous imprisonment for rioting, killing, arson and related charges, was transferred to Sasaram jail. Raghuram soon became his follower.

Keshrinath preached inside the jail, "Consider this. You have two brothers. One of them says... I want to live separately. Well. You give one-third of the land to him and one-third of your house. Things are done in this way. Right?… Can he say, after the property is split, that the whole belongs to him?"

"No."… "How can he say so?" … "Never."

"That is what has happened here. Jinnah Sahab said he wanted a separate home for them. They got it. Pakistan. But some of them still remain in India! And Gandhi was supporting them. So Nathuram Godse had no option, but to kill him."

Mohan had no quarrel with him, for he felt whatever the man said was logical; but the day they attacked Bashir, a Muslim prisoner who was his friend, Mohan fought them single-handedly. Then, bruised from face to toe, he was transferred to another ward.

As soon as he came to the other ward, a better one without ruffians, a man, who looked like a professor, congratulated him, "You did a great job, risked your life to save a Muslim from a pack of Hindu wolves." This man was Birbhusan, a Socialist, who was in jail as a 'political prisoner', though the separate category was not recognized by law.

Mohan's throat still hurting him, he was not inclined to talk. Otherwise, he would have said he did not try to save a Muslim, he stood by a friend.

Birbhusan was rather disappointed to know Mohan was illiterate. He was a middle-aged man, quiet and bearded, with good intentions that led him to undertake a mission of educating Mohan Ram. One day, he took a piece of paper, sketched the outline of a bird and placed it before Mohan. "What is this?" he asked.

Mohan stared at the picture blankly.

"Come on Mohan. What is this?" Birbhusan asked again.

Mohan looked on at the sketch, shook his head and stared at Birbhusan like an injured dog, the sharpness of his eyes being replaced by bewilderment.

"A bird. Don't you understand?" Birbhusan too was confused.

"A bird? So little!" Mohan was amazed.

"Yes. It's a sketch of a bird. Isn't it?"

"Yes," Mohan agreed quickly, happy to be able to wriggle out of his embarrassment.

"Then why didn't you say that?" insisted Birbhushan.

"Never seen such a small bird," Mohan muttered in dismay.

Anybody else would have stopped the attempt of educating the 'rustic idiot', but Birbhusan was different and he hated to fail. So, when Mohan Ram's term was over, he could write his name, the first one from the Chamar-*tola* of Puraina to be able to do. He also knew about Socialist leaders such as Narendra Dev, Ram Manohar Lohia, Achariya Kripalani and J P, who were often uniting and then disuniting with the merger and split of Socialist parties.

After the completion of his term, Mohan was let loose in a world of grand uncertainty, with the *haveli* still haunting him often, but now only in the dead of the night.

About a couple of months later, still moving on aimlessly, he met a saffron-clad sadhu, an ascetic who had left his home to know God. Mohan stayed with him for a couple of days, during which the sadhu rarely talked to him, but shared with him his food. Then, on the night of Deepawali, the festival of lights, he spoke to him after lighting some tiny earthen lamps. "Son, do you know why we light lamps on this particular night?" the old man asked.

Mohan only shook his head and uttered, "I am a Chamar."

"So what? Your forehead says you will do great things."

After a minute's silence, Mohan said, "I can't do great things for I have no competence. I am a Chamar."

"Competent people seldom do great things. For doing great work, one needs a great purpose."

Mohan did not understand it, and mumbled again, rather sadly, "I don't even know about Deepawali. Maybe Ramchandra returned to Ayodhya this day."

"That was added later on," the sadhu dismissed him casually. "A month before Deepawali, the spirits of our forefathers come down to earth to get water from their descendants. On the night of Deepawali, the biggest Hindu festival, we urge them to go back to their abode and to help them return, we show them light, which is called *Ulkadanam*."

Suddenly, Mohan asked, "Whom do you call a Hindu?"

"Whoever believes that God himself comes down to earth to salvage dharma and who burns the dead is a Hindu."

"Are Chamars Hindus?"

The sadhu took a drag on his *ganja*, a hallucinating drug, and said, "Sure."

"Then why don't they allow us to enter the temple?"

The sadhu, who had a grim voice and sharp eyes, shook his head, "They don't know. Barring anyone from entering a temple... is a sin." The sadhu took another drag and sat quietly, his eyes closed for a couple of minutes. And then he said, "We, living souls are actually a part of the great soul that is infinite. The sun, the moon, the stars, the jungles, you and I are all parts of that great soul. The hills know it. The sun knows it. We have forgotten it because we have taken the shape of living souls. Try to find this consciousness within you and you will understand everything. Just perform your dharma. The sun's dharma is to give heat and light, and it will do so until it burns itself out. Follow your dharma like the sun."

Mohan fell silent, wondering what his dharma was: scaling the dead carcass as his forefathers had done, or fighting the *haveli*?

After a long pause, and by then the drug was affecting him, the sadhu mumbled, his eyes almost closed, "Don't brood. Your forehead says a lot about you. Go ahead. You will challenge the gods, then the gods will retaliate... after that you will see through the stones."

Mohan was rattled; he cringed, "What does that mean?"

Suddenly the sadhu woke up again, and said, "I don't know. You yourself will realize it when time comes."

"How?"

"When time comes, it itself tells one that it is there. But nothing happens before time. The sun does not set in the morning... it always sets in the evening."

Confused to the core, Mohan asks, "Then what shall I do?"

"Follow your destiny. Don't resist it."

The next morning, the sadhu was not to be found anywhere. Mohan was hungry, and he too decided to leave the place. This time his journey for days finally landed him to the north-eastern part of Bihar, in the neighbourhood of a railway-town called Katihar, which was far away from Puraina. He saw a few people eating something inside a makeshift camp atop which a red flag fluttered in the gentle breeze. Hunger emboldened him to go near the *badka log* and ask, "Can I get something to eat?"

Someone said rudely, "No."

As Mohan turned back, a bespectacled gentleman in *pyjama kurta* called him back, and asked him to sit and eat with them. Mohan chose the corner of the tent to sit on the ground, but before the amazed eyes of the others, the man insisted that he sit on a chair. Mohan refused and finally said, "I am a Chamar."

A Chamar had no right to sit along with the *badka log*, the gentry, but this man continued to insist, until someone else intervened, "Dada, he is not your comrade. Let him sit there."

Mohan was about to leave after eating, but the 'dada' forced him to stay back. Then he almost dragged him through the meadows up to the dingy lanes of non-railway space of Katihar, and from there a couple of kilometres more to reach a small *pucca* house. He unlocked the door and asked Mohan Ram to come in.

Mohan could see the room standing at the door; a room of *badka log* with books piled in one corner, a table fan, and a cot. He did not know what the man had in his home was the bare minimum for a gentleman, as for him a room containing a table fan itself was a symbol of wealth that only upper caste men were entitled to, and he declined to enter the room. But the man compelled him to stay there, declaring that the Communists did not believe in castes. Mohan did not understand the statement, but stayed there for the night.

SUJIT SINHA, the schoolteacher comrade, was not a Bihari Kayastha, though people regularly mistook him for one because of his title; he was Kayastha, true, but a Bengali.

His father was an officer of the Indian Railway. His transferable job had brought him to Katihar from where he retired and went back to Ranaghat in Bengal, where the joint family had shifted from Dhaka just before the partition. They considered themselves lucky to avoid the misfortune that befell the Hindus thereafter in East Bengal, before and during the partition of the country. Out of the hell in time, his father wanted to live in perfect peace, but Sujit was like a bone in his throat. While his father went to Ranaghat, Sujit stayed back in Katihar and despite his brilliant academic background, chose to join the Communist Party.

In those days—it was the late 40s—the word Communist evoked various reactions from various people: sympathy, hate or indifference, but the commonality was fear. The Communists could either be loathed or be saluted from a distance, but not desired at home. So, his father was furious and decided to disown him. "He is haunted by the ghosts of communism, has denounced God and therefore has no place in our home," his father proclaimed in a gathering of the full family that included all the brothers and cousins of Sujit's father and their wives, sons and unmarried daughters. And then he proclaimed, "Someday, he would land in jail."

Elevating his father to the place of an astrologer, Sujit went to jail just after Independence when the Communist Party made an abortive attempt to initiate a revolutionary process. That was under the leadership of a young BT Ranadive, who armed the cadre with less of guns and more of a slogan that dubbed the newfound independence a sham. Sujit's aunt, who loved him the most, was so sure he would never come back that she suffered a stroke and was partially paralysed. Sujit was released two years later, when the Communist Party denounced its earlier attempt to revolutionize society through an armed rebellion and removed BT Ranadive from the post of general secretary, probably to send signals to Nehru's government that they would now behave.

Sujit believed Ranadive's path was right, but with the latter's decline, he was forced to follow the diktat of the party. Now, a free man again, Sujit went to meet his ailing aunt secretly, without his father's knowledge. His mother was also there in the dimly-lit room where he met his paralysed aunt, who asked a question with great difficulty, "Why do you risk your life for the party?"

"Because I dream of a better life in this world. If I do something else, I will be safe and well-off, but people about me will still be starving, suffering and dying. That will destroy my own individual world."

"Everybody dreams, my son... everybody does... but at night," Sujit's mother piped in. "Then, Baba, why do you have to dream during the day? Why don't you dream at night and work, like others, during the day?"

Sujit smiled wryly before saying, "You won't understand, Ma. If I do something else in the day, I won't be able to dream at night. I can't leave this dream behind me. It's my life. It's the only thing that makes me feel my life is not going waste."

When Sujit again came out of the house, opting for a life of dreams, his mother too was in tears. It was only then, at the age of 26, that Sujit realized his mother too had an existence of her own, an existence subdued by the presence and domination of his father.

In those days, the Communist Party had a measly presence in the state of Bihar. It had a lone member in the first legislative assembly from Begusarai, and even that was won in a by-election. During the second general election of '57, the tally in the state assembly rose to five. Faced with such a limitation, the party was trying to build itself in some pockets of the state including the Katihar-Purnia belt where Sujit was active. When EMS Namboodiripad became the Chief Minister of Kerala, the first Communist to form a government in India, that too in '57, Sujit convinced himself that the parliamentary path too was worth trying. But the government was soon dismissed by Jawaharlal Nehru, and while the party took it as a conspiracy of the CIA, Sujit again turned sceptical about parliamentary democracy.

Those days of post-Independence were hard, and issues like food adulteration, hoarding or black marketing and acute shortage of food were the mainstay of the campaign of the Communists, and for raising these issues, they were often harassed, jailed or even beaten. Trade Unionism was a risky business as employers often implicated them in false cases and even killed the more radical workers who believed that the party was there to fight the capitalists. Under these circumstances, living with a dream for changing society was actually like living a nightmare.

The senior leaders of the party hoped for a possible disintegration of the Congress in the state and looked out for 'a progressive section' in the ruling party. Lala Singh, an old Communist who, after independence, had almost retired from politics, was expecting that the Congress would soon disintegrate on caste lines. "See, Mahesh Prasad Sinha and Krishna Ballabh Sahay have lost the elections," he told Sujit, sitting on a cheap rug in his own house. "This is due to infighting among them. Even Rajen *babu*, despite being President of India, was interfering in favour of Anugrah Narayan."

"Right," Sujit muttered without being sure of the relevance of it to their party. He could not comprehend how the Communists would conjure up an alliance of forces with the help of the 'progressive section' of the Congress to overthrow such a system.

As he remained bogged down with the problems of the jute mills—the party had given him the responsibility of dealing with these unions—Sujit often wondered when a real labourer would become the leader. He believed the party would make a dent only when it would be able to carry the majority of the poor in the state, and for that, he thought it fit to have leaders from the lowest rung of the society, the actual toilers who work in the mills, in the mines and in the fields. So he took Mohan Ram to his home to see if a rustic rebel could turn into an adept comrade.

That night, Sujit went to bed happy and excited. But the next morning, he found the young man missing and the door of the room open. He went out searching for the young man, and after an hour found him near the bus stand. He went up to him and asked him softly, "Where do you want to go?"

"I don't know," Mohan replied indifferently. And then pointing to a bus he added, even more reluctantly, "They will not take me. I have no money."

Sujit brought him back again, gave him some food and then said softly, "We… Communists fight the landlords. If you stay with us, you will see. You will also have to fight them. But you can't fight them alone."

"Do the Communists want to demolish all the *havelis* where the landlords live?" Mohan asked.

Sujit was taken aback by the question that was asked rather casually, without betraying any malice, as though challenging him to decipher the tinge of hidden hatred. He looked on at Mohan's face for a while, and then nodded emphatically.

MOHAN RAM was in a new world, adapting to a new life, being polished and chiselled, learning the basics of Marxism and vowing to fight for the proletariat, all because he felt the day when the Communists would attack and demolish the *havelis* was not far off. He was put in the agricultural front, attended meetings and listened to the leaders, none of whom ever asked him to sit at a distance, none of whom ever reminded him that he was a Chamar, and it was a world upon his heart.

Over time, the leaders started seeking his opinion, giving him a dose of confidence, but at times, the leaders themselves shuddered at his radical positions.

During the day, he travelled through the rural areas, and in the night came back to share the room, where a radio had come to accompany the table fan. Mohan called Sujit Sinha Comrade *babu*, as he could not imagine calling a gentleman 'comrade'—the word that almost seemed like a first name to him.

Till midnight, he read the books that Sujit gave him, books on primary sciences, history and on Marxist thoughts, all in Hindi, and in the morning, he asked Comrade *babu* each and every question that came to his mind. The range of his questions was quite astounding; starting from 'what is the significance of those constellations of stars?', or 'how do camels go without water for days?' to 'at what stage of revolution we are in?', or 'what is the difference between objective and subjective conditions?'. Sujit indulged him to the extent that he even explained to him what he himself was doing and why, or where he was going and for what: "I am going to Islampur in Bengal. This place was taken out from Bihar and was added to the Dinajpur district of Bengal. When the area was in Bihar, our chief minister Shri Krishna Singh gave land to the Santhals and other tribes on lease for nine years. But now, West Bengal is not abiding by that. True that they need land. Thousands of refugees from East Bengal, now East Pakistan, have settled in that district. But for that they cannot deny the tribesmen."

Mohan noted down every point in his mind and could repeat everything, including every minute detail, even after months, marvelling leaders such as Sujit, who took to calling him whenever they needed such details.

Mohan began to be known in the locality as a firebrand comrade, who was prepared to fight for every genuine cause, for a vendor beaten up by the police, for a worker cheated by his employer, or a sharecropper rejected by the landowner. He often clashed with the police, mostly without prior permission of the party, and Sujit Sinha found it difficult to impress upon the young man to be 'responsible'.

Then came a day when Mohan got his first jolt in a world that he thought was a part of his heart. In a remote village, a pregnant woman was killed by the police who opened fire to quell a hungry mob looting a truck of the Food Corporation. Mohan, accompanied by many villagers, stopped the police from taking away the body of the woman, and decided to take the body to Delhi without a clear notion of the distance. He coined a slogan hitherto unheard of: 'Nehru's police have killed her, let her body be taken to Nehru.' An angry mob shouted the slogan before the alarmed policemen, who started retreating as the mob swelled.

Faced with such extremely volatile situation, the district level leaders of the Kisan Sabha, who had reached there to take the lead, were compelled to follow Mohan and embark upon a long journey with hundreds and hundreds still coming out to join the procession that was heading to Katihar. In the night, when the procession was still away from the city, Sujit came to Mohan with a couple of newspaper stringers and Ramjatan, a firebrand labour leader of Katihar who could bring life to a halt with a call for strike.

"We have to stop this, Mohan," Sujit said as Ramjatan nodded. "Our leaders think this is anarchy. If you proceed... thousands of men will join you and nobody will be able to stop them. Not even you. No government in any civilized country can allow you to go on for days with a corpse, which is decaying."

"Comrade Mishra told us that this is making a mockery of the laws of the country," Ramjatan said sadly. "You know... they always think of permissible limit of rebelliousness. I told him that we will try to ensure that we Communists are law-abiding good citizens."

It was the same Ramjatan who would tell Mohan another day that the Communists would never attack any *haveli*, for the leaders believed in measured rebelliousness to attract people towards them without hurting the system too much.

On that night, when the procession bulged and took menacing dimension, Sujit convinced Mohan to give up. In the presence of the district collector, a truce was negotiated between the administration and the party—the administration promised to send relief material for the starving and ailing people, and in lieu of the promise, the body was handed over and was cremated at night.

Mohan was shocked by the interference, and for the first time, an annoying and harassing point took root in his mind: these people would never attack any *haveli*. And it was reinforced by Ramjatan a few days later.

Soon after that, Mohan landed in jail, but this time because of no fault of his. A section of the communist leaders had him arrested during the 1962 Indo-China war that divided the communists badly. One section that followed Russia's proposition of peaceful transformation to socialism took completely nationalistic stand and condemned China; the other that believed in China's line of armed revolution declined to accept China as an aggressor. Sujit belonged to the pro-China faction and told Mohan and others that the majority of party leaders, who were dependent on Russian support, direction and money, were going to compromise the proletarian interest. He claimed that this section was driving the party away from the path of attacking the *havelis*. Thus Mohan was happy to go to the jail, imagining that it would accentuate the division in the party. And the party really split two years later, when unlike many others Mohan was still in jail. Mohan was happy to know of the split, for he had a faint hope that it may prune the party of those elements who would never be in favour of demolishing the *havelis*.

Once, when Sujit went to meet Mohan in jail, he asked, "Comrade *babu*, how long do you think it will take to change things? For revolution, as you call it?"

Sujit realized the young man whom he had inducted in the party was turning restless, and to ease the situation, he mumbled, "*Karmanye vadhikaraste ma phaleshu kadachana.*"

"What does that mean?" Mohan was baffled to hear the Sanskrit verse.

"When Arjuna, one of the most competent warriors in the epic called *Mahabharata,* saw many of his relations and friends on the other side with whom they were going to wage a battle, he developed cold feet. What will I gain by killing them? That was the question in his mind. Then Krishna, the God, said this: 'To action alone hast thou a right and never at all to its fruits; let not the fruits of action be thy motive; neither let there be in thee any attachment to inaction.' It means you have the right to work only, but no right to its outcome."

"Why?"

"It is a philosophical concept embedded in an epic. This particular part is known as the *Bhagavad Gita*, a religious book, in which Krishna tried to explain the concept of dharma. How to explain that? Dharma is not religion. It is something like…"

Mohan muttered suddenly, as though waking up from sleep, "I know that."

"What?"

As though in a trance, he tried to recollect something. "The sun's dharma is to give heat and light… It does its work honestly. It will do so till it burns itself out."

Sujit was perplexed; he asked, "Who told you that?"

Mohan smiled. "A sadhu."

After sitting silently for quite a while, Sujit explained, "You never told me this. But I was joking. We Communists don't believe in the concept of *Gita*. There will be revolution, and as I have told you, it will start when subjective and objective conditions match each other."

Mohan nodded, "The rotten reality and the urge to change that."

Sujit took a few seconds to realize what Mohan had said, for he had never used these words while explaining the tenets of Marxism, and then remarked, "That's correct."

A while later, Sujit said, "You will be released soon. And after that, you should help us in a big way."

Mohan was perplexed, for he was all ready to work as a whole-timer of the party, which meant his body, mind and soul were mortgaged to the party. In what way could he help more?

"You must marry Comrade Ramia," Sujit clarified.

"Marry! Why?" Mohan blurted.

"She is a brilliant comrade. But her father… he is a teacher at the municipal school… wants to marry her off. You have to save her. We do not have many women comrades and we do not want to lose her."

"But why me?"

"I can't answer; the party has decided it," said Comrade *babu*, one of the top decision makers at the district-level of the new party, which still had no different name to distinguish itself from the old one, as both the parties were claiming that they were the real Communist Party of India.

Suddenly, Mohan began to chuckle in an unusual way; he rarely laughed and even a funny situation brought only a semblance of a smile to his lips.

Sujit spluttered, "What's it, Mohan... What's the matter?"

"I have understood why I have to marry her," Mohan said, now in a quiet, indifferent voice. "She is a Chamar. Will the caste comrades marry her? You are right, Comrade *babu*. I have understood the party wishes me to marry her because the party does not believe in castes. Don't worry, Comrade *babu*, I will marry her."

It was the first severe blow that unmasked the party before his eyes; the new world in his heart broke into pieces, each shard raising embarrassing, upsetting questions.

Mohan married Ramia a few months later, but never forgot that she was imposed on him, a constant reminder of the caste-character of the Communists, who claimed to have denounced caste! And when the party proposed him to move to a far-away village called Dulatpur to spread the organizational network of the new party, he did not take Ramia, who was still working among the women, along with him. He did not even bother to come to Katihar on the day Ramia delivered a big dark girl with brown eyes like her father's.

Mohan was again arrested at the beginning of the Indo-Pak war, again without any particular reason; it was what the government dubbed as preventive detention.

In the jail, after a long time, he dreamed of the *haveli* again. It appeared in the form of a jail where among the wardens were both Pullu Yadav, the head of the guards who had presented him with a long scar on his temple, and Comrade *babu*, the Communist, who compelled him to marry Ramia.

Comrade *babu* sat outside his cell and said, "You must learn to wait for the time when the subjective and objective situations match; only then you can think of armed revolution."

"But how will you run the gun then, Comrade *babu*? You never handled a gun, and by then, you will be old. The gun will become too heavy for you."

At this, Comrade *babu* became furious, opened the bars to enter the cell and started beating him severely as other wardens joined him.

Mohan woke up at this stage, and wondered why Comrade *babu* had turned into a warden, and how he could tell him something so easily that in reality he never even intended to utter before him.

Released from the jail after a month, he went to Comrade *babu* and asked him why people dreamt and how the dreams could be interpreted.

"It's not true that dreams are any sort of premonition," Comrade *babu* explained. "What we see in our dreams are actually what we think of in our subconscious level... that is fear, anger, anxiety, love, lust or anything, of which we do not think consciously because of our refinement. Civilization has taught us not to think of many things... all these are reflected in our dreams."

As Comrade *babu* came up with further details, Mohan got distracted, for he had picked up the essence: our dormant desires, alternatively the subconscious mind, come into the open in a dream.

Mohan went again to Dulatpur, where he had worked earlier too; but now the time was changing and destiny was charting out a new course for Mohan Ram, who was born out of a dead mother's, a dead time's womb.

Dulatpur was situated just outside the reach of the turbulent River Kosi that rushed down impetuously, laden with sandy remains from the north, to turn the fertile fields into arid wastes after the monsoon. The river nearer the area, Mahananda, did inundate the village once in a few years, but the water did not log for more than a few days, and in fact, helped the land to regain fertility.

But in those days, a severe drought tore apart the lives of the people, further pauperizing the poor, forcing them to eat gruels and to die silently. Mohan came to know that the situation was not something peculiar to that place; it was the same all over Bihar or Bengal. Late in winter, when the trees had shed their leaves, the news came from Bengal that the police tried to suppress the food movement led by the Left by taking up guns against the agitators. In Bihar, Ram Manohar Lohia, the Socialist leader, took the lead in the food movement and the political situation in the country became unpredictable and explosive. It seemed that Indira Gandhi, the new Prime Minister, was losing gradually but inevitably.

Meanwhile, Mohan tried to organize the agricultural labourers to take possession of the land of big holders, but the people were not prepared to follow him. "The lords will then take more tribal workers who come from Chhotonagpur during the agricultural seasons, and we will die," they told Mohan plainly. Mohan was frustrated and thereafter he concentrated on picking up some young men, Hindus and Muslims, and indoctrinated them so that a core was formed for further radical activities. And it was from one such youngster, Saifur, that one day Mohan heard something that he would never forget. "I overheard what the elders were discussing last night," Saifur told Mohan. "They said what you tell them is right, but they cannot win against the lords for they have no gun, while the lords have guns."

Mohan heard it in rapt attention and nodded, and then sat silently for a long time, looking as usual at the distance, as though seeking answers to riddles of creation that eluded even the greatest philosophers. He was clueless, but again destiny came up to lead him, this time in the shape of one Panu Moitra, a Communist who appeared different from the others. He drew a picture of a future that was different as he delved in the possibility of an armed rebellion. He then talked of one Charu Majumdar, a comrade from north Bengal. "He is an old comrade of Siliguri, son of a schoolteacher," said Panu. "During the days of split, he was with Promode *babu*, but he always wished Jyoti *babu* should not come with us."

"Why?" Mohan asked inquisitively.

"You know often a Communist Party is infiltrated by men who are actually rightists. The real Left leaders lead the party to a point... and then the rightists masquerading as Communists hijack it. It has happened everywhere, it will happen again. The leaders will betray the true Communists. Charu *babu*, and we all, feel that Jyoti *babu* or Namboodiripad or Surjeet... all Politburo members of the Marxist Party... are all rightists."

"I know," Mohan commented, looking at the distance.

"Back to our point," Panu started again, "in those days, the relationship between Jyoti *babu* and Promode *babu* was so strained that while they were lodged in the same jail... Dumdum jail... they never came out to take a walk at the same time. Later, they joined hands. Charu *babu* was campaigning for an armed struggle through leaflets during the days when India attacked China. Union Home Minister Gulzarilal Nanda used those against us, to show us as traitors. The leaders said it was not our line... we did not hold China as the aggressor, but we never thought of joining hands with China. Later, Charu *babu* agreed to abide by the party line, but clandestinely formed a Maoist group. In this group, we talk of a revolution by the peasants, armed struggle by them and creating free zones."

Mohan was interested, though he did not know that his destiny had sent this man to him to unsettle him once again.

Those years were turbulent with people demonstrating against severe hunger, and it led to the ouster of Congress from power in nine states. But Mohan was astonished to see that his communist party supported the same government in Bihar that included ministers from the others communist party. In Bengal too, both the communist parties joined hands.

But soon, the first deadly blow was served by the radical Communists in West Bengal. It was as though destiny was showing Mohan Ram that the time had come for him to challenge the 'gods', as the sadhu had told him years ago. It all started in the northern part of Bengal, in the foothills, in tea gardens. From March 1967, peasants of Naxalbari, Kharhibari and adjacent areas in north Bengal bordering independent states of Nepal and Sikkim started carrying on their movement openly. The police had to register 60 cases of loot, 41 cases of forcible cultivation in the other's land and 9 cases of occupying land. But the movement changed its course from 23 May, when it became so radically enthused that the police imposed curfew and clashed with the militant peasants in the village of Jharugaon under the Naxalbari police station. The police went there to arrest some offenders whom they had implicated for criminal cases, but the villagers refused to let their comrades be arrested and attacked the police, in which a police sub-inspector, Sonam Wangdi, was hit by an arrow. He later died in a hospital.

The militants intensified their campaign for collection of arms, traditional arms like bow and arrow and a few guns. The state retaliated on the morning of 25 May when the police fired at an irate mob in Prasadjot in Naxalbari, where tribal women had led a procession with bows and arrows in their hands, totally oblivious of fear. The police firing killed five of them: two women, two children and a man.

Soon Promod Dasgupta, the firebrand leader of the parliamentary Marxists, came up with a new theory, the only rhetoric the Communists in those days used to identify as the root of all evils. "All these are part of a conspiracy hatched by the CIA." But, by then, the Maoists in India had found their path; the path of Naxalbari. After the name of the place, the Maoists in India came to be known as Naxals, alternatively Naxalis or Naxalites.

On 21 June, a poster appeared within the campus of the University of Calcutta, a few hundred kilometres down the map towards the Bay of Bengal. It read: "Spread the fire of Naxalbari to villages all over India."

On 28 June, New China News Agency flashed the news of a peasant upsurge under the leadership of Maoists in the Darjeeling district of West Bengal in India. Peking radio carried the news immediately, and

Peking Review came out with a long article on 5 July: "Spring-thunder over India." A spark can set a prairie on fire, it argued and predicted the final victory of the Indian revolution, without delving into the details. It inspired hundreds of urban youths, and they began their journey towards disaster and death.

A little away from the epicentre of the uprising, in his tiny den in Katihar district, Mohan read Charu Majumdar's writings: "It is moreover necessary to organize small and secret militant groups for conducting the gun collection campaign. Simultaneously, with propagating the politics of armed struggle, members of these groups will try to successfully implement the programme of gun-collection."

And, in secret meetings with his rustic followers, in the dead of the night, Mohan too preached, "Chairman Mao has enriched this path shown by Lenin. He has taught the tactics of people's war and China has attained liberation along this path... Charu *babu* says in Vietnam, in the Philippines, Burma, Indonesia and even in our country in Nagaland, in Kashmir and Mizoram, the same line is being followed."

Sujit Sinha, his mentor, was not impressed. He explained, "The situation in our country does not warrant an armed struggle. Charu *babu* wants to establish himself as a great leader. That's all. I tell you, revolution does not only depend on the desire of one leader. Charu *babu* is trying to advance the revolution. It's only his subjective desire. It would fail… it would fail."

"So what is the right path?" Mohan asked with a sincere look, without betraying his real intentions.

"At the moment, we can follow a line that Pramode Dasgupta is planning. It will be based on two things: one, class-based front, where our front will be based on peasant-worker's alliance, and not with any other bourgeois party, and two… partial partisan war, whereby we will stubbornly control those areas where we are strong."

Two years after the beginning of the uprising, after another round of election in Bihar, in which Mohan's party drew a blank, he decided to wage his final battle for demolishing the *haveli*s. Little did he know that the final victory that he thought was only a battle away would remain beyond him all through his life.

He went to Katihar to meet Ramia and to tell her that he was leaving the party. He thought Ramia would be shaken and would decide to sever all relations with him like so many other comrades who denounced their marriage for ideological differences. But the woman, whom he ignored all the years they were supposed to share, told him solemnly that she would always be by his side. When he explained further that Comrade *babu* would now treat him as an enemy, she merely said, "They are leaders, but you are my husband. I have to follow you."

Mohan stood shocked and betrayed, betrayed by his own deeds, by his destiny, by Ramia's philosophy of life. Why she revealed her true self so late when he would not be able to reciprocate, he wondered restlessly. He repented for being distant from her, and as he looked at her to confess his deeds, he found her gaze fixed on his face—her small eyes in the round face sodden with love and respect—and for the first time, he realized that from that particular angle, she looked beautiful! But he did not have much time, and he kissed her sleeping daughter on her forehead and took leave from his wife. "I may not come back for a long time," he said sadly, "but I want to be victorious."

"I will wait for you," Ramia said faintly as her voice choked.

Back in Dulatpur, where the winter crops were ready in the fields, Mohan asked the sharecroppers to take the whole crop away to their barn, a move that challenged the right of the landlords to possess much bigger land than stipulated by the law. This angered the landlords so much that they sent their private armies. They came with sticks and swords, while brandishing a couple of guns. That was always sufficient; but this time, what confronted them from the other side were guns secured by the Maoists from a local dacoit gang of the Backwards.

And at night, in small gatherings of radical youth, Mohan declared, "The time has come to establish yourself. We are on our way to final victory."

The situation was grave; the landlords went to the police who readily came forward to protect the law, for the policemen sincerely believed guns in the hands of the lords were part of law and order, but those in the hands of the tillers led to anarchy. Local administration contacted the party leadership at Katihar, and as the leaders saw in Mohan's movement a clear reflection of Naxalism, and a repetition of what had happened in Mushahari of Muzaffarpur, they expelled him from the party. It was Sujit Sinha, the Comrade *babu*, who proposed the expulsion.

Within weeks, with the state determined to have its way, the rebellion was crushed, and Mohan had to leave the area. His Maoist friends, however, took charge of Mohan, and took him across the border of Bihar, to a 'shelter' in Bengal.

13

The Present Continuous (1985–86)...

BEFORE KILLING a man, God kills his wits. It is an adage that haunts Mahendra Chamar, who feels a terrible end is approaching him, and as a prelude to that, his memory is being washed away by the waves of time that will ultimately form a black hole, leaving him to grope with the invincible darkness.

For over a year now, he has been encountering this black hole, a few hours of ordeal of not even remembering who he is. It all started one sunny morning. His head turned heavy for a while and then everything went blank, though physically he remained stable enough to ask himself who he was. Then it took to visiting him after a gap of a month or two.

During the attacks, his brain works, his body responds, but he faces a total blackout of memory for hours; even afterwards, his memory remains somewhat eclipsed for a few days as his head mists up. Then, gradually, everything starts reappearing. The doctors say his brain is dying. After some time, such fits of amnesia will recur more frequently and the duration of the blackouts will increase, and after many such attacks, someday his memory will go blank; he will be left in a dark zone where he will move about oblivious of his identity.

Mahendra wonders about his future and thinks of his past, sitting in a small room of a Home run by a protestant priest, Father Lal. The

Father, who believes in 'liberation theology' and is not antagonistic to the Naxalites, is busy distributing milk and loaves of bread to children, almost none of whom is a Christian.

After rescuing him from the hospital, his comrades kept moving him from one place to another in Madhya Pradesh, but apprehending that he would never come round, they brought him to this Home, where he has been staying for about two years, often lying meekly on the cot like a wounded dog, and occasionally, taking a stroll or trying to read.

Once the doctors spelled out that they could do little to save his dying brain, he thought for ways to fight this disease; he was prepared to die, without resentment, without taking umbrage, but what seemingly was in store for him was something dark.

One night, the sadhu, whom he had met long back, appeared in his dream. "You will challenge the gods, and then they will retaliate; after that, you will see through the stones," the sadhu said, sitting in front of a fire, his appearance exactly the same as it was when he had met him.

Mahendra looked at him, and something came to his mind that prompted him to ask, "Seeing through the stones? I didn't understand the words then and I don't understand them now. What do you mean?"

"You yourself will realize the meaning. Just remember when time comes, it itself tells you that it's there."

"I know about consciousness of the people to fight for a just society. But what is this consciousness that comes from within to tell us the time for change has come?"

"It means 'know yourself'. When you will be able to know yourself, you will know everything."

As in dreams, he could formulate his next question after an inordinate delay: "But... I still don't understand. How do I try to do that?"

"You are a part of the supreme consciousness... Follow your destiny," the sadhu closed his eyes as he did years ago. "I told you that the gods would retaliate. But when you faced common miseries like loss or death, you felt the gods had retaliated. Fool. Gods have started retaliating only now. If you can face it bravely, you will be able to see through the stones."

The same scenes appeared quite a few times, like a merry-go-round, and later, when he woke up to a new dawn, a bit cloudy but warm one, he sat quietly for a long time, wondering about the sadhu, the dream, and the future. And days later, he reached the conclusion that to defeat the gods' design, he should learn to live in the present, an endless present that would have no past and no future, like time itself.

But why all this happened to him, he often wondered sitting in the dark. Why he was destined to fight from the beginning of his life? Why was his daughter lost? Why his second wife had to elope with the betrayer, Bhola, and got killed? Why so many of his acquaintances had to die? Why was he destined to forget everything?

He did not know the answers, but he knew that he would have to live a lonely life, and would have to create a new reality for himself, where he would have no future, for future would always be a point of reference in comparison with the past. At times, he felt restless wondering about the new reality that he himself would have to invent to live on, as he knew he would forget his comrades and the shared dream for which so many had laid their lives, and even worse, he would not be able to recognize Chini, his daughter, even if she was found.

In those days, Father Lal often came to him and discussed a lot of things to distract him from his worries—the problems faced by the PLO after being forced by Israel to abandon Lebanon, or how Lech Walesa of Solidarity was fighting for trade union rights in Poland after being awarded the Nobel Prize. What struck Mahendra was the fact that Father Lal always supported people's movements for freedom and better life, irrespective of ideologies. In one such afternoon, when he was reading a novel by Prem Chand, the Father announced, "Something serious has happened."

Mahendra lent his ears, and looked back at the Father.

"Indira Gandhi has been killed," the Father's tone betrayed anxiety and disbelief.

The next few days poured in more disturbing news from all parts of the country and particularly from Delhi—as the PM was killed by her Sikh bodyguards, Congress workers organized themselves to take revenge on ordinary Sikhs, while the state machinery abdicated its role. "The brave soldiers of the Congress are showing their bravado by killing thousands of innocents." Father Lal told Mahendra and grumbled, "Forget about other places, thousands of Sikhs have been killed in New Delhi, the capital of India, and Indira Gandhi's son, Rajiv Gandhi, the new Prime Minister, has said… tremors are felt if a big tree falls. He is himself endorsing it. What a leader!"

In the next general election, people sympathized with Rajiv Gandhi, but the Father was no more interested in that, for he was busy fighting for the victims of gas leak from a Union Carbide plant in Bhopal, a horrific industrial disaster in which more than 15,000 people were killed. "We have information that the West Virginia plant of the company has an advanced computerized safety system and there they don't store this deadly gas, MIC," the Father told Mahendra. "Here they did not even inform the authority that they had stored so much of MIC. This is mass homicide by the multinational, who like all other MNCs has treated India as a land of animals, and violated all norms."

"That is what we are," Mahendra remarked with a sad smile. "They know that anybody can do anything in this country after bribing the ministers and other men in high positions. Don't blame those MNCs."

"The government has allowed the top man of the company to go out of the country," said Lal, who was one among a small group of persons who had started fighting for compensation for the victims, a fight that was fated to continue for decades. "People must ask Arjun Singh why as the Chief Minister he failed so miserably. He must quit politics. He has no moral right to continue."

"Why blame him alone, Father? Anybody else would have done the same thing," said Mahendra.

"But then, how can we bring in change?"

Mahendra smiled again. "You have to address the root, Father. You have to challenge the gods. When a landlord rapes a low caste woman, no one is bothered in this country. Not even the family of the victim. The landlord is a god. Gods can do no wrong. And such millions of mute people are the voters and they think people like Arjun Singh of the Congress or that man, Patwa of the BJP, they are all gods. They will never amass enough strength to challenge the gods. That is the limitation of your electoral system."

The following summer—by then, he had a few more attacks of amnesia—Comrade Biplab, literally revolution, the secretary of the Unity Group, came to meet him one day, and without any prelude, asked, "People say you talk of gods these days. Is it true?"

Mahendra pondered over the intent behind such a question, and concluded that the leader was trying to ascertain whether he was still a revolutionary, or had he deviated from his earlier faith. He chuckled, as though the laugh would convey his real feelings, and said, "I feel that God is a force that dominates, scathes and brutalizes our lives... the lives of the Untouchables, Backwards. We have to challenge and defeat the gods. In that way, I feel more comfortable."

As Biplab gaped at him, he added, "You know, in my village, the Dusadhs had long ago boycotted the Hindu temples. They built their own temples after inventing their own gods. That was a way of challenging the gods and a society that is said to be created by the gods."

"I think essentially we don't have any difference," Biplab said a while later. "But why do you take recourse to such obscurantism? Don't you think whatever happens has a cause? Don't you think everything can be interpreted by cause and effect? I am sure you don't believe God created the universe."

"God is often synonymous with Nature."

"But you talked of challenging the God," now Biplab sounded harsh. "Now you say God and Nature are synonyms. But how can you challenge Nature?"

Worn out by the long conversation, Mahendra answered after a long pause, "God or Nature, whatever you call it, fixes destiny. This earth will be no more some day. Life will perish. That is destiny. You can challenge it and find some other planet to where you can transport some lives and defeat Nature."

On that day, the conversation ended there, but actually it is still continuing, in a vague way, inside Mahendra's head, spreading its branches in all directions. It will continue, Mahendra knows, until he invents the new reality: a present continuous...

Mahendra sees another man with Father Lal, who is through with the distribution of milk and loaves, and feels he knows the other man. For a few minutes, he cannot remember who he is. Then, he suddenly remembers; he is Shambhu Guha Niogi, a former Naxalite who, for years, is living with the poor miners in the Dalli-Rajhara belt and fighting against the savage exploitation the miners face. He waits for the duo as he knows both of them will come to his room.

AFTER LOSING all his dear ones, Shyamlal now follows Stephen like a shadow. The shadow, however, cannot pronounce, like many others, Stephen's name properly and calls him Istiphen. He is afraid that there can be a quicksand anywhere, waiting to cave in and drag him inside, into the darkness that resembles death. But he is sure no demon lives under the ground. For a couple of years now, he has turned himself into a shadow of Stephen, only because he feels Stephen knows where a quicksand awaits human beings, and can rescue those trapped inside.

While Shyamlal sees Stephen as his guru, Stephen has his own guru whom he calls Babaji, a man with long curly hair and an unkempt beard. Shyamlal had heard about this man being a rebel when he was in his village. Afterwards, Stephen had narrated how this man fought the non-tribal landowners, money lenders and contractors. But Shyamlal had not seen this man earlier, and so he feels excited as he looks at him.

Babaji is standing at the edge of a small valley, his gaze fixed on the distant hill called Ranchiburu, which has given the city of

Ranchi its name, and Stephen is standing silently behind him, along with Shyamlal, for more than 15 minutes now, waiting for Babaji to turn back.

He turns back all of a sudden, a soft light reflects from his eyes, and he smiles at Shyamlal. "I know your story," he says softly. "Someday, we will be able to free our land from outsiders. And then tribesmen will no longer lose their parents, children, or their land only because they are tribals." Babaji smiles again and walks a few steps forward, sits on a block of stone while twinning his fingers around a small earthen pot from which he has been quaffing *mahua*. He asks Stephen to bring another jar of *mahua*, and when Stephen is gone, Babaji tells Shyamlal, "Follow Stephen. He is one of my trusted lieutenants. Ten years ago, he led a team who faced the firing from the 'diku's… the rich men, but did not budge. Ultimately, they killed five men of that village, four Muslims and a Bihari."

"Wasn't that Kutchi? But Istiphen said you led that movement?"

Babaji smiles, and without uttering a word weaves his fingers through his beard while looking at the hill and the peak that is now hidden beyond a veil of cloud. The sky is not heavily overcast, but different shades of clouds have clubbed together about the peak, creating a veil of mist.

"My father was a schoolteacher," Babaji says after a while, his voice gruff and laden with intense feelings. "He organized the tribesmen to fight the exploitation of moneylenders-cum-landlords and inspired people to send their children to school. One day, he was murdered. I was in college in those days. The question before me was so critical. My father wanted me to be a professor. That was his small dream centred on his son. But he had another… bigger dream… of liberating the tribal people. I chose the second dream…"

The darker clouds are mellowing, as though being diluted, and their hue loosing the intensity of darkness as Babaji speaks on.

"But I shunned my father's non-violent means, and took up arms. I fought for years. Then Indira Gandhi… the Prime Minister… sent a proposal to me… to surrender and contest election to force the government to make concrete steps for amelioration of our people. That was about 10 years ago."

Shyamlal is overawed. "I never knew that," he mutters.

Babaji waves his hands in the air. "Then we contested election and had an alliance with Congress in 1980. But we could not achieve much in terms of real change. So now, we are to intensify our stir. I heard you often ask about the Naxalites. We have among us a few Communists, but they are not Naxalites. Apart from that..."

Babaji takes another long pause and then says, "They don't believe in God, all these Communists. And they fight among themselves. Just a week ago, one of the Maoist groups, MCO, killed five men of the other group, Unity or whatever they call it. Neither has a cadre of even 100 men, I am sure. But they are killing each other. And they are led by outsiders... mostly Bengalis. But the Jharkhand movement is led by the Jharkhandis, and not by outsiders. Just after Independence, in our proposed Jharkhand, we, the aborigines, were the majority. Now we are about 30 per cent. Soon we will be one-fourth of the population. Unless the Jharkhandis fight for their rights, everything will be lost."

"How we are getting reduced?" Shyamlal asks.

"Outsiders are overtaking us. For centuries, our people have left this land in search of food... gone to the tea gardens of Assam and north Bengal, gone to work as labour to Bengal and north Bihar. And now, our girls are leaving in throngs to all parts of the country to work as domestic help."

Shyamlal finds Stephen walking up towards them with a bucket full of *mahua*, the country liquor. Babaji also notices him and says, "Stephen often remains obsessed with a hill shaped like a bird's head. He became an orphan at a tender age, worked in Vitry... that is Victoria mine near Dhanbad and... finally was settled in Koderma. He worked in the quarries and mines from a young age. He was beaten up, often remained half-fed, but finally became a *sardar* of the coolies. And then he joined us." Babaji lights a cigarette and looks on towards the distant hill that has become hazy now as grey rain clouds approach them.

Shyamlal cannot see the horizon anymore; rain clouds are advancing fast, from the hills towards the valley, reducing the visibility and bringing in sprays of water that pricks his forehead like the 'peace water' sprinkled by Hindu priests after a puja. Now Babaji starts running and as Shyamlal watches his speed, he feels amazed.

Minutes later—by then they all have sheltered inside—the rain starts falling incessantly, hiding from the human eyes the hills, the trees, the skies, the surroundings. Babaji sits down and drinks the liquor to his heart's content, looking at the downpour that creates a hard sound as it falls on the big flat rock by the side of the cottage. Suddenly, another man, drenched and gasping, enters the cottage. "Have you heard it, Babaji?" he cries. "In Santhal Pargana, the police had fired on Santhals and killed 15, including the former MP, Father Anthony Tudu."

"Killed? Where?" Stephen reacts immediately.

"At Sanjhi. They were protesting the nexus between money lenders and police."

"Fifteen killed!" Babaji exclaims, closes his eyes and remains silent with his hands locked and his body still.

When he opens his eyes, they are burning, but his voice is low and placid, "Did you notice how the rain started? It happens often. It drizzles for a minute or two and then comes down heavily. Popular upsurge also takes place in the same manner. If we can motivate people to fight for few months, then the downpour will overwhelm the whole world."

Though he does not understand the relation between the rain and the movement, Shyamlal is amazed and convinced.

"I HAD given up hope, but I am now reassured," Harry says with a semblance of smile as he pushes back his chair, his hand outstretched to reach Raj Karan's.

Raj Karan, the Superintendent of Police, Task Force (anti-Naxalite Operations) of Bihar, wears a French-cut beard that gives his longish face with piercing eyes a rugged look. As he stands up, Harry realizes the man is over six feet with broad shoulders, tanned skin and a firm posture, and for some strange reason, he feels more assured, as though a brawny figure is indicative of determination.

"The first time we erred in not guarding our *haveli* properly," Harry says while standing up. "The second time I relied upon a don, who failed. He took so much time that the Naxalites took that bastard Chamar out of the hospital. This time I feel I have found the right person. But don't forget your promise… you must hand that Chamar comrade to me… alive."

Raj Karan's face shows no expression and he does not even nod; he just stands still, as though waiting for Harry to leave.

Coming out from the Police Headquarters, Harry enters a restaurant and after ordering coffee with chicken sandwiches, looks at the road through the tinted glass windows and recapitulates what has happened over the last few days.

His thoughts go back to Titiana, a tourist from Central Asia, whom he managed to impress and get into his bed, and then told the tragic story of his life. She asked, "Have you avenged the killing?"

"The law is there," Harry told the girl.

She stood up, arranged her hair in a bun and murmured, "I am a Turk by blood… from my father's side. I believe you yourself should avenge it."

Harry did not sleep with her again, for he saw the shadow of his wife, the illusion, in her; and the next day, he went to Banaras to meet the family's priest and astrologer, who lived in a house on the banks of the Ganga, the mighty river revered as *punyatowa*, the sacred water.

"Tell me what to do… why are women trying to thrust upon me a role that I am not willing to play?"

"These women are directing you towards your goal. You are a part of Shiva, and they are *Shakti*, the power," the astrologer said grimly.

That night, when the lights were off and he was trying to get some sleep, Harry found his eldest brother's son, a victim of the massacre, standing near him sporting his cricket uniform. He was a good cricketer and many in Allahabad thought he might get a place in the cricket squad of India if he progressed well; but he was killed when he was 16. He murmured to Harry, "You must do something, uncle. They deprived me of my body, you must do the same to them."

Then Harry saw the astrologer standing near the door and beckoning him to walk across the Ganga.

"That's impossible." Harry cringed.

But the astrologer said, "You are a part of Shiva. You can walk across the water."

Harry resisted, but both the astrologer and his nephew mocked at him for his inability and started walking across the Ganga, forcing Harry to follow them. However, while they walked across steadily, Harry went down with each step, tried to swim, but his arms and legs were too slow to keep him afloat. When he was about to drown, he woke up.

The dream started haunting him. Why should they together swim across the river, a dead boy and a living old man? And why had his nephew started pleading with him to do something? What could he do, particularly when the culprit had escaped? With all sorts of questions crowding his mind, he went to the astrologer's house again, but found the house shrouded in a pall of gloom. And then he came to know that the astrologer had died in the previous evening.

The waiter comes back and places the plate of sandwich and the coffee set on the table, and after arranging everything, goes away without a nod or a smile, bringing Raj Karan back to Harry's mind.

With a small bite at the sandwich, Harry returns to his earlier thoughts.

He decided to meet the officer called Raj Karan when he heard from his friends in the police that the officer from Haryana cadre had come to head a task force to wipe out the Naxalites from Bihar.

Harry pours coffee into the cup as he reaches the last leg of his thoughts.

Now that he has met Raj Karan, he is confident that something is really going to happen after so long, something bloody, something awesome, something that will exterminate the animals called the Naxalites. He has pleaded with the officer to hand him over the body of the Chamar—he was sure the police would find him—and the officer has tacitly agreed.

The Chamar's body will pacify his uncle, his wife and surely his nephew who appeared in his dream. Harry sips his coffee and mutters to himself, "At last, light has appeared at the end of the tunnel. God is gracious."

KARMA GETS a message in the form of a letter that carries a particular fragrance that he associates with the *firangi* nun, Sister Lillian.

She cannot write Hindi well, and that is obvious to even Karma, who has not studied in any school ever. He opens the letter and feels the Sister's presence in the fragrance that fills his heart with a feeling that is inexplicable and, to a large extent, irrelevant. She has asked for his help to create health awareness among the masses, as in the villages around her school in the last one week two people have died—one was a woman who needed an operation but declined to go to the hospital, and the other was a man who after being bitten by a fox did not take anti-Rabies injections. "You fight for changing the society. If you do not put stress on the consciousness of the people then what is the point?" she has asked.

It is not for the first time the Sister is arguing the point, but Karma is confused, as his leaders are not interested in the subject.

When he met her for the first time—he went to her to demand regular levy from the school—he was charmed by her personality and appearance. But she declined to pay the money, and said, "You say you try to ameliorate the condition of the people. And what do you think we are doing here? Making money? We are trying to educate the children of those hapless persons for whom… according to you… you are working."

Karma had no answer to that, for he was not prepared for such an encounter, and withdrew on that day. But a month later, he again went to meet her, this time with another writ—the school kitchen must provide food for comrades if they come to seek food.

"How often will they come?" she enquired.

"Maybe once a month," Karma said cautiously, as this time he was determined not to budge.

"That can be managed," she agreed and turned her back to him all of a sudden.

After a fortnight, when Karma, along with three other comrades, went there to ask for food, the Sister looked at him with indulgence, and commented, "So you asked for it for yourself."

Karma was hurt and retorted, "I came to rescue an old woman whom the villagers were to kill, suspecting she is a witch. If you don't want to give me food, don't give. Provide for the others."

Suddenly, the Sister became apologetic and said with a sad smile on her pink lips, "Why should I not provide food to you? Come."

Since then, he has met her few more times, and has discussed, on her initiative, a number of things concerning the rural poor—issues such as spreading education and health awareness, and taking an initiative in providing employment. Often, Karma could not reply to her queries, either because he was not confident about the answers, or he suffered from an inferiority complex before the educated nun, from whom a particular fragrance filled his heart. He has discussed her suggestions with the leaders of the Unity group in which Comrade Mahendra's Red Salute group has merged, but they have not given it much importance.

With the letter in his hand, Karma feels now he has a second chance as he has become a member of the central organizing committee of the People's Unity group, and is travelling with Comrade Biplab, or Revolution, the secretary of the Unity group.

Karma looks through the window of the slow-moving train on its way to Balaghat, an area rich in manganese ore and jungles full of teak and sal woods. "How long will it take?" Karma asks, for he wants to assess whether broaching the topic will be effective now.

"Another hour," Biplab answers confidently.

Karma hands him the letter from Lillian with a succinct foreword, "Sister Lillian has again written to us, and you know what she wants us to do."

Biplab reads the later carefully, but without saying anything and without returning the letter, he starts reading a book written in Bengali.

A few hours later, drenched in the untimely rain and worn out by fatigue from the journey, they meet Nagjyothi, literally 'glow of the serpent'. He is one of the top leaders of the southern Naxalites and they meet in a hamlet not far from Balaghat.

Karma has no clue why Biplab is meeting Nagjyothi, whom he had seen only once when this man, along with Comrade Sainath and Comrade Rambabu, went to Kalipura to meet Comrade Mahendra. While the four were closeted in a hut, Comrade Baguna told him that this 'trident' from the south met Mahendra at least twice a year. The thought saddens his mind, for it reminds him that Baguna was killed a week ago, and the police said they had to fire on him as he was trying to escape.

"We must merge our groups fast and make way for a mass upsurge, Comrade Biplab," Nagjyothi says, sitting in a small one-storey house.

"We have discussed it," Biplab says slowly. "But many of our comrades are not willing to accept your version of international question and are not prepared to tolerate those parts where you have criticized Charu Majumdar."

"Charu Majumdar was... no god," Nagjyothi's voice becomes shrill. When he speaks in Hindi, groping for the words in a language that is not his, he talks with a certain hiss. "This is the problem with you. We say... we do not support annihilation theory. It can be resorted to only in exceptional cases. And we say... mass movement must continue. Charu Majumdar was wrong to denounce mass movement. These are the two points where we... differ. What's the problem with it?"

Karma does not understand the whole of it, for Nagjyothi is using English words like 'annihilation' and 'mass movement', but he gets a rough idea of what is being discussed.

"There's a growing feeling, maybe a misconception... that you want to lessen the importance of armed action," Karma hears Biplab mumbling.

"Not at all," Nagjyothi retorts. "We were the first to give sanctity to money-action, and that was five years ago. We have allowed 'bank robbery', even extortion from contractors or government servants. Why? We feel we are an alternative state power, and wherever we will be able to establish people's power, we will do this. But why do we need money? Because we need to... buy arms. Traditionally, we depended on traditional weapons and some arms we looted from the police. But that is not sufficient. So it is not true that we are not stressing the point of armed action. Not true. But..." Nagjyothi's voice sounds laden with dismay, "Strangely, Comrade Mahendra agreed that 'mass fronts' and 'mass movement' should flourish along with 'armed action'."

"Comrade Mahendra!" Biplab heaves a sigh. "He is a great loss for us."

"He is better now; why do you count him as lost?" Nagjyothi asks.

"He undergoes a fit of... memory blackouts. And he talks about God and destiny. I think he is a lost case. It happens. He fought for so many years. I had seen him when he was active in Bengal during Charu *babu's* time. And then that injury. His brain is affected."

"But thinking about God... very sad," Nagjyothi's voice reflects concern. "I think his brain is really damaged."

Staring at the kerosene lamp that is suddenly glowing very brightly, indicating that the fuel is almost burnt out, Karma wonders whether Biplab and the southern leader have any right to comment upon Comrade Mahendra. He strongly feels that a mere superior position does not make someone really superior to all those who are below one in the hierarchy. Emboldened by his thoughts, he overcomes his edginess to say, "He always used to refer to gods. He said we are fighting against the designs of the gods who have created society and the caste system that has turned us into slaves. He told us that the Communists have always refuted the existence of God. But that doesn't work in this country, which is the land of gods. Here we have to fight and defeat the gods."

The lamp goes out. Karma cannot see the reaction on the faces of the leaders, but now that he has spoken out and expressed his mind, he does not care any more. Sceptical and scared of a reaction, one often prefers silence, but when one has already spoken out, one does not bother anymore and is ready to face the consequences.

After a long silence, Nagjyothi says, "Sometimes some people intrigue us, for they see things differently. We can't understand them… Whatever. If you feel he is finished, I am interested in him. You can give him on lien to us."

Karma remains seated uneasily and, in a flash, remembers what Mahendra had told him about five years ago, on a similar dark night, "We are trying to unite the various groups of Naxalites. We seek such mergers to reach the ultimate goal of making a comprehensive military strategy that we believe is essential for the revolution to succeed. For us, the central strategy is formation of an arch of influence that would be built from the western coast of Maharashtra-Karnataka up to the Himalayan Kingdom of Nepal through the corridor of the jungles of Andhra-Madhya Pradesh, Orissa, Bihar and Bengal, a 2,000-kilometre long arch that would cut off India's south and east from the north and the west."

As he remembers it, he says, without caring for anyone else, "Probably he will love to work for you, for he always dreamt of the arch that will be the corridor from where the revolutionary fire will spread."

"You know about the corridor?" Biplab croaks.

Before Karma reacts, Nagjyothi says in a tone that reflects sarcasm, "Don't forget he is Mahendra's comrade. When we fought for cheap liquor to be given to the toilers, Comrade Mahendra told us that the notion that toilers need liquor was totally false. Later, when the wives of the workers revolted against it, we realized how right he was. Then we started campaigning against liquor."

Karma feels tempted to ask whether they can raise health issues, but decides to remain mum, apprehending that Biplab may get upset.

The idea distracts him, makes him inattentive for a while, and when he comes back from his thought, he hears Nagjyothi saying, "We have to fill up the vacuum and I am sure we are the only force who can do it, for no other party in this country thinks of the poor. But for that, we have to create a social base. The ideal situation will be if we can run schools and even hospitals, apart from carrying on our cultural propaganda as we are doing now."

"Cultural front is your great strength," says Biplab. "You know that Karma?"

"No," Karma mutters uncertainly.

"They write and enact dramas and sing songs to convey our message and thousands of people gather to see them," Biplab seems enthusiastic. "In Bihar, though we have some bards and cultural troops, still they are far, far ahead in this."

"It's nothing," Nagjyothi says suddenly, and now he speaks fluently in Hindi. "We have to expand much more, keeping that corridor in mind, and we must encourage many more open activities. We have to establish ourselves as a very big force, as a political party that will shape the future of the country."

While returning to his base the next day, Karma feels both happy and sad. He is happy because he will now go back to Lillian with the message that some of the leaders are thinking like her. He met Nagjyothi separately in the morning to tell him about the Sister's proposal. Nagjyothi agreed at once, and said, "Years ago, Rambabu told me that these should be our motto. We all agreed. A sort of cultural revolution. Rambabu will be here soon. Discuss it with him." Then he broached it with Rambabu, who used to visit Kalipura along with Nagjyothi and Sainath, and after the discussion, he is now confident that united Maoist forces will surely work for a total change—for imparting education, for raising all sorts of consciousness, for cultural movement; all together for creating a new man. What was more heartening for him was a fact that Rambabu told him: Comrade Mahendra was very enthusiastic about this total change.

Rambabu also asked him to exert pressure on the leadership for unity of all factions, but Karma feels neither his leaders will agree to merge the organization with the southern group, nor will he be able to exert pressure on them. The thought makes him sad.

MAHENDRA TELLS the Father that he has decided to go to Panchkuian, where people are carrying on a non-violent resistance against a company that has managed a lease from the government to set up a factory on the pastoral land of the villagers.

It is actually Sainath's plan. Better known as 'the protruding nose', he is the main leader of the People's Revolution Group in central India, and was a regular visitor to Kalipura along with Nagjyothi and Rambabu. Now he wants Mahendra to help them implement a delicate plan of turning Panchkuian into a People's Revolution Group base.

Father Lal feels Mahendra is not fit to take up such responsibilities, more so after another recent attack of amnesia that had left him physically and psychologically down for some days. He looks on at a distant chimney that is emitting smoke and distorting the otherwise bucolic setting at the back of the Home, and shakes his head, "I can't let you go."

"But I have no other option," Mahendra says softly. "I have to do my duties."

The recent attack of amnesia was much more vigorous, for it continued for almost a day, after which Mahendra realized that he had totally forgotten his early childhood till the day when he was tied to a banyan tree. He could not even remember why he was tied to that tree. He knows that someday he will forget everything, but it is not bothering him anymore, as he has learnt to live with it, and has regained his calm.

If we are a part of the great consciousness that is the force driving the universe, we too have powers to lead our life to where we want to reach, he has concluded. Destiny is the winding path that will take people where they want to reach. For him, his path is an endless endeavour to create his own world. "Seeing through the stones means creating my own reality, my own world," he has concluded, though he still does not understand the meaning of the strange phrase. But he is confident that by carrying on with his work, he will be able to create his own world, and then, see through the stones.

With this confidence, he met Sainath in a village near the mines and agreed to go to Panchkuian. Sainath was keeping long hair and Muslim-type beard and was wearing a dishevelled look that did not match his revolutionary image; it was a good disguise.

When they met, Sainath asked him, like he did in the older days, "Do you think what Russia is doing in Afghanistan is right?"

Mahendra replied, "One has to fulfil one's duty, one's dharma. The sun gives us light and heat, and never relents from its duty. Each action can be adjudged through this."

Sainath looked at him curiously while the long lugubrious siren dared the miners to go under the earth. Almost a minute later, Sainath asked, rather nervously, "Who decides what is whose dharma?"

Mahendra replied, "The positive forces of the universe. And destiny too plays its role."

"You believe in fate?"

"Not fate, destiny."

"What's the difference?"

"Just now a brick can fall on my head. That is fate, which I cannot change by my action. But destiny can be changed. You have chosen your destiny by becoming a Maoist. At different points, life provides us with options, and according to your choice, you fix your destiny. You had options… to lead a peaceful life as a teacher, or a government employee, but you have chosen a path…"

They went inside a hut, sat on cane stools, and Sainath again came back to the context of Panchkuian. "If you work with us, you will become a symbol of unity," he said in a serious tone. "Whenever I meet you, we discuss about unity. Now, a majority of your comrades have joined the Unity group. But they have rejected our proposal for a merger of Unity and our People's Revolution. If you join us…"

"I think Raul, who now works in Orissa, will also join you," Mahendra said softly. "My erstwhile comrade is working in Malkangiri region, and trying to unite other smaller groups who were also working there."

"You are lost in some thoughts," Father Lal says and scrutinizes Mahendra's face. "Whatever you say, I can't allow you to go."

Now looking on at Father Lal's worried face, Mahendra says, "Father, when time comes, one has to go."

"I don't know, but if you have another attack and forget yourself for longer duration… very few people will understand you there."

"How does it matter?" Mahendra mutters. "It is better to work than be idle, though work will not change anything."

"Then why should one work?" Father Lal asks.

"So that those who do not follow dharma are punished. That is what Krishna, whom people consider as God, said in the *Bhagavad Gita*. If you fight and defeat the wrongdoers, that is good. But if you don't, then time will do it. So, if you consider those millions of years of life on earth, it makes little difference whether you work or not." Mahendra looks at a bull trudging through the road, and adds, "Someday there will be no human being, no earth, not even this solar system. So why should we work? Only because doing some work is better than sitting idle."

"But being a Marxist, how do you believe in what God said?"

"He was not a god. He was a human being and the greatest philosopher the world has ever seen. In those ancient times, any philosopher had to preach in a religious garb." Mahendra speaks casually, as though he is discussing about crops or cattle.

The Father's forehead turns furrowed, and he asks, "If you believe in Him, why do you kill people?"

Mahendra looks at the Father, and sighs. "He himself had asked to fight against *adharma*, that is... in brief... derailment from humanity."

For a while, the Father stands still, for this is the first time he hears such an interpretation of the Hindu holy book. He had never thought that someday a Maoist would justify his action quoting from books belonging to the realm of religion, and that too with such solid logic. Isn't it there in other religions too? The crusade in his religion, jihad of the Muslims? Won't those terms, if interpreted in secular context, lead to the same conclusion that you fight for a just world? And of course, the Marxists believe in that, fight for peace, as they put it.

Mahendra turns his head and looks straight—his eyes have now lost the fire that earlier scorched people and forced them to look away—and says abruptly, "Now, I will have to go, for that is my destiny. But someday a letter may come here from Katihar. If ever it comes, please contact me and send it to me."

"I will," the Father says readily though his eyes have questions.

Mahendra remains quiet for a while, and then, without knowing why, he reveals a part of his secret for the first time. "I had a daughter. I lost her after my first wife died. We lived in Katihar in those days. If my old comrades find her, they will send the letter."

"Oh!" Lal's face seems clouded. "I never knew that. I thought your wife was killed and your son is being raised by one of your comrades in UP."

"He is my second wife's son," Mahendra says in a tired voice.

"I never knew this," Lal mutters.

"No one knows it, except my comrades who are in the Marxist Party, who did not leave the party with me to join the Maoists. And they do not know about my second marriage. Probably you are the first person..."

"I understand," Father Lal mutters without knowing why he says so, and nods a number of times as he gets absorbed in difficult thoughts. Suddenly he asks, "But why would you go when you are not well at all?"

Mahendra looks at the distance and explains, "I know for sure I will not live to see the revolution. But if… in my lifetime, I see the Maoists have united… I will die with a hope. Unity of all our organizations will be a great boost, and only then, our real struggle against the state will begin. That is why I am going. I am with the Unity group, and also with the southern Naxalites. This will help broaden our unity, and will create a happy world for me."

Father Lal shakes his head, but does not say anything.

14

Glimpses of the Past (1940–80)

WITH A few hundred workers and rising profit, his paper mill was doing quite well; but in those days of the turbulent '60s, Harry could see the elements of disquiet building up.

In Bengal, the character of labour was changing under the initiative of the Communists, and Harry had no doubt in his mind that the change would surely lead to anarchy. Seemingly justifying his worry, union leaders of the paper mill suddenly served a strike notice on him. Harry and the manager of the mill, Mr Kapadia, were nervous, but the labour officer, one Ganguly, taught them how to turn this into an advantage.

"Sir," he told Harry politely, "they demand 8.33 per cent bonus and an increase in wage. About bonus, I think we can afford about five per cent and the workers will be happy. The wage hike is the main problem. I feel we can raise wages by five rupees per month across the board after allowing the strike to go on for a month. We won't show any interest in breaking it. And when things will be settled, we won't pay the wage for this one month."

"What do we gain by this?" Harry's asked.

"By not paying the wage for a month, you square it off with the increase in salary bill, and by one month, you clear your stock... afterwards you don't have to pay idle wage..."

Harry thought over it quickly and exclaimed, "Wonderful!"

Ananda Ganguly, the labour officer, said softly, "Sir, this is the technique the Marwaris use in the jute mills."

Then Harry came to the crucial point, "But how would you have the settlement after that? The workers may not agree."

"Sir, it's simple," Ganguly smirked. "Common workers are poor hapless fellows. A month without wages is terrible for them. The union leaders are the persons who create all the problems. In the name of workers' interest, the Left unionists brazenly seek to strengthen their political base."

Ganguly then explained his plan as Harry heard in rapt attention. "The more powerful union in our office is the Communist union, AITUC. I think they enjoy 80 per cent support. But we have the Congress union too, INTUC. I will ask the INTUC leader to oppose the strike call. Then in AITUC, there are two groups. The Communists have split their party recently. But, on the labour front, they all belong to AITUC. Now the most militant leader is Barin Ray, who is with the new Communist party led by Promode Dasgupta. This group claims that they are the real CPI. We will corner him by using Tapas Bhowmik, who belongs to the original CPI."

As Ganguly leaned back on the sofa, exuding his confidence, Harry asked, "Would it be so simple... dumping Ray?" He asked in Hindi while the labour officer spoke in Bengali.

"Sir, we have to arrange for a few bottles of good whisky for Tapas Bhowmik and thousand rupees for the top INTUC leader."

"Money I understand. You bribe the Congressman. I have heard you can do it with some of the leftist trade union leaders too. But why the whisky?"

"Tapas *babu*'s father had left him at least a few hundred thousand rupees. He is the president of at least 10 unions in 10 factories. He would have become an MP had the Communists not split. You can't offer him money." Ganguly looked about him and whispered, in English, "Different gods are satisfied by different flowers."

Harry saw in Ganguly the potential of a very successful business executive, and muttered into his ears, "You will get the money. I will provide it from my personal account. Rs 3,000. You don't have to account for it. Just do the work."

And Ganguly did it. The workers were on strike for 40 days, and when the management felt production should start again, Ganguly successfully managed everything and the mill opened a week before Durga Puja, the biggest festival in Bengal.

Harry got the news at home, and then came out for a stroll since it was a fine afternoon; the sky was partly cloudy and the locality quiet. He went down the lanes and reached Kumortuli, the locality of the potters, who were busy making idols of the goddess Durga. Suddenly, his eyes caught the breasts of an idol, high and tight, still to be painted, and they reminded him of his guard's wife. A moment later, Harry felt ashamed of his thoughts while looking at the idol, and apologized to the goddess several times before hurriedly turning back for home. But the guard's wife haunted him all the while as he walked down the narrow lanes, as he crossed the main road, and even when he lingered for some time at the front of his house in a bid to cool down. Inside the house, he realized he had no escape from the image and decided to have his way. He asked the guard to leave at once for the factory to have a look at how things were moving there.

"Master, we have to lock the door. Let me ask my wife to do so," the loyal guard said. "The cook and the caretaker have gone to the cinema. So, apart from you, only Motia… my wife… will be at home. You know this is a bad time…"

Harry was relieved to know that no one else would be there. He himself came forward to lock the door, for the first time in his life, insisting the guard to leave at once. After locking it hurriedly, he walked a few steps, as though possessed, and wondered where to go, for he had no idea which of the many rooms on the ground floor allotted for the servants was occupied by his guard. But then he heard a faint sound of a song from the radio and eventually it guided him to one room, where he found Motia, a dark well-built woman, lying on a cot with the radio beside her.

She got up hurriedly as he entered the room, her eyes betraying fear and confusion, and the first thing she did was switch off the radio. She thought the *malik* would rebuke her for making a noise. But as the master stood silent, she realized without looking at him that he was looking at her bosoms, and she pulled her veil down to cover her face. He looked on at her heavy and shapely breasts covered by a blouse studded with sequins, at her belly shimmering in sunlight reflected from the mirror, and at her long thick curly hair. "We have to lock the door," he muttered, as though he was bound to repeat the instruction.

He was in his late 20s and was experienced in these games. Still, at that moment he was confused, for till then he had only had prostitutes and did not know how to approach a woman who was not known for her easy morals. But as he let his body to take its own course, the woman did not resist him; she only became too stiff, almost turned into a body of flesh and blood without life.

In the next three months, Harry slept with Motia at least once every week, and though she never resisted, she always turned into a lifeless entity, as though she had no desire, no feelings, no expressions. It irked Harry and gradually he lost interest in her.

A few months later, the guard came to him to convey good news, "My wife is pregnant, *malik*." As Harry looked on in confusion, he said, "Everybody thought she was barren. That is why I stopped going to village. Now I can go." Harry realized that she was carrying his child. He took out two 10-rupee notes and while giving the money to the guard, a tall stout man from his native village, got slightly worried—if the child were born fair like him that might lead to some talk. But the child, a son, bailed him out by going upon his mother.

During those days, Harry was also feeling the heat of the changes taking place in rural India, a sort of churning and mild tremors loosening the base of feudalism even in his village. While Bengal was having a radical face-lift, Bihar was changing slowly with the Socialists emerging as a growing force in the state, and the Communists raising their heads in Bhojpur region. The legislative constituency called Puraina was much bigger than the Thakur's *khas taluka*, but the *haveli* had its place of respect throughout the constituency; that helped Sampat Singh, the pawn chosen by Badhe Thakur, to win from the constituency thrice. But, in a by-election held after his untimely death in 1965, Hukum Lal the socialist made history by defeating the Badhe Thakur's eldest son.

Hukum Lal had contested from the constituency once before, in 1962, replacing the earlier candidate of the Socialist Party, another Yadav, who had contested twice without any luck. That earlier candidate was a Krishnauth, a sub-caste who claimed to be the most superior among the Yadavs, while Hukum was a Gareri, a lower sub-caste. When Hukum Lal became the candidate, the old guard of the *haveli,* Pullu Yadav started campaigning among the Krishnauths and Majarauths (another sub-caste to which Pullu belonged) not to vote for a Gareri who had replaced a Krishnauth. It ensured Hukum Lal's defeat. But he took lessons from that and realized that if he could somehow manage the Communists and the Bhumihars, he would win. He did it in 1965. The Communist Party did not field any candidate in Puraina, and Hukum Lal consolidated the votes of the Backwards and a section of the Bhumihars, thanks to Subhash Chaudhary, a doctor by profession.

Subhash Chaudhary had come to the area a few years ago. He opened his chamber in Sahar, a nearby town, and also bought a small house in Khatura, a village in the north of Puraina, to treat patients in the villages on the weekends. He treated poor patients without charging any fees from them, and even gave them free medicine, a gesture that made him popular in the area within a short time. He then campaigned among the villagers to take from the health centre TABC injections, a single-dose vaccination for a range of diseases. He did his best to ensure that they immunized themselves by announcing that he would not treat anyone who had not been vaccinated.

One day, a car stopped in front of Chaudhary's chamber and the Badhe Thakur alighted from it. "I have come to congratulate you, Doctor Sahib," he said. "Only a doctor can compel the people to go in for vaccination. You have done a marvellous job. The entire village has been immunized."

Chaudhary stood up, neither excited nor worried, gestured towards a chair to ask him to be seated, and stated, "The mission has failed."

Badhe Thakur remained where he was, just two steps inside the room, and asked in astonishment, "Why?"

"The Harijans have not undergone vaccination."

"So what?" Badhe Thakur seemed puzzled.

"We may not count them as human beings," Chaudhary smiled wryly, revealing the crude fact that caste-men had never counted the Untouchables while enumerating the number of villagers. "But medically, they are human beings, and if they are infected, the disease remains. And the virus of the disease remains active."

Badhe Thakur stood pondering for a while, and while turning back, muttered in English, "I get your point."

As he went out slowly from the chamber, Chaudhary stayed in and kept on looking until the landlord's car, an Austin, roared to start. He later came to know that the car went straight to the *haveli* from his chamber—by then the road connecting the villages in the locality had been laid to bear light automobiles, thanks to Sampat Singh, the then MLA—and soon after the drum beaters were called. By the evening, it was announced in Puraina and its neighbouring villages that if cholera broke out in any *tola*, the whole *tola* would be thrown out of the locality. On the next day, the Untouchables and some other most Backward caste men and women came to the health centre, many of them mortally scared and crying for vaccination.

It was this Subhash Chaudhary who mobilized a large section of the Bhumihars in 1965 by-election against Badhe Thakur's eldest son, a Rajput. He reminded the Bhumihars that in the state politics the

Rajputs were the main rivals of the Bhumihars, and it was pointless to make the next Badhe Thakur also an influential politician. The Bhumihars saw logic in that and voted for Hukum Lal.

For this, Lal was greatly indebted to the Doctor Sahib; but among the Yadavs, he continued to preach the supremacy of the Yadavs. "In 1912, Gope Jatiya Mahasabha was established in a bid to unite all the Yadavs. It said, 'we all are the descendants of Lord Krishna.' The slogan gradually united all Yadavs and Ahirs from Punjab to Bihar. We demanded the status of Kshatriyas, like the Rajputs. We started wearing a sacred thread, participated in movements for protection of mother cow, and rebelled against oppression. But then Bhumihars tried to stop us from wearing the sacred thread. They killed five of us. I was young, and had just joined the Railway in those days… might be 1935. Then conflicts went on in Lakhisarai, in Barahiya Tal, in Sheikhpura. That was why I decided to join the Socialists. Our task is to establish the rule of the Backwards…"

As Badhe Thakur came to know about the campaign that threatened the *haveli*, he again went to meet the doctor. "Why did you join hands with the Yadavs who are hostile to the upper castes?"

The doctor was candid enough to reveal the reasons, "You will understand everything if I tell you that I am the grandson of Ramasis Chaudhary, whom you excommunicated and compelled to leave the village three decades ago."

"Ramasi*ji's* grandson!" the lord of Puraina was visibly upset. Standing at what seemed to be his favourite place, just two steps inside the doctor's chamber, he shook his head thrice, and then said, "But do you know why I excommunicated your family? They organized a nude dance, and were not repentant. Tell me Doctor Saab… you do so much for the welfare of the people… judge me from my point. Was I wrong?"

The Thakur, whose son had been defeated by the railway man, sounded tired and beguiling.

The doctor took time to reply, "You were right from your point of view, Badhe Thakur Sir. But that doesn't matter. My grandfather died on my lap. The last thing he said was… go to Puraina and avenge of the insult. I was 10-year old. I asked him how. He said, by evicting the Thakurs from Puraina. I promised him… 'I shall try'. It was my promise to a dying man. My father tried to dissuade me. But I came here to keep my promise. I am bound by that."

"You feel you can evict us from Puraina?" suddenly the landlord's voice hissed in anger as his eyes wore a sharp, cold look.

"No," the doctor smiled wryly. "Thank God, I promised him… that… 'I shall try'. I didn't promise 'I shall do that'. So…"

As Harry came to know about it and compared the situation in his native village to that prevailing in Calcutta, he could see the future; there would be upheavals that would attack the feudal and semi-capitalist structures. Harry had urged his family to move out from Puraina and invest everything in business, but his father remained adamant. "People don't respect a capitalist," the landlord said grimly.

Soon thereafter, Ganguly advised Harry not to invest money in Bengal, predicting turbulent days ahead that would ruin the state. "The situation is turning worse day by day," he uttered clearly even after five pegs of whisky, sitting in the drawing room of Harry's house in Bagbazar. Harry, with his glass of Coca Cola, heard him attentively, for he believed people told the truth under the influence of liquor. Ganguli then explained his point, "The Communists are creating problems everywhere. And River Ganga is drying up. That will kill our Calcutta port. Calcutta will turn into a desert soon."

Harry asked Ganguly, "Then what should we do?"

"Bit by bit, get your investment out of Bengal," Ganguly, whom Harry valued as his trusted lieutenant, replied.

Harry had his investments in the tea gardens of Darjeeling, in a pharmaceutical company to make a cream that claimed it could make dark girls fair, and in a venture to export cotton garments. He accepted his lieutenant's proposal and discussed it in detail for long hours.

It was about then that Harry found the first woman who was exclusively his, the widow of a Bengali worker who had died in the paper mill in an accident. Harry was marvelled by such women and often wondered whether women were a different species. Motia, the guard's wife, had never talked to him earlier and after she had the baby, Harry never entered her room: but two years later, one day she came straight to his room and said, "I want another son." And Champa, the wife of a man killed in his factory, was prepared to be his lover only for a secured life: wasn't it strange?

But his wider concerns soon overwhelmed all other pains and pleasures as the political scenario in Bengal got murkier: he heard about a group of miscreants starting a radical movement in north Bengal, the Naxalites, who were soon joined by throngs of middle-class Bengali boys, as though they all had turned into pyromaniacs.

The violence that started in villages was spilling over to the city of Calcutta, threatening the very existence of the upper middle class, though the real rich like Harry were beyond the Naxal's reach. That, however, was not assuring enough for the rich; but to their satisfaction, the state and the police under the leadership of the able Chief Minister S S Ray retaliated effectively, and the movement dissipated, though in memory of the violent days, the trams in the city still chugged along the rails with slogans for peace inscribed on them: *Benche thakun, banchte din, hingsrota barjan karun* (Live and let live, shun violence).

Then came the war with Pakistan, resulting in regular blackouts in Calcutta, followed by the birth of a new nation called Bangladesh. The non-Bengalis discussed among themselves whether West Bengal would try to secede from India to join Bangladesh—"After all, people in both sides are Bengalis. Who knows!"

Harry's mother died soon after, making the *haveli* more distant, more irrelevant and somewhat absurd to Harry. His whole focus was on earning profit and expansion of his business. He began to take out his money to two different places, Kanpur and Delhi, and launched a new company to produce plastic products, for which he established a factory at Gurgaon, a yet-to-be developed suburb of Delhi. Then he set up another small plant for his pharmaceutical company in Kanpur. He took Champa to Kanpur where he bought a house, and found a sardarni, tall and stout, called Harminder—most of her family was killed in partition riots and she was raped—to look after him in Delhi.

But new worries started shadowing him as the Naxalites became active in the Bhojpur region, some 600 kilometres away from Calcutta, and reached Puraina, his native village. He was tensed when he heard that three Naxalites active in the area had been killed, though who killed them was a mystery, for neither the police nor the private army of the *haveli* was involved.

Soon after, Badhe Thakur invited everybody to celebrate his eldest grandson Chandra Pratap's 16th birthday in the village. It was to be an event, as Badhe Thakur believed adulthood started from 16. But Puraina was a place that Harry hated; electricity had reached the village a few years ago, but telephone lines were yet to be laid out. He apologized to everybody, maintaining that he would not be able to make it to Puraina because he had some urgent meetings.

Hours after the scheduled night of celebration, early in the morning, Harry heard the telephone ringing in his house in Delhi. He woke up and picked up the heavy black receiver.

"Haloo!" the other side sounded rustic. "I want to talk to Shri Hari Pratap Singh of village Puraina. Hari Pratap Singh. Hallo!" It was an unknown, unconcerned and hoarse voice.

Harry uttered in disgust, "I am Hari Pratap Singh."

"Namaskar sir, I am the SHO of Puraina police station. Forgive me, sir. I am compelled to convey some terrible news. But this is my duty." His words were apologetic, but his voice did not betray an iota of concern. "There was an unfortunate incident at your *haveli* last night. A group of miscreants attacked the *haveli*. I am sorry sir. They killed five of your family members identified as Ravi Pratap Singh, Surya Pratap Singh, Krishna Pratap Singh, Narayan Pratap

Singh and Chandra Pratap Singh… I am sorry sir. Don't worry about the others. Now there is full protection. Haloo… Are you listening, sir? Haloo!"

"Haan," Harry said vaguely, as nothing had registered in his head that seemingly had turned blank.

"Sir, if you can come early. The bodies are kept… crick…" The line got disconnected.

He could not and did not believe what he had heard.

Afterwards, though it was very difficult for Harry to forget the image of five bodies lying in a row, wrapped in white sheets, he turned to business and women to keep himself busy. But often the trying image haunted him even in his otherwise beautiful dreams, as though it had been etched in eternity to remind all the lords of their utter helplessness. He earned more money, invested more, and found more women, who, attracted by his performance, were ready to share their body with him for favours, or even for fun.

"The concept of chastity is restricted only among the middle class," Ganguly, who had by then come to Delhi to assist him, told him while drinking a glass of rum with soda. "Ninety per cent of women belonging to the middle class or influenced by middle class values are followers of Sati or Savitri, the symbols of chastity. The rest are liberated, be they above or below the middle class. They smoke, drink, and share bed with many partners. The women who readily sleep with you are those liberated ones."

Harry was now going to Puraina regularly, at least once in a couple of months, to see his uncle who guarded the *haveli* with a futile zeal like an old warrior fighting against the ghosts. During those visits, he witnessed how the region was changing, how mindless tractors were replacing the sad bullocks, canals were bringing in miraculous water, buses were carrying the locals on the tarred roads while more people were migrating for a job in the offices or mere manual work, depending on the category they belonged to. The big and middle farmers were prospering. Harry felt a real scope for capitalist farming was emerging there following the path of Punjab and its famous green revolution, but he would not risk investing in the Maoist land.

Harry merged his various companies into one and named it the Puraina Haveli Group of Industries to immortalize the memory of his father and his uncle, who belonged to two different poles, but shared the same pride for the family. In those days, he was assisted by Madhav Pratap, nicknamed Sanjua, the son of Harry's uncle. Sanjua was only a year older than him, but he too died young from a disease that doctors diagnosed as meningitis. Harry then broke a family tradition and inducted his eldest sister's son, Raghu Prasad, into the family business. Before that, everything remained restricted among the sons of the family only.

Harry sent Raghu Prasad to Calcutta, where his only interest was the paper mill. Everything else had already been shifted out of Bengal, where a Communist government was in the saddle after the assembly election in 1977. "It's a bad time for us," Harry told Raghu Prasad. "First, Indira Gandhi lost at the national level. She declared emergency. Society was learning discipline. Trains were running on time. The labour force understood that they could not do whatever they liked to. They learnt a lesson from the railway strike led by that rogue George Fernandez. But now, I don't know what is going to happen. Prime Minister Morarji Desai is a disciplined man, but people like Fernandez are with him in the cabinet. And in Bengal... it is lost."

But then, 23-year old Raghu Prasad asked something that made a deep imprint on Harry's mind, "I want to know, just for my own understanding, why can't we influence these Socialists and Communists? They all need money. They have to contest elections. And we can provide them with money. What do you think?"

Harry did not respond for a while. They were sitting on the first floor of their newly-acquired house in Dover Lane, which was a part of the posh and developing south Calcutta. Then he said, "True. Very true. And if I carry forward your assumption, the logical conclusion is that we capitalists should not align with any political party, but we should compel all political parties to follow our agenda."

Harry tried to influence Bengal ministers, but when that did not work, Ganguly came forward with another thesis. "As long as there is this man called Promod Dasgupta, industrialists would be seen as enemies of the people. If Jyoti Basu outlives him, and still remains the chief minister, you shall have a chance."

Through time, Harry further diversified his business, and started propagating before other industrialists or bureaucrats in every gathering his idea of a 'rightist revolution'. He spoke of a radical change of political economy, by which he implied an economy unshackled from every control and liberated from the bureaucracy. He asked them to be above politics and pressurizing all politicians to follow this agenda for economic growth. At times, he realized that he had turned into a perfect combination of his father, who delved into difficult ideas, and his uncle, whose mantra of life was business.

Harry was still trying hard to make the police act and bring the culprits of Puraina to book. He felt happy when Mahendra was arrested, but just after that his uncle got him married to his cousin Sanjua's widow, and his life started taking a bizarre turn as his wife constantly badgered him for revenge, medieval style.

15

The Present Continuous (1986–87)...

PASCAL FERNANDEZ, the joint director with the IB, the intelligence wing of the central government, says smilingly, "I think, Cobra, you are in trouble for that line in your poem. 'Flood is a good time to make money... put your conscience in the pocket to lick the honey.' Have I quoted correctly?"

Ashok Sharma, the Romantic Cobra, nods. "As a poem, it is rubbish," he says softly. "But it conveys a point. They make money from everything... my fellow police officers and those in the administration. Last year, when I went to Samastipur and other areas, I found no relief had reached those people ravaged by the flood. The state and the central governments allot so many crores of rupees for the affected people, but hardly 10 per cent of that reaches them. The rest is eaten up by officers like us, the contractors, the politicians and some influential locals."

Pascal waves his hand in a bid to stop him, "I understand. But would you be able to do your work, when the whole department gangs up against you?"

"Let me see. When I was the SP in Hazaribagh, they said my next job would be that of DIG, Magadh Range. But when I became a DIG, I was given Intelligence. And that was good. Now I know how corrupt politicians are, how closely they are related to criminal gangs and how they are encouraging these criminals to gain prestige and power. It's another matter that nobody cares. But this will help me to throw light on corruption."

"They will complain to the Home Commissioner, to the minister... and maybe all of them are involved."

"They have started doing that," the Romantic Cobra says with a sigh. "But you know, I too have made courage the mantra of my life."

Pascal turns to him, "I need such courageous men by my side. Join the Central Reserve Police and get transferred to Delhi."

They are travelling from Gaya to Patna in an Ambassador car that roars through the bumpy road at about a speed of 60 kilometres an hour, compelling the driver and the guard, sitting on the front seat, to keep their eyes on the road. Ashok takes his time to understand the proposal, and is enthusiastic. "I have no objection."

"Good, I knew it," Pascal says confidently, and to work out the arrangements, asks, "What about your wife and... I believe you have a daughter?"

"My daughter studies in Darjeeling. My wife..." Ashok stops suddenly.

Pascal looks at him and asks, "What about your wife? She is a doctor in Patna Hospital, isn't it?"

As Ashok nods, Pascal continues, "I met her when our investigation about the escape of that Naxalite was on. She is a nice lady. But... if you don't mind... a bit stubborn. Will she come with you?"

"My wife does not stay with me anymore," Ashok Sharma reveals in a sad voice. "She has built a full-fledged TB centre. It's about hundred kilometres from Patna. In fact, in five minutes we will be passing through an area which is about 10 kilometres from that place. She stays in that centre these days. When I was elsewhere, she was in Patna. When I came to Patna, she left the city... I come here if I manage to get leave. But she..."

Pascal looks straight, between the heads of the driver and the security person, but he is not interested in the vista of the road and its surroundings. As Ashok Sharma breaks into a pause, he turns towards him again, as though to remind him that he is yet to finish his sentence.

"She has not seen her daughter even once in the last one year," Ashok says coyly. "She does not allow her to come here, lest she is infected. Nor does Rani manage time to go to see her."

For a couple of minutes, Pascal sits quietly. He listens to the muffled horn of their air-conditioned car as it cuts through a bazaar area, watches the scared reactions of the locals who jump out of the road, and appreciates in his mind the nerve of the driver who does not slow down even when someone is just 10 yards from his wheels. "She is a noble lady," he then comments cautiously.

"No doubt. I salute her. But she has become too noble for our daughter."

Pascal realizes he is on the brink of a sensitive personal zone and prefers to be quiet for some more time.

Ashok breaks the silence a while later, "It all started after Mahendra Chamar escaped. The first few days she was scared that the Naxalite might try to kill me. She was abnormally scared. She was very courageous as such. But, God knows why, she panicked and developed some sort of a nervous disorder…"

"You arrested that man, didn't you?"

"Yes, I mean I led the operation."

"So her fear had valid reasons."

Ashok looks at Pascal. "I don't deny. But she was not like that earlier. For her, duty was above all. She never wavered when I went to nab dangerous criminals. I don't know what happened. And then she decided to work for the TB centre."

Once again, the two sit quietly as the car rolls on. After a few minutes, Pascal suddenly asks, "Sharma, you said that place is nearby?"

"Which place?"

"The TB centre?"

"Yes."

"Can we go there?"

As the car turns towards the village, Pascal changes the topic, "You know, I want you to be in the central force because I believe you have a beautiful mind. I am going to be busy with the extremists of Punjab. I hate to be in uniform, but they have decided to put me there. I believe all these problems, northeast or Punjab or Naxalites... should be handled with extreme care. And for that one needs a soft mind."

The car hits a bad stretch, caused by a few hours of shower on the previous day. It moves slowly as though to create the right ambience for Pascal's words. "A lot depends on us, on our approach. We have always had two schools of thought in the intelligence department, and I presume that they have been there right from the beginning. One school believes in brute force; don't bother about the root cause, just finish off the rebels. The other believes in the healing touch; find the root cause, give space, and use force selectively. I belong to the second school, but I know we are an insignificant minority, an endangered species. However, this is the only road to a permanent solution."

"You mean the Naxalite problem should be handled with care? But, sir," Ashok almost mumbles, glancing at the senior IPS officer through the corner of his eyes, "the government here doesn't share that view. The man who is given charge of this Special Task Force believes the Naxalites are bandits, and should be killed. That's how he wants to finish them off."

"Who's the bugger?"

"One Raj Karan. From Haryana."

Pascal nods for a few times before saying, "You never know, even this man's efforts may yield results. Naxalites were crushed by SS Ray earlier and now they have come back. But SS Ray and his officers carried the day. Now this Raj Karan may succeed for the time. But I have a hunch that Naxalites will come back again, taking lessons from each defeat. They will emerge stronger."

"You think so?"

"Definitely. I feel we are never learning a lesson. We are using the same old method. And, Sharma, you will always confront buggers who do not understand anything, but hold key positions. What's even more dangerous is that these idiots don't know that they don't know. And worse still, you will find lots of people, or buffoons, who are greatly impressed by the performance of those idiots!"

"Right sir," Ashok agrees from the bottom of his heart.

Pascal, known as a quite man, suddenly sounds sharp, "Don't leave space for those mediocre lots, though they will always be in great numbers. They will defeat you time and again. It's true that they rule; but isn't it also true that the world moves forward because of ideas that come from thinking animals?"

Half an hour later, they are on the gate of Arogya, the TB centre, a two-storey large rectangular house surrounded by a set of white cottages. "The road for the last 10 kilometres was terribly bad," says Pascal as he comes out from the air-conditioned car to look at the white building, and is hit by the summer heat that creates a shiver in his body.

Inside Arogya, as they wait for Rani in a room without even an air-cooler, Pascal observes, "It seems that they don't have much money and life is hard here. But she was accustomed to a life of luxury."

"She was. That is past. For the present, she has this life of penance!"

"Penance! Why?"

"God knows," Ashok sighs.

Rani comes after almost half an hour. "A patient was in a critical condition," she says apologetically. "I was trying to revive his breathing."

"How is he now?" Pascal asks with concern.

"He is dead. We could have saved him if we had a ventilator," Rani states with as much indifference as is expected from a doctor. She sits besides Ashok and asks, "What would you like to drink? Fresh lime water or tea?"

Pascal says, "Nothing. We have to leave within half an hour."

Rani looks at Pascal, to whom she was introduced some three years ago, and then turns to her husband. With a sad smile, she mutters, "You are such busy people."

Ashok tells her that he hopes to join the central police and will be going to Delhi. Rani listens quietly, and then she nods like a soldier resigned to her fate.

Pascal realizes Rani has lost weight, and seems to have lost the glow on her face, making her look older. "Why has she chosen this life?" he wonders. But he is not surprised, for Rani was always different— confident and perhaps arrogant, though her conceit is coated with humility. He had seen wives of many of his junior colleagues, who behave in a way as though they too are his subordinates, but this woman is an exception.

A little later, when Ashok and Rani take him about the centre, Pascal realizes that another one-storey building is hidden behind the main one, and behind those, there are about 10 huts and a sprawling garden. "These huts are for patients who come with some relatives for treatment from far-away places," explains Rani and takes them near the rear building and stops. "This building is for more difficult cases… for those from whom chances of contamination are very high."

"Won't we see that building?" Pascal asks lightly.

"No," the answer comes from the Romantic Cobra. "This is the *Lakhsmanrekha*. You cannot cross it. That is for patients who are highly contagious. She cannot allow you there."

"But you work there for hours," Pascal wonders, now looking sharply at that building that has turned into a note of exclamation in his mind. "And I know for sure there is no preventive for TB. It's different in a hospital. But you live here."

"I am not alone," Rani smiles. "We are seven people all together. Three doctors and four nurses."

While leaving, Pascal tells Rani, "I greatly admire people like you. You are much more important than chief ministers and prime ministers, all self-seekers. If you need any help, never ever hesitate to tell me."

"Sure," says Rani. "I may need your help for importing equipment and machines."

After sitting in the car, Pascal repeats his words, "She is a noble lady. You are really blessed, Ashok."

For the first time, Pascal calls the Romantic Cobra by his first name; earlier he had always addressed him only as Sharma.

WHEN KARMA meets Stephen and his shadow called Shyamlal, the valley has turned nearly dark though the peaks are still visible, perhaps to remind the world that height means enlightenment. Karma looks at Shyamlal for quite a while, and then mutters, "Haven't I seen you before?"

"Maybe," Shyamlal replies with a degree of bitterness that surprises Stephen. "I lived in Kalipura. Your leader came there and misled us. We were swayed. And we lost everything."

Stephen sits on a stone slab and the other two follow him to sit nearby.

The place seems like a mall, though the concept of a mall is not known to the local residents who earn their livelihood on a daily basis by crushing stones, plucking leaves, making leaf plates and doing any odd job that comes up in the absence of regular agricultural activities.

"We confess to making wrong moves there by allowing the road to be constructed," Karma says. "But, Comrade Mahendra did not want to blot out an opportunity of work for the villagers. That was a mistake."

"Why? Couldn't the police reach our village if the road had not been there?" The dark has engulfed them now, and in that blinding dark, Shyamlal carries on, "Why blame the road? What about Bhola, who betrayed you? He accused me of being a Naxalite and put me behind bars."

"We have killed him," Karma divulges calmly, as he gets a strong odour and realizes Stephen is consuming liquor.

"That's good. But many things you do are not quite good," Shyamlal mutters darkly.

Karma is startled, but not being sure whether the explanation will come automatically, asks, "Such as?"

An impenetrable darkness now shrouds them so completely that all of them are reduced to silhouettes and no one can see anybody's face.

"You people hide in a place and the villagers have to give you shelter. But you don't think of them. When the police come to know that they sheltered you, these people face a lot of troubles and often land up in jail, and are tortured. Like me."

"But," Karma now says firmly, "people love us and that is why they give us shelter. They trust us and they want to change the conditions..."

"Wrong. They support you because you have arms."

"Arms! Yes, we have arms. But weren't the people of Kalipura with us?"

Shyamlal's voice turns grim and he says something in Mundari that Karma does not understand. Shyamlal then turns to Hindi, "Yes. I never supported you. And there were a lot many like me. We knew you would bring disaster."

"Why didn't you tell us?"

"Because you had arms."

"But those were for fighting the police, not to intimidate you."

"Who knows? Who will argue with a man with arms? And in Ridki, two days ago, the Naxalites killed a person because he argued with them."

"Where is Ridki?"

Stephen interjects, "You don't know? It's near Kolebira."

"They are not our comrades. They belong to the MCO. They even attack us." Karma rues their relationship with the other Maoist organization and adds, "We have made truce with Emancipation group. But MCO is different."

Shyamlal retorts, "You know who is what. A handful of people divided into hundreds of groups! Hoh!"

Now Stephen interferes, "Stop squabbling. We have come to discuss something."

But the shadow does not even spare the body. Shyamlal retorts, "It will be futile. They carry arms. We believe in a mass struggle. We are going to launch mass movement, aren't we? And they are led by outsiders."

Stephen says calmly, "Be patient. I have also suffered, Shyamlal. My ancestors were evicted from a village where a hill raised its head like a bird's... even with a crest. Imagine it. How great that place was! And that hill was an abode of the gods. But you have suffered more. You have lost your entire family."

"Entire family!" Karma cringes. "How?"

"That's a long story," Stephen mumbles. "He was in jail. When he came out, he searched for his family, his wife and sons, wherever he could. Even I helped him later. But they are lost."

For quite a while, the three sit silently, and the darkness gradually fades as the stars appear in the sky and human eyes become accustomed to the dark.

A bird flies fast by and Karma, attracted by the flutter, looks at it: a white owl that people consider a good omen. He brings down his gaze and wonders how to show his compassion for this man called Shyamlal, but he cannot decide on suitable words. He gives up the attempt and says, "I would like to request you, comrades, to join us if you want to achieve anything real for the tribesmen."

"That's not possible," intervenes Stephen. "For some limited purpose, we may work together."

Now Karma gets prepared to convey his position as plainly as possible, clears his throat and begins calmly, "We express full solidarity with you. But our ideologies are not palatable. You fight for a separate state..."

"And if we don't get that," Stephen announces grimly after quaffing almost half the bottle in one go, "we will start campaign for a separate country, like the Sikhs who are demanding Khalistan."

"True, but there we differ. We want social change for all people. We want equality of all. Not only for tribal people or Harijans. Nor do we go by geographical demands. We don't support the killing of Muslims or Hindus, or Jains."

Suddenly, Shyamlal retorts, "But your leader, Comrade Mahendra, said he would give us back our right over the jungle and land. Now why do you say you don't want to fight for the tribals?"

The three sit like ghosts and without understanding each other's position fervently argue among themselves, vacillating from one topic to another, often fighting over points of agreement and at times agreeing on issues that are definitely divisive!

"If you don't fight for us, there is no give-and-take between us," Shyamlal announces all of a sudden.

"That's not the point," Stephen rebukes him. "But you are no big force, Comrade Karma."

"We have our mass fronts and someday we will prove our strength," Karma says confidently.

For the next few minutes, everybody sits silently, absorbed in different compartments of thoughts, looking at the crescent moon that has arisen from the horizon.

Suddenly, Stephen speaks up with a slur, "You'll prove your strength? No strength. You are ghosts. We will show you our strength. We will rule." And then, he starts singing a Hindi song that Karma counts as a cheap one: *Jhumka gira re, Bareli ke bazaar me, jhumka gira re.* (The earring has fallen off; the earring has fallen off in the market of Bareilly). He starts moving towards the edge, as though haunted by an urge to be alone so that he can communicate with the darkness.

As Karma looks at the man shambling on towards the edge, his senses are swamped by a sense of anguish that makes him repent his decision to come to this place.

"I DIDN'T know that from north to south, India is 3,000 kilometres, and from east to west, it is 2,500 kilometres," he says looking at the fields for which a battle is going on, his eyes reflecting a sort of sadness. "That makes it so difficult for a new force…"

The listener, sporting jeans and a cotton kurta, wonders about the identity of the speaker known as Mahendra *baba*. He sees an opportunity and says, "At times, I feel you are a Naxalite."

"Even if I am, why should you object? Don't you think Avnish*ji*, if the Naxalites were strong, no company would have dared to claim this land? No government would have dared to lease it to any company?"

Avnish Jogleker does not want to hurt the man who is clearly unwell, often suffering from fever and at times forgetting even his identity. So, he puts forward his point in a friendly way, "The problem is Mahendra *baba*, I am scared of arms. It can cut both ways."

"What option the poor people have when they become victim of injustice everywhere... when they are denied nourishing food, good schools, treatment in a standard hospital... denied of everything?" Mahendra coughs, and looks at a large board set on bamboo poles, placed strategically on one side of the tarred road. The rectangular board is divided into two—the left has words in English, and the right in Hindi. At first glance, the board seems like an innocuous advertisement of some cheap but quality manure, but a closer look reveals that it is a message from a liquor company that now has entered into other fields. 'Land belongs to Goodwill Mines and Metals, a company promoted by Goodwill Distilleries,' it says. Below that there is a rough blueprint of the proposed plant, beneath which, in smaller letters, further details are given: 'A prospect of development. Order issued by government.'

"Do you think armed struggle will achieve anything?" Avnish asks. "I heard your cadres tied up a landlord with a tree near an ant-hill and poured honey on his body. The ants ate him for days. It happened in Gadchiroli recently. I assume the landlord was a notorious man. Still, do you think this was proper?"

Mahendra looks at the distance, his eyes contorted, and suddenly he remembers Chhote Thakur of his village. He closes his eyes, and a while later says, "We have no other option. We fight against the system, not against the individuals. But again, the system consists of individuals. Isn't it?... Delhi, or even Bhopal, the capital of this Madhya Pradesh, cannot hear the voice of the likes of Panchkuian. The day I came here someone told me this land is the pasture for livestock of at least 10 villages and about 4,000 people live in these villages. The government knows that the board—Goodwill Distilleries' prospect of development—is immoral... a warrant for destitution. But, you know, the government will only yield when locals will take up arms. Then funds will come, and the ultimate tragedy will unfold."

"What tragedy?"

"Then the Naxalites will be defeated, eliminated, and the locals will again be left to their luck. This country is ruled by hundreds of those... Goodwill Distilleries."

"But, you don't condemn the savage way of killing the Maoists resort to?"

"What will change, Avnish*ji*, if I condemn it?" Mahendra's tone suddenly turns acerbic. "We haven't started it. When the poor retaliate, when they create anarchy, it becomes intolerable for our civilised society. But this is such a high civilization that cheating the poor, evicting them from their homes, denying their livelihood, allowing them to die without treatment for they do not have money, or killing them slowly by huge indifference, nothing is intolerable. What is intolerable is retaliation. But that is human dharma. Human beings for ages have fought *adharma.*, and the fight will Go on, either in the name of Lord Krishna, or Marx or Mao, or Gandhi, or someone else."

With the divide between them assuming an insurmountable dimension, both of them fall silent and start thinking about some past experiences that they have not shared.

Mahendra ruminates his initial days in this region, the days that widened his understanding of reality and introduced him to people such as Chhote Pandu, who came to him with some other young men and a woman named Kamla. "The elders are cowards," chuckled Chhote Pandu. "Some of us are also cowards. If others become courageous like me, we can defeat the *sharab compani.*"

Mahendra expected the others to burst out laughing, but their faces told him that they all agreed with Chhote Pandu, prompting him to ask, "Are you the most courageous man?"

Mahendra says without looking at Avnish, "People in this area believe Chhote Pandu is the most courageous man."

Avnish turns to Mahendra in astonishment as his words sounded unrelated to what he was saying earlier. Till Mahendra broke the silence, Avnish was thinking about his meetings with various officers, the district collector and even secretaries in Bhopal, to convince them of the need to withdraw the lease that he thought was immoral, and also illegal, for tribal land could be leased out only if the tribal panchayat gave its assent. One day, after he came out of the room of a government secretary without getting any assurance from him, a stenographer whispered to his ears while passing by, "You are making futile attempts."

Avnish was startled and after realizing what he was told, he asked the man to explain his words. With indifference in his eyes, the man muttered, "Goodwill has lots of money. They are the largest brewers in this state. They can do and undo things."

"You mean these officers are on their payrolls!"

"Don't forget the ministers, sir," the man said nonchalantly.

As the man turned away, Avnish again stopped him to ask what would happen if he moved the court. The man answered, "They will forge documents and bribe the judges."

He has just recollected those words when Mahendra makes the remark about Chhote Pandu. Avnish knows why Chhote Pandu is considered the most courageous man, and he explains, "A sadhu told his mother that though she would not live long, her son would live for a hundred years. His mother died a month after being told that her days were numbered. When he grew up, Chhote Pandu came to know about the prediction and since has done daring things, for he believes he would not be harmed however dangerous his mission is. And you know, when this notice was put up, I tried my best to reverse the order. But I don't know why the rich of this country want to strangle the poor." Avnish heaves a sigh and shakes his head. "Then Chhote came to me and said, we have only one option left. What's that, I asked. We will squat on the land when they come to take possession, he told me. We convened the panchayat and discussed it, and we could take the decision of physical resistance because of Chhote and a girl called Kamla.

"I know her," Mahendra discloses.

A wall of silence divides them again, and Avnish starts wondering how the locals have changed. He remembers how they, years ago, were awestruck when he showed them photographs he had taken in Melbourne, where he went to raise funds. But Avnish knew the art of bridging distances and said, "*Arre*, what is there in those foreign cities? Yes, they are rich and fair in colour. And you have to go there by a plane. That is something like a bus, except that the doors are closed and it goes through the air. *Baas.*"

They had never even touched a motorcar; but as Avnish put things in place, it became easier for them to understand. But, an elderly man asked, "Do you see gods when you go through the air?" A relevant question, because the Hindus believe the gods reside in the skies.

Under the gaze of so many inquisitive eyes, Avnish took a few seconds to wriggle out of the situation, "Are you mad? Gods live in much higher altitude. No one can go there."

And now the same lot, those simple and straight people who remained docile for generations, are prepared to confront the mighty *Sharab Compani* against all odds. "Everything has changed magically, and I believe the common man has infinite strength," Avnish remarks without looking at Mahendra.

Mahendra was thinking about the possible options before the police, and he gets slightly distracted by the comment. "Can you tell me how the locals have changed?" he asks, as he wants to understand the change and formulate a thesis to be submitted to Sainath. Chhote Pandu and a few other young people from the locality have gone for arms training. Mahendra had convinced them that the only way to fight state-terror was through counter-terror; but now he himself doubts his thesis, particularly after witnessing how by peaceful physical resistance the locals thwarted another attempt of the administration to acquire the land. They sat on the ground, and the number of the squatters rose to many hundreds, forcing the police force to retreat.

"I came here many years ago, with a mission, with a determined belief that the rural folk need education," Avnish starts a long story. "My friend Kamlesh Jha was also with me. We thought the people of the Ashram were wasting time by teaching some craft to men… there were no women those days… and by imparting moral values. Budha *Baba* heard our plan but said nothing. *Baba's* son, known as Raj *Baba*, said, 'You can try it out. I won't say it will fail. But I must tell you one thing. Their immediate need, as we conceive it, is not the same as they conceive it'. I still remember those words." Avnish scratches his thigh and continues, "Within a few months our mission failed. No one was interested in education as boys and girls went out to the fields or elsewhere in search of employment early in the morning. It was an experience that repelled both of us. Kamlesh decided to quit. But I had no place to go."

"Why?" Mahendra asks.

"I was the youngest son of a prominent industrialist, but the door had shut behind me. I left home after I picked up a quarrel with my parents and I could not go back there, begging for mercy."

"Such things happen. It's time that decides everything."

As Avnish stares at him to get at the bottom of what he has said, Mahendra asks, "What happened after that?"

"After that?" Sitting in front of the hut, which has been Mahendra's abode for the last one year, Avnish looks at the distant fields where people are taking their cattle, something that the brewery hopes to stop. "Then I stayed here and circumstances compelled me to be at the helm of this Ashram, for Raj was terminally ill. Budha *Baba* died a couple of years ago, but his son died many years ago."

Avnish remembers how, at that point of time, Raj's condition was deteriorating day by day. The doctors in Raipur suspected he had cancer. There was hardly any treatment for it in the mid-60s in India, and if he was to be treated, he had to go to Europe or the US. But he was adamant not to go anywhere. His father had established the ashram for the people, argued Raj and told everyone that he could not waste money on his treatment. "He wanted to live as any other man here. He wanted to die like them too," Avnish tells Mahendra

"A great soul," Mahendra mutters.

"Avnish goes back to his story. Raj was the descendent of a Tamil Brahmin family though for years the family had lived in Hyderabad in Andhra Pradesh. A year before Independence, Raj's father Radheshyam Iyenger, known in the ashram as Budha *Baba*, crossed over to the province of the then Madhya Bharat, and founded the ashram to fulfil the dream of Mahatma Gandhi's *gram swaraj* in the heart of this tribal land. He was happy with a small ashram and believed in teaching people by setting examples before them. Raj tried to expand it, but had fallen ill in the midst of his mission."

Avnish looks at Mahendra, to confirm if he is still interested in the story, and finds Mahendra all doubled up, with his chin resting on his folded knees, his eyes fixed at some distant object.

"A month later, Raj's condition deteriorated further," continues Avnish.

One evening, Raj became restless in pain and asked Avnish to call his father. As Budha *Baba* entered the room, Raj said, "*Pitaji*, I forget everything. I am dying but my mind is restless..." He stopped and gasped, and a while later said, "Tell me something to bring back my calm."

"That was the first time I saw him so restless." Avnish tries to overcome the echo of emotion from the past, coughs twice, and continues: "Even Budha *Baba* looked on for some time with bewilderment in his eyes. But soon he composed himself, sat by the side of the frail body of his only son and seconds later began to recite hymns: *Na jayate mriyate ba kadachinnayang bhutwa bhabita ba na bhuahh/ Ajo nitya saashwatohayang purano na hanyate hanyamane sharire…"*

(The soul knows no birth, no death and despite several births it never grows, never decays; it is enduring, eternal and old. When the body dies, the soul does not.)

Basangshi Jirnani yatha bihaya, nabani grinhati narohparani / Tatha sharirani bihaya Jirnayanyanii, sanyati nabani dehii."

(As the birds leave their old nest, as the human beings pick up new garments, the soul too leaves the worn-out body and adopts a new one.)

"Budha *Baba* recited these verses from…" Avnish takes a break to rid himself of an ant that has bitten him, and hears Mahendra *Baba* completing the sentence by muttering the words "the *BhagavadGita*".

Avnish is marvelled by the old man's knowledge, and says, "Yes, the *Bhagavad Gita*. He recited those verses with a rare glow on his tormented face, closed his eyes and recited the next verses, as though in a trance. I still remember vividly, how the dilapidated room turned into a sort of monastery. I wondered whether Raj could internalize the Sanskrit verses of the *Bhagavad Gita* at that stage, but I found a profound calm pervading his blackened face. It was in his blood, the language, the verses… those were a part of his soul."

The sun hides under a tiny reddish cloud that filters and passes on the rays, filling that part of the world with a magical colour that is seen very rarely.

"Maybe I am boring you with my spiel," Avnish says coyly.

"No, I am listening. Carry on."

"That night, Raj sank into coma," Avnish says sadly, his tone reflecting the gloom of those days. "He died 10 days later…"

A week after his son's death, Budha *Baba* retired to a room and closed all its windows and doors. He explained the reason: he wanted to see through darkness, to see the other face of the world. Avnish felt the idea weird and said, "When a night vision binocular will be invented everybody will be able to see through the dark."

Budha *Baba* remained silent for a few seconds, and then, as though emerging from a prolonged meditation, he said, 'That won't see through death. Darkness includes death.' I realized my mistake."

The tiny cloud that had given the world its magical look drifts away and the sun comes out, enabling the world to retrieve its original face marked by green pastures and tall trees, a few human beings and cattle, a few clusters of huts and a one-storey *pucca* house that is known as Bapu Ashram. Looking at the fields, Mahendra blurts out, "Seeing through death! Strange. Is it same as seeing through the stones?"

"What? Seeing through the stones? What does that mean?"

"Forget it," Mahendra says hurriedly. "What happened then?"

"Since then, the charge of ashram was on my shoulders."

"You brought the ashram to its present shape, I heard. You introduced crafts training for women. Didn't you?"

Avnish nods. "I tried to make my existence meaningful. The glorified word is service."

"Yes, that's what everybody tries to do… making their existence meaningful by working sincerely in an office, or by social service, by becoming a sadhu, or else by taking up arms to change the system. One has to build up one's own world."

Avnish nods again, and then, as though he has suddenly remembered something, says, "So, you are a Naxalite?"

"If I say yes how would you react?"

Avnish takes a few seconds to reply, "A year ago, a couple of my friends came here from Austria. They travelled through the Chhattisgarh region and before leaving they told me that had this been Europe, the whole population would have turned into Maoists. But let that be. I will ask you this, why you have come here?"

"To assess whether the Naxalite movement can spread to this area where you are resisting the liquor company," Mahendra is candid. "I had decided to come earlier. But it was delayed as I fell ill. But after coming here, I saw how you thwarted the attempt to take away the land. Now I feel that there is no need here of any armed movement. You have aroused the people, who can take care of themselves."

Avnish laughs wryly—it is a laugh that betrays his sarcasm—and then asks, "What will happen to your comrades then? Haven't they contacted Chhote Pandu and Kamla?"

"I will ask them to withdraw. After all, whether you follow Mao or Gandhi, you try to unfold the greatest good for the maximum number from the bottom. The end is important, the means comes after that."

"Gandhi said, the means justify the end," Avnish throws his words in the air, without expecting any answer. At times, he can be harsh, but at the moment, he does not want to hurt the old man.

Mahendra looks at the distant pastures and mutters, "I was a Marxist. I believed that the end justifies the means. But now, I am not so sure. What happens if you take up the wrong means assuring that you would reach the coveted end, while you actually work for something else? It has happened in Russia. It is happening in China now under a new leadership. Rightists masquerading as Communists have taken control."

Avnish is again amazed by the awareness of the man who looks like a commoner, a poor Harijan or tribesman in shoddy clothes, living in a wretched hut. He asks, "You have told me that you are a Naxalite. Aren't you afraid that I may reveal it to the police?"

"I know you won't," Mahendra replies casually.

"Why? How?" Avnish feels irritated by the answer.

"I have read it in your eyes."

"How do you read Pravin Jain?"

"He is not straight; he has a lot of things to hide."

Shaken, Avnish asks, "Have you talked to him?"

"Never. Why have you made him the second man in your ashram?"

For a long time, Avnish does not utter a word, but looks on at the cattle for whom there is not much food as after a long dry spell the grass has turned into hay and plants are mostly dying. Then he turns towards Mahendra and reveals hesitantly, "He was chosen by Budha *Baba* a few days before his death. In those days, Budha *Baba* lost his sight completely. That was quite natural, as he had spent years in a dark room. Pravin came here two years ago. That was in 1985. He asked me if he could join the ashram. I took him to Budha *Baba*. And then… it was weird… but as soon we entered the room *Baba* asked, 'The other man with you, has he come to join us?' I said, yes. At once he said, 'I was waiting for him. I knew he would come. Now I can die in peace.' And then he instructed me to accept him as my colleague, and asked him to accept me as his elder brother."

"You abide by it, but he doesn't," Mahendra says gently.

"He tells people that he is the chosen one. He says Budha *baba* could not breathe his last until he had come. Maybe it is true. Budha *baba* died a week after he joined. He has strange ideas. He believes that the Aryans did not come from outside, but were Indians, and from here, they spread to other areas. He feels the first proponent of atomic theory was Maharshi Kanad, an ancient Hindu scholar. He feels what our ancestors said about atman, the spirit, is the basic of science. They said atman changes form but never even a smallest part of it is lost or added. Modern physics say the same thing about energy and matter."

"He is from the RSS, which is now swarming this region," Mahendra says plainly. "It might be so that some RSS people planted him. Perhaps they told Budha *Baba* that they believed someone would come to join the ashram, someone great, and he naively started believing in that."

"I don't know," Avnish shakes his head uncertainly, revealing his indecisiveness. "But he has made great sacrifices. He was a teacher in Bilaspur. He has left that city and now lives here with his wife and two children. I have accommodated him. Isn't it what I am supposed to do?"

Mahendra does not react initially, but then he says, "You should act firmly according to your belief and judgment."

"I can't," Raj sounds resigned, "Because I don't have unflinching faith in anything. If I become ill, I won't go anywhere for treatment, not because I am principally against it, but only because Raj *Bhaiya* didn't go."

Mahendra nods and says, "Often following an idol in a blind way brings disaster, but often it provides so much solace..."

"Because of my indecisiveness," Avnish now says tautly, "I am watching helplessly as your comrades, Sainath and Rambabu, are all set to take over our movement."

"They are good people," mumbles Mahendra. "But I will tell them to help you indirectly, without coming into the picture."

AFTER A week's futile attempt to make Rambabu speak, the authority registered a number of cases against him and kept him in a solitary cell in the jail, probably hoping that someday the Naxalite would be so overcome with frustration that he would start revealing everything. But sitting in the cell, Rambabu wonders about only one thing: why he failed to follow his sixth sense on that afternoon when the scoundrels surreptitiously came up and laid their hands on him.

His sixth sense for imminent danger was something bizarre; it created a sort of cold discomfort deep within him, in his body, in the flow of his blood. He had always known it as a premonition of a catastrophe, and was experiencing it when he stood at Kazipet station, waiting for a train that was supposed to take him to his destination. Still, he failed to react accordingly.

He was arrested while going to meet Comrade Mahendra, under instruction from his leader Comrade Raghupati, who felt every leader of all the Maoist organizations should be briefed about the differences that had cropped up and virtually split the southern Naxalite organization. He had a long discussion with Raghupati about the points to be briefed.

"When Comrade General Secretary expelled Pamula for using bombs in Anantpur district and thus killing not only targets, but their families too—women and children—we were solidly behind Comrade GS," said Raghupati, as though to convince himself. "But now, he says all policemen cannot be our enemies. If you consider the class theory, that's right. But what when they come to kill us? Since 1980, when our organization was reborn, we have lost so many comrades. And now GS wants to contain violence. Excellent! But we will never accept this."

"I don't know," Rambabu whispered, "but I feel Comrade GS will ultimately talk about participating in elections by floating another mass front… as the Emancipation has done in Bihar. They have floated the Indian People's Party to contest elections."

"Yes, raise that point. We must go and convince everybody connected with us," Raghupati again sounded confused, perhaps because he was suffering from a guilty conscience.

But, for Rambabu, things were clear, convincing and straight; without revolutionary zeal and fighting spirit, without an elaborate military preparation and proper perspective, a Maoist organization cannot carry forward its work. His faith in the invincibility of such a proposition was hardened by his knowledge that a section of the LTTE, the militant organization fighting for creation of an independent Tamil state in Sri Lanka, was ready to support them by providing sophisticated arms and ammunition. The condition was that they should leave Tamil Nadu for the LTTE. He chose to brief Mahendra first, because Mahendra was a leader who did not belong to their organization, but strangely, despite his infirmity, was working for them at Panchkuian. "In a world where people fight over minor issues obsessed with their ego, where ambition blurs vision, and the Maoists are no exception, Comrade Mahendra is different," he thought as he set out to meet him.

At the railway station, he stood near an iron bench packed with men sitting almost on each other's lap, and suddenly felt a shiver go down his body. He had to wait for an hour for his train which was running late. He was not too uncomfortable standing on the platform, but the cold discomfort within his body started bothering him. He looked about him, but found nothing suspicious. Then, unwittingly, he allowed his past to take over his thoughts. He recollected how such a feeling haunted him in the early 70's, when he regularly heard the stories of martyrdom or arrest of his comrades. In those days, the teeming flock he joined turned into a dwindling force, and death seemed to be on the prowl every moment.

He left his school and his family when he was in the 10th standard. His two elder brothers and a younger sister, apart from his widowed mother whose morose appearance still haunts him, lived in a village in Medak district of Andhra Pradesh. He went northwards to a village called Hasimpur in Karimnagar district. The day he arrived there, the landlord, Kasim Tariq, was liquidated by the revolutionary force, and Rambabu was immediately inducted into the guerrilla squad, without much training, as the local leaders believed training was subservient to determination.

They carried on for some time and their support base had widened when the debates started in the organization. Was the area a liberated zone? Was the theory of annihilation right or wrong? Had Comrade Charu Majumdar gone wrong? And then came Nagjyothi, the Glow of the Serpent, who said all these questions were emanating from the thoughts of Reddy with whom the revolutionaries should have no link. That was the first time he saw Nagjyothi, a stout, dark and middle-aged schoolteacher.

But, after a few months, strife and polemics again cropped up; some supported one Comrade Pattanaik and others backed Comrade Sathyanarayan, obfuscating their real goal and tactics. In another few months, everything was in the doldrums. Some left the organization, some were caught by the police, and a few were killed by paramilitary forces. Rambabu and others took refuge in the jungles and carried on the task of providing guerrilla aid to the surrounding villages. Nagjyothi came again during those days to convey an urgent message from the leadership: comrades must not live in the jungles, should be in the villages among and with the people like fish in water. After he had left, the guerrillas discussed it among themselves and rejected it, as the villages were open to attack. And with each passing week, the cops advanced further, recovered the land lost to the guerrillas, and the Maoists were pushed further inside. The last bastion of the flock to which Rambabu belonged was a remote village about which they survived for the next three months. It was during then that Rambabu first felt a cold discomfort deep inside him, though he did not know it was a premonition for a catastrophe that would turn everything to mere insignificance.

His comrades, however, invited the catastrophe by their daring adventure, despite objections from him and Ramalu, who was the most senior comrade among them. They killed a police constable with the false conviction that such action would arouse the level of consciousness of the local people, and the next morning the paramilitary forces surrounded the village. They made all the inhabitants stand under a scorching sun for hours, thrashed the men and finally molested the women. All they wanted to know was where the Naxals had vanished, to which direction of the forest, a question to which none of them provided the answer though everybody knew it. After ravaging the village for hours, the cops left before dark, fearing retaliation from the invisible men.

It was obvious that the cops would come back more prepared to launch an upgraded offensive and would forage through the jungle. That night, members of the *dalam* debated among themselves whether they should disperse so that they could come back after the storm blew over. Rambabu emphatically opposed the idea, condemned it as an escapist attitude and announced that he would stay on and fight, if need be, alone. The next morning, when the sun peeped softly through the leaves, illuminating small geometrical shapes all about his body, Rambabu woke up from a dream in which he had wrestled with a bull for hours in tiring repetitive scenes, and to his deep dismay found himself all alone with his comrades' guns dumped near him.

"*Andaru velli poinaru* (all of them have left)," Ramalu suddenly appeared before him and smiled wryly.

Along with Ramalu, Rambabu spent the next couple of years in that village, with no immediate plans or programmes. In those days, Rambabu was trying to recruit his comrades with an eye on regrouping the organization. He worked in isolation, for he had no knowledge of the outside world, having severed all connections with it in a bid to fully integrate with the rural people. Then Ramalu died suddenly, after suffering two days of fever. A couple of months later, one day, the village elders called him and asked him if he was prepared to marry Tulari, a teenager who was fond of him, and he agreed after pondering over it for a few days. It was, he reasoned, a sign that he had succeeded in his mission to mingle with the locals. He even took her once to the temple town of Kondagattu, where she offered puja in a temple while he stood outside.

Then again, the outside world came calling in the form of Nagjyothi, who seemed more sagacious after the disaster. "Everybody thought our movement is over. But that's not true," he said in his characteristic style. "As you have continued our work here, the others have worked somewhere else. And now, it is time to consolidate. It will take time. The leaders are still in jail. But we will start by coordinating among us."

Rambabu suddenly asked, "*Ee rozu tareek emiti?*"

"20 August."

"1973, isn't it?"

An amazed Nagjyothi stared hard at him before nodding. And then he said, somewhat reluctantly, "I think you need rest."

"No," interrupted Rambabu, "I need some help. For the last two years, I have lived with a dream… of a new sunrise. If you have come to tell me the time has come to act, you must arrange for two things, arms and money. You can do it. You have connections."

It began to drizzle and they walked towards a hut, stood under its shade and kept talking. "But why do you think we need a lot of money?" a while later Nagjyothi asked looking at the rains, then lashing at the fields and jungles, accompanied by lightning and thunder.

Rambabu had to raise his voice high to be heard, "Because you need arms, you need to run schools, hospitals... provide for employment."

"Schools? Hospitals?" Nagjyothi was repeating the words in disbelief. "You think we should do that?"

"You must. Otherwise, how can you liberate these Harijans, the Girijans, and the Backwards? How can you liberate the Lambadas who have to live outside the villages? Without education, what will these folk do?"

Nagjyothi heard him out before replying, "You will have to begin it... the effort, I mean. Then we can adopt it. Our backbone was the Harijan-Girijan combination, and other Backwards plus Muslims. And see... after our movement... last year during the assembly elections, the Congress decided to nominate many more Backwards, Muslims and women. They announced it with so much fanfare. 'Indira Gandhi wants social change,' they campaigned. Pooh! They have renominated the Brahmin chief minister Narasimha Rao. This Rao is a revivalist. With the death of Sanjivaiya, their Harijan face is also gone. We must act fast. This is the time."

Rambabu heard everything attentively for he was out of touch with the world. Then he asked, as though as a recheck, "What is your opinion about the Telengana movement and demand for a separate state?"

"That is a fight between the different groups of the bourgeoisie. Telengana leaders such as Chenna Reddy are trying to reap the benefits out of the genuine grievances of the people."

"This is sub-nationalism, and if people aspire for this, why should we oppose?" Rambabu said emphatically.

After that meeting, Rambabu began to work on the cultural front. He wrote one-act plays depicting the atrocity of the police or the landlords, the dream of the common man to hit back at them, a dream that becomes reality with the appearance of the Naxalites. But again, the cold discomfort came back, and he recognized it as a premonition of impending danger. Soon, an internal emergency was proclaimed in the country, and the administration armed the police with special powers.

After the emergency, things began to look up. But then Comrade Rajaramaiah was arrested and another period of internal strife followed. There were some who advocated a radical line, while some argued that boycotting an election could not be seen as a strategy. But all those were put to rest when Rajaramaiah jumped bail and returned to form a new organization, the People's Revolution Group, in 1980. It was called a group as it recognized that only after the merger of all such groups, factions and cells, the party would emerge again. Rambabu found a place in the Telengana state committee, something beyond his expectation, and he was told that people from Maharashtra, Madhya Pradesh and organizations active in Bihar would join them. Smaller organization and leaders from Maharashtra and Madhya Pradesh soon joined them, but no group from Bihar agreed to do so, though the parleys went on, and even in Andhra Pradesh, two smaller groups insisted on keeping their separate identity. In less than two years, Rajaramaiah was arrested again. But this time, they were more organized, and other comrades filled up his absence. They directed lower units to follow Rajaramaiah's line: 'Assert yourselves now, put more stress on frontal organizations, avoid killing as far as possible.'

Rambabu was now entrusted with the charge of the cultural front in the Telengana. They, the Naxalites, now considered Telengana as a separate state and had a separate state committee for the region. Rambabu worked with the people's theatre, an open front consisting of students and some intellectuals, some of them famous revolutionary poets. His main aim was to lead the people towards a cultural revolution, and he often pondered about setting up schools and hospitals. But on a night in December 1983, he was summoned to Bangalore, the capital of the neighbouring state of Karnataka, and as he reached his destination, a hotel in the city, he found Raghupati in the room sitting with Kuppuswami, another central committee member, and two strangers. A plan was already in place and Rambabu was to implement it. He had to succeed, for a mistake might end in the death of Comrade Rajaramaiah, the General Secretary, who was in Osmania Hospital, chained to his bed.

"You must be very careful, as a lot depends on it," said Kupuswami. "You know they arrested Comrade GS again in Nagpur and planned to liquidate him. A parliamentary Communist leader of the city… BB Bardhan came to know of it. He went to the office of a newspaper. The journalists enquired with the police, and after denying it initially, they acknowledged that Comrade GS were arrested along with some others. That's how he was saved and then sent to Andhra."

The operation turned out to be a cakewalk. The comrades fired at the chains that shackled the top leader and took him out. But, just a month later, the party decided on something that was too shocking for Rambabu; he was appointed the chief of the cell for security of Comrade GS. "You have nerves and courage to lead our army, and our head of the guerrilla force Comrade Rambabu has selected you for this job," Nagjyothi, who knew his preferences well, said and added, "We don't have much choice."

Rambabu believed all those who would be working for the main organization should never be put in open fronts, but no one heeded to his advice. And now, he, a man who travelled through the villages enacting street dramas, was inducted in the 'army'! And soon, the days became turbulent. The Telugu Desam Party, when it was formed four years ago, benefitted from their tacit support and came to power. But suddenly, they turned hostile. Every day, news reached him of some comrades being arrested, someone being killed in encounter, real or fake. The police were picking up boys and threatening the girls in small towns to create fear psychosis. Starting from the late '60s, for more than a decade, the Naxalites had threatened the landlords and rich peasants who fled their villages in the Telengana region in fear, leaving behind hundreds of square kilometres of a fertile zone for the Maoists. The Maoists distributed land to the landless, negotiated with the middleman or government officials for the price of the farmer's products, and levied taxes on the rich. But now, when the state was retaliating, they were losing everywhere. And top leaders like Comrade GS or Comrade Nagjyothi were planning more open action, as though the state would leave that space for them.

Rambabu believed it would not, but Nagjyothi insisted that the Naxalites would never be able to fight the might of the state unless they fight with the vast majority of people with them. That would require less arms and more mass movement. But, by then, Rambabu had transformed himself into a staunch believer in arms, and was very close to the chief of the armed wing, Comrade Raghupati. He had no hesitation in grabbing the opportunity when told that the LTTE, the rebel Tamil organization of Sri Lanka, was prepared to provide them with arms. At the instance of Raghupati, he met LTTE men. But Comrade GS and Nagjyothi were totally opposed to the concept of upgrading the arsenal. GS said, "We don't need sophisticated arms as we are not a terrorist organization."

For Rambabu, the rift was more saddening as Nagjyothi, with whom he has shared years of hardship and planning, joys and woes, was on the opposite side.

Engrossed in his thoughts at the railway station, Rambabu ignored his premonition, and came back to the present only when the train he was waiting for rumbled in.

"Comrade Rambabu," someone whispered from behind. Rambabu turned back, forgetting he was not supposed to respond to that name, and found an unknown face behind him. Quickly, he collected himself, and his left hand went into his side bag, towards the cold butt of his Mauser. "A message has come from Comrade Rajaramaiah," the man continued whispering as though he was Rambabu's old soul speaking. A couple of seconds passed by before Rambabu saw it through; no one in the organization would refer to Comrade General Secretary by his name. He decided to proceed towards the compartment again, keeping a vigil on the man from the corner of his eyes, his fingers on his Mauser. Suddenly, someone from the other side punched his jaw so hard that he fell to the ground. Rambabu took out his revolver, but someone put his foot tightly over his wrist and kicked the firearm away. Another person, a third man, kicked his face just beneath the temple.

"Had I been alert, they would have never got me," Rambabu tells himself. After he was arrested, they had forced him to stand on a slab of ice and his feet still bear the pain and slight numbness that it caused. His right heel pains again and Rambabu folds his leg to touch the spot, which had earlier turned into a sore. Then he lies down with a deep faith in his mind that someday he will succeed to break the jail, though he has no inclination how.

16

Glimpses of the Past (1940–80)

ON THE very first day of Mohan's life in a Naxalite den in Bengal, his exalted idea about the new force was despoiled by a bizarre question from another comrade, "Have you ever enjoyed killing anyone?"

Mohan looked over a meadow, his sharp eyes showing annoyance, for he thought the bearded urban youth wearing a stiff appearance was ribbing the rustic ghost that he was. But seconds later, when he fixed his stare and scanned the man's face, he realized it was a serious query. It brought another bizarre question to his mind: does this man suffer from severe constipation?

"Comrade, have you heard what I asked?" the man who was about Mohan's age, about 30, asked again.

Rather shaken by the questioner's insistence, Mohan Ram replied gruffly, "Sometimes we are compelled to kill somebody. But there's no reason to enjoy the killing. Is there?"

"You won't enjoy killing a class enemy? You have to come out of such petty bourgeois mentality. You must." The spectacled lean man jabbered in a manner that seemed unacceptable to Mohan. "You should kill the class enemies by your own hand. One is not a real revolutionary if one's hands are not tinged with the enemy's blood. Every member of our guerrilla teams should have first-hand experience of annihilation."

The room in which Mohan and other comrades were sitting were full of newspapers that two boys were utilizing as posters by scribbling on it: "China's chairman is our Chairman. Long live Indian revolution." Or "Boycott election, Parliament is a pigsty."

Confronted with this man at the onset, Mohan wondered whether Comrade *babu* was actually spot on in his assessment of the Naxalites as a bunch of anarchists and romantic idiots. Otherwise, why should one feel happy about killing another human being, unless one had personal enmity?

Like a professional lecturer, the other man started again, "See Comrades, we have to change everything. We should strike at the root of everything… the schools, for example. This bourgeois educational system is a rotten one. This should be abolished. And to do it, you have to threaten the teachers, and, in case they disobey, annihilate some of them. These middle class people… you know comrade, are timid in nature."

While Mohan looked at the man in disbelief—he knew the school teachers were poorly paid lower-middle class men—he heard him saying, in Bengali, "*Comrade, eai khatamer tattoi sangshodhanbadider theke aamader alada karche abong prakrito biplabite parinata karchhe* (Comrade, this theory of annihilation makes us different from the revisionists and turns us into real revolutionaries)."

At night came Prabir Samanta, the one in charge of the region, a healthy middle-aged person with greying hair and a bushy moustache that gave him an appearance of vigour and solidity. He sat with Mohan in the night and asked all the details about his life in the party in a way as though he was going to write his authorised biography

All of a sudden, Mohan asked, "Why do you put so much stress on annihilation? What does it mean?"

Prabir fell silent for quite some time and observed a cockroach on the wall minutely. After a couple of minutes he said, "I often drink local liquor. You do?"

"Never."

"You told me you are a Chamar. Generally, those below the middle class strata do not have any inhibition about boozing. But you have," Prabir said sombrely. "All our middle class comrades would be shocked if they hear I also take drinks. I once discussed it with Comrade Charu Majumdar. He agreed. He has no inhibition."

"It is not a very important thing for a man and often it creates a lot of problems in poor men's life," Mohan retorted as his patience suddenly ran out. A second later he said, "You have not answered my question, about annihilation."

"You met Comrade Subir this morning," Samanta sighed heavily. "He puts too much stress on this. This is a tactical thing. It is related to the idea of combining mass movement with guerrilla actions. As far I understand it, as Lenin said, we have to use force and yet develop such forms of struggle in which people's direct participation will be there. But now, despite a revolutionary situation in this country and in the whole world, we cannot proceed much with mass movement. So, tactically, we have to put a little stress on annihilation for the time being..."

"What you said is perfectly right. For preparing the people, we have to use arms. But not for individual terror... isn't it?"

Samanta nodded feebly.

Before Mohan could ask anything, he heard a woman's vibrant voice, "Hei Comrade, I got late in the fields, but have you called a meeting tomorrow?" And then, as she entered the room and noticed Mohan, she muttered, "*Hei baba, natun comrade batye. Kuta hote? Koilkatta to na* (Oh, a new comrade indeed. From where? Not from Calcutta)."

"She is Budhni," said Samanta looking at Mohan, and then, turning towards Budhni he said, "He is Mohan from Bihar. An old-timer."

"Mohan!" Budhni repeated banteringly and began to giggle. "But where is his flute?"

"Flute? He is not the real Lord Krishna that he would carry a flute." Samanta answered indulgently. "He carries gun."

Mohan was enchanted by the voice and the cryptic comments of the woman called Budhni—a lanky dark woman, with a red hibiscus pinned with her hair and a bangle of flowers girdled at her wrists, wearing a short shoddy sari that failed to hide her body.

"Budhni, we will meet tomorrow in the village. Now go," Samanta rebuked her in a voice that betrayed affection.

As Budhni left the room, Samanta commented, "She talks too much, but I have never seen a woman more courageous than her." A couple of minutes later, he added, "Tomorrow I will take you to a village called Sontalia... a tribal village with some low-caste Bagdi and Bauri population... Budhni, her husband and others are our leading force there. It's on the verge of the jungles and has all the possibilities of becoming a base area. Centring that village, we will spread our work in other areas."

Then Samanta asked Mohan to use assumed names, "You speak Bengali well. I suggest you to work as Mohan Kahar in this locality."

The next day, they reached Sontalia, a quiet village with scattered huts—plain hay-stacked roofs over bamboo poles, in some flimsy sheets of jute acting as walls. The terrain was rugged, the soil dry and the people as poor as the Untouchables of Puraina.

The village became Mohan's first base, from where he started his work almost in the same fashion as he had done on the other side of the border, enthusing people not to work as bonded labourers, not to cower before the rich and influential, and urging them to remember that all men were equal. A couple of months later, he led the villager's revolt against a money lender, ordered him to be killed after the people's court decided so, and realized he too had started following the bizarre but alluring theory of annihilation.

Then the inevitable happened. One day, when Budhni and Mahendra were sitting together, and in a gorge in front of them, two snakes coupled up, they too got trapped in the net of primal instinct.

Thereafter, life became different.

With the leaders regularly stirring up dreams of a great success, with a wild love beckoning him from near the gorge, Mohan was now a changed man. In no time, he was hailed by all as a firebrand militant leader, nicknamed a 'cheetah'. In the land of myths and heroes, one more icon had been added, and as he realized that, for the first time in his life, Mohan felt he too was important and worth something. His past started fading into insignificance, and though he remembered his wife and his daughter at some dark nights when he stood alone staring into the distance, he realized they too were turning into distant memory.

But the initial euphoria began to evaporate after a few months; the first signs of cracks became evident in the Communist Party of India (Marxist-Leninist) or CPI (ML). Mohan heard about it from Samanta, who was in a rather pensive mood one day, "Mohan, I am discussing with you something that I won't with the others. One is this theory of annihilation. Some people are taking it too far… maybe they have the blessings of Comrade CM… Charu Majumdar… In short, CM. Second thing is that there is no central control and people are doing what they feel like. Again, CM supports this. He feels the ground level comrades should have full freedom. It probably means there is no need of leaders who are in between… between Charu *babu* and the cadres."

Samanta broke into a pause to breathe—he had started suffering from asthma—and whispered, "The third thing is the debate on protracted war versus short war. We knew it would be a long battle, maybe decades before we win. But now some people have started saying that by '75… five years from now… the revolution will be completed and we will be victorious. Once again, this theory has the blessings of CM. He is now planning to propagate the possibility of a third world war that will facilitate our revolution."

"How?"

"I don't understand that either."

"Why don't you discuss it with him?" Mohan asked softly.

"He won't listen," Samanta replied and shook his head.

Mohan was amazed; it saddened his heart as he told himself that in all the parties, the leaders are the same.

A while later, Samanta asked, "With the troubles within Congress, Indira Gandhi supporting VV Giri for the post of the President of India and the ensuing confusion… do you think it's a revolutionary situation?"

Mohan thought for a while and then, breaking his tradition of silence, gave vent to his feelings, "Had you been born a Chamar, or for that matter in any low caste family, you could see the difference. It's always a revolutionary situation, and yet, never a revolutionary situation. You can't enter the home of the upper castes, can't go to their temple, can't sit with them. You don't get food for days. You get less for the same work. Or you get nothing. You work as a bonded labour. And you are beaten anytime; your women are enjoyed by them. And if you touch their women? Maybe death… Or you may get something worse…"

"You mean the situation is really like this?" Samanta wondered.

Mohan laughed wryly, a laugh that would have irked any other leader. But Samanta was different; he looked on questioningly at Mohan, prompting him to explain, "You won't understand. You are not a Chamar. You are a gentleman."

"But… don't you feel they would now join us?'

"Not so easily. A dog remains loyal to his master even if the master beats it. Can you provoke a dog to be disloyal? It's the same."

Samanta stopped as he saw Chandan, a young comrade from Presidency College of Calcutta, entering the room.

Many such young boys had joined them, and it often intrigued Mohan as to why they joined them when they had homes, clothes and food. When he shared the thought with Budhni once, she giggled, "Some of them often look at me secretly," she revealed. "But if I go near them, they shrink. Except one. Comrade Badal."

Mohan asked, his tone not congenial, "He had you?"

Suddenly, Budhni hissed like a snake, "Why should he alone have me? I decide whom I shall have. I don't sleep with sly foxes."

Trouble brewed soon after that. The Maoists came to know from two leaders who had secretly travelled to China that Peking had abandoned and virtually orphaned them. China felt the movement in India had gone astray with its denouncement of mass movement, with its stress on bizarre theory of annihilation and delving into the prospect of a third world war. Chinese leaders advised the representatives of 'spring-thunder' to seek indigenous solutions to their problems. Then, with the state showing the canine teeth, news of disasters and desertions started pouring in; and the first major jolt was from Midnapore, where the movement had earlier taken a legendary dimension.

In a secret gathering, Samanta blamed Charu Majumdar for the failure in Midnapore, "Comrade CM denounced the movement for possession of land and harvest as a form of 'mass movement', which he categorized as a reformist movement! The party, once entrenched among the masses, got alienated from the people. Our comrades attacked the police camps in Bengal, in Bihar ..."

"Comrade, you disparage our great leader Comrade CM," suddenly shouted someone. "We will not tolerate it." It was the same man, Subir, who shook Mohan on the very first day. He still believed in the infallibility of theory of annihilation, as well in guidance of Charu Majumdar, whom many comrades like him had elevated to the status of a demigod.

A couple of days later, Mohan went to Calcutta along with Chandan and Badal to arrange for arms and money, and took shelter in Badal's house at Bali, where he was introduced as Mohan Kahar. There Mohan met Badal's cousin sister Rani, a medical student. Little did he know—and he was not supposed to know—that his destiny would bring the same woman close by him many years later, when as a doctor she would be treating a patient called Mahendra Chamar, and would help him escape.

A fortnight later, when news came one evening that the police had started searching houses in the area, Mohan acted as an urban guerrilla for the first and last time in his life—only to make way for Chandan and Badal to escape. He crossed over the roofs of the houses and fired at the constables, who could not guess from which house the shooter was operating. As the police made a retreat, waiting for reinforcement, Mohan clambered up the highest point to locate an exit route, and then escaped towards the rail line to board a train.

It took him a couple of days to be back in Sontalia, where Chandan was waiting for him. "Badal has left us… he has surrendered to the police. That night itself. His uncle is an influential man. He would escape punishment, I believe. I was worried for you."

As Budhni heard it, she giggled and remarked, "I knew he would flee. He was a slippery character."

Some days later, he learnt about his wife's illness while he was in Jamshedpur. In those days, he travelled regularly from Birbhum-Bankura-Purulia districts of Bengal to adjacent areas in Bihar, Dhanbad-Giridih-Ranchi-Singhbhum, to brief the comrades as instructed by border committee secretary Prabir Samanta, and to hear their views. He reached Jamshedpur, which had not forgotten an early morning swoop in which hundreds of youths were arrested by the police. "Many of them are not in jail, neither have they come back, none knows where they are… We will not see them again," comrades told him and added, "Do you know that our students fought with the police from the roof of the Jamshedpur jail for two weeks?"

"We have heard about it. It happened in November."

That evening, when Mohan was leaving Jamshedpur, a comrade aged about seventeen or eighteen came running, dragged him to a corner, and mumbled, "The police attacked KMPM High School and beat up the students mercilessly. Three students have died. They were below 15."

"Take help from teachers and guardians… lawyers… and try to mobilise people to protest this," Mohan whispered to the young man.

"Later Comrade. Now I want to leave this place. Otherwise they will kill me."

Mohan looked at the panicked face of the young man and felt a strange sort of compassion for him. "Take that train to Calcutta," he pointed to a train stationed in another platform.

Before fleeing, the young comrade handed him a letter. It was from another comrade and revealed his wife was critically ill.

Back in Sontalia, he narrated the situation to Samanta and Chandan, who heard him out silently. Samanta was sick, his stout body showing signs of decay as he had developed asthma. "What you say is totally contrary to what is there in a map that Chandan has brought," he appeared fraught and depressed. "It shows almost the entire area as a free zone. Our party has distributed it."

Chandan said, "It is becoming terribly confusing. We are raising questions, but..." he shook his head in despair.

The next morning Mohan met Budhni and others in the jungle adjacent to the village and advised them to set up a series of people's courts in the villages and try the doctors and lawyers who charged high fees. In the evening, he met Budhni again near the gorge, where they spent hours together, without knowing that it was their last evening with each other. Budhni was looking across the gorge, towards a slope that gave the impression that it was the edge of the world as it suddenly disappeared from the view. Mohan had noticed earlier that Budhni often gazed towards that direction, and he asked lightly, "That place is always the same, why do you look at it with such interest?"

Budhni giggled. "Not at all. The slope changes colour. Last summer it was reddish brown. During the rains, it became grey. In the winter... see it has turned green."

"It has turned green long back, during the midst of the rainy season."

"So... you too know it. Then why did you say it's always the same."

"Basically it's the same," he argued.

"Only for those who cannot see. This world changes everyday. That mahua tree, it was only this much before you came," she said, pointing to her waist. "Look at it now... it's so big."

Mohan nodded, and suddenly broke the news, "I will leave tomorrow to see my ailing wife. I have told Comrade Samanta about my plans."

Budhni, who was looking at the moon steadfastly, nodded and then commented, "Tomorrow or day after it would rain heavily."

"How do you know?" Mohan asked lightly.

"See the ring-like halo about the moon. Whenever the ring is thick and closely knit about the moon, it means it would rain heavily. If the ring is loosely knit, a bit away from the moon… it means there would be rain soon, but not a very heavy shower. I learnt it from a Bengali gentleman. He was an old man and told me that it is an old saying by an ancient lady called Khana. *Dur sabha, nikat jal; nikat sabha, rasatal.*"

Staring at the moon, at the thick close ring about it, Mohan deliberated about what Budhni said in Bengali; he did not know it would save his life another day.

"You must go," she said a while later, and then, as though in a trance, she muttered, "I will wait for you."

The next morning, when Mohan started for Siuri the sky was clear, but when he was boarding a train to Katihar in the early afternoon, it turned cloudy.

The cloud was also in Katihar, and as soon as he came out of the station, five policemen emerged from thin air; there was no way he could escape. He was swiftly whisked away to Munger in an Ambassador car that denied him a last meeting with his wife.

He was again put up in the Munger jail, where news about their movement poured in regularly, as though the high walls about the compound were porous. The first of the series was quite enthusing for them: the Naxalites had attacked the Rupsakundi police station in Ghatshila, killed two policemen and looted nine rifles and 105 rounds of ammunition. But Mohan knew it was a stray piece of chivalry by some guerrillas, and would not save the meteoroid from dying. As the leaders too saw the apocalypse coming, they began to emphasize on carrying what they described as 'class struggle inside the jails'—it essentially meant planning a jailbreak—that mostly failed, but succeeded in some cases as in Dumdum, where 50 comrades escaped though the cost was high. In *lathi* charge and firing, 32 were dead and about hundred injured.

Then came the bad news—Comrade Sashanka, secretary of West Bengal unit, was killed by the police in Maidan in central Calcutta.

And then came the worst—in Baranagar, at the suburb of Calcutta, the Naxalites killed the secretary of the local 'Nava Jivan' club, and in retaliation the Congress Party carried out a purge on a massive scale with a leader of the Marxist Party acting as an indirect accomplice. According to the locals, scores were killed, and for the next few days ,the roads about Baranagar Bazar were strewn with bodies of suspected Naxalites, many of who were innocents.

It was in the jail a few months later that Mohan heard the news of his wife's death, and it came on the same day when he got to know about the first split in their organization—SN of Bihar had formed a parallel Central Committee after being expelled from the party.

The warden who informed him about Ramia's death also asked him if he wanted to attend her funeral.

"No," Mohan said. "Tell your officers I don't want any favour from them. I don't take favour from the piglets."

"You are beaten so much, so much… still you won't be straight. You need a stronger dose!" mumbled the warden.

Some months later, on an afternoon when a heavy storm started blowing along with heavy downpour, when the siren blared to warn prisoners to get inside the cells immediately, Mohan noticed a long ladder propped up against the boundary wall of the prison. Masons working there forgot to remove the ladder as the storm had hit them suddenly, compelling everybody to run for shelter. In no time, it became dark with visibility falling to one metre, and as though to confirm the adage that fortune favours the brave, power supply got disconnected as the storm caused a short-circuit somewhere. Mohan was sharp, but cautious, like a tiger stalking its prey. He noticed a jail employee had taken shelter under the watchtower, approached the man from behind, overwhelmed him, and took off the clothes he wore; then he sported those, giving him the appearance of a guard. A moment later, his eyes were set on a thick, long rope lying there, as though waiting for him! As the darkest clouds rumbled overhead, as lightning struck every now and then, Mohan climbed the ladder and when he had scaled the wall, he tied the rope tightly to the ladder to slither his way down on the other side.

The rest was easy.

He reached his earlier base at Siuri, from where an old comrade hurriedly took him away to a far off place, to Panu Moitra, who narrated to him the story of a grand disaster. "We shall have to start afresh, Comrade Mohan," he whispered. "The party is splitting. Everybody wants to be a leader. And in the mean time, most of our comrades are in jail, tortured brutally and many of them killed in the name of fake encounters. You knew Chandan, isn't it?" He looked at his face, and continued, "His mother was sick. He went to see her. But the police was alert and he was arrested. Since then, there is no news about him. The local police denied that they arrested him. Not even a fake encounter death in this case. This is a new strategy. Chandan has just vanished."

"They have killed him?"

"The body has been either cremated secretly or thrown into the Ganga."

Mohan felt chill run down his spine; he never knew when Chandan, the young man with glasses, quite and sombre, to some extent like Comrade *babu*, had made inroads into his heart. A while later, Mohan asked, "What about Comrade Samanta?"

"Samanta is absconding. He is critically ill and comrades have recently shifted him to Calcutta. Comrade Charu Majumdar is also ill."

"What about the villages?"

"Most of our comrades have died in encounters with the Central Reserve Police. Budhni was arrested and raped in the paramilitary camp. Then she snatched away one's revolver and killed a *Jawan*. The others shot her dead. Sontalia and other villages… those in the north… all are immunized now. Before that, we fought bravely. You remember, we stopped selling of liquor even in towns like Siuri, Bolpur, Rampurhat? Many schools were closed. A system of people's court was gradually emerging. The money lenders were forced to return the mortgaged property. Our comrades…"

While Panu was going on about how the paramilitary forces and the police had let loose a reign of terror, Mohan sat still, without expression or movement, as though he had turned into a spider that could linger for hours, and even days, at the same spot. Mohan could not hear anything, as his heart was asking his head a question that seemed to him a riddle, "Why did all the three say the same thing and not keep their words?" Munni said it, Ramia said it and Budhni said it; they vowed they would wait for him, but they did not keep their promise. Comrade Budhni, like Munni, was raped before being killed, and again he could do nothing at all. Why was it so? Why? Were they all dying to mock him? Was it a part of a conspiracy that destiny had hatched to show how meek, how irrelevant he was despite all his efforts, his pride, his political life and his guns?

Mohan knew it was all over, but he was not willing to yield, and a week later, he shifted to another place more than 150 kilometres southwest, from the bank of Mayurakshi to the bank of Kasai, where a few comrades were still working among the villages adjacent to the jungles. But, there too, the end came abruptly after they clashed with a small dacoit gang operating in the area, without knowing that the gang was sponsored by the officer-in-charge of the local police station. Soon, on their trail were hordes of paramilitary *jawans*, compelling them to move back into denser areas of the jungle. On that night, Mohan sighted the thick ring of a halo about the moon, and deducted, as Budhni had taught him, that it would rain heavily. Clouds really gathered the next morning. It started raining from the afternoon, and turned into a heavy shower after midnight. In the early morning, when it was still dark, the comrades tried to escape from the jungle, but a distant post of Central Reserve Police sighted them and began to fire their light machine guns.

All his four comrades and a local man, tall and dark, died in the firing: the police identified the fifth man as Mohan Kahar.

Mohan escaped with a bullet in his left armpit. With terrible pain and fever, he finally reached Ranchi, where his supporters took him to a doctor, Anirban Jana, a sympathizer of their movement. He suspected that the wound might turn into gangrene, which meant death in those days. The doctor was whispering this to his comrades, but Mohan overheard it and intervened. "Doctor Sahab," he said, "it doesn't matter if I die. But before that… I just want once to be in Katihar. Can you give some medicine so that I can survive a week?"

He wanted to meet Chini, his daughter, before dying.

But the doctor did not allow him to go. Keeping him in his house, the doctor fought with all bacteria and viruses, and eventually succeeded. And then one morning he told Mohan that Charu Majumdar was dead. "He was arrested from his hideout in Calcutta," Jana said sadly. "One of his comrades informed the police. He was kept in a lockup at Lalbazar, the police headquarters. Twelve days later, he has died in the same lockup. Police said he had died of a heart attack. They must have killed him."

Mohan heard everything, but said nothing; he just sat quiet for a long time. It seemed that the 'spring-thunder' was over; but he decided to carry it on, if needed, from scratch.

THE MAN, who was a top cop of Calcutta, was tall and heavy and as he talked about different subjects, Pascal Fernandez, a young IPS officer, who had joined the service only 10 years earlier, looked at him with admiration. "This man," Pascal thought, "is now known all over the country for his iron fist with which he has demolished the urban guerrillas in Calcutta, but he is not at all a dull brute."

Sanjib Gupta, the Bengali officer, offered him a drink. "I am drinking some Scotch," he bragged, and asked him casually while topping his drink, "Would you like to join me?"

"No. Thanks, Sir, I don't drink," Pascal said.

"Good," the veteran officer smiled. "Let's discuss business now. It is good that you have joined the central intelligence now. Our Prime Minister, Indira Gandhi... I often meet her... is concerned about these anarchists. I think that is why the authority has asked you to prepare a report. I will help you in your assignment. But before that, tell me about Andhra. It's strange that the two most affected states are Bengal and Andhra, which are separated by some 500 kilometres. What is the nature of problem there?"

"Sir, I can tell you about an incident," Pascal said, smiling tensely. "There's a village called Kahikatoa, where a constable from our nearby camp... Surrendra Rao ...used to visit regularly. He was sent from the camp to keep a watch on the village. One day... that was 12 May 1969... the villagers apprehended him and handed him to the guerrillas. The next day he was presented before the people's court where the locals, marginal farmers and agricultural labourers, tried him and awarded the death penalty. But the leaders told them that this man, who was himself poor, was just complying orders of the... as they say, the reactionary bosses. So no purpose would be served by killing this man, they argued and let the man go. He came back the next morning and told everybody what happened. He also acknowledged that he had donated twenty rupees to the Naxalites."

Pascal found the senior officer frowning, but decided to continue, "A day later we suspended the constable alleging that he had a nexus with the Naxalites. Probably, he was too embarrassing an example for us. Later on, I talked to him. And I felt he had not lied."

The Bengali officer nodded with a smile. "So what is your conclusion?"

Pascal, who in the last half an hour had witnessed Gupta's wide spectrum of knowledge as he talked on different topics with equal ease, was nervous for a moment. "I think," he said hesitantly, "somewhere we are going wrong and though the problem has been resolved for the time being, it may reappear."

"Why?"

"Sir, the *Hindu* wrote the origin of the movement was the trade union movement of Girijan, the hill tribes. I agree, sir. Mao Tse Tung or Charu Mazumdar did not inspire this. It was a revolt by the so-called low-born men and women. Sir, when I was the SP of Khammam, I saw the tribal labourers being killed for a small crime, or often for nothing. A woman who owned 50 acres of tobacco land burnt a Harijan boy alive, but none came forward as a witness when I booked her. Then in Takulapalli, that was February 1968, a Lambadi boy did something minor for which a gang of goons under instruction from a minister attacked the entire Lamabadi village…"

"Who are these Lambadis?" the Bengali officer sought clarification.

"They are a poor and backward tribe. The goons attacked and ransacked their village, torched their huts, molested their women and beat up their menfolk. I could do nothing, Sir, for it was the rule of the Reddis. But, my point is I am not sure whether landlordism will survive under police protection. Our Home Minister Vengal Rao said the movement had a social base. In 1969, we furnished figures and the government estimated that Naxalites had 10,000 activists in Andhra…"

"10,000!"

"Then we arrested so many, sir, killed so many, declared different areas as disturbed areas," Pascal continued enthusiastically. "In my district, Khammam, several places were declared disturbed and central paramilitary forces raided those areas. We lodged conspiracy cases and so many other cases. But see, sir, how many eminent persons came up against court's order to hang Pattanaik and Paidia. Even Jayaprakash Narayan and Harekrushna Mahatab have protested."

"What about that controversial letter?"

"It's forged, but it was a good attempt. It was to be seen as a letter written by one Rao, the jailed Naxalite leader, to one Reddy, who is a landlord and a relative of another top leader. It said fake currency notes of three and a half million rupees would come from China via North Korea, which the Korean embassy would send in a parcel. The letter said the landlord would get ten lakh for this service. A well-planned letter, but the foolishness is staring at your face. The letter revealed that Chinese Chairman Mao had ordered a press in Sanghai to print ten million counterfeit notes of rupees hundred denomination and this money will be distributed among Indian Maoists. Why should a Naxalite write it to someone…"

Before Pascal could proceed, Gupta said, "That was foolhardy. No Naxalite would give such details to someone who is a landlord."

"Right sir," Pascal concluded and was waiting for further queries from his senior, which did not come for quite a while.

"It seems you don't believe that the movement will be wiped out," Gupta commented after he had almost finished his drink.

"Sir, I know you are a hardliner. And successful. Sir, I don't want you to see me as a dove. But I feel, unless the root cause is addressed the fire cannot be doused for ever." Pascal said this knowing the other man had crushed the urban guerrillas, who had created terror in Calcutta, with an iron fist.

Gupta gulped down what was left of his drink, and lit a cigarette. "Hawk or dove, none should close his eyes to the root cause, the socio-economic reality. I fully agree. But when the problem comes before us, we have to be ruthless. Good God! In this country, human right is not a criterion as it is in Europe."

Pascal preferred to remain silent and it worked. After filling his glass, Sanjib Gupta started again, "To crush such nasty things you need strong laws too. This time we were lucky. The Naxalites even violated their rule book. They were crushed in Midnapore first. That point of time, I was in the state intelligence. The urban boys went there to live as 'fish in the water'… that was what their literature said. You have to read literature of the Communists to understand them. Whatever, they were supposed to live there with the poor, but didn't even know the basic facts. The tribesmen who come to work as agricultural labour from the Chotanagpur region of Bihar, the most wretched lot, stay in the employer's cowshed in the agricultural seasons. So, those poor fellows had no option but to be with the employers. They can't risk the cowsheds, you understand. And the locals would not join the Naxalites, because once identified they would lose their jobs. The landowners would go for a seasonal tribal hand in place of the local worker. Even apart from that, an urban boy among the rural folks can be easily identified."

"Right, Sir; but in Andhra, most of the middle-tier leaders are rural folks."

"That's dangerous. I can tell you here, in Bengal, it won't be revived in the foreseeable future. But, if it is so, Andhra would be a different story." He nods and strokes his glass with his finger: "Must be so. Otherwise, why that state is witnessing such uprisings regularly. The '40s, '50s and again '60s. Why? One has to look for the root cause."

The man then went on giving more details about Calcutta, bragging about his role and often censuring the general police force as timid, unfit and a corrupt lot.

While scribbling down his points, Pascal felt happy to note that despite being a rabid hardliner the influential senior officer endorsed his assumptions about the root cause. 'When I submit my study-report I will conclude with this man's quote,' he thought and turned the leaves of his pad back a few pages to underline the quote: "Hawk or dove, none should close his eyes to the root cause, the socio-economic reality. I fully agree. But when the problem comes before us we have to be ruthless."

WHEN MOHAN joined a new force that had emerged in the Bhojpur region, his birthplace, he was a broken man, a different man.

In Bhojpur, the movement, also branded as 'Naxalite' movement, spread under the leadership of one Master*ji*, who was earlier with the CPI(M). He was so severely beaten up by the upper castes for promoting a Harijan candidate during the election that he had to be in hospital for six months. Once he was discharged, Master*ji* lay low for a couple of years, and devoted himself to imparting physical training to the youngsters. The upper castes, happy that he had been humiliated, did not give him much thought, till three of the Bhumihars responsible for beating him were killed in the village called Etwari. Master*ji* went underground when the low caste boys, the new Naxalites, had amassed enough strength to fight back the landlords. Facing an unforeseen challenge, the lords turned towards the police and the administration; but the fire was spreading fast, and the message was clear, '*Etwari ek chingari*,' Etwari is a spark...

Before reaching Ara to meet Master*ji*, Mohan went to Katihar, but to his shock he found that his father-in-law had left the town with Chini, his daughter, for an unknown destination. Two of his old comrades from the Marxist Party promised him that if ever they got any news of Chini's whereabouts, they would send a letter to an address that Mohan had provided them.

In Bhojpur, he assumed his new name, Mahendra Chamar, to avoid the trail of his past that had ended with the death of Mohan Kahar, as recorded in the police department. Despite his personal tragedies, he was enthused by the new dimensions added by the 'Maoist Committee' led by Master*ji*, who had accepted 'honour' of all the 'low born' as the main slogan, though that excluded the upper caste poor from the ambit of the downtrodden for they never suffered from lack of honour.

Honour simply meant freedom from being raped, tortured or killed!

Being instructed by Master*ji*, Mahendra went to a new place to 'furrow the barren land'. He took with him a few documents that he had carried for years, and a small book called the *Bhagavad Gita*, a Hindi translation of verses with the original Sanskrit. When he felt tired and dejected, when the thought of Chini stared haunting him, or when news came of some comrade's death and he wondered how this flow of blood would cease, he read that book, considered to be at least three thousand years old.

"Comrade," someone called him softly on one afternoon when he was reading the *Bhagavad Gita*. "We have provision for two more days. We have no money. You ordered to get camouflage uniforms like the army, but…"

Mahendra just nodded.

The comrade saw the book, and asked, "Isn't that a religious book?"

"Yes. But it also tells the eternal truths of life."

Encouraged by the answer, the comrade asked, "From my childhood, I was taught that killing human beings is a sin, very big sin. Does this book say anything about that?"

"This book says doing your duty is the only way. The man, Krishna, whom people describe as God, was actually a great philosopher. He prodded the people to do what one has to do for preserving justice and truth. We are actually doing that."

During those days, Mahendra was careful not to repeat the mistakes of the 'spring-thunder' rebellion that failed ignominiously. His mantra now was different—avoid a clash until you are strong enough to take on the offensive by landlords, police and of course, the army, which would come at the end.

Then, one night Mahendra saw, for the first time, a dream that would reappear innumerable nights spreading over months and years!

A little girl was lying on his chest, cajoling him hard not to go out to work…

"But I have something very urgent to do. A fight is going on and I have to go today," Mahendra appealed to her.

"*Ka tum tir leke larhte ho bapua* (Do you fight with arrows, Papa)?"

He laughed. "I think we need arrows."

"But whom do you fight, bapua?"

"The landlord."

"Landlord! What a funny name! Hee hee." She giggled, and became thoughtful.

On the first night, the dream ended at this point as someone called him. As he woke up the comrade said, "Comrade Sadhu Ahir has come."

Sadhu Ahir, a Backward, who for a long time led a group of dacoits kept the link between Master*ji* and him. He came to tell him that Master*ji* was no more. After a shoot out for hours, he was killed by the private army of landlords a couple of days back.

Then, over many months, when Jayaprakash Narayan, the Socialist, came to Bhojpur to change the landlord's hearts so that they donated land to the poor, and when he went away to fight the Congress and was arrested, Mahendra heard of many such deaths of his comrades, and one of them was Sadhu Ahir himself.

During the early days of Emergency, Mahendra and his two associates, Comrade Shankar and Raul, whose actual name was Rahul, carried on their work as silently as they could, and their team, moving northward, reached Puraina. The local poor did not know that Comrade Mahendra was Mohan Ram, who had left their village long back, but they were attracted towards the Naxalites. But just then, unknown assailants killed young comrades at a place close by Puraina. Shankar was furious and wanted to retaliate immediately, "The Thakurs of the *haveli* have killed our men," he said emphatically. "We must attack the *haveli* and kill all of them."

Shankar assumed Mahendra would not agree, for he never allowed killing of any innocent, a term by which he understood 'those not involved directly', but to his big surprise, he saw Mahendra nodding. "Their sin is now spilling over," Mahendra muttered as others looked at him blankly wondering why he used the word 'sin'. Shankar arranged hundred odd supporters to be present along with the armed comrades, and the operation was carried out by the Naxals on a dark night, when they surrounded the *haveli*, dragged out in the open Badhe Thakur and Majhle Thakur and their two sons and a grandson, and gunned them down.

Mahendra believed in the use of guns instead of conventional weapons, for guns were symbols of might and they convinced the people about the invincibility of the Maoists.

But Shankar found Mahendra a sad man when he came to know that Chhote Thakur was not killed. "We will do it another day,"

Shankar said, but that failed to cheer up his leader, who shook his head, "No, not again."

The police became overactive in the area after the incident, and announced an unusually large sum on Mahendra's head, as though to console the *haveli*. Feeling the heat, Mahendra withdrew his comrades from there and sent Shankar eastwards, and Raul to the south to spread the message to new areas. By then, the second secretary of the Maoist Committee, Comrade Manik, who took charge after Master*ji*, was killed, and new faces came up to lead an almost non-existent organization. Mahendra had no contact with them; he just carried on propagating a dream, but a couple of years later his dream itself was challenged by the new leaders. They felt what was going on in the name of Maoism in Bhojpur region was rabid casteism, often unrelated to Marxist theories. By then, the political scenario in the country had changed vastly; Prime Minister Indira Gandhi had, after suddenly deciding to have an election to legalize her rule and refurbish her image tarnished by imposition of Emergency, lost out to the Janata Party, a motley conglomeration of the Socialists, centrist like old Congressmen called Congress (Organization) and the rightist Jan Sangh (known as the Hindu Party). There was an air of jubilation—prompted by the end of autocracy and installation of the first anti-Congress government at the centre—and the changed environment helped the new leaders of the Maoist Committee to reappear in the Bhojpur region. They renamed their organization as 'Emancipation', and in their bid to purge the organization of undesirable trends and characters, they castigated Mahendra for attacking the *haveli* and sought an explanation about his work in Kalipura and other areas. They sent notices to Mahendra, but the letters met with a deafening silence! They sent emissaries who went back with strange answer from Mahendra, "I am always with those who are determined to blow up the *havelis*; go and ask your leaders whether they are in favour of that."

Soon after the new leaders decided to launch a frontal organization that, according to Mahendra, Shankar and Raul, was an opening for a political body that would participate in electoral politics in the future. That made the rift complete and Mahendra severed link with the organization established by Master*ji*, but the leaders from the organization tried to persuade him again. They invited three of them for a final meeting. At the end of the meeting, Mahendra stood up and as usual fixing his gaze at some inanimate object, at that moment on the wooden table around which they were sitting, said in a grim voice, "Our leaders told us that Parliament is a pigsty, that election is a mechanism to perpetuate the bourgeois system... Once upon a time, we broke off from the Communist Party to form the Marxist Party with the hope that it would work for revolution. But they failed us. And then our leaders said, at the time when we, the Maoists formed our organization... they said... those Communists who remained in the older parties are sold out to the system...."

There were sounds of gunshots—it was the outskirt of Arrah town, and that day of May was the day of *lagan*, an auspicious day for marriages—coming from the courtyard of a nearby house, from where a marriage party was setting out towards the bridal home with guns and liquor.

Mahendra waited for the sound to die, and then said, "Those leaders who told us all these are dead. Now you are heading towards parliamentary politics. A day is not far when you will become a parliamentary Maoist party, a stone-bowl made of gold!"

A Bengali comrade mumbled, "We are still debating that."

"Debate it," Mahendra said politely. "I know the outcome. You will join parliamentary politics... I know, because, now you are sold out."

There was a deafening silence in the room, as though a lightning had struck in, but the Bengali comrade tried to cajole him again, "Comrade Mahendra, despite differences, you are a valued comrade. We salute your contribution. Please try to understand that time has changed and we have to change."

Mahendra replied with extreme politeness, "Comrade, you are educated people. You have infinite knowledge to justify every decision you take. But I am a rustic ghost. I cannot change."

Afterwards Mahendra formed the 'Red Salute' and carried on his work, while Comrade Raul sought Mahendra's permission to go to his home state Orissa, to the Malkangiri region, where a couple of his old friends were trying to form a new base keeping the experience of Master*ji* in mind. "If Bhojpur can do it, why not Malkangiri?" Raul asked Mahendra, who nodded and allowed Raul to leave.

As the days passed, a new myth was created over a vast area, a myth of Mahendra Chamar, or Comrade Mahendra, a myth that attracted hundreds of young men and women. In those days, he had started sporting the army uniform, and his charisma attracted Damni, a young woman, whom he married after some time. A son was born to them a year later.

Once in two years, Mahendra visited Katihar too, but each time he got the same answer from his old comrades—Chini could not be traced.

At times, gazing at the vast emptiness of the horizon from the edge of the hamlet called Kalipura, Mahendra ruminated his past, thought about the comrades who had died and about those whose whereabouts he did not know, like his daughter or Prabir Samanta, and the thoughts inevitably led him to one query, why all these happened?

17

The Present Continuous (1987–88)...

MAHENDRA LOOKS at the perched earth being soothed by light rain as he travels in a bus to Dantewara, and wonders about the irony—though it is raining now, in early winter, not a drop was to be had during the monsoon. The bus comes to a halt and the comrade accompanying him mumbles, "Mahendra Baba, we have to get down here."

The summer was severe all over Chhattisgarh. It burned the grass and the plants. The cattle died as fodder and water turned scarce with each passing day. All the railway stations witnessed unusual crowding as people boarded the trains to Bombay, Bhopal, Nagpur, and even Delhi, and among those leaving, at least half were women, some carrying children on their laps. They left their cold hearth and empty home to avoid stalking of death, to seek 'fortune' somewhere else, to work as daily labourers in construction projects, in hotels and shops or as 'day and night domestic help', euphemism for a sort of slavery.

The shadow of disaster was looming on Panchkuian too, and the women were working extra hours on their crafts—coloured potteries and bamboo works—to sustain their families. Many new faces crowded the Ashram, mainly those who had ignored the training and a few from distant villages, for a quick lesson. Towards the end, the desperate villagers arranged for marriage of frogs; the bride came from another village while the groom belonged to Panchkuian, and with their last savings, the locals gave a feast after releasing the newlywed in a pond inside the jungle where a puddle of water still existed. Thereafter, the worst struck them.

Mahendra comes down from the bus, and walks with his comrade. He stays for a day there, and then another comrade takes his charge and he moves southward, to reach a village in a forest in Orissa. There he found Comrade Sainath and Comrade Raul waiting for him in a hut.

"They said it's Dandrakhol reserve forest, but I don't see much forest here," Mahendra quips as he leans back against the wattle that runs the risk of breaking down under the weight.

"Jungle! Hahh," Raul Raut smiles sadly. "When I left you to work in Orissa... that was towards the end of '78, almost a decade ago... this place had a dense jungle. Then they decided to build a road to Gupteshwar. That was such a nice excuse. They felled trees at least 10 times more than what was required for the road. The local tribes were also happy, because they got some money for felling the trees or constructing the road. That was the beginning. The felling continued. And it continues even now. The businessmen, the forest department and the police, everybody is in it. So much money they earn from this illegal business! Now you know, local tribesmen cannot fall back so much on the forest when the crops fail or in non-agricultural seasons. The time is not far away when they won't be able to collect anything from the forest—the bamboo shoots or sal seeds or roots or mahul or the dimri fruits which they eat."

"I suppose you have no class enemies here?" Mahendra asks a while later, his voice betraying a strange sort of indifference.

"No," Raul starts laughing as he remembers a debate among them in the past, when they were in the Emancipation group. Both Shankar and he believed that class enemies existed everywhere and the initial battle had to be fought against them, as that would raise the consciousness and confidence of the rural proletariat, preparing the base for struggle against the state. They presupposed the existence of a layer of class enemies as an axiom. But Mahendra told them that in many parts of the country, the class enemies did not exist at all, and that was why during the spring-thunder days, the Naxalites could not make much headway in south Bihar. He argued that in those places the Maoists would have to target the corrupt government officers and the failed state. It did not convince them then, but so many years later, Raul knows that Mahendra was correct.

After a while, looking straight at Mahendra, Sainath reveals apologetically, "We wanted you to leave Panchkuian, for what has happened there was dangerous for you."

"It was foolhardy," Mahendra retorts without malice. "If they had not attacked the police, that young fellow... Chhote Pandu... wouldn't have been killed. He attacked the police with only two of his comrades. And there were probably 25 or 30 armed policemen. You know, the locals believed Chhote Pandu would live hundred years for a sadhu had predicted so. And the boy was so daring because he believed in that bogus prediction." Mahendra heaves a sigh and continues, "What has happened in Panchkuyan will not help any progressive force. The local movement will be finished. They have also arrested Avnish, the man who led the resistance and ran the Ashram. Now the Ashram will fall in the hands of Pravin Jain, the RSS man."

Sainath mutters looking at Raul, "I tried to convince my comrades that we don't need armed activities there."

"Aren't you the secretary of that area?"

"True. But it is also true that we didn't instruct Chhote Pandu and his team to undertake any armed action. Believe me."

After a few seconds Mahendra says, now his voice sounding worn-out. "I understand, Comrade. Arms have their magical charm. Sometimes I feel it's good that I am forgetting everything."

"But now we will be more dependent on arms," Sainath smiles sadly.

Sainath has removed his beard, and has given his hair a crew cut, depriving it of the tousled look it wore earlier; he looks different now, seems younger and agile. He looks at the ground and almost mumbles, "Comrade, you remember so many times we have discussed about the broadest unity of all the Maoist groups. Even a week back Comrade Rudra, our Nepali comrade, came here and urged for unity among the Indian Maoists. My wife was also present in the meeting. But now Peoples Revolution Group is badly divided. I told you about the division earlier. But now it seems irreconcilable. It has turned into a fight to finish. Our central committee has become dysfunctional. I am working on my own. Raul is doing the same. Nobody knows what is what."

"To which side you belong?" Mahendra utters a few words after a long gap.

"We don't know. We are confused." Sainath looks at Mahendra to anticipate his opinion. But he fails to read his comrade's face, and decides to reveal his mind, "I would say we failed to have a comprehensive plan. Comrade GS miscalculated the risk from the beginning. He could never imagine that Rama Rao, whom we tacitly supported in the election and who said *laal salaam* to us would launch such offensive against us. Hah... But the other group led by the young fellows... they have gone to the other extreme. We need arms, of course," Sainath argues in a way as though he wants to convince himself. "Raghupati is the chief of our armed wing, and I feel he is putting stress on military strategy only. And... he may win... because he is the top military commander."

Mahendra does not respond for a while. Then he says, "I want to go back to Bihar."

Sainath looks on at his comrade, watching his eyes turning dull, and tells him, "I will send you back alright, but sometime later. A grave incident took place close to the town called Dharwal in your state. Your comrades of Unity group called a meeting there to protest against the intended eviction of the Harijans from their huts. Earlier, the Harijans lived at the back of the village. But now a new road has come up that passes through the vicinity of the Harijan *basti*. So the upper castes have decided to turn the rear into the front and evict the Harijans from there. To protest that move, unarmed comrades and sympathizers, men and women of the *tola*, assembled in the local school ground. And…"

"I know," Mahendra interrupts him, his eyes not reflecting any shade of emotion. "When the meeting was on, the police blocked the only exit point and opened fire on them. It's a repetition of Jallianwalla Bagh in free and democratic India. As many as 35 or 36 were killed."

"Now MCO comrades have retaliated," Raul chips in.

"I know," Mahendra says in the same repetitive way, without a tinge of emotion. "The MCO has killed 60 upper caste men in a village."

"They said they retaliated in this way," Raul mumbles.

"They have killed 60," Mahendra repeats and adds, "including many innocents. Thank God they spared children and women."

"At times, I feel this is the right path. Eye for eye," Raul says vaguely.

"Comrade," Mahendra looks at Raul and mutters, his voice reflecting the determination he had in the earlier days. "It is expected from them, the police and the administration. They will kill us, because we are poor, and more so because we are low-born men and women. But we Maoists should not behave like them. We must behave like civilized people."

"Shoo," Raul suddenly shouts and throws a stone towards something, compelling Mahendra and Sainath to look at that direction. "Isn't it only a cat?" Sainath asks in surprise.

"These are feral cats, quite dangerous," Raul states while looking at the fleeing animal. "These were earlier in these Gadaba huts. But the local Gadabas now cannot even feed themselves and there is not even a mouse in their huts. So, those cats have gone to the jungle… Did I tell you that forest department had not allowed them to plough their land last year because the plots were inside the jungle? And this year, there was no scope as the drought had parched the earth all over Orissa."

"All over India," Mahendra corrects him and asks, "Are there tigers in the local forest? I imagine other areas are still forested."

"Earlier there were, the locals say. But those have vanished more or less from Koraput. They have made and are planning to make so many power projects here by felling trees… Balimela, Machkund and what not. The reservoirs of the Kolab will eat up a vast area of the jungle and will go close to Koraput town itself."

They sit silently for a while and Mahendra looks at the bald hills at the distance, and the plantation on the lower slope of the hills.

"That's cashew," Raul says. "The tribesmen earn a little from this, but the middlemen make a huge profit. We have to take it up." Raul waits for a while, then looks at Mahendra and wonders whether this man is really lost. He thinks about something and says, "It seems the MCO is changing. They are ready to discuss the path of revolution and have promised to stop attacking us."

"Almost all of their leaders are Bengalis, both MCO and Unity," Mahendra mutters unmindfully.

Raul fails to understand the logic, looks at his leader, and continues, "But if the truce works, it will be a great step forward. I have told Samaresh *babu* that this fight should stop. By killing each other we gain nothing."

"But that is not the Maoist path… such mass killings…"

"I am not getting into that, as I agree with you," Raul tries to put forward his point calmly. "But like you, Samaresh *babu* interprets the situation in the Indian context. He feels if caste domination has to be cracked, then this is the only option. Whatever, at least this may be a new beginning for a broader unity in Bihar."

"My old friend Comrade Rudra… from Nepal… is also insisting for that," Mahendra sounds distant. "Here in south-central India, PRG is virtually split. There in Bihar, we are uniting. But if it is unity for killing the innocents, what do we do with such unity?"

Raul looks at him, then at the distant cashew trees, and comes to the point, "I agree. But, probably we have no other option. The state machinery everywhere is killing our men. So the PRG comrades are adopting new techniques. To free some of the top comrades, the southern Naxalites have kidnapped six IAS officers about six hours back. The message came to us just before you arrived. One of those officers was very sincere and someone told me that this man was shocked to know that so many girls are compelled to go out for work to distant lands where many of them take up prostitution. One such girl told him that it was better to be a prostitute than a worker in the brick-kiln where one had to work during the day for money and be raped in the night for nothing. Anyhow, now we are on the alert, because, if need be, those hostages maybe sent outside Andhra, to us."

"Kidnappings by the Maoists!" Mahendra says in a way that exposes his alienation.

"You are shocked by all these, I understand," Raul says in a low voice, his eyeballs moving between Sainath and Mahendra. "But they have done it to free some comrades."

"And Comrade, we seek your advice." Sainath now says quite grimly. He gets up, walks a few steps to be seated beside Raul, and then continues, "The way Comrade Raghupati is clamouring for sophisticated weapons, do you think that will make us look like terrorists? Both Raul and I believe that ultimately Rambabu's team will survive."

Mahendra thinks for a while, and then he says, his words appearing like a faint echo of the past, "I don't know. I only know that the struggle, the resistance will always be there. Irrespective of you, me, Comrade GS, or Comrade Rambabu... arms or no arms... it will always be there as long as there will be hunger, poverty or... criminal inequality. It will be there because it is the dharma of the human beings to fight against injustice. But only those who would be able to carry on this fight without expectation will succeed... though the fight will never end."

"Will never end?" Sainath reacts sharply, his voice betraying incredulity at what he has been told.

"Never, because man's effort to create a new world will never cease," Mahendra sounds firm, so firm that no theory, no ideology, no argument will ever reach his ears any more.

Sainath gapes at him, and for the first time he realizes that his erstwhile militant comrade has turned into pure absolute enigma, transcending the barriers of time, faith, conviction and even existence.

"True, Comrade," Raul tries to cajole his leader for one last time. "But you used to say that we are what we believe we are. So, we believe the experiment being undertaken by Comrade Rambabu, though fraught with danger, has some..."

Suddenly, Mahendra cuts him short, "I will not be there to see the results of all these experiments, Raul. I will not be alive... at least mentally. Just remember that leaders have betrayed the people time and again, in every country, in every organization. One becomes tired of fighting and makes compromises. Some go over to the other side." Mahendra breaks into a pause, his eyes no more reflecting the burden of memory he carried for so long. He looks straight at Raul's eyes, and says, "If you feel, join PRG. But just see, just ensure... that no one spoils the blood of the martyrs. All of them died true; but are still alive in us. Even I, when I will forget everything... or if I die... I will be there, within you, within Comrade Karma, within Sunder Besra who is languishing in a jail."

He then turns towards Sainath and continues, "Don't forget me, Sainath, don't forget the martyrs. And don't forget, we work for making things better, not for spilling blood. If you believe in eye for eye... there will be no end to that. That never makes a better society."

Thereafter, for a long time, they sit quietly, till Mahendra retires in the hut and lies down on a cot. For some reason, both Sainath and Raul feel they have heard their once-upon-a time leader for the last time. But they do not dare to share the thought with each other. In the evening, they leave to visit another village and come back at lunch time the next day. When they look for Mahendra, the comrades tell them that the old man has left. Someone saw him going towards the main road when the day broke, and thereafter no one has seen him.

AS THE jeep stops at a spot where two more jeeps are parked, Rambabu looks tensely at the cops who have come to unchain him. He thinks quickly about how he shall react if the cops try to stage a fake encounter. "I will turn it into a real one," he tells himself as he alights from the jeep.

It was still dark when the guards woke Rambabu up and told him tersely, "Get up fast and wash your face. You have to go somewhere."

In the jail, it was always better to abide by the guards, and Rambabu had learned it the hard way, still nurturing a bruised leg and a sore eye. He got up and asked, "Where? You know?"

One of the guards shook his head, "We have been instructed to make you ready in half an hour. Someone is coming to take care of you."

Just an hour later, Rambabu was seated in a police jeep with his hands chained to a shaft attached to the front seat. They offered him his old trousers, a new tee shirt and a heavy pullover, but it was still too cold and Rambabu was shivering in the early morning wind of December. An officer was sitting in the front row, his face grim and fingers on a revolver. His walkie-talkie divulged secret information and poured out commands, while one unintelligible phrase kept recurring, "Sergeant Charlie has failed…. Sergeant Charlie has failed…"

The jeep sped past the city, the forlorn roads, the sleeping suburbs, and went ahead towards lonelier areas where the fields still bore the marks of devastating drought of the past months. The highway allowed a clear vista through the tall trees and Rambabu saw the first signs of a new dawn breaking over the hackneyed earth. He looked on for a while, and then suddenly he started worrying about the intention of the cops. "Where are they taking me? Are they going to stage another fake encounter?"

For the last 10 days, after being bruised by the wardens with whom he had picked up another fight, he was in the hospital, totally cut off from the world. Only last evening he was brought back to the jail and was put in a place like a condemned cell. "And then in the morning this sudden journey... things are not explicable," Rambabu told himself and looked at the constable sitting beside him in the jeep, a lean man with a simple and confused face. "There may not be much time left," he thought to himself. "To kill me, they will first have to untie my hand, and I shall at once snatch the pistol of this constable. The rest would be interesting."

But the jeep showed no signs of slowing down; in fact, it was roaring down the road so fast as though it was in a terrible hurry. Rambabu looked at the reddened sky and the clouds gathering on the horizon, and with his plans for retaliation ready in his mind, he wondered why clouds always came together near the horizon when the sun rose.

The jeep braked suddenly, giving a severe jerk, and then again picked up speed, and the husky voice in the walkie-talkie came up with a question, "Smith, Smith, are you on your way with Rambabu?"

The officer sitting in the front leaned forward and answered in English, "Smith speaking... Smith speaking... we are on our way... hope to reach bang on time."

"Peter, Peter, what about Rajendra?" The husky voice asked again.

The reply could not be heard. But the voice carried on questioning entities unknown to Rambabu, "Tommy, Tommy, are you with Chelliah?"

Suddenly, the whole thing became a little clear to Rambabu; he was being taken to a place where Comrade Chelliah and Comrade Rajendra, both of whom were in jail, were also being taken to. So three jailed comrades were being brought to one place. Why? Before he could proceed further down the lane of his thoughts, the husky voice lamented again, "Sergeant Charlie has failed."

Rambabu felt bored and remembered how they tortured him for so many months. They tried it out day in and day out even in the jail, but failed to extract even a word from him, as though his lips were glued, and the only sound that could pass out of those rather thick lips was a shriek, the only protest against torture. Then burning cigarettes were pressed on his palms, thigh and afterwards on his belly, and when that failed to open him up, an officer told him that next it would be put on his penis. Rambabu shuddered, but did not give up, though he knew the threat was real. But the cops could not work on their threat because of an unexpected intervention by the court—a human rights organization moved the High Court to prevent such brutal torture, and Rambabu later came to know the organization was led by one Kannan. The court asked for a report from its own medical officer who severely indicted the police and that spared Rambabu's penis.

Now, after a couple of hours' journey, the jeep suddenly stops at a spot where two more jeeps are parked. As the cops unchain Rambabu, he quickly looks at the cops and plans how he will attack them if he sniffs danger. If the cops have a plan of killing them staging a fake encounter, by shooting them from the back, he resolves to make it a real one and alights from the jeep. He feels pain in his left eye that has been twice damaged in third degree sessions he underwent in lock-ups and in the prison.

Just then, a senior officer comes in front of him and says, "You are being released. They have told us to release you here and to ask you to proceed towards Ramocha. That's on this side…" The officer raises his hand to show the direction but a fly distracts him. He waves his hand to get rid of it and directs him towards the jungle as the fly comes back to sit on his nose.

Rambabu sees his two comrades there, ready to venture into the jungle as soon as he joins them. Rambabu walks up to them and looks back to see whether the cops are aiming their guns at them. No, they were standing like innocent men, looking at them helplessly. The three comrades walk along the road and take a turn to enter the jungle, wade through slush and water on a strip of lowland. "Why have they released us?" Rambabu asks.

A man appears suddenly to tell them that the tube wells are vomiting blood. It is the code, and the comrades feel relieved. They walk on with the fourth comrade to meet their other comrades waiting close by.

"I think I can smoke a cigarette now," says Chelliah.

"Cigarette! From where did you get it?" Rambabu sounds rather curious.

Chelliah, who is the most senior man among them, says jokingly, "Hoary hair pays brother, you won't understand. The jailor himself gave it to me."

"Jailor! You are lucky. Where were you?" Rambabu asks casually as his eyes scour through between the trees for the comrades.

"Khammam," Chelliah says and takes out a cigarette from a brand new packet. "The jailor was good. I smoked another one when I was waiting for you. You were late..."

"But why have they released us?" asks Rambabu.

"To get back the six officers our comrades have kidnapped," answers Rajendra.

"Kidnapped?" Rambabu sounds puzzled.

"But... for that they have released us!" Chelliah wonders aloud.

"That's because of another reason," the fourth comrade says smilingly. "They decided to yield only when National Security Guards, the elites among the central commandoes, failed. And see, even with the British law that is still in vogue in our state, whereby the tribesmen languish in jail and do not get bail like the others, the state has failed to extract words from the villagers. I salute the common man of this country."

Rambabu realizes the Charlie who has failed is NSG.

Before others can react, three comrades appear before them and salute the three freed from the jail. One of them is very close to

Rambabu, Comrade Krishna. "We have succeeded!" Krishna sounds jubilant. "Comrade Raghupati says whenever the state will attack us in its fullest strength, we must retaliate with all our might. He is sure the strategy will work. And it works, you see. When he told me to kidnap those six officers, I was scared. But now we have won."

"Yes," says Chelliah.

"What about those officers in our custody?" Rambabu asks anxiously.

"They will be released as soon as we reach our area," answers Krishna. "They have given us safe passage… I will inform them and then they would be released… maybe tomorrow."

As they walk on through the jungle, Krishna allows the others to go a bit ahead of them, and then tells Rambabu, "Comrade Raghupati planned this only for you, as he feels you are the person who can negotiate with the LTTE properly. Meanwhile, I have convinced all others like Comrade Sainath and Comrade Raul. I have told them that we can get everything from the Tigers… guns, explosives, mines… everything. But between you and me, it is difficult to ascertain who is actually in the top leadership of those Tigers, isn't it?"

"No one," whispers Rambabu. "Their top leadership is not concerned much about us. Even earlier, I have negotiated with the middle rank and the main negotiator was not an active warrior. I met another LTTE man in the jail. He told me that our PM Rajiv Gandhi virtually kept their leader Prabhakaran under detention in Delhi and forced him to sign the peace accord. Since then… they are looking for opportunities to retaliate."

As Krishna looks at him in amazement, Rambabu smirks and adds, "Earlier when they contacted us, they felt that India will remain a friendly force, particularly Tamil Nadu, and they will take advantage of the situation. So, they wanted a pact with us. We will not go to Tamil Nadu, they will give us arms. Now, probably, they will not mind even if we go to Tamil Nadu. They will help us, because they also want to hit back at the Indian state."

AFTER LEAVING the hut where Sainath and Raul sheltered him, leaving his known world, Mahendra now traverses from one place to another, from one district to the next, without knowing the reason. He follows his dreams in which the sadhu, who many years ago predicted that he would be able to see through the stones, guides him from time to time. Amazingly, being instructed to do so, he has decided to forget his past with all its remnants, his name, his struggle, his daughter, his life, and even his dreams that he has nurtured for so many years, giving a nice burial to Comrade Mahendra.

The sadhu appears again and urges him to set out for his quest, to see through the stones. "You have defeated the gods again," he says.

"How?"

"They wanted to defeat you by making you worried, by making you repent for your deeds. But you don't care anymore. Every punishment fails if the punished does not break down before it. As you are not cowed by the fear of losing your memory, they have failed again. Now you set out on your mission."

"Where shall I go?"

"Whichever way the path goes…" mutters the sadhu grimly as he disappears from his dream.

Mahendra sets out the next morning on foot, and moves towards the east, leaving the cobbled road behind, along the meadows, until he is worn out. Then he sits down under a banyan tree and closes his eyes to avoid the midday sun that irritates his eyes and his deteriorating vision.

Within minutes, he falls asleep.

Hours later, someone shakes him to wake him up, and opening his eyes, he finds an old man wearing a white dhoti and a white *chadar* looking at him with utmost care and anxiety. "Who are you?" the man asks.

Mahendra looks about to see a partly cloudy twilight that has filled the whole surrounding with a reddish glow, and answers, "A traveller."

The stranger takes him to a small ashram that belongs to the Vaishnavite sect, and assures him that he may stay there for as long as he wishes. "You eat something… we are vegetarians, and take rest. Tomorrow morning, we will talk again. You are not a *mussafir*, but if you don't want to tell me who you are, you need not."

Almost a week later, the man, known in the Ashram as Chandidas Gosain or simply Gosain*ji*, asks him again, who he was. "You are not a commoner," he tells him with a semblance of smile on his lips. "That day, I saw you reading the newspaper I brought from Gaya, and you were reading an article on Bofors controversy. No commoner will read that. Even I do not understand that."

"I know nothing," Mahendra turns cautious. "It's in the newspaper."

"True, but there are so many things about us. Only the wise knows the meaning of those." Chandidas pauses, looks at the tall lean man, and asks, "Are you scared of someone? Is that the reason you don't want to disclose your identity?"

Mahendra is sitting in the open, and Chandidas has taken his seat beside him, as though he is his old friends. The sun has set a while ago, and now the shadows have started falling, compelling the birds, the cows and the men to return home after a tiring day.

"I was a Naxalite," Mahendra reveals suddenly, not knowing why.

"Naxalite!" Gosain seems crestfallen for a few seconds, then recovers to mutter, "You were, well, okay… But then, what are you up to now?"

"I want to see through the stones… But I know everything has a time. Nothing happens before time, and nothing remains without happening when the time comes."

Gosain thinks for a while and then mutters, "You are blessed. I think with God's blessing, you will be able to see through the stones."

"I don't believe in God. All through my life, I have challenged the gods, in whatever form they are."

"Doesn't matter. That was your imagination. God is God. He can neither be worshipped, nor challenged. But I believe you will succeed in your mission."

"Do you think it's possible?" Mahendra asks with great hope in mind.

"Very much. A stone is the embodiment of truth. The scientists may tell us its physical and chemical composition. But there is another dimension of everything, the soul. With God's blessings, you will be able to see that."

"I don't know. I am confused. I have left my comrades behind. That is like betraying the cause for which so many had laid down their lives."

"Lord Krishna and Radha's love is known in the world as the epitome of love. But then Krishna left Vrindavan… left Radha, never to come back. Why? From his small individual world, he went away to the bigger world. He salvaged dharma and went back to his abode of perpetual bliss."

"But in my case," Mahendra seems crestfallen, "this is going back to individual world from a bigger world."

"Gosain, you know so much, and you don't understand this?" laughs Gosain, who calls others Gosain too. "The world of truth is the biggest world, and one who sets out for the quest of truth, sacrifices everything… his individual world, his small collective world, and even himself. For truth, you can sacrifice everything. But truth cannot be sacrificed for anything."

Mahendra sits silently as darkness engulfs them and bells ring in the temple inside the ashram. After quite a while, he asks, "What is truth?"

Gosain laughs in a way as though he has won a duel. "Gosain, you know the answer. Simple men and women may not get at the bottom of it. For them the answer is: Truth is God. But surely, you are not so simple. You want a broader meaning."

"I want to hear it from you," Mahendra insists.

"You want to trap me. Well then, truth is something that is not illusion like this world or our lives."

After another long gap, as he suddenly remembers the distant past which he often cannot recollect, Mahendra says, "The government had fixed a good price on my head. Now you know it. Won't you try to get it?"

"Mohammad, the Prophet, said a camel may go through the eye of a needle, but a rich man can't go to heaven. Why do you want the doors of heaven to be closed for me?"

"But you are a Hindu. Why are you referring to Mohammad?"

"They all are great men," Goswain folds his hands. "Buddha, Shri Chaitanya, Mohammad, or Jesus. Why should we differentiate among them? All of them are persons to be remembered at dawn."

"Then why do Hindus and Muslims fight?" Mahendra wonders aloud, without expecting any answer, for he knows the world is full of puzzles that have no answers.

A day later, Mahendra has a severe attack of amnesia that keeps him down for a few days, and when he recovers, he finds all the past incidents in his head have tangled up; it is as though his memory has been fogged, and nothing can be seen so clearly as to notice their distinct features. He also develops a new symptom, a faint but constant buzz in his ears, like a bee has settled down inside his head.

The only thing he remembers clearly is that a sadhu comes to him regularly to guide him to see through the stones, which means seeing the truth. He feels his time is nearing the end, and early next morning, he sets out again, without knowing where he is supposed to go. In the afternoon, he reaches a village, where a young man shelters him and feeds him for reasons best known to him. They are Koiris, a Backward caste; but as Mahendra cannot remember to what caste he belongs to, they give him the benefit of doubt and conclude he must be like them, a Backward, and treat him as such.

After a week, Mahendra tells the young man that he wants to leave, for he does not like to be a burden on him, and to his surprise, he finds the young man's eyes turning wet. "What's the matter?" he asks.

"You look like my father." A drop of tear rolls down the young man's eyes. "He worked so hard to raise us, but when our turn came and we thought we will let him rest, he died. By serving you, I serve my father. Don't leave me."

Mahendra decides to stay there and wait for the sadhu to come back.

Weeks pass by, and then months, and then even years. Mahendra waits on and on, but no sadhu comes in his dream to guide him.

PART III
After the Doom

18

The Present Continuous... (1991–92)

LIFE, LIKE a river, often takes an unexpected turn to embrace the unforeseen, unsettling the course of the past that allows it to survive, or often to thrive.

Mahendra Chamar knew it when he had not lost his mind, but even now, his life moves through the same craggy terrain of unforeseen ups and downs, of expectation and frustration. He was settled in the village where a young man sheltered him, and could have lived there till the end, but destiny was still playing its tricks. He was frustrated as he had not been able to see through the stones, though the phrase no more seemed to him as opaque as it was earlier. He did not know what he would achieve by seeing through the stones, but he attached much importance to it, probably to make meaningful the present that had neither a past nor a future.

At times, Mahendra read the newspapers and came across headlines like 'VP new PM' or 'Union Home Minister's daughter kidnapped', or 'Lalu Prasad Yadav elected CM'. But these things did not touch the core of his heart, and he read them with such indifference as though his soul had transcended his body that had fought, lost and fought again. He spent his days idly, often staring blankly at the meadows rolled out up to the horizon, often trying to solve the problems of the locals, or by making earthen toys.

Thus, when it seemed that his life had really settled down in a slow small world of frustration and sustenance, suddenly it began to move again; his past started reappearing in his mind, though in incoherent bits.

Now, nearly three years after his arrival in the village, many such bits of his past flash before his eyes, but neither can he connect characters nor recollect their location in the frame of time, and they seem to him mere compilations of visuals—a boy being beaten after throwing a stone at a huge iron gate, a little girl lying on the chest of a young man, a man preaching in darkness... Such visuals are galling, like something showing in parts while keeping the whole out of reach, and Mahendra curses the visuals.

Every evening, when the light fades over the horizon and the birds finally fall silent, Mahendra lies down on a charpoy, his toes rubbing against each other and his gaze fixed at the sky where stars appear one after another, like their light has just reached the earth after many light years. The sky changes continuously, every hour and every night, Mahendra knows with his limited knowledge. It was Comrade *babu* who taught him about planets, stars, comets, and meteoroids; and all that he learnt in those days is still preserved in the cells of his brain though the image of Comrade *babu* has got washed away. Mahendra lies quietly and enjoys the screech of a few bats that fly for a while and then rest by hanging from a big tree, listens to the bark of the dogs that chase invisible enemies, and observes the wheels of a bullock cart that comes back home.

The young man who gave him shelter often sits beside him and asks, "What do you search for in the sky?"

"You see," Mahendra says softly, "the stars remind you that you were not here many years ago, you will not be here many years later. But then, why are you here? You are here only to make this world a better place for your successors, so that one day this earth turns into heaven."

On one such evening, someone else says, "My mother died a year back. But I have seen my mother in my dream last night."

"It is our subconscious mind," Mahendra makes an attempt to explain a dream. Then he realizes he has forgotten the explanation that someone gave him long back. It creates a sort of uneasiness within him, and he goes to bed with that.

On that night, when wind rustles through the trees heavily as a prelude to a storm, the sadhu appears again in his dream. "You are wasting your time," he tells Mahendra.

"But I don't know what to do. Why did you leave me?"

"I am leaving you forever. I will not come back."

"But why?" he cringes and clacks his tongue.

"Because I do not exist."

"What does it mean?"

"I exist because you exist. I am your subconscious mind."

"What do I do then?"

"Go. Get going."

The sadhu disappears and Mahendra wakes up wondering what it was all about. After a long contemplation, during which the storm rises and then fizzles out, he realizes whatever he has seen in his dreams emanated from his own mind, and whatever direction he has received was actually from his own subconscious identity. He starts pacing in his small room and suddenly, as though struck by a lightning, he remembers Comrade *babu* and his explanation of a dream. Thereafter, his head starts reeling as he begins to remember certain parts of his life that remained buried under his mind—he was born as a Chamar... he became a Communist... then he joined the Maoists... his daughter was lost.

He stays awake for the rest of the night—often remembering something and forgetting it minutes later—and just when the meadows started bathing in the soft light of the dawn, he leaves the village where he has stayed for three years. He starts walking towards the west. He walks on for days. At times, a word or a name calls to his mind a part of his past, but it does not linger for long. What is constant in his mind is, as it was, that he has to see through the stones, and he starts believing that it is the panacea for all his worries! With that thought at the back of his mind, he wanders aimlessly, eats whatever he gets and then reaches a place where many TB patients are waiting to see a 'goddess', a doctor who treats poor patients without charging anything.

"What is her name?" Mahendra asks someone.

That man passes the question to the next one, and that man to the next, each to the other, till all of them confess that they do not know the name of the goddess, whom they simply call Doctor *didi*. But Mahendra is interested to know the name and ultimately the guard tells him that the goddess is Dr Mrs Rani Sharma. The name calls to his mind Dr Rani, kindles his memory of the hospital in Patna, and he decides to meet the 'goddess', to ascertain if she is the same Rani.

When he meets her, he is happy to see the same Rani, the Queen, who has turned much leaner and a bit sickly. She, however, seems to be much more excited to see him, though she takes time to discover the old Mahendra through his long tangled hair and beard grown over the years. Then she says, "I never thought I will see you again... That was 1983, when your comrades took you out. This is '91. But you have grown so old in these years. What's wrong with you?"

"I did not know that you are Sharma; I was hesitant to meet you."

"I am Sharma," Rani smiles, and then she tells him about her husband, revealing to him for the first time that the man who got him arrested was her husband. She tells him that she was scared that Naxalites or Mahendra himself would take revenge on him and suffered from a deep sense of guilt, and finally decided to work for the poor for the rest of her life to atone for disloyalty to her husband.

Mahendra sits quietly when the story is finished, compelling Rani to ask, "What are you pondering over, Mohan *dada*?"

"I never knew it. Otherwise, I wouldn't have asked you to keep it a secret that I was all right," Mahendra says sadly, as though repenting his deeds. "You can now tell him that I am here."

"Why?"

"He can arrest me."

"He is now with the Central Reserve Police as an IG, and… there is no question of sacrificing one's brother for one's husband."

"You are not sacrificing me. I am done for."

"How?"

"I forget everything. Often for days, I do not recollect who I am… So I have set out to realize what a sadhu told me long, long back, that I will challenge the gods and then they will retaliate and finally I will be able to see through the stones."

Another doctor rushes in to brief '*didi*' about a patient's critical condition, and Rani tells him that she will be there within five minutes.

Mahendra gets up and tells her that if she has no intention to hand him over to the police, then he will rather leave.

Suddenly Rani comes close, bends down in a bid to touch his feet, and she actually does that, making him dumbfounded for a while. "Bless me," Rani says.

"Bless?" he mutters confusingly. "I am a Chamar. Nobody touches the feet of a Chamar and we cannot bless anyone."

"You are the noblest man I have seen. You are my elder brother and you have to bless me so that I get the same husband, the same daughter, same parents and also you as an elder brother in my next birth." Rani almost chokes.

Mahendra raises his hand uncertainly, hesitation stops him twice, and then mutters, "I bless you. You will get the same parents, same husband and daughter."

"What about you as brother?" insists Rani.

With his eyes turning cloudy, he shakes his head and mutters, "That is impossible, my sister. We live in two different worlds. You are an upper caste… I am an Untouchable. Somehow, by quirk of fate, we met. But accidents can't be repeated. But I bless you in each birth you transcend from a queen to a goddess."

Thereafter, without saying anything more, without looking back even once, he walks out of the room, out of the house, out of the premise.

He then goes on and on.

ASHOK SHARMA, the Romantic Cobra, asks, "Have you heard about Phoenix?"

The intelligence chiefs from Karnataka and Madhya Pradesh, VDS Gowda and RN Basu nod, while the man from Andhra, TR Narayana Reddy asks, "Talking of the mythical bird that burns itself and again rises from the ashes?"

Ashok looks at the younger officers, and says, "When I think of the Naxalites, and particularly about one character, Mahendra Chamar, what comes to my mind is the Phoenix. On Mahendra Chamar I will come back later. But let me deal with the whole force first. By 1972–73, we were sure they were over. They resurfaced in Bhojpur just about then and again we crushed them. But since mid-1980s, they were again active in parts of Bihar and Andhra. We did our best to stifle them out. This time, they are refusing to die. Now they are very much present in Chhattisgarh region of MP."

Narayana Reddy opens his mouth for an update, "From 1989, they have AK-47 and other sophisticated arms. And from all indications available to us, they will use more sophisticated arms from now on. The southern Naxalites has about 50 *dalams*... one *dalam* is eight to twelve men... average is 10. So, it means they have about 500 armed cadres."

The Romantic Cobra bends forward to look at the papers lying in front of him. While foraging through them, he tells Reddy, "Shekhar, your IG is in their hit list."

"He tried his best to eliminate them, much of which is not known to the world outside the jungles and hills," Reddy mumbles.

"Yes, I was trying to locate this table," Ashok Sharma suddenly turns enthusiastic after finding a sheet of paper. "See the spurt in violence, I mean in Andhra Pradesh, over the years. In '81, there were only 53 incidents in the state and 10 were killed. But in '87, there were 252 incidents and 63 people lost their lives. That year they kidnapped our officers also. 1988 witnessed the killing of all together 59 people in 453 incidents. 1989, being the election year, violence increased. But it did not come down significantly in the last year, and this year we have elections again for Parliament."

As Ashok takes off his reading glasses, Basu adds, "And now they have these deadly AK-47s. Local police will be helpless against them."

"Right." Ashok repeats the word thrice. "We have to upgrade the armaments of the local force. When in Andhra they are using Kalashnikovs, soon we may find it in Dandakaranya. But what about Bihar? There is a group called Unity group, which is close to the southern Naxalite group."

"The important question is," Basu says, "how closely these Naxalites are related to the LTTE."

"My information is that they don't have high-level contacts with LTTE. Just some ex-LTTE men…" Gowda waves his hand to show his confusion.

"But it is only natural that they would get more help," Ashok tells the others. "We went to Sri Lanka as Peace Keeping Force and then started killing them. They will retaliate with all their might. And the reports we have from Tamil Nadu are very disturbing. They may try killing some bigwigs."

It is a hotel in the coastal town called Visakhapattanam where they are sitting; the Romantic Cobra on the bed, and the others on chairs that they have dragged by the side of the bed. The rooms on this side of the hotel overlook a swimming pool with an adjoining lawn where a party begins, and the sounds of music blared out from a loudspeaker trespasses the rooms like a giant wave of the sea.

"Hey ho," Narayana Reddy exclaims. "What's this?"

They wait for a few minutes hoping that the volume will be down, but when it does not happen, Reddy calls up the reception. They wait for a few minutes, as all of them are sure that steps will be taken immediately, for in this country police officers most often have the last word.

When the volume is lowered, Ashok Sharma says, "The situation is pretty bad. One of my central police officers recently wanted to raid a village. But those from the state police did not dare to enter that village. They said those areas were out of bound for them. 'We never go there. It's their area. No police team had entered those remote villages in last five years. We have no permission.' That is what they said."

As Narayana Reddy nods indifferently, the Romantic Cobra continues, "Our officers asked what would happen if they entered the village. They said the force won't find even one of them. They are from the village and if they come out after storing their arms somewhere, no one will understand who they are. Some 15 such villages fall under that police station, and if the station does not declare truce, the Naxals may blow up the police station. They said the Naxalites, if they desire, would attack suddenly, perhaps in the dead of the night, ransack the station in some minutes and then will disappear in the jungles. They just vanish in the jungles without any trace. So... you have to buy peace with them if you want to go back home after completing the period of your posting there. Same situation in southern Bihar and northern Andhra. The villages are ruled by the Naxalites. They distribute land, collect levy and adjudicate over crimes in kangaroo courts."

As Reddy nods, Basu suddenly says, "The problem is, in big cities, no one knows about this situation. Forget about Delhi or Bombay, not even in the state capitals."

"The upper echelon of our society wants to monopolize every facility for themselves; we have seen that during the Mandal controversy," Gowda comments. "Government decided to reserve jobs for socially and economically backward students, and the upper caste men, students, media, political parties, everyone tried their best to throttle it."

"But that was done on the basis of caste," Basu disagreed. "VP Singh could have done it on the basis of economic criteria. But he chose caste to further his political..."

"Aren't most of the Backwards like washer men, barbers, iron smith, masons poor?" Gowda, himself a Backward, retaliates smilingly.

Ashok raises his hand and intervenes, "All these are true, but that does not concern our job. The upper middle class or the rich in the big cities… they don't care for the poor, true. I have seen young girls, dressed like fairies, throwing biscuits at the footpath dwellers and enjoying the fight over the crumbs. Given a chance, why shouldn't those footpath dwellers turn into Naxalites? True. All the Backwards are those whom the scriptures call the Shudras, born to serve the upper castes, true. However, there aren't much government jobs now. They are abolishing posts. Whatever, as police officers we can't do anything on these points, apart from just what we are doing now, discussing these things among us. The point, however, is that the apathy or callousness of the government bosses is allowing the Naxalite situation to deteriorate. The question is what we can do about it. Someday, it will threaten the upper echelon's very existence. That will affect your sons and my daughter. That worries me. No development, not much scope of work, no nutritious food, no medical facilities, no social security at all. By social index, most of the remote villages of India are Sub-Saharan Africa. This is the breeding ground of violent dissent, isn't it?"

Both Gowda and Basu agree at once.

"I had a meeting with Bihar officers," Ashok comes back to his topic. "Naxals are spreading their organization throughout south Bihar. They are provided with the basic infrastructure by the peasant committees and hold their sway by dispensing instant justice from the people's court while Red Army gives them necessary protection. Now, bloc level officers also attend those people's courts when summoned. And I think people like Mahendra Chamar are working as link men between these organizations."

"I believe you mentioned the name earlier. Who is that Mahendra?" asks Basu.

For the next five minutes, Sharma briefs the others on the man called Mahendra Chamar, and then concludes by saying, "How his comrades took him away from the hospital is a mystery. But since then, he remained traceless. Strangely, we have traced him after so many years and that too in Andhra. It became clear when that man, zonal commander of the southern Naxalites… Krishnababu or something who was killed…"

"Krishna Raju," Reddy corrects him.

"Yes. The Andhra police got a diary from him and after some months, I took it from them and got it translated. There was a mention of Mahendra Chamar. It seemed that Comrade Sainath of PRG had a discussion with Comrade Mahendra on some important issues like using sophisticated arms and the extent of violence. From what he wrote, it seemed that Mahendra had a different view and that view was haunting Krishnababu… no Krishna Raju."

For the next three hours, they discuss the probability of interconnectivity among the southern and eastern Naxalites and the possible fallout of it, at times with utter seriousness, and at other times, in a relaxed mood.

A little while later, when the officers are having their dinner in the same room, the phone starts trilling to break the deadly news to the officers—Rajiv Gandhi, the former PM, is assassinated at Sriperampudur in Tamil Nadu, where he had gone to campaign for his party for the parliamentary election.

"Our worst fears have come true," Ashok Sharma tells others after a gap of about half a minute, during which all the three officers were absorbed in their respective shards of thoughts.

"Surely, it is the handiwork of the LTTE," Reddy adds immediately. "Only they use human bombs."

HARRY HAS turned into a strong votary of new economic policies unleashed by PV Narasimha Rao as Prime Minister with Manmohan Singh as his Finance Minister. "The Asian elephant will now wake up," he tells people who matter, the captains of industries.

Many of them ask, "How?"

"The government is unshackling the elephant, you understand. What is liberalization? You don't have to go to the government for permission for everything you want to do. The end of licence-permit era. The government is finally saying goodbye to the very form of controlled economy, those bogus concepts of socialism. Now more investment will be coming, from foreign and domestic sources. It will be a real competitive market."

"But would we be able to face the competition from the world giants?" the sceptics ask him in small gatherings.

"The question is," Harry tries to convince the others, "if there are good students in the school, won't you send your ward to that school? Would you say my son won't be able to face competition and that's why I'd rather teach him at home? Your son's future will be doomed then. It's the same. You have to face competition and thrive. Some old industries will die. Like jute industry. That's dead. Who cares! But there will be many more avenues."

"Like?"

"That will unfold," he says emphatically.

While some laugh at him for such views, some businessmen and industrialists who belong to his close circle, ask, "How will we benefit from it in the near future?"

"Easy. The tax structures will be changed and I believe will be rationalized more and more. We pay huge tax compared to developed countries. That will come down. And at a later stage, the labour laws will be relaxed, liberating us from the unions."

"How are we to shield ourselves from the competition?" asks his friend Chiranjiv Singh, sitting in a restaurant in a five star hotel in Delhi. "Top industrialists are favouring it. But we do not belong to the elite club."

Harry nods, and then whispers, his voice grave, "For some reason, God has never allowed me to settle with what I have. He destroyed my family. Even the industries I started with were ruined. The paper mill that I developed was a victim of labour unrest and turned unmanageable. It has gone to liquidation though I am not worse off from that. I will sell the land… it will make me richer… and that's the tragedy. Your unit becomes sick, you sell it off and you become richer. So many people do that deliberately. But if you are sincere, it's a shock. For me, an industry is a challenge."

"True," Chiranjiv looks about the hall, notices a group of young men and women laughing and enjoying themselves, and nods.

"For all these years, we have had no new avenue before us," Harry shakes his head to show his disgust at the state of affairs. "Now many will open up. I don't know when, but as it will unfold, we will have to grab the opportunities."

Harry knows even some of his friends, who are not so ambitious and are afraid of traversing along a new path, considers him a bit crazy. He had said in the past in various seminars that Indian polity should take a rightist turn shedding the dead weights of Nehruvian political economy, which later on was dubbed as socialism by Indira Gandhi, and the big players agreed. But most people thought that it would never happen. But as India was on the verge of defaulting in foreign debt servicing, as the government had to mortgage gold, as devaluation became imminent, the rulers were forced to change track. Now when such new avenues are unveiling before them, his friends are trying to cling on to the old order; but Harry is not surprised, for he knows majority is always scared to accept a new system.

Harry feels enthused when the biggest Chamber of Commerce, of which he is not a member, invites him to speak on the subject of liberalization. Their public relations man met him and said, "We need more like you from the middle segment of entrepreneurs… with modern outlook, free from feudal mentalities." Harry has accepted the offer as that is what he wants to be remembered as, 'a modern industrialist free from feudal mentalities'.

But destiny has scripted something else for him, and as he cannot change it, he still has to find time for a hidden, secret second agenda that he is bound to follow; he must find the man called Mahendra Chamar.

It is strange that as years pass by, as he fails to find that man, his mind also hardens; now he wants to exterminate the whole population of the Maoists. It is even stranger that with this grit hardening his mind, his passion for women has subsided. Now, he is prepared to cover the tortuous journey to achieve the end, for now he feels he will not to be satisfied only with Mahendra Chamar's blood.

SHYAMLAL, WHO once fell inside a deserted mine, is working in full swing, trying to mobilize people for a final battle to get a separate state of Jharkhand. But often even those who work under him do not accept his words as the last ones on other subjects!

To draw a parallel between the rising sun and their burgeoning movement, he has said that the sun remains soft when it rises and that is why it is so red. But a younger man, Ratua, has rebutted him and has argued that the sun is always the same and it does not rise or set in actual terms. His authority thus being challenged, Shyamlal is fuming at the moment. He asks, "Then why in the night you can't see it?"

"Because the earth rotates… in the night, the sun is seen from the other side of the world."

"They see sun in the night also?" Shyamlal is unnerved.

"No," Ratua, an Oraon boy, tries to clear the air of confusion. "Now it is day for half the world and night for the other half."

"How funny, morning and night at the same time!" Now Shyamlal sharpens his attack confidently, "The earth rotates! And what about the sun? It remains fixed? Listen friends, you see the sun above your heads now. Ratua says, it will always be there."

The older people titter, and an irritated Ratua storms out of the sitting, away from the cool shadow of the trees, towards a cluster of huts at the distance. Younger fellows follow him.

"The schools actually inject insects into their heads," comments another elderly man Jatin Oraon, who is a member of the 'parha', the Oraon area panchayat. The elders—four of them are sitting together now—share jokes among them. But Shyamlal does not take part in it as he has suddenly remembered something else, something that has left him perturbed.

A few days back, he saw Stephen, whom he calls Istiphen, meeting a Muslim trader in the same village where once the Jharkhandis had fought and killed a few landowners and middlemen. The trader, Henayat Khan, was one of those who treated tribesmen as slaves and, even after the killings, continued the old trade with the help of the police. As such, Stephen meeting this man was worrying; but that was not all. He came back to the hut he shared with Shyamlal a while later, and started counting a wad of notes that he had obviously got from the bearded trader.

Shyamlal could not resist himself from asking, "You have taken money from that trader?"

Stephen almost flinched, as though to avoid the deadly lunge of an invisible snake, and asked, "Who told you?"

"I have seen you entering his house."

"You followed me when I went out?"

"Yes."

"That's not done. We do something that the leaders instruct us to do. You shouldn't have followed me. But now... don't discuss this with anyone else. This man wants to buy peace with us and in return, he is ready to pay us. And we need money to mobilize people and strengthen our movement."

Shyamlal had stuck to this man for seven years and considered him as his leader, and he had no intention to challenge him. But, afterwards, a weird thought has started knocking his mind: if all the *dikus* who exploit the Jharkhandis want to buy peace and pay bribe, what happens then? What will be the significance of a tribal state, even if they get it? The *dikus* will carry on their trades, and tribesmen and other Jharkhandis will work on like slaves in the mines, fields and everywhere else! Would that not reduce all great promises to the people into a load of nonsense, all their fights to ridiculous triviality, like they are crows rearing the fledglings of the cuckoos?

"See this book. See what is written here: The earth revolves round the sun and rotates on its own axis. It takes 24 hours…" Ratua, who has come back with two other boys, shouts. He reads the paragraph that explains what Copernicus and Galileo had said centuries back, and the elderly persons listen to it glumly. They cannot contest it anymore, for it is written in a book, and they all believe something in print cannot be wrong.

A while later, Jatin asks, "What is written there about solar and lunar eclipses? It is not due to Rahu and Ketu?"

"What do you say Jatin *chacha*!" Ratua addresses Jatin as uncle and explains the whole thing reading aloud from the book. The elders sit huddled together, peeved with the fact that whatever they knew throughout their lives was wrong.

"Hey, you *Chachas*, why you sit together sadly?" Ratua again sits near the elders with questioning eyes and turns towards Shyamlal, "You said we have to be cautious nowadays. Tell us what to do."

Suddenly Jatin retorts, "You are all grown-ups. And we are old fools. Will you listen to us?"

Ratua gapes at him for a while and then begins to laugh, his white teeth flashing in the backdrop of his dark face. "What do you say, Jatin *chacha*! You are all elderly men. You know so much. These things you don't know because you didn't attend schools. So what? You are our guardians. My father never went to a school. Should I disobey him then?"

The elders are overwhelmed. They are all smiles now; they appreciate Ratua, and even poke fun at themselves for their ignorance. "That is why the schools are so important," Jatin comments.

HE MOVES on for days together, often resting in some place for a day or two, and again resuming his aimless journey as he does not realize how to see through the stones; often he goes without food, and at other times, the villagers see him and mistaking him as a sort of a god-man, offer him something.

Several months later—by then his journey has taken him to a village in Chhattisgarh region of Madhya Pradesh—he hears a local man asking others not to go towards the highway the next day.

"Why?" Mahendra asks.

"*Dadalog* (the big brothers) told us that a big officer would be passing through that road for who they have planted a mine there."

"Officer? Who?"

At this, the young man gets irritated, "*Hai Ram*! You know them? If I tell you that he is an IG of Central Police and his name is Ashok Sharma, what is that to you?"

Mahendra gets startled. Still, he says with as much reluctance as to appear disinterested, "Nothing. That man will be in Raipur. When will he come?"

"Hey! You know so much!" The young man drags him away from others, and says, "I am a Naxalite. You know, who Naxalites are?"

"Yes," Mahendra mutters. "Those who fight."

Satisfied with the certificate, the man now reveals, "Tomorrow he has a programme. He will come in the afternoon and we will blow him up."

"Great. They deserve it," Mahendra agrees at once, and then, with an appearance of nonchalance, he asks, "How far is Raipur from here?"

"Eighty kilometres."

Mahendra boards a bus that takes him Raipur at night, and goes to Father Lal, who is not in the Home, but is expected to return the next morning. He spends the night in a dingy room that others allot him and in the morning, when he finds that the Father is back, he asks him for the telephone number of Ashok Sharma, an IG of Central Police stationed in Raipur. After a while, the Father gets him the number, and asks, "What will you do with it?"

"I shall make a call," Mahendra reveals as he finds his brain is working well and the buzz inside his head has subsided. "Would you help me to a public call booth?" he asks the Father.

"You can make a call from my room."

"No," he shakes his head. "Lets go."

At the PCO, he asks the Father to dial the number and ask for Sharma, the IG. With bewilderment in his eyes, the Father dials the number, asks for Sharma and transfers the handset to Mahendra.

After he heard the sombre 'Hello' from the other end, Mahendra asks, "Ashok Sharma?"

"Speaking," the voice says.

"Rani Sharma's husband?"

"Y-e-s… But who's on the line?"

"You have a programme… down the road that goes to Jagdalpur… but don't go. They have posted a mine to kill you."

"What! Who?" the voice turns agitated.

Suddenly, Mahendra feels a faint buzz in his head again, gets confused and mutters slowly, "The Naxalites."

"But… who are you?… Hello…"

Mahendra takes the receiver off from his ear, tries to remember his other name as what comes to his mind is Mohan Ram, and then he puts the receiver back to his ears. "*Log hame*," he starts the sentence hesitantly, and as he remembers his other name, he continues, "*Mahendra Chamar kahate hai*n. (People call me Mahendra Chamar.)"

For a few seconds, no word comes from the other side. But when Mahendra decides to hang the phone, he hears the voice again, "Why are you trying to save me? Why are you telling me that there is a mine on my road?"

Mahendra hesitates to answer; he knows certain riddles cannot be explained by words, and even if one attempts to do so, one cannot convince anyone else. Still he mutters a few words that come to his mind, "You have a lot of things to do… to create a new world." And then, assuming that the other end will ask more questions that he cannot answer, he hangs the receiver and turns back.

Back at the Home, he asks the dumbfounded Father for a favour, "I want to tell the leaders of our organization about this. Will you help me?" He then dictates the Father a few lines and asks him to deliver this to any Naxalite whom he knows.

"But," the Father intervenes, "You have not explained in the letter why you saved this man."

Mahendra looks on. The world reels slightly before his eyes and the buzz in his ears intensifies. "Time will tell them," he says plainly, as though surprised by the Father's ignorance.

"But, why did you tell that man that he would create a new world?"

Mahendra thinks for a while like listening to a faint echo coming from the past, and then says, "Everybody should create his own world. That is what one is supposed to do."

Father Lal stares at him, his eyes betraying curiosity with a contrasting combination of empathy and confusion. "Where had you been these long years?" he asks a while later.

As the buzz makes him feel sick again, Mahendra thinks for a while and then confesses, "I don't remember."

The Father nods for a few times, and then asks, "But why a Naxalite saved a police officer, Comrade Mahendra?"

Mahendra tries to remember why, but fails and says, "To see through the stones." He starts walking and adds, "I must leave now."

"But you are visibly very weak," Father Lal tries to cajole him for the last time. "In these few years, you have become 20 years older. You look like an old man, like of 70 years, though you are… we calculated it once… just about 50 only. When you came to my Home seven years ago, you were not like this. You are committing suicide. Don't do this. Stay here."

Mahendra looks at him blankly and mutters, "After all, we are entitled only to carry on our work. There's no escape from it."

19

Glimpses of the Future (1999–2000)

AFTER THE people put off the kerosene lamps, allowing the fireflies to twinkle elegantly, the villages turn dumb and vague in the dark. The only sounds that can be heard even then are the drones of the cricket, the occasional call of the jackals, and intermittent rustling of palm and date leaves as the wind tries to penetrate them playfully.

"It's strange that in these months I have not asked you what happened in your life since that night," Karma says in a sad voice.

From the other part of the cot, Lillian mumbles, "Me too."

"Our life was all the same," he says. "I became close to Comrade Rambabu who belonged to the PRG. He wanted me to put pressure on our leaders to merge our group with the PRG, and I tried my best."

"And what about your top leader?" Lillian decides to continue the dialogue, for after months Karma is talking of all these things. It seems to Lillian that he has suddenly come out of the gloom that had enveloped him from the time he came to know that his days were numbered. She knows that a few months back, Karma's organization Unity group has merged into PRG.

"Comrade Raghupati?" Karma smiles. "I met him only once. But they have taken over and are carrying on the organization well. I was the first to be a witness to their training by an erstwhile Tiger. He taught us to lay mines…"

"You have made bombs?" Lillian asks without any interest.

"I know how to make it. Our common explosives are made of ammonium nitrate, potassium chlorate, sulphuric acid and sugar. All these one can buy from ordinary shops. For a mine... gelatine stick is better. A chemical timer can be used with any explosive. Basically, you can make it from fertiliser and fuel oil, or the mixture of nitro-benzene and salt..."

"Enough," Lillian intervenes suddenly. "No more about killing machines. But how your new general secretary displaced your old leader? Comrade Rajaramaiah was quite a name."

"Rambabu compelled all his units and the fraternal units like us to support Comrade Raghupati. His attitude was simple: either support us and get sophisticated arms and ammo, and, more crucially, training... or get lost. It worked. All of us were under attack. Think of Dharwal killings. The police killed our 36 unarmed comrades. We needed sophisticated arms to fight back the police, the landlords. So... apart from the earlier GS and Nagjyothi, and another CC member of their organization, all others supported Rambabu. Thereafter, Comrade Rajaramaiah was replaced."

"Everybody accepted him?" Lillian asks casually.

"Yes. I attended a meeting where Rambabu told us that they would be replacing Comrade GS with Comrade Raghupati. I remember that day vividly... 1992 autumn. I met Rambabu near Wani town in Maharashtra... they call it Black Diamond City... and as a pillion rider, I went with him across the Khuni River. We stopped at Kopamandav village for tea, and then crossed Penganga from whose bed sand was being taken in trucks. Then we entered Andhra and reached Adilabad. The motorbike turned left on Ashoka Road from the roundabout and went to MG Road, the busy bazaar with all sorts of shops. There were Sainath and his wife, Comrade Bindu, whom I earlier met near a pond behind a bus stand at Mulpalli in Gadchiroli. Then there were Comrade Rudra and Comrade Chhatre, both from Nepal. At that point, they belonged to two different groups. Now all of them have merged their units and have given the call of people's war in Nepal. Whatever, in that meeting Rambabu pleaded for providing shelter to some of his comrades and rued that his organization had no elaborate plans to send comrades elsewhere when at one region they were under attack. Rambabu understands military strategy. Comrade Bindu agreed to shelter them. All of us agreed with Rambabu that Comrade GS should be removed, though actually only the party congress could remove him and not the CC. But who cares! The only condition was they should not denigrate Comrade Rajaramaiah publicly, in any of their mouthpieces or booklets."

Lillian is interested to know about Nepal where Karma went before falling ill, but she does not dare to raise that topic, fearing that Karma may then come up to the point of his illness. So she asks something different, "People say you are adopting different tactics now."

"Many things have changed. Now our guerrilla squads move out of danger zones to other states and we have elaborate plans about that. We have identified new areas where we should enter. Comrade Rambabu feels we should study the socio-economic conditions of those new areas and then prepare plans. And …"

"You do that?" Lillian asks, this time really inquisitive.

"We are planning to do it. Many bright young boys are likely to join us. They can survey an area and give us detailed reports. Another thing is… we now ask people to be involved with other organizations, political parties or social organizations, and to carry on the main tasks secretly. There are new plans about military strategy also. We will work silently till we reach a position when we can give a call for people's war. We are not averse to make truce with anyone. We discussed all these. Just after that I fell ill."

"You have been to Bastar many times. It has dense jungles?"

"Only at a few places."

"Tell me of such other journeys," Lillian tries to keep him on.

"Once I went to Warangal where a meeting with Comrade Krishna Raju… he was killed in an encounter later… was scheduled. But he was not in Warangal. From there, I was asked to board a train that took me to Vijaywada. Then a comrade guided me to another train and asked me to get down when it would reach Narayanapuram. There someone was waiting for me. After stepping down from the platform, we crossed the road and a canal flowing parallel to it. Then we ambled down a lane that turned left just a while later. My guide asked me to wait outside a double-storey house with a whitewashed wall, and he went inside, only to come out a minute later with a motorbike. Then we hit the highway again and started moving to the same direction as was the train. Afterwards, we diverted from the highway, and in Tadepalligudam, we came across a procession with goddess Durga. You know, they worship Durga from the day of Dusshera, just opposite of what is done in Bengal and Bihar where Dusshera is the last day... and in the procession there were jokers, Kali, Shiva, Ravana, people on stilt with various masks, and in that crowd was Comrade Krishna. Imagine!"

"Why was he in a religious procession?" Lillian asks with a small frown.

"That was the place where he used to take shelter. There no one knew he was a Maoist."

"You people travel so much and have seen so much," Lillian sounds involved, and less careful. "You told me just before getting ill you had gone to Ayodhya hills."

"Yes. With Comrade Rudra, who took me to Nepal. I went on the full-moon night of Buddha anniversary for a hunting festival. The Santhals call it *disum sendra*. I bathed in Bamni waterfall with the comrades, drank the water of Sita Kund and ran with them to hunt in the jungles. Comrade Sanju Tudu held my hand tightly and supported me through the unknown land in the dark. Though our team could hunt only a tortoise, no deer or boar, they were jubilant and after roasting the hunt, we ate it after midnight."

"You are so lucky, you have seen so much," Lillian says.

"I think Comrade Mahendra saw much more... but then he lost his mind. So sad! He started saying... time answers all our questions and nothing happens before time."

"That's true," Lillian says seriously. "At every crossroad, life offers you different options. Only those who can read the time choose the right path."

"How?"

"It cannot be explained. For ages, people in this land have tried to do these things. Some have interpreted life by time, some by magic, some by something else. But I believe, these concepts represent eternal truths, and by showing respect to these concepts, you can advance much more, even beyond science. Man is not attached only to the material world, but also to spiritual world. Western philosophy and science cannot reach there."

A frog croaks from within the room, but neither of the two shows any concern. They will be alarmed if only a snake or a scorpion is found. They sit silently for a while, and then Karma says, "Tell me what happened to you."

She comes up with words a while later, "All that I told you a while back were at the back of my mind even then. I was sure that by running a school the way we were running it, we could not provide real education to those tribal or Harijan boys and girls. But the authority was not bothered. The Fathers were pressuring me to try to convert the tribals. I felt that was wrong. By making the tribesmen Christian or Hindu, we will kill their culture. As in the wildlife, we try to protect the endangered species; so in human life, we have to protect every faith, every way of life, or else we will lose our root and our diverse ways to attain divinity. And the time was turbulent too. You remember I once told you that I didn't believe Lal Krishna Advani was playing with fire stoked by the temple movement only to get to power."

"You disagreed that day when I said he might arrange riots to come to power," Karma smiles. "Now you see, he has come to power and has forgotten those Mandir and Hindu issues."

"Yes. Even then, you gave me the example of Jinnah, and you said often politicians play with the lives of the people to come to power." Lillian speaks in a serious tone. "But I was not prepared to play the church's game. I was not prepared to convert anyone. I pretended that I was trying. I called the villagers every Sunday in the afternoon and told them stories about *Joshua Baba*. I knew they used to come to have the snacks and… also enjoyed the stories like one in which Jesus turned water into wine. They wished all water could turn into wine." Lillian laughs and Karma joins him.

"Then Michael, that cook who thought I would be able to stop the advancement of the mines, one day came to me to tell me that he was leaving," Lillian again turns sombre. "Mines had come up to Barhi, and his village was served a notice of eviction, and he blamed me for doing nothing for him. I was so puzzled. I did not know in those days what could I do. I did not know that people's resistance could be organized. I was a mere slave of the Church. Then we went to see him…"

"And that night," Karma heaves a sigh.

"Yes."

That evening, while coming back after visiting ailing Michael, they were chased by a few men who did not belong to the locality, and Karma dragged Lillian inside the jungle, fearing that the rogues' target was her body. They managed to escape, but were lost in the jungle. Then a heavy downpour drenched them. Fortunately, they found a deserted cottage, and after being sure that it did not belong to snakes and scorpions, they entered it. Then slowly, furtively, the dark night spread its spell and engaged the two, a Maoist and a nun, who had been attracted to each other even before, but had suppressed the tender feelings assuming those were improper and indecent.

"You have suffered a lot for me," Karma mutters repentantly. "You became pregnant…"

"That gave me the strength to leave the church," Lillian continued with her story as she remembered a bright morning.

On that morning, a midwife examined her sitting beside the river Rombi with her instrument of experience, and then said, "You have a seed inside your belly. Hail thee … you be a mother. You are blessed."

The tribal woman did not bother to ask her who the father was. It did not matter to her ,who believed a mother and a child made a full circle. A tribal midwife whose root was not yet severed from Mother Earth was not polluted enough to question the legitimacy of a seed, of a life, which was the most tangible and most valuable gift of Sing Bonga, the supreme God.

Amazed by her indifference, Lillian asked the midwife whether she was not inquisitive about the father.

The midwife looked at her face for a while, and then said softly, "Look there, you see the jack fruit growing up… bigger and bigger it will grow… water and light will nurture it. It was a seed—a seed of that tree. That tree is the mother. But where from the pollen came? Who knows?… The tree will not be able to answer. She would say air delivered it to her. It came in the mild breeze in the autumn."

As she listened to the rustic uneducated woman, she realized that the magic of life had also drawn her into the eternal flow of life that started from an amoeba and down millions and millions of years was still blooming every day and every night. As she looked about her, she could hear a new message in the rustling of the leaves, in the hum of the bees, in the babble of the River Rombi: Hail thee mother!

Lillian's voice chokes as she recounts that day, and Karma spreads his hand, his wavering hand, to place it on Lillian's palm. They sit quietly in the dark and listen to the calls of various nocturnal creatures who have replaced the creatures of the day, as though to show there cannot be any void in this universe. After quite a while, Karma asks Lillian, "That girl was talking of a new millennium. What is that?"

"They say today is the last day of the second thousand years of the Christian calendar. Tomorrow will be the first day of the third millennium. First January, 2000. But actually it is not so. The first millennium did not end in 999, but in 1000. The last day of the millennium is still a year away, though the world is celebrating the day a year earlier."

"Why?"

"People say that it is the effect of consumerism. The church aids the market economy. And you Hindus have forgotten your traditions. I am talking of those in the cities. They are now celebrating Valentine's Day, which was earlier limited to the Christian world. This, in fact, helps the Hindu fundamentalist organizations."

"All these will happen now," Karma says gravely. "I am not for any religion. It is the opium of the masses. As the opium makes a man forget his pain, so religions distract man from the real causes of their miseries. You won't agree, I know. But even you left the Church."

"That's because they are fraud," Lillian avers. "In the name of education, they were planning conversions. And I told you... seeds of love gave me the strength. Whatever, that girl Nidhi will come again. While leaving, she asked me about our relation and when I told her that I am your wife, she seemed amazed. She thinks a Maoist and a nun make a better story. They all are like that... frivolous."

After a while, Karma makes an effort to say 'I really love you', but what he actually says is something different, "If we had not met accidentally two years back, we would have never met again."

"That was again according to the laws of magic."

"Must be. But you didn't tell me even then that we had a son."

"I told you that I believed you were my husband."

"That's why I came to you when I fell ill. And only then you told me... about our son," whispers Karma.

After a long silence, Lillian asks, "Do you want to see your son?"

Karma thinks for quite a while and shakes his head slowly, "No, don't create disturbances in his life. When the Comrade who had raised Comrade Mahendra's son after his wife was killed by us came to Father Lal and wanted to know whether he would reveal to his son that he is only the foster father... the Father advised him not to do so. Because it would disturb the boy who would never find his real father."

Lillian heaves a sigh, "Maybe you are right. Our son knows Agnes as her mother and Ajith as his father."

Karma does not utter a single word, but sits silently, allowing the night to unfold its charm and to encompass two human beings sitting together.

A while later, Lillian says, "At one point of time, I believed every male person is a dog. But then how everything changed. That's magic."

"But why is there so much injustice?" Karma asks immediately, probably relating to some thought of his mind. "What does your God do about it?"

"God created human beings," she repeats the answer she has given to many in the past. "He gave us immense potential to be good and just. He filled our hearts with love. But we have disobeyed him. He can't be blamed for that. He has not failed us; we have failed Him."

"How will things change then?" he asks a while later.

"How things will change?" Lillian takes time, hears the frog croaking again, and decides not to repeat the customary answer, "I don't know. I don't know whether man will ever again turn into the man God wanted to create. But being human beings, our only task is to make endeavours to attain divinity."

"At times, I feel all these had not happened," Karma sighs. "Had I been born in a society where a few people did not deprive many others, my life would have been different. Then I need not have fought all through my life. How different, how beautiful it would have been then. We could live together, our son, you and I."

She feels Karma is losing faith in life and decides to intervene, taking recourse to her old thoughts, for she has not found any alternative to those. "For the betterment of the whole mankind always a few will have to fight. Jesus laid down his life. Gandhi did so. There will always be good and evil and a few will have to fight for others… to defeat the evil forces."

He sits silently for a while and then says, "That's why Comrade Mahendra used to say that we should carry on our work without expectation. Probably, like you, he too knew that this fight would continue for ever."

A lightening cuts across the higher altitudes and Karma looks through the window, waiting anxiously for the rumble to reach his ears, but it never comes. A while later, Karma opens up his heart: "It's true… this world is ruled by magic. I had a comrade, a young boy. When I last met him, he told me that he would come back to me after a couple of days. That night, in the jungle shelter, a snake bit him. They ran out of anti-venom injection and he died."

Lillian nods, and mumbles, "No one knows what God desires."

Thereafter, they sit together silently, communicating to each other without uttering a word, as they have done many times in last few months, and have learnt through their experience that message of love is independent of words.

20

The Present Continuous (1993–94)...

WHEN HE reaches village Domri, Mahendra finds a pall of gloom has covered the locals only because a centuries-old banyan tree at the centre of the village is dying. Legend had it that once the tree was pulled down by the mighty Son when it had inundated the area, but within 72 hours, it stood up again, all by itself. That was a miracle, the people were sure, and devotees thronged about the 'divine' tree to offer puja, after which huge crops bequeathed fortune thereto unknown to the locals. Since then, for many decades, devotees had come to the village, Hindus and Muslims alike. While the Hindus offered puja to a blackish stone considered as *Shivalinga* on one side of the huge cluster of trunks of the ancient tree, the Muslims tied threads after offering prayers to the adjacent *idgah*.

Mahendra does not have any great feeling for a tree, but Ramjatan Ojha, who looks after the place, has. He is on fast since the day he realized the ancient tree is dying. "If the tree dies, all our prosperity will be lost again," he says, breaking in tears.

"That tree is not dying," Mahendra says emphatically and clacks his tongue. "It is committing suicide."

"What?" the locals cringe in shock.

"For the gods, all human beings are their children," Mahendra says thoughtfully. "Hindus, Muslims, Christians—everyone. But for all these years, we have seen innumerable riots in our land. And now, the whole country is trapped in hate. You believe there was a temple. Ram was born at that very spot where the mosque is. Who had seen it? And the Muslims believe a mosque cannot be given up. That would be sacrilege."

Mahendra does not know how he says all these, nor does he understand how he is repeating something he has read in newspapers in recent times, for he never felt concerned when he read those.

"Then what we will do?" the locals seem baffled.

"Ensure that in this area no one has any ill-will towards the other community. The ultimate truth of life is love. Practise that here and let us see whether the tree survives." Mahendra stops, and then adds something that he himself does not understand well, "The trees are embodiment of love, and truth. Always remember that."

The villagers agree at once, but Mahendra does not wait to see the outcome. He leaves for some unknown destination within a few days, and moves on towards the east with a man called Hafiz, who has discovered in him the power of foretelling the future. He is not rich, but has enough money with him to feed both of them, and so Mahendra does not have to ask anyone for food or shelter, and after a very long time, he travels by a train! A fortnight later, they settle at a small town called Tundi in Dhanbad district. Hafiz has a friend there, Abdul, living in a small house near the police station. Abdul gladly asks the duo, one his friend and Muslim, the other unknown and Hindu, to stay as long as they wish to.

A week later, Mahendra has another fit of amnesia that curiously cures him of the buzz inside his head!

Days pass by, and without knowing what to do, Mahendra moves about the small township called Tundi in small steps, and when overcome by lassitude, he sits on the balcony of a house or just outside the precinct of the police station. One day, a man comes to meet him, and claiming a long acquaintance seeks answer of a bizarre question: "Why did you save the IG from the mines?"

Mahendra fails to recognize him, fails to remember any IG, and though the man seems disheartened—he says that leaders will expel a legendary comrade if no explanation can be put forward—Mahendra sends him back. With mist pervading his head, he cannot think properly, but he remembers one thing very clear—he should strive to see through the stones. So, one day he tells Abdul and Hafiz that he is leaving them, and sets out in yet another effort to see through the stones.

He starts his journey again and a few months later he reaches another place that seems to be a known locality, a village where he might have lived some time though he does not recollect when. He approaches the place, wondering whether it is his native village, which often appears in his dreams and as he sees a man sitting beside a pond, he asks him, "What is the name of the village?"

The man looks at him, and does not find it interesting to talk to the bearded tall dark man with tangled hair. "Puraina," he says reluctantly, and turns his head towards the pond again.

"Puraina?" Mahendra mutters, as the name hits a chord in his heart and starts resonating. Puraina… Puraina… Puraina.

In his mind's eyes, he sees an iron gate… someone throwing a stone at the gate and the clank… Puraina! And then a stream of memory resurfaces; it brings him back to the day when he arrived at this place after a sojourn in distant lands and met Munni, and again left promising her that he would come back and marry her…

He looks about and as he feels giddy, he clutches the branch of a tree just by his side, wondering how it is that the gate of his memory is reopening, allowing him to see from Puraina where Munni was raped and killed, to Kalipura. He sits down under the tree as he remembers his daughter Chini who was lost, and looks at the skies which has turned soft blue just after the sunset. "Even if there is God, He must be a very cruel entity," he tells himself. "Otherwise He wouldn't have given me back the memory of Chini." He turns angry and shouts like an imbecile violent man, "Hey God, if you want to fight me, appear before me. Don't fight like a coward, you tormentor."

Soon after, he winds his way back, away from the village.

ASHOK SHARMA, the Romantic Cobra, sighs, "I don't understand what is happening. First, the DSP saved me. Otherwise, I would have been there in the sky so long ago. But that was understandable. What about this Mahendra Chamar? Why he rang me up to say that Naxalites are laying mines for me? Why? And it was true. Our men detected two Claymore mines while the third was blasted by the Naxalites, through a remote control device, hurting two of the minesweepers."

His wife, Dr Rani, smiles and her white teeth shine, though her emaciated appearance and the dark circles about her eyes show that she is in poor health. "I know why," she says almost apologetically. Getting up from the chair, she goes closer to her husband to sit on a cane chair beside him.

As the Romantic Cobra, who has not written a single poem in last five years, looks on at her in shock, she starts revealing an untold story that started with Badal, her cousin, and ended with how she concealed facts from the police. Then, as an anecdote, she mentions about Comrade Mahendra's visit to the centre. "I don't believe in their ideology," she says with great satisfaction, "but how can I claim that I do not believe in basic qualities of a warrior who is fighting for a cause? That is why I failed to report it that he was out of semi-comatose. That is why I failed to report that he came here. This visit was, however, not important. He is now just a shrunken shadow of his past. He forgets everything. He has a clot in his brain. It will kill him. But 10 years ago, I really cheated you, and that was why I decided to open this hospital to atone for that crime against you."

"Wait a minute," Ashok Sharma stops her. "Why do you think it was a crime against me?"

"Because I did not tell you."

"So what?" the Romantic Cobra seems perplexed.

"Because you are a police officer who was …I mean concerned officer."

"So what! If what you have done is according to your conscience, then it is no crime. At least, no crime against me."

Rani's eyes sparkle from within the dark circles about them. "You think so?" she asks and adds, "In fact, I sought solace precisely in this argument. But I lost my mental peace. Then I met the Maharaj who was with Ramkrishna Mission. He did not want to know what my problem was. He just said, repentance dilutes the crime, but even after that if one wants to do penance, one can devote oneself to the service of mankind, in any form. And then I decided to take up a full-time service."

With a very big grey area as to why she left everything to work in a remote area away from everyone being cleared, the cop mutters, "It was, might be, a crime against the state, but..."

"I don't care," Rani utters forcefully, and as her husband stares at her, she adds, "The state cannot change my conviction that I did the right thing by not disclosing the fact, by not betraying my elder brother."

The two sit quietly for sometime, and then, Ashok wonders aloud: "Anyway, it was no crime against me. I am not the state, and I don't know whether I would have done something different had I been in your place. You acted against the state. But... even that is vague. Had it been so that the Naxalites could manage to come to power, they would have rewarded you. Basically, you acted against the government. Sometimes we also act against a government, against a government in a state under instruction from the central government or even against the wishes of the central government. Ultimately the state, the government or intelligence agencies, everything is run by a few people, and in this country, most of them are corrupt men and women. But you have atoned for a crime that you didn't even commit."

Silence reigns over the room, barring the flapping of wings by a few pigeons, who live the whole life, eat, make love and sleep, on a tiny ledge above the windows.

After a long pause, Ashok tries to cajole her, "Now that your husband is out of danger... and you are not well... leave this place and come along with me. We will see good doctors."

Rani smiles again, "Now it's a different story that shows atonement is independent of crime! Now I can't leave this place. Let me die here. Now I will be able to die in peace."

"Why are you talking of death?" the Romantic Cobra feels unnerved.

"Because I see it coming," Rani confesses in a way as though it is nothing serious. "As a doctor I know, I will live maximum a couple of years. This is July 92. Maybe to '94, or perhaps '95. I have got a resistant variety of TB."

"No!" Sharma cringes. "I don't believe it."

Rani smiles sadly, but does not say anything, and as the pigeons too fall silent, the vacuum gets filled up by the clock that ticks like a time bomb, a dissonant note that distracts one from the concepts of life, death or even time itself. After quite a while, Rani gets up, walks slowly towards the wooden chair placed before a typewriter, and hears Ashok asking, "Had it been known that I wouldn't be upset about not being told the truth, you wouldn't have opened this place?"

Rani sits on the wooden chair and smiles wryly before answering, "Maybe not." She takes out the paper from the clutch of the typewriter and looking at it says again, "But if you ask me whether I regret now… I don't. In these years, we have saved at least 700–800 patients; 800 human beings who would have otherwise died. On an average, a hundred patients in a year. So many others are under treatment. I have written to the government, along with other NGOs and doctors, that the grave danger is the dropout factor. They are now contemplating a scheme called 'directly observed therapy, short course' or DOTS that may come into force soon. I have introduced it here. Basically, we administer drugs to the patients here, before our eyes. Otherwise, they make a mess. So… I wouldn't regret the decision, though it is true that I have ruined your life."

"I wouldn't regret it either," Ashok says. "But maybe we have not done justice to our daughter."

Rani says, her eyes still on the typewriter, "She has joined medical course and wants to serve in this centre. It shows we have not lost out. But…"

Ashok walks up to her and asks, keeping his hand on her shoulder, "But what?"

"I may not see the day when she will become a doctor," She says in a grim voice and adds, "But I will make a request that will show how cruel I am."

"What's that?"

"After me, you take charge of this centre."

Ashok moves away and stands at the door from where he can see the whole compound, the nearby 'nursing centre' where 'outdoor' patients are attended and, at a distance, the hospital, where extremely bad cases are admitted. "But I am not a doctor," he wonders aloud.

"What we need is a good administrator," Rani rings out from behind.

"If it is so, I can join now," Ashok says emphatically.

Rani turns her head to look at him with incredulity in her eyes, and then says, "You may join us after a year. That way you can take over in a smooth way while I am alive."

"Surely I'll," Ashok Sharma nods. "But before that I will take you to Delhi, to AIIMS. I don't believe that there is no treatment."

"You are challenging me!" Rani smiles the most bizarre smile anyone can conceive of. "Don't forget I am the last word on TB. This is a rare type and medicines can support me for that much time… just a couple of years."

WHEN HARRY meets Bisheshswar Singh, an almost-old man who wants to fight for changing Hindu society, he remains unsure about the man's consideration for leading a private army. Some agree to work for money, some for women, some for fame, he knows and waits for the man to open up.

"We have to raise an army, like the regular army where I have spent many years, and there should be strict discipline," the man with heavy and translucent glasses says arrogantly. "The first thing we have to ensure is that no upper caste man should ever have physical relation with the Untouchables and other low caste women. It is only because of such transfer of seeds from the upper caste males to the low-born women, that we have created this problem of rebellion."

"Do you think so?" Harry asks nervously while wondering why he is raising this upper caste army to fight the Naxalites. He has failed to lay his hands on Mahendra Chamar, true; the Naxalites are killing people belonging to the upper castes, true: but does that mean he has to take lead in wiping them off? He does not think so. But every incident of such mass killings rekindles his memory of five bodies wrapped in white sheets and five pyres burning side by side. That has brought him here today to choose the supreme commander of a united upper caste army.

"It's not me Sahib, it was laid down by our ancestors, the sages," the other man answers grimly. "Precisely for this reason they prohibited marriages among the castes. But now upper caste men do *Gandharva* marriage with the lowly women. …"

"What is that?"

"Sleeping with them to satiate the sudden surge of physical need."

Harry thinks of the woman kept by his uncle, with whom he too had slept once and tries to imagine what caste she belongs to.

"Some low-born people are becoming rebellious because they are grown from the seeds of the highborn," the other man explains. "This will destroy our society, which was preserved for 7,000 years."

"7,000!" Harry sounds surprised.

"Yes, the Aryan civilization in India."

"Seven or five? Some even say three."

"The western world always tries to denigrate us," Bisheshswar avers. "They don't have a living ancient civilization surviving and thriving to date with its social and religious structures intact. Not anywhere in the world. They cannot even imagine it. They tried to destroy us by imposing English on us, by banning Sati, encouraging widow remarriage and allowing divorce."

Harry ponders whether he should nod, but he takes so long to decide that his reaction becomes meaningless. Bisheshswar has, by then, gone much beyond the old topic, "Every action has an equal and opposite reaction. The time has come to retaliate and restore our caste system to its old glory."

"But," Harry decides to vent his scepticism, "the government says caste considerations are banned. How would you advance them?"

"Government! Hooh!" Bisheshwar Singh pours out a sound that may be interpreted as strong disagreement, or even contempt. "Our first Prime Minister Nehru was a sahib... more western than oriental. Since then, the same tradition is carried forward. Family control is against the wishes of God. Ask any Muslim. They shudder at it. Ask any pious Hindu. Ask the Christians, the Catholics, and see their reactions on divorce, or on abortion. But our leaders have decided to be modern, even by destroying our civilization."

Harry does not utter a word, for he has understood that the man whom he confronts is highly knowledgeable and dangerously obstinate; he tries to think about his Calcutta days where he saw those Jan Sangh supporters and heard their discussions from the adjacent room. He wonders whether, like them, this man is also a Muslim-hater, and he asks. "Do you think Muslims are also destroying our society?"

At this, the man looks for a few seconds from behind his heavy lenses, and then spews out a sound that Harry again fails to interpret. "They are a different religion and have right to live with dignity," says Bisheshswar.

"But they say our lower castes have adopted that religion."

"So what? They have gone out of our fold and communalism is a heinous crime against humanity."

"Then why not casteism?" suddenly Harry feels argumentative.

"Of course casteism is equally bad," Bisheshswar sighs and adds, "one has to understand that casteism means efforts to change the social equilibrium by using the caste sentiment. It's same in case of communalism. Communalism means efforts to change social equilibrium by using communal feeling. Both are equally bad."

Harry takes almost a minute to realize that according to this man what the Naxalites, or to some extent the Socialists, try to achieve is casteism; and then it comes to his mind that Socialists and their offshoots are dubbed 'casteist' by everyone, even by the media. "I think you are right," Harry says after realizing the thesis, "though I felt whoever thought in caste term was a casteist."

"This country revolves about the caste system and the day that structure is diluted, the country will be in great danger," the old man says audaciously. "The middle class is the victim of detachment from reality. They say reservation should go because it is meaningless. It should be based on merit. Wrong. There should be bar on lower castes. They should not get any intellectual job. Because… it is known for thousands of years… that only upper castes have merit. Others are lesser human beings. Brahmins should be the first priority of the government and then Thakurs and Bhumihars and Kayasthas and so on."

Harry is amazed by the man's philosophy. He appreciates it as he has a penchant for shocking views. But he wants to be sure that the man is not lunatic, and asks, "How do you prove that the lower caste men are inferior?"

"Silly question," the man sounds annoyed. "I don't have to tell you that Ramchandra, the god, killed Shambuka, the low caste man, for he violated the societal norm and learned scriptures. But I can tell you that there were another group of human beings, in the ancient times, who were called Neanderthals. They were lesser human beings and were exterminated by our ancestors. In the same way, the lower castes are lesser human beings. If scientists study their genes, it will be evident."

Harry nods uncertainly, and to conclude the discussion comes to the point: "What will be your consideration? How much money?"

"I heard many leaders are with you... Congress... BJP. Good. But are you the person who will look after money?" Bisheshswar asks plainly and, as Harry nods, says, "You have to take care of the entire army and provide for everything. Remember, it will be named Ranjoy Sena after the great warrior Ranjoy Singh, and it will not be just a conglomeration of various landlords' armies. It will be an independent army to finish off the army of the devils."

"And how much money for yourself?" Harry asks again.

"I need a *dhoti* every year, and a blanket every five years. Apart from that my food... two chapattis in the morning and two at night... any vegetable and a litre of milk."

Harry wonders what the man is talking about, but before he can decipher anything, the man adds, "And yes. If this spectacle is broken, you have to provide money to repair it."

Amazed, Harry just manages to utter: "And the cost of your treatment."

"I have no illness," the man says boldly, and adds, "Except that I want to fight the blight."

Harry is happy to find this man and decides to tell his friends—some landlords, a few politicians and some police officers—that the grand army to take on the Naxalites is in safe hands.

Stephen wanders like a mad man, his hair ruffled and eyes sad.

Shyamlal, once considered his shadow, has left him; and before that, he spat at him. "You are a crooked man, a corrupt man," Shyamlal thundered. "Once you told me that all through your life you were searching for a hill shaped like a bird. You said you have dedicated your life to this cause as you felt these were interlinked, finding the hill and... creation of Jharkhand. Hohh! All bluff. Liar. Actually, you were hoodwinking us by fabricating stories about nonexistent things. Essentially, you were after money. A corrupt bugger. Chiih!" He spat on the ground and, like a possessed man, shouted, "You are worse than a jackal, than a bore. You swine. All the tribesmen like me will only loathe you and your leaders. I am leaving you to join the Maoists."

Then he spat aiming at his body, turned back and went away.

Stephen could not utter a word, for his tongue was stuck in disgrace. Since that day, his conscience is lashing him like he is the grimiest mongrel. He was not hurt so much because Shyamlal called him a corrupt bugger, for it was true. While handing lakhs of rupees coming for election campaign, like all other middle level leaders he always kept aside ten per cent for him. It is also widely known that even top leaders including Babaji had taken money to vote for the government in the Parliament. Essentially, he was hurt for Shyamlal had thought that the hill shaped like a bird's head was a fabrication. What a disgrace for him and his forefathers! He decided to find out the hill first, and then show it to all to prove that his forefathers had not lied. And so, he set out to find the hill. And after ten days of blind wandering, he came across a man who too had heard about a hill shaped like a bird. "But," the man said, "That hill... is..."

"Is what?" Stephen asked impatiently.

"Is the hill of the *bongas*," the man's voice cracked in awe.

"Where is it? Tell me."

As the man described the route, Stephen got up and prepared to leave.

"Don't go there," the man cautioned him. "It's very remote and in a deadly zone. Surrounded by strange hills and jungles. Nobody goes there. And, if anyone climbs the hill he too becomes a god and never comes back."

Stephen looked back for the last time, and left.

Now, after another couple of days, he is still wandering like a mad man, passing through an uninhabited zone at a time when the shadows are still tall in the west. Tirelessly he walks on, mostly through the feet of the hills, stopping at times only to ascertain whether he is on right track.

Another couple of hours later, he stops as he realizes that his endeavour has got him to a place where on all sides there are hills like eagle's bald heads and jungles of dwarf trees and plants. The place looks strange and deadly. There is not even a single tall tree and the tallest ones are only a little taller than him. The earth is blackish, as though the red soil Chhotonagpur plateau has been covered by coal dust. There is hardly any bird, barely any animal except lizards and chameleons. Almost no rustling of the leaves. No babble of any stream. It is like a land of the dead. He climbs up a hill that has a smooth slope, and looks about. While the deafening silence of the surroundings unnerves his weary soul, he gets a severe jerk as he turns to the north-west. Just a kilometre away, beyond a gorge, stands a hill that has an awkward shape at the top resembling a bird's neck, while a huge slab on it may be in interpreted as the crest. He comes down and though his energy is at the ebb, he runs towards the left to get a better view of the whole of the hill, to ascertain whether the hill is really like a bird's head.

A while later, he reaches a spot from where it is evident that the hill is shaped like a bird's head!

He again runs, this time towards the hill, though he does not know why.

As he reaches closer to the hill, his soul starts undergoing a change. When he reaches at its foot and starts climbing it, he gradually feels calmed by the presence of a ubiquitous spirit all about him. Higher up, he loses all attachment to his life. He sheds all his worries. He bears no malice towards anyone, and strangely, no love for anything that he possesses. He mind turns vacuous, and eerily calm, as though all his senses have gone numb. What remains in him is a bizarre unreal attraction for the top of the hill, as though he is in a strong magnetic field and the pick is the magnet.

He climbs on with the sun above his head. Twice he slips, thrice he stumbles his feet against the edges of the rocks, but nothing deters him from getting higher and higher. He has no feeling of hunger or thirst, has no organic reaction like pain, strain or breathlessness, like he has turned into a soul without a body. He has no purpose, no desire. No fear either.

Another couple of hours later, he stands on the neck of the bird, on which stands a very big slab of stone: the crest of the bird.

He starts climbing the slab, the walls of which are almost plain and straight, almost impossible to even clamber; but it is so very strange, the slab seemingly holds him tightly so that he does not fall. He goes up like a lizard, as though he also has thumb-pads, and ends his journey by reaching the topmost point of the hill.

He lies down on the top—a soft, blackish mould-bed—exhausted and deranged, and in his head a question emerges that he does not understand: 'How do I save my creation?' He ponders deeply over the question, but when the sun sets and from the east dark clouds start moving in, he falls asleep.

Within an hour, the dark clouds cover the whole of the sky surreptitiously, like they have come with a message that can be delivered only in darkness. As the clouds rumble, Stephen hears the sounds of drums and opens his eyes to see hundreds of men at the foot of the hill, clad strangely, spears in their hands, praying to him. He asks them: "What do you want?"

"We are coming from the west, Great Bonga, and we do not know, please tell us, should we proceed?"

"Why have you left the place where you were?"

"Outsiders came and defeated us."

"Who are the outsiders?"

"They are strange people, fair and tall, and many in number. They chant mantras, clear the jungles, make villages in the plain land and worship the fire in which they pour ghee. For hundreds of years, they lived in villages and we in the jungles. But now they are advancing, cutting off jungles and pushing us further back."

Stephen thinks for a while and mutters, "The Aryans! Well, who are you?"

"Munda tribesmen."

"Well, you proceed to the east, though misfortune waits for you there too. You will become slaves of the machines and mines."

He again slips into a sombre sleep, and again he is disturbed by the sound of *dhamsa*. He looks below and sees another group of tribal population. "Who are you?" he asks.

"Bhils," they cry.

"Why have you come here?"

"Oh, great god, save us, or we will be finished."

"Why?"

"Outsiders have taken over our land and we are threatened by them."

He thinks for a while, and then thunders: "That is your destiny. You will even forget your language. You will have no identity. But, you will survive like that for many centuries to come."

"Should we proceed to the east?"

"No, go back to the west."

They go back with heavy hearts. But, after a while he again hears a babble. "We are Chero tribesmen, and we seek your permission to stay here," the men below tell him and offer sacrifices. "Should we will call our land Palamou?" they ask in folded hands.

"Yes, and be here till you are struck by destitution and oppression."

After sometime, again some people wake him up with their shouts and cries. "Who are you?" he asks again.

"Great Bonga, we are the Santhals. Save us. Earlier we were tortured by the fair people of the land. Now fairer people have arrived."

He thinks for a while and mutters, "Yes. The Englishmen."

"Should we proceed farther west?"

"No use. Go back to the east. You will survive as labourers in the tea gardens and serve the landlords. You will be in a wretched condition."

As they go back, he smiles: "All of them will become rebellious… they will fight the Englishmen as well as other older *dikus*. Their rebellions will be crushed and they will live in this land where people will not believe that a hill shaped like a bird's head ever existed. They will be evicted, killed, left to die by the outsiders ruling over this land. And then, there will be no hill shaped like a birds head…"

After a while, Stephen really wakes up. He hears deafening sounds of thunders, but remains unperturbed. He sees blinding lights coming down from the skies, but he does not feel scared. Soon the rain starts sweeping the valley and pounce upon him with all its might; but it has no effect on him. He lies prostrate, waiting patiently for the last, for he knows he will never be able to save his creation. He does not want to descend from the hill either, for he knows the world below is a grimy place.

He waits patiently for a long time, and then a thunder hits the top of the hill shaped like a bird's head, as though to pay tribute to the god lying on it.

Under the tremendous impact of the thunder, the crest at the top that has soaked in the impact of many such thunders through millions of years suddenly cracks and starts rolling down. It splits into several large chunks, all of which roll down towards all the sides, get divided into further chunks, thereafter are broken into smaller and smaller chunks till they reach the ground below.

HE WALKS on with a question in his mind, "Where should I go?"

In the last few years, he had covered many hundred kilometres, often east to west and then again to east and again to west, but that was entirely different journey for his brain was dying then. Now that his brain has recovered suddenly, the burden of memory not only hurts him, but brings to the fore questions. He was daring and somewhat content when he had no memory, but now he is worried and sad. Suddenly, he remembers Kalipura. He remembers his comrades told him that the hamlet had turned desolate with abandoned huts in ruins and wild shrubs growing everywhere. Still, he decides to go to that place as his mind tells him that to see through the stones he must go there for one last time.

A week later, guided by his clairvoyance, he does reach there: he approaches the desolate hamlet at the dusk and moves forward slowly, with his eyes fixed on the slightly uphill path and his heart throbbing in unknown expectation. When he reaches the spot from where he used to look towards the horizon, he understands a storm is brewing, as he smells dust particles in the air. Then he smells burnt coal, something that is not expected unless an earthen oven is lit, and he realizes that it is coming from the left to where the hamlet called Kalipura was situated.

He dodders up to that place to come across a few huts, not very old, and one burning earthen oven. He walks up to the nearest hut, and finds a lanky woman looking intensely at him. Seconds later, she lights a match and makes fire out of some dry leaves about her to see the stranger better.

"Are you... aren't you... who are you?" she asks.

For a moment, Mahendra feels giddy; but his sensory organs have sent him signals that prompt him to ask, "Are you Bijuriya?"

"Yes, but..." she cannot complete her sentence.

"I am Mahendra."

She looks on at him dumbly and after a while asks, "*Comret* Mahendra! Are you sure you are not a ghost?"

"Ghost!" he wonders for a while. "I am not sure. But not a Comrade anymore. Maybe... a ghost... that is what I am."

She almost shouts, "Don't rib me. Tell the truth."

He sits next to her on the veranda of the hut, and asks for water.

Handing him an aluminium jug, she mutters, "We knew you were dead. Where were you so long?"

Mahendra tries to recollect where he was, but he finds he can remember only those days when his memory was not eclipsed; the rest has turned into a bundle of clouds. Just then the storm hits the hamlet and as Bijuriya shouts a warning, someone rushes to take the oven inside. She throws water on the smouldering leaves and, while taking Mahendra inside by holding his arm, says, "We are five families here and we light up only one oven and share whatever is cooked."

"But," Mahendra mutters, "I heard you all left Kalipura..." He stops without finishing the sentence and then adds, "I destroyed your lives."

"No," Bijuriya answers confidently. "It happened because we didn't leave the village even after the bamboo trees had flowered."

He tries to remember hard and then mutters, "Yes."

"But, you *comrets* are very cruel," she says suddenly.

"Why?"

"You ordered them to kill your wife; but she was innocent."

"My wife!" he tries to understand the meaning of the word.

"Have you forgotten your wife?" she asks.

Mahendra realizes Bijuriya is referring to his second wife: "I didn't order anyone to kill her. But how was she innocent? They killed her because she eloped with the traitor, Bhola."

"No," she retorts. "Why don't you try to know every side of it before you reach a conclusion?" Bijuriya sounds acerbic. "She did not elope with anyone. That foxy guy told her that you were dead and the police was after her. She believed him because he was associated with you. He took her along with him and then kept her forcibly... threatened her that her son would be killed if she tried to run away. From her I heard that you were dead."

"You knew my wife?" Mahendra is trying hard to collate the facts.

"No," Bijuriya seems overcome with emotion. "I saw Bhola. I saw him and wondered who the woman was with him. Then I came to know everything."

A thunder hits a nearby tree, and after the blinding heavenly light comes a resonant metallic sound that continues for quite a while, like millions of glass jars being broken. But Bijuriya does not shudder, not even flinches a bit, and just looks on at the outside, waiting for the sound to die. She has amassed so much courage in last few years when the world had pounced upon her that nothing mundane can make her shudder any more.

"She planned to come with us when I met her," she says after a while as the world becomes quiet again except for the sound of rain. "But before that could happen, the innocent woman was killed by you..."

For a long time Mahendra does not say anything, and then he heaves a sigh that expresses his fragility that for years he tried to overcome by using the identity of a Maoist as a cladding. "I killed them all," he mutters so lightly that even Bijuriya cannot hear it. "I killed my first wife by indifference. So, Chini was lost. I killed Damni by making wrong moves. I knew it was not arms that decide everything. It's consciousness..." Mahendra started like he is going to explain everything, but the effort fizzles out even before it starts.

Hours later, when the sky has cleared and cold breeze has started blowing in, Bijuriya sits beside Mahendra and whispers, "I did not want to hurt you. But..."

Suddenly, Mahendra retorts, his voice clear and confident, "*Aur kono chara nehi tha* (There was no other option.)"

Bijuriya fumbles, and then asks what the comment was about.

"I have thought about it and reached my conclusion," Mahendra says in a way as though he is talking to himself. "Whatever I did was correct. I had no other option. I was born a Chamar, whom the rest of the world did not consider a human being. We are Untouchable. If they touch us, they become impure. They won't be impure if they touch dogs, cats, or snakes. But..."

He takes a pause, scratches his legs and starts again: "They will address me as '*tu*'. They address each other as '*aap*'. They address their children as '*tum*'. But we are always '*tu*', because we are not human beings. Even young upper caste boys addressed my grandfather, who was a doddery old man, as '*tu*'. They will address me as '*tu*' now, because I do not possess arms anymore... When I was in the Communist party that participated in elections, they said they would teach upper caste poor men to be respectful to poor Untouchables." He smiles wryly, as though he has convinced his audience, and as Bijuriya looks on, he continues: "That would take centuries, I knew. I heard, when Jagjivan Ram's mother... Jagjivan *babu* was a very big leader and minister at the centre... went to attend the marriage of Rajendra Prasad's son, she heard Rajen babu's wife muttering to her daughter-in-law... 'don't touch the feet of this woman, she is a Chamarni'. I don't know whether that is true, but most likely to be true."

He smiles again, and waves his hand in a gesture that can be interpreted as anything: maybe acceptance of fate or frustration emanating from his defeats, maybe rejection of the system or subjugation to the ultimate! "I knew the only way to get elevated from '*tu*' to at least '*tum*' was by taking up arms. For that I have sacrificed everything. I did it for all of us, for our wives and children… because I wanted to promote our lot to *tum* from tu."

"I didn't want to hurt you," Bijuriya repeats with concern, as she had never heard Mahendra talking to her at such length in the years she knew him. "I just feel that one should check the truth before reaching a conclusion."

A while later, Bijuriya goes inside; but with all his energy dissipating after the long speech, Mahendra remains seated at the threshold, wondering what truth is. His rational thinking or return of his distant memory does not amaze him, for he is so shocked that he has forgotten about his disease: he stares on without seeing anything, thinks about Damni's killing and argues with himself about truth.

The moon that has appeared in the clear sky after the rain looks at him from down below, from a puddle at his front; the nocturnal birds flutter their wings but can hardly see an insect all of which has been washed away by the rain; call of the jackals condenses the silence of the night.

Mahendra remains seated at the threshold, wondering what truth is, and how to get at the bottom of it.

The moon vanishes from the puddle and goes behind the tall trees; the nocturnal birds get tired and stop fluttering their wings; the jackals go so far away that their calls are not heard anymore.

Mahendra wonders about truth. Did he kill his near ones by his acts, or they were destined to be killed? Why Krishna said even if Arjuna did not kill those who had deserted dharma, He himself as Time would kill them? What was the truth then? Was it Arjuna who killed his near and dear ones; or was it Time that killed them and Arjuna only resorted to his karma?

The moon withdraws as the first lights of a new day breaks; the nocturnal birds go back; the jackals hide themselves in the jungles. Just then, Mahendra stands up and without bothering about his aching knees and reeling head, shuffles towards the nearest tree to tell it: "Now I can see through the stones. Till the time I didn't know that my wife was innocent... an innocent was killed by the comrades... I couldn't see through the stones. Now that I know it, I see through the opaque walls of one-sided truth."

The tree dangles its leaves, a few drops of water stored in those fall down, and the first crow caws from above as the sun illuminates the highest mound known as the 'abode of the spirits'. "Seeing through the stones means seeing the truth," he shouts. "Others don't know what truth is because they cannot see through the stones."

Bijuriya, who has woken up, comes running down to him and touches him from behind, feels the man's body is almost burning and, in fact, takes her hand off from him. "*Comret*," she cries in anxiety.

Mahendra can neither see her, nor feel her touch or hear her cry. He shouts again so that the tree may hear it properly: "You know why one cannot see through the stones? You don't know? Ha ha ha..." His loud laughter almost echoes through the endless time that has held sway over the earth, the skies, all the suns and the moons in the universe, the gods and the demons, and even the Time itself.

The tree answers, "You can't see the truth."

Mahendra stares hard at it for a second and asks, "What?"

"Tell me, what is truth?" the tree challenges him.

"Truth? There is nothing called truth. It depends on how you see it. There are only different shards of truth. There's no whole truth."

"You haven't and you can't see the truth," the tree tells him again, "because you have eyes. We know the eternal truth because we cannot see."

"Do not challenge me, I warn you," Mahendra retorts fiercely.

Bijuriya raises an alarm and others start coming out from their huts.

The tree sways all its leaves and branches as all other trees join the chorus: "We know the truth... we know the truth..."

The world starts shaking before Mahendra's eyes, and the morning light starts fading, as though time is withdrawing its flow and is going back to its own womb.

"You can't see truth," the tree whispers again.

"But I have tried to see it for so many years!"

"That was seeing through the stone... knowing the reality as a whole," the tree mocks him as air rustles through its leaves.

"Maybe," he yields. "But we human beings pass on reality as truth."

"You have seen through the reality that is opaque from each of its sides," the tree announces. "You have seen through the stones."

"No one should look through the stones either," he says, his voice cracking as he realizes that now that he has seen through it, he has outlived him. And then he sinks into the dense dark that resembles death; but is not death.

"He has fainted," the others shout to each other and take him inside Bijuriya's hut.

Hours later, when he regains consciousness, he turns into a man who is absolutely without memory, who can neither recognise anyone, nor remember even his name.

PART IV
Postscript

21

Glimpses of the Future (1999–2000)

SHYAMLAL TRUDGES slowly through the track that leads to Kalipura. In between, he takes a break to sigh heavily, and then resumes his journey like a harassed animal returning to its lair. It is a lonely wintry night, but he is not scared of any ghost or demon, for he has learnt his lessons from life; he knows ghosts or demons do not exist out in the dark or inside a ditch, but among human beings only.

He stops for a while, looks back at the road, and his eyes go towards the *dhaba* which is still open, expecting some hungry truck-driver to drop in. He wonders why this food outlet in interior land has illuminated tiny bulbs to decorate a board on which in Hindi someone has written with a blue chalk: Welcome 2000. "Who cares to observe the English new year in villages?" he thinks to himself and walks towards Kalipura after wrapping the *chaddar* tightly to protect himself from chill wind sweeping across the land.

He has rebuilt Kalipura, the hamlet where he was born and where Bijuriya came as his bride, the hamlet that was deserted after flowering of the bamboo trees and an encounter between the Naxalites and the police force. Of course, it was Bijuriya, who started the resettlement there, but when he reached there, he decided to carry forward the work along with Bijuriya. They started visiting old inhabitants who were living in different places, and their two sons, raised by the monks of the Hindu Mission, joined them.

"We have to arrange for work so that the residents have a means of livelihood", their eldest son Jagan told them and took them to the local member of the legislative assembly. The MLA, Surendra Nath, who belonged to Emancipation Party, heard them attentively, and then said, "If you are really interested in rebuilding the village, I will help you. But this is something strange… rebuilding a village. Why do you want to do this?"

Shyamlal answered, "Because we are like trees and our roots are there."

The MLA looked askance at him, and then nodded, "Well said. The whole nation has forgotten its roots. But you are trying to find it. Well said. … But, about means of employment… what were your occupations earlier?"

"Our village is in the badlands, and only when the rivulet brings water we can go for some coarse cereals," Shyamlal explained. "But from that we cannot meet both ends. However, we know how to make baskets from bamboo and from other…"

"You know handicrafts, yes… understood," the MLA stroked the table in his front with his fingers. "I shall try to arrange for a dealer of the Modern Handicrafts to buy things you can make out of bamboo or any other material. They are a private company, but I trust them more than corrupt government officials. These people do business in a proper way. You will also train there to learn other crafts…. And I tell you frankly, they will donate some money to our party and that much will be our additional gain." And then the MLA asked Shyamlal, "I hope you will not be active for the Jharkhand Party here?"

"I have left politics," Shyamlal shook his head to show his disgust. "Anyhow, we were not fighting for this truncated Jharkhand. It is now south Bihar only. They have forgotten districts of Bengal, Orissa or MP."

"In MP, they will create Chhattisgarh state," the MLA says indifferently.

As Shyamlal remembers that day, he turns back towards the road through which now buses ply, and his eyes locate the shade where a signboard reads: Modern Handicrafts. It is a warehouse built by the company, which depends on Kalipura and other villages of this region for supply of various products that it mostly exports.

On that day, at the end of their conversation, the MLA told them, "It is strange that you people have come to me." As Shyamlal and others looked at him with questioning eyes, he explained, "This is the village from where police arrested Comrade Mahendra after an encounter. And…"

As the man took a pause, Shyamlal could not desist himself from asking, "You knew Comrade Mahendra?"

The MLA laughed and asked, "Where is he now? I heard he had lost his mind."

"He is a lost man," Shyamlal revealed sadly. "I was with him for months. He could not even remember who he was."

"What happened then?"

"One morning, I found he was gone. I could not trace him afterwards."

"His comrades do not know?"

"They don't care," Shyamlal said gruffly.

Through the years, while he was rebuilding the hamlet passionately, Mahendra was always there in his mind, and in between, he took a break to renew his efforts to find the man. He never thought that he would ever be successful in this venture either, and he is still not sure whether what he has achieved can be called success.

"Shyamlal," someone calls him from the dark.

Following the sound, he looks at his left and after staring on for a few seconds, he realizes from the silhouette that the other man is Abul Mian. "It's good that you have come back," says Abul. "A child has fallen ill and I am going to get some medicine from the doctor." As Abul rides his cycle, Shyamlal remembers how this man, a Muslim, who was not among the old inhabitants of the village, came to live here and taught the villagers to make statuettes of plaster of Paris that now fetch them some extra money. He is going to a doctor of the health centre residing in the next village on the road.

Shyamlal reaches his hamlet, which has swelled so much in size that it can now be called a village, and looks at the houses that the government has helped them to build, wondering how greatly the village and the lives of the villagers have changed. This village will not go under Jharkhand state, which is likely to be formed soon, he knows, but he has no worry for that. After all, what is important is the lives of human beings and he would have been happy if all the villages of Bihar could change like this. But in other places, people are still not conscious of their rights and do not have a people's representative like Surendra Nath, who tries his best to do something for his people and keeps on travelling throughout his constituency. "People manage to get food nowadays, but they must also assert their rights... for jobs, for low-cost houses, for irrigation," Shyamlal mutters to himself and walks past the tube well that they got installed by the government.

A few steps ahead, he finds Bijuriya sitting at the veranda of their small tile-roofed *pucca* house, her cheek resting on her palm. As she sees him, she stands up, waits for him to reach her, and asks, "Any news?"

"I reached there too late," Shyamlal heaves a deep sigh.

"What does that mean?" Bijuriya's eyes are contorted.

"He was in Puraina, but three years back, in 1996, he was murdered."

"Murdered!" Bijuriya gets a start. "By whom?"

"By the landlord's grand army. Ranjoy Sena."

"Oh god!" Bijuriya almost breaks down. "He had left everything, but they didn't forget him! They are so cruel!"

Jagan, their eldest son, comes out and looking at the grim faces of his parents, asks, "About whom are you discussing? Who has been killed?"

"Comrade Mahendra," whispers Shyamlal.

"Oh. I see. Today a constable came for you. He told me that the police is again looking for Comrade Mahendra," Jagan reveals to his father. "One person, yes... Harry Singh... his relatives were killed by Comrade Mahendra... and now that Harry Singh has gone missing. In that connection, the constable came to enquire about the comrade. He will come again tomorrow."

"Let them search all the corners of the world," Shyamlal mutters grimly, and adds, "Idiots."

THEY WERE already in their respective cots placed in two corners of the room when they heard knocks on the door followed by a muffled voice calling Karma. For a few seconds, Lillian lingered like a trapped animal and wondered whether it was someone from the police who earlier in the afternoon came to the village to pick up two Harijan boys for stealing a cycle.

Lillian is still waiting. But Karma is not scared of the police, as for him it makes little difference if he dies in the custody, and murmurs, "It seems a comrade has come."

"Comrade!" Lillian whispers and gets up, lights a candle and goes out with it to see who has arrived. Half a minute later, a man enters the room and asks, in a low voice, "Comrade Karma, tell me who I am?"

The man's face cannot be seen from the cot on which Karma is sitting as the candle is with Lillian standing behind the man.

"The voice has similarity with someone I knew... Sunder Besra... but..." Karma stops as he feels it cannot be Sunder for after being identified by Bhola, the traitor, he is in jail for long years.

"Who says you are ill? You're fine. I am Sunder," the man says excitedly.

"You have broken the jail?" Karma asks without any excitement.

"No," Sunder replies casually. "They kept me inside for nearly 17 years, and one day they said, enough is enough. Get lost. That was in the month of Sawan."

A while later, as they settle down, Sunder Besra says, "Comrade Ranjib and Comrade Raul told me that you'd be here. They asked me to visit you. I am a free man now. So, no risk is involved."

Lillian goes out with the candle. Sitting in the dark, Karma asks, "You met them?"

"Yes. I have met many comrades in these four months."

"You have started working again?"

"No," Sunder smiles and his white teeth glimmer even in the dark. "Everything has changed. Our organization has turned so big. We all have merged with the southern group PRG. Unity group has joined them, Comrade Raul has joined them and they have grip over Andhra and Bihar and parts of Karnataka, Maharashtra, Madhya Pradesh, and Orissa. But, none knows where Comrade Mahendra is. I feel I'm an outsider here."

They sit silently for a while and Lillian comes back with the candle and an aluminium bowl, which she hands to Sunder.

"Oh, great. *Sattu* with mustard oil and green chilli. My favourite food, you know Sister." Sunder seems happy.

"I have left the Church," Lillian smiles.

"I know," Sunder concedes at once. "In fact, I didn't know you when I went to jail. I have heard of you now. I have called you sister in the Indian sense. We are all brothers and sisters, isn't it?"

"Oh, sure." Lillian says emphatically. "If you think I am your sister, tell me... why you feel like an outsider? I heard you saying so."

Sunder eats voraciously, a clear sign of being hungry for a long time, though he has not betrayed it earlier, and only after being half way through, he says, "I was surprised to see our cadres. They get food and a little bit of money. Some of them have joined us only for that. Many of them have no commitment and they know nothing about Marx or Mao. That was unimaginable in our time."

"True," Lillian agrees at once. "But they are at least fighting for the uplift of the poor."

"Right," Sunder nods. "But at many places they are stopping the administration from building a road... somewhere a bridge. But people want these things, and there is nothing wrong in ..."

"Those will not change their plight, you know that," Karma intervenes.

"I know," Sunder says while eating, "but what have we provided for the people in return? Their wages have not increased significantly, their products do not fetch them much higher returns... in Palamou region, jungle-mafia have felled thousands of catechu and teak trees, and we could do nothing to stop this or to confer the rights to the jungle-villages."

"That region is controlled by MCO," Karma grudges.

Sunder does not attach any importance to the intervention. "What have we done for the people? We have made deals with the contractors and traders. We are flushed with money, while the people whom we serve, who are often harassed by the police, remain as wretched as they were. At many places, comrades have redistributed land, which is a great work. But that is nothing when you compare that with opulence of the cities. We run schools at one or two places, but the Hindu chauvinists RSS runs many more schools."

Karma remains silent. But Lillian comes forward, "What's the way out?"

"I don't know. But probably we have grown too big too fast. We have sacrificed quality for quantity. In south Bihar, if police really tightens the noose some day, nine out of our ten comrades will flee. They will just vanish."

"That's more true about the MCO," Karma whispers. "They are much bigger here... in Bihar."

"I heard they would merge with People's Revolution in coming years," Sunder now takes on Karma's point. "They are debating it and on this issue MCO has split. Comrade Shankar is not willing to join PRG, but Samaresh *babu* is willing. So, eventually, they will be part of the whole. And our comrades are not too different."

As Sunder finishes his food and licks his fingers, Lillian asks, "A little more?"

"No, this is enough."

"Then what is to be done for the poor?" Lillian raises the question again. "Don't you think you should open schools, run health centres, make them aware and conscious, before you try to revolutionise them?"

"Maybe... I don't know," Sunder sighs. "But our government has now adopted new strategy... to push the poor so interior that they become invisible. Government takes away little land they have in the name of development, urbanization, industry and dams... Narmada... Tehri... what not. Why? Because we need development. New Economic Policy. We have to make upper ten per cent richer... and we have to please our masters sitting in the World Bank. This is the time when one should strive to unleash mass movement. Where is that? Rather, the Hindu chauvinists have taken advantage and have spread their network."

Lillian is amazed by the knowledge of the man who is an aborigine Naxal and had been in jail for many years. "An indomitable spirit is never asphyxiated," she tells herself, "like a sapling of a banyan tree, it pokes its head even from a fissure in the concrete to tell the world that life is bound to be victorious over all odds and difficulties, affliction, and agonies."

"Well, you can discuss these things tomorrow." She takes the aluminium bowl from Sunder and tells him, "You lie down in the other cot."

"What about you?" Sunder asks.

"I will manage it there," she points to the other room. "That one is roofed with concrete. That becomes hot. Bit, it's a wintry night. No problem."

"Have a cot there?" Sunder gets up.

"No," Lillian insists. "But don't worry. I will lie down on the holdall with which I move if I go out for some days. It's comfortable." She goes out immediately, leaving the candle to the comrades, assuming that the two will carry on their conversation for some time.

"I think while in some places comrades are doing good work, we need to open up much more," Sunder sits down and says in a plain tone, like he is talking to himself and trying to organise things in his mind. "We need to unleash mass movement. I think Comrade Rambabu's death is a great loss."

"Comrade Rambabu is dead?" Karma cringes.

"You don't know? That was a month back. He was in a hotel in Bangalore with Comrade Sainath and Comrade Rampal, another CC member. They're picked up by the police and were killed in a jungle."

"Comrade Sainath!" Karma sounds shaken.

"Yes," says Sunder, and as Karma falls silent, probably in shock, he adds: "Two of those three whom we called 'the trident' during Kalipura days, are no more. But the police didn't know that they were killing the sober faces of the movement. Rambabu, Sainath and Rampal were trying to put pressure on Comrade Raghupati to shift towards a line of mass movement, so that the state realizes our strength."

"Mass movement. How? We are all banned in Andhra," Karma mumbles rather indifferently.

"I know. This is natural that the state will ban you, will kill you. But we should not counter them only by brute force. We must transform the people into a radical force. Those three went to Bangalore to discuss these propositions and…"

Karma cuts him short to say, "This line of sophisticated arms was propagated by Rambabu himself a decade ago… during the days when they were preparing to replace Comrade Rajaramaiah, the then GS."

"That's something strange," Sunder agrees. "The same man was now advocating a different path. But, we also learn from our experience. Probably, he realized the limitations of arms a decade later. It happened to me too. In jail, in the initial days, I used to protest a lot of things. Why should we be given bad food? Why should we be treated as criminals instead of political workers? So many things.

For that they used to beat me… they punished me by putting me in solitary confinements. They were wrong. I was right. My demands were just. But after years, five… seven… eight years… all my expectations left me. I stopped expecting human behaviour. I stopped expecting standard food or anything else. I took life as it was."

"You are really a changed person," Karma whispers.

"I got a strange officer in the last part of my jail days," Sunder treads through the path of memory. "He was courteous, and he believed a jail is a wrong place to keep criminals. Everybody should be given opportunity to rectify the wrongs he has done, he believed. I told him that the concept is not applicable to me. Because I didn't do anything wrong. He told me that killing a person is wrong. I said, I killed class enemies. He then told me the story of a local judge. That man tried the case of those who were accused of a massacre in south Bihar. A month before the verdict, the MCO comrades started threatening him: you award capital punishment to anyone, we kill your daughter. He has only one child. He pleaded with them… he had to abide by law. He stopped sending his daughter to the school, but awarded capital punishment to three of the accused. But, did he do anything wrong?"

Karma looks on at Sunder's face, waves his hands in the air and finally says, "Though I do not agree on most of the points you have referred to earlier, in this case I am confused… but, I am sure that he wouldn't have awarded death sentence if the convicts were from upper caste or rich people."

"That's also true," Sunder concedes. "Then a few days back, a tribal comrade from MCO told me that in their organization, tribal comrades are looked down upon by Yadav comrades, who are their middle level leaders."

"That is true only about MCO. They are a Yadav-dominated organization. They supported the party led by Laloo Prasad Yadav."

"No, Comrade," Sunder heaves a sigh. "Blaming MCO is escapism. MCO will merge with your PRG soon, if they denounce their line of mass caste-killings, and if leadership issue is settled."

"Leadership is not a problem. When we merged with PRG, Ganapathy offered the post of general secretary to Jogen *babu*, who was the real brain even during Comrade Biplab's time. But he declined the offer because of his age. Now our GS may relinquish his post for Samaresh *babu*, the top man of MCO. They have split, you said…?"

Suddenly Sunder chuckles, and says, "God knows how many times Comrade Shankar will split organizations. He left us to join MCO when Comrade Mahendra was in hospital, in our most critical time, and now…"

Both of them sit silently, lost in their different course of thoughts, while a nocturnal bird skirls from a nearby tree.

Quite a while later, Karma asks, "Has MCO agreed to stop following the line of mass killings?"

"They will stop that, Comrade Raul has told me," Sunder reveals and turns thoughtful. "Now they feel it is not needed any more. For over a decade, they have followed it. They attacked villages and killed 10, 20, 30, or 60 men from a particular caste. They did it to rouse the Backwards and the Harijans in north Bihar. They feel now people have reached a stage of higher consciousness."

"But the landlord's army, Ranjoy Sena, also does that. They will not stop." Karma ponders about the possibilities.

"That's the problem," Sunder nods. "But Samaresh *babu* told me that they would attack the Ranjoy Sena bases and finish them off. He is confident."

"I hope they would shed their Backward caste character also," mutters Karma.

"But then, wasn't Ramakant a very important comrade of your organization, of the unified PRG in Bihar?" Sunder suddenly starts chuckling.

"Of course." Karma is surprised to see Sunder chuckling. "He is very bright and bold, though a bit arrogant. What is funny about it?"

"He has left you."

"What!"

"Yes. And the reason is… a Harijan, Tulsi Chand, was placed above him. Being a Rajput, he could not tolerate it. He was prepared to work under the guidance of Bengali *babus*, but not under a Harijan. He said this organization is being dominated by the Harijans and that's why he left. Not only that, he vowed to kill Harijan comrades."

"My god! He will become a major threat." Karma almost shudders.

"Maybe," Sunder sounds tired. "But Comrade, I am only confused. You know, you have worked without Comrade Mahendra for long. But for me he was the only leader. He used to say arms are subservient to people's movement. I believe in that. Time has of course changed. Comrade Rajaramaiah, who was the GS of southern Naxalites in those days, surrendered to the police and has died. Nagjyothi, who used to come to Comrade Mahendra along with Rambabu and Sainath… spends his time in the local CPI party office. Everything has changed."

"We have advanced a lot since then," Karma whispers. "Now we are working even in Bengal. Earlier we thought what the parliamentary Communists have done there… they are ruling that state for more than twenty years without break… we thought it would be difficult for us. But actually, they have done little for the poor and we are advancing fast there. You know when they realize it that we are advancing… Communists, Congress, BJP, whoever is in power, they launch various schemes for food, work and so on to alienate us. But probably now people will understand that if the government can eliminate us, all those programmes will vanish."

"It happened in Midnapore during spring-thunder days, Comrade Mahendra told me."

"Then Sunder," Karma almost pleads, "don't you think we are on right track?"

"I don't know. The world has changed, and new tactics will have to be adopted. Judging by our striking power, we have gained enormously. We have killed the ex-IG of Andhra. We kidnap officers or MLAs or others in Andhra, in Maharahtra, Chattisgarh, anywhere. We can strike at anyone in different states. We are still acquiring new arms, more sophisticated mines… and trying to get something called rockets."

"We don't have that yet," Karma intervenes.

"Maybe," Sunder sounds indifferent. "But, we have to think of different factors. Why is it so that the Hindu chauvinists have spread over the whole of central and northern India? Why have we failed to do so? How they have won the hearts of the people? By hate campaign only? By their fervour against the Muslims, the Christians? Maybe, but that cannot be the sole factor. Somewhere they have touched the chord of the millions. Maybe it is a reaction against too much westernization, a sort of cultural retaliation. Unless we analyse and understand these trends, we will never be able to raise people's consciousness to a higher stage."

"I don't know much," Karma concedes a while later. "You know I was an orphan raised by a washerwoman. But I can tell you one thing. We also think of these things. We have formed united forum of Maoists of all the countries of this region…"

"Leaving India and Nepal, no Maoist party is a recognizable force in any other country of the region."

"Agreed," Karma says and feels a bit depressed. "In India, we have decided to take more women, like the comrades of Nepal. Soon you will see half of our comrades will be women. Once this happens, we shall be able to penetrate in new areas much faster. And we have decided to allow those who are tired of fighting to surrender. They may later work for spreading our support base. People will listen to their stories and will be inspired. They will seek permission and we shall allow it. Our people's courts will allow much less execution…"

"These are all about arms and tactics," Sunder says abruptly.

Karma looks at Sunder's silhouette with invisible irritation in his eyes. "Without arms, you will be killed like Shambhu Guha Niogi of Chhattisgarh," he sounds acerbic. "He did fantastic work among the tribal mine workers. But he didn't believe in armed protection. One day the industrialists send a hitman who killed him in the night. Government arrested the killer, but didn't touch any of those industrialists. Without arms, you will be killed, I will be killed, all of us will be killed in the same way. And everything will be over."

Sunder remains silent for quite a while, and then says, "I don't mean we will surrender arms. But I am afraid that this dependence on arms will someday take us to the agents of ISI, the Pakistani agency that is fuelling trouble in India by luring the Muslims…"

"I know," Karma cuts him short. "Some years back, even one important comrade in Andhra left our organization to join the Jihadi forces. But are we prepared to take help from ISI?"

"Everybody denies that. But it may be via media. We are trying to link us up with Naga and other militants taking refuge in Bhutan and Bangladesh. They are connected with ISI. So… Whatever, I feel we must take advantage of the situation in the country as a whole. I am talking of human rights, media, democracy, whatever form…"

Karma cuts him short: "Are you also in favour of participating in elections?"

"Time changes, and one has to …"

"Principles do not change," retorts Karma.

"Right. But why not tactics? Modern world will not allow Maoist takeover through arms. Not in India, not even in Nepal. Sanctions will be imposed. Multinational force will come. So why not try to convert your base for electoral practice, without succumbing to bourgeois system as the parliamentary communist parties have done."

"Maybe," Karma nods uncertainly. "But if the leaders anywhere want to surrender arms, our cadres will throw out those leaders."

"I know," concedes Sunder. "I understand your point that such tactics may be adopted only when you are capable of shaping the democracy in a way so that you can take over. I won't disagree, Karma. But still I feel that the democratic system must be utilized."

Karma nods sceptically and gets absorbed in difficult thoughts.

22

The Present Continuous... (1995–96)

HE LOOKS on at the man who is calling him by the name 'Comrade Mahendra', but his eyes cannot penetrate the waves of time, and he shakes his head.

"Aren't you *Comret* Mahendra?" the man asks desperately.

"I don't know my name," he mutters. "But who are you... you said?"

"I am Shyamlal and my wife is... was Bijuriya. We lived in Kalipura. You came there one day. You told us to fight for a just society. And so many things... do you remember? *Comret!*"

"Bijuriya?" he asks, his eyes contorted and face reflecting torment.

"Yes. She was as beautiful as a... as a... as a river, a river filled up to the brink."

"Bijuriya!" he repeats as his wrinkled forehead develops deep creases.

"Yes. You know, Bijuriya is lost. And also my two sons."

"Bijuriya?" he asks once again, this time almost in a trance, and Shyamlal stops carrying on the conversation.

Mahendra feels a whirl deep inside his head. Something very vague, very distant, a hamlet draped in mist, appears before his eyes; the sky is hazy, the hill of the spirits is dark… and… and… a woman is there. "She had a birthmark on her thigh, close to her belly?" he asks.

Shyamlal would have been angry if anybody else had asked him the question when he lived with Bijuriya; he could have hit him hard, even if it was Comrade Mahendra. But 12 years later, his whole existence with Bijuriya has turned so distant, and so tenuous that it has no potency to make him angry. He simply nods.

A few seconds later, Mahendra's eyes suddenly flash and turn sharp. "Bijuriya!" he says loudly, "Your wife. Yes. She is there."

"You met her?"

"Yes," he nods, his eyes losing the sharpness.

"Where, *Comret*, where?"

"Where?" he looks about him, and repeats the same question thrice.

"Can't you remember, *Comret*?" Shyamlal asks tensely.

With the sharpness gone from his eyes, he shakes his head in a way as though he is ashamed, for he cannot remember anything, not even his name.

For next more than one year, Shyamlal stays with him. He opens a tea stall by the side of the road, and whatever he earns, he spends on them, hoping that some day the comrade will remember where he had met Bijuriya. He has little hope though, he knows well as he regularly finds Mahendra arguing with the trees on something like 'seeing through the stone', a clear indication of the fact that the man has lost his mind, and probably will never be able to remember the name of the place where he met Bijuriya. But he is not interested to go back to work with the corrupt Jharkhandis; he is not prepared to work for the Maoists; he rather likes to spend time like this, selling tea during the day and listening to Mahendra jabbering strange things in the night.

"Never try to see through the stones," Mahendra often alerts him. "Otherwise, you will become senile, like me."

"How can one see through a stone, *Comret*? It is opaque." Shyamlal says lightly.

"Nothing is opaque, except truth. Only you have to see it from all sides."

At other times, Mahendra laughs in a benign manner and mutters, "I am a mad man and that is why I speak nonsense. But, there was something at the root of all these... but... but I don't remember."

Shyamlal feels that Mahendra has long back overcome his identity of a Naxalite, and has turned into someone else, someone very strange, someone who can see through the mist that covers the human lives from birth to death, and that is precisely why he fails to remember anything else. One evening, he sits beside Mahendra and tells him, "*Comret*, this life is blind driving... as though the man who drives the bus is driving it blindfolded... isn't it? Can you tell me how we can see the future?"

"Future?" Mahendra thinks for a while, and then answers, "There is no past, no future. There is only truth. Truth and illusion. Only trees can see the truth. From a seed to a tree, to a seed... there is no past, no future."

Shyamlal cannot grasp it, and asks, "Then what one is supposed to do?"

"You perform your duty, though that will not change anything..." Mahendra utters the phrase he often repeats. He has told Shyamlal that it is a mantra in Sanskrit that he cannot remember anymore. He seems sleepy and adds, "*Aur kono chara nehi hai.*" There was no other option.

"But I cannot fight with guns as you did," Shyamlal says a while later.

As though waking up from a dream, Mahendra answers, "A gun is a toy. We have no death, no birth."

"Then what shall I do?" Shyamlal at last asks the question that is haunting him since he is spending time aimlessly, waiting for an almost impossible day when Mahendra will remember where he had seen Bijuriya.

"You will create a new world," Mahendra says a while later, his voice reflecting a sort of confidence that he had in good old days. "A world where everybody is equal, where love rules and hate has no place."

"How do I do that?" Shyamlal sounds puzzled.

"You yourself will understand that when the time will come."

Still terribly confused, Shyamlal asks, "How will I understand that the time has come?"

Mahendra lies on the cot, closes his eyes and then mutters, "*Samay khud tumhe batabe* (Time itself will tell you.)"

Mahendra is ashamed of the fact that he cannot remember the place where he met Bijuriya; but one fine morning, he remembers something in a flash, and cries out, "Shyamlal, go to Kalipura, go to Kalipura."

Shyamlal is so startled that for a while he cannot utter anything and only looks on at the comrade's eyes, which he finds bright and revealing, to some extent like the burning eyes he had in old days. "Anyone lives in Kalipura?" he asks after regaining himself.

"Go to Kalipura... near the catechu jungle." Mahendra insists.

That night, when Shyamlal is asleep, Mahendra sees a glow out in the meadows and starts following it, as someone tells him from within that far away there are trees waiting for him. He leaves the area to embark on another journey towards his future about which he has no concern anymore. He understands that his days are numbered, for he often feels he has no strength left in his body to walk even a yard more and settles down wherever he is—on the side of a meadow, in front of a house, under a tree in the jungle. When he regains strength, he follows his heart that seems to guide him to his end.

Several weeks later, he reaches a *tola* of the Harijans, which seems to be known to him, and out of curiosity that visits him only for once, he asks someone, "What is the name of this village?"

"Puraina," answers the other man.

The name strums a chord in his heart, but it dies soon. Still, he decides to live there as he feels that his journey has come to an end.

A couple of days later, at the end of the *tola*, he finds a statue, a black one made of clay and plaster of Paris, and he asks the locals, "Whose statue is this?"

"Comrade Mahendra Chamar's," a passerby says casually and goes off.

For some reason, Mahendra chooses a very big banyan tree near the statue to live under it. With his long white beard and wrinkled skin, he looks like a very old man, and one or the other villager, a Harijan or even a Backward, offers him food everyday. If some day none of them gives him anything, a young man from the Harijan-*tola* called Chedilal comes with some food. He tells him that he is the grandson of Birju, and the great grandson of Budha Chamar, who died after being shoved off from the path of the Thakurs. "You look like my grandfather who has died years ago," he says.

Chedilal is a wonder youth of the *tola*, for he has gone to school, the first boy from the Harijan-*tola* of Puraina, and can even count.

While living under the tree, Mahendra develops a bizarre habit: every morning, after waking up early, he plucks some wild flowers and offers those to the statue which has turned cumbersome as its right ear has fallen off after a heavy rain. Often a passerby laughs at him, and asks, "Do you know this statue was installed by the MCO comrades? You know who this man is?"

"*Hoga koi sadhu-mahatma* (Must be some saint or great soul)," the old man answers with a smile that exposes simultaneously his faith and simplicity.

People laugh at him—'a mad man'—and go away; but someone, people say he is the son of the minister Subhash Chaudhary, arranges to make a hut for him and Chedilal works it out with the help of a few more Chamars. Mahendra lives there, talks to the trees and waits for the end.

The end comes abruptly. It is early winter and the trees are still green and sparkling, as though inviting Mahendra to talk to them, to debate the essence of life, of earth and of creation that has made his life riddled with holes.

"Do you ever go mad?" Mahendra asks the banyan tree.

"We never turn mad, because we have always seen the truth."

"You don't have eyes," Mahendra turns querulous.

"We see through our existence, through our stems and trunks, through our roots, through the leaves and flowers and fruits. There is no ending to it. That is why we grow all through our lives."

Mahendra feels tired and says, "Then convince me that you see truth."

"That is why we don't fight," the tree answers.

In the last few months, Mahendra has almost stopped talking to human beings, and has communicated with the trees only, particularly the old ones who stand about him like grand old men. Mahendra asks again, "If I say I am not convinced, would that make you angry?"

"We don't know what anger is," the tree answers.

"I know," Mahendra nods, thinks for a while and then asks, "Then tell me, how you see truth when you don't have eyes?"

The tree, as the wind runs through its leaves, says, "First tell me whether we trees can move or not."

"You can't move," he says, smiling foolishly.

"Wrong. You try to interpret things with your eyes. That's why you can't see truth. We move through seeds, through generations, through time. You will never understand it. We are embodiment of truth."

Mahendra nods and mutters, "I think I knew that."

The tree ignores him and goes on, "You can't see truth for your vision is coloured by passion, excitement, aspiration, power, thoughts and... your mobility. Only trees can see truth that is eternal."

"Then tell me what is truth," Mahendra insists like a lost soul.

The tree cannot answer for a while as the air has stopped blowing, but Mahendra waits eagerly and looks about him to watch whether the leaves of the distant trees have started swaying. After a long gap, the answer comes, "Truth is... whatever is created... will be destroyed."

The tree falls into silence and though the air blows again, it does not answer any other question, compelling Mahendra to go away towards a small plant whose flowers have endured the dew of the cold night.

He trudges with a profound feeling as his heart has turned composed and placid, like the water of a big idyllic lake. He plucks a few flowers from the small plant. At this, the plant giggles, and he remembers that long back, one small girl also used to giggle like this lying on his chest, though he cannot figure out who was she.

After a while, he dodders towards the statue which has become discoloured and lost both of its ears, and like everyday, he offers flowers at its feet. While doing so, he finds a few people on horseback at a distance, but they do not mean anything to him, and he ignores their very existence.

"The trees do not know the whole," he tells the statue. "They believe the ultimate truth is that whatever is created will be destroyed. But they do not know that there is something even after that. They do not know ultimate truth is performing one's duty without expectation. Isn't it so?"

Those men come closer in a way as though they are zeroing in on the statue, and as he turns back after offering flowers to the statue, one of them leans down from his horse and asks, "Hey Budha, whose statue is this?"

"Must be of some saint or great soul," Mahendra replies gently.

"Great soul! What is written there?" the man on horseback puts his finger towards the nameplate, but Mahendra does not care to look at that.

"Who is Mahendra Chamar?" the man asks again.

"Must be some saint or great soul," Mahendra again replies gently.

"Hey Budha, who are you?" someone shouts angrily.

The word 'Budha' suddenly throws some light inside his head, and staring straight at the man, he replies, "I am Budha Chamar."

"Chamar! Then keep off," the man, who has turned irate, thunders. "We will break this statue."

The man hits on the head of the statue with an iron rod and blows off half the face.

Suddenly Mahendra shouts, "Hey, don't do that."

"Why?" the man asks in rage and bending as much forward as possible hits the head with a heavier blow, this time pulverizing the rest of the head.

"They must be resisted, or else the muggers will kill this great soul," Mahendra tells himself and hugs the body of the statue, to protect it from being vandalized, as though it is an old friend.

The man shouts, "Get off, or I will kill you."

Mahendra enjoys the rage, looks at the ruffian and mumbles, "So what? You cannot kill my soul."

"Get off," the man shouts at top of his voice.

As the old man does not move, the attacker raises a crowbar and shouts for the last time, "Get off."

"*Nahi*," Mahendra retorts, as he enjoys, to his heart's content, his resistance.

"Don't hit that man," someone else croaks from behind.

But the man who has broken off the head of the statue is so overcome with rage that he hits the old man's head with the crowbar as hard as he can.

Mahendra's head cracks, blood splutters out as he falls on the ground, and for a few seconds, his body shivers like a just-beheaded goat; then it becomes still forever.

SUBHASH CHAUDHARY looks at the mirror and wonders whether he is the same man who years back came to Puraina to make an attempt to fulfil his words to his dying grandfather. He had only one aim, and for that, despite being an upper caste Bhumihar, he joined hand with Hukum Lal the railway man, a socialist, known as the champion of the Backwards. He reached closer to his goal when he started defeating the *haveli* in the elections and the rest was scripted by destiny!

He still remembers the day when he told the last Badhe Thakur of the *haveli* that he would carry on his attempts to drive them out from the village, to avenge for the insult of his grandfather; he remembers the cold ferocious look of the landlord, before which his spirit stooped, though he did not betray his feelings and held his ground firmly.

"Poor man, he could not match my brain… or luck," Subhash, the doctor who challenged the *haveli*, mutters at his image, smirks and walks away from the mirror.

Minutes later, he sits on the armchair at the first floor balcony from where the bustling in the house is heard clearly. He sees his supporters moving about in the ground floor, and in the sprawling garden, preparing for god knows what. He thinks unmindfully that he has witnessed the onslaught of history, and was instrumental in it only marginally as far his own efforts were concerned. He believed he would be able to marginalize the *haveli*, but he never thought that he would be able to drive them out from the village, and thereby be able to complete the circle of revenge that started with the organizing of a nude dance. "But only a little bit of arithmetic and you gain so much," he smirks as he enjoys the placid beauty of the landscape.

When the Naxalites first started working in and around Puraina, he just did his arithmetic properly and arranged for killing three of them, being confident that the blame would be on the *haveli*. He could foresee that the red force, known for their bellicosity, would avenge for it! And they really did it, though their 'revenge killing' was much more horrific than he could imagine; the locals were dumbfounded to see five members of the *haveli* killed.

In the following years, he became a prominent leader of the Janata Party in the Bhojpur region, and when Hukum Lal died rather prematurely, he was elected to the assembly. When Laloo Prasad came to power, he was in the House for the fourth time. "I became a minister, and forgot my last words to my dying grandfather," he tells himself. "Chhote Thakur was still in the *haveli*, and unless he was evicted, I was not supposed to forget my promise. But I did not care; it was only incidental that Chhote Thakur fell into the pond, and died the next day that marked the end of the *haveli*."

Looking at a few people who have huddled them outside the gate of his house and are trying to raise some banners on a 'tempo', a big three-wheeler, he wonders how the priority of life changes with time.

"But I did not seek money," he starts countering himself, "I started my life with a charitable dispensary. I only sought to help Hukum Lal the railway man, the founder of socialist movement in Puraina. But he died all on a sudden and I became an MLA; Janata Dal defeated Congress and I became a minister; people offered money on their own and I became a millionaire." A smile appears on his lips as he concludes, "We are all destiny's children. We can do little. It is destiny that spreads its hand of help; some can grab it, others fail."

His son comes, and handing him a cup of tea, he mutters, "Our man has come. He says MCO may go against us in the future."

Subhash Chaudhary does not attach any importance to it, and sips his tea calmly, while his son continues: "They helped us in the '95 election. But the leaders are now expelling those who worked for Laloo*ji*'s candidates. The Maoists now want to shed its identity of a Backward-dominated organization helping the Backward-dominated party."

"Give it a short shrift. Not important."

"But," his son hesitates and then adds, "They attacked the *haveli* once. They may attack the contractors under me."

Subhash Chaudhary laughs again: "Just see. They may ask for money. Just give a hundred thousand and they will protect you."

"Another thing," his son says again. "An hour back, Ranjoy Sena men came to demolish the statue of that Naxalite... Mahendra Chamar. They have killed the old loony man who used to stay near the statue."

The leader turns at his son with a mild frown, then shifts his gaze towards the front again, and mutters, "Barbarians."

As his son goes away, he again wonders whether he is the same man who came many years ago to this area with the mission of wiping out aristocracy. He has wiped out the old aristocracy, and while all over Bihar some Yadavs have become a sort of neo-Brahmins, dominating every possible sphere with the active help of CM Laloo Yadav and his associates, in Puraina he has established a new aristocracy of his family, of an upper caste Bhumihar family.

Finishing his tea, he stands up as he will have to leave for Patna within an hour. Looking at his supporters busy discussing god knows what, he tells himself, "They will always be there." He knows it better—poor self-seeking workers will be there with every politician who has money, irrespective of ideology, belief, caste, creed, religion or even performance, because in this country money talks. "*Paisa bolta hai*," he repeats in his mind, feels a strange sort of pleasure and turns to move into the room.

HARRY GETS down from the horse and sits under the shadow of a tree as he is sweating even in the early winter. After futile attempts of many years to find and kill Mahendra Chamar, he has demolished the statue of that Chamar built by the Naxalites, and at the moment that has filled his heart with profound happiness.

"Had that mad man not been there, we could have demolished the statue rather peacefully," says Pran Kumar. He is a top commander of the Ranjoy Sena, the landlord's army, though he does not know who Harry is.

"Your men could have spared him; they killed an innocent." Harry repents.

"You think so?" Pran asks.

"Of course. He was a mad man. When he was asked who he was… what he answered, did you hear that? He said, he was Budha Chamar. There was a Budha Chamar in Puraina, but he was *budha*, I mean old, very old, even 50 years ago."

"They often use the same names," Pran says casually, while looking at something else at the distance. "But how do you know that?"

"That's another story. But, he was an innocent mad man," Harry laments, without knowing who exactly his men have killed.

Pran Kumar, known as the right hand of Bisheshwar Singh, the founder of Ranjoy Sena, does not say anything, but slowly slinks away from Harry.

"Its good that apart from a couple of politicians and Raj Karan, the police officer, no one knows that I have formed this organization of brutes," Harry tells himself, and wonders why Raj Karan, who was once in charge of anti-Naxalite operation in Bihar, took so much risk to help him.

Harry recalls what Bisheshwar told him last night, "During the last operation, after entering Harijan-*tola*, Pran killed three persons of a family, and then an elderly woman came running up. 'We are very poor, Master, what do you want from us? We have nothing,' she begged as others were being rounded up. Pran Kumar replied, 'We only want your lives. That's the only thing you can offer.' He killed the slattern the next moment…"

Harry had earlier tried to convince Bisheshwar that as Naxalites never kill a woman or a child, Ranjoy Sena should also follow the same principle, but the old man rejected him with disgust: "You are talking in a way as though the Untouchable Harijans or Backwards are human beings like us," he averred. "They are not. They are lesser humans. The Harijans should not be treated as human beings at all. No criteria for them."

Pran Kumar was as loyal to his commander as a dog to his master, and precisely for that reason Harry asked Bisheshwar to allot the task of breaking the notorious Chamar's statue to Pran, and informed the top man that he too would join the mission in disguise. As Pran did not know Harry, before they set out for the operation he lectured him on the code of conduct, "No molestation, no rape. This is an ideological matter. We don't consider them as human beings. If it is so… their women cannot be desirable objects. Keep it in mind. Even female apes have holes, but you don't fuck them. Same for the Harijan women."

After the operation, they retreated quickly. After a couple of kilometres, they got divided into three groups to avoid any suspicion by any villager or an onlooker. Pran Kumar kept only Harry with him as he was his custodian. Then they took a turn beside a small mound and reached near a lake, which was shimmering in the late morning after appropriating the sun in its womb.

Sitting under the tree, alone in the vast field, Harry suddenly wonders, what is he doing here, instead of spending time with his wife, whom he has asked to join him in business and who has amazingly excelled in that job. 'This killings and counter killings will go on,' he tells himself. "Naxalites kill twenty, Ranjoy Sena kills 30, Naxalites kill 30, Ranjoy Sena kills 20… this will never end. How long should I sponsor them… and why?"

Then he gets distracted again as he thinks of Chhote Thakur's death. Chhote Thakur was found half drowned in the pond that was dug a few years ago and beside which he used to sit at every afternoon. When brought home, it was detected that he had suffered a cerebral attack and lost his ability to speak. But the doctor, who came from Ara, advised to keep him at the *haveli*, as the hospital was too far away. While being shifted to the main *haveli* from the outhouse quarter he built, Chhote Thakur moaned, as though he wanted to say something that no one could understand. The next day, in the early afternoon, he was found dead in the first floor room, his eyes wide open and almost coming out of the sockets, the tongue stuck out in a way as though someone strangled him, though his neck bore no mark of pressure.

"It's something bizarre," said the doctor who again came from Ara. "If you want you can send his body for postmortem. But I am sure they will find nothing, though it is not natural death."

"What do you mean?" asked Maya, the illusion.

"He was scared, terrified… after sighting something… living or whatever… and that is the reason," answered the doctor.

"What do you mean by living or?"

"That's bizarre… I saw another man dying like this, and it's up to you to believe it or not… the villagers said he was killed by a ghost who, they said, had killed three others before that man. All of them died in the same fashion… just like this," concluded the doctor and looked back at the dead.

The doctor's words had tremendous effect on everybody, and all together, they decided to leave the *haveli*, except an old servant Gitram, who had vowed to die there. Maya claimed she did not believe in ghosts, but for her son's sake, she too decided not to visit the *haveli* ever again. Gradually, Harry almost forgot the village, though he carried on funding Bisheshwar Singh. But his wife, the Illusion, again prodded him to action. One evening, when he told her how Ganguly, his long-time associate, had broken the labourer's resistance in the Gurgaon unit by getting two of them killed, she reacted furiously, "You have murdered labourers of our factory. That's ghastly."

Harry was irritated and asked, "If we can try to kill Mahendra Chamar, why not a ruffian labourer?"

She looked at him strangely and said softly, "The Chamar broke our family, while the labourers belong to our extended family. And you have failed to kill that Chamar. You have proved that you are not a real man."

And that is why he is here, on the fields in a remote area of Bihar, spending time with the criminals and roosting under the shadow of a tree. He laughs in disgrace. He remembers that once, looking the lion atop the gate of the *haveli*, he told his uncle that he would change his destiny. He decided to protect the lion king from being maimed, but forgot everything later on, allowing the king to turn into a broken pieces of marble. That probably turned into the last anathema for the family. "But what could I do to stop all these that has deigned me to the level of a warlord?" he ponders in resignation to his fate.

Then, deep inside his heart, he broods over his lost dreams of shaping up into a modern person without feudal taints, into a modern industrialist. Soon, sitting like a broken man, he decides to tell his wife that Puraina is a closed chapter for him, that it is not possible for him to gift her tuft of that Chamar's hair, and for that he is even prepared to sign a divorce paper.

The decision soon turns into determination and pacifies his mind. He gets up while wondering where Pran has vanished. He turns back, and as he moves towards the pond, he finds Pran, awkwardly busy at a distance with a girl, evidently a Harijan. When Pran comes back, he shouts, "This is not done. You were with a Harijan girl."

"I am sorry," Pran Kumar mutters without caring.

"I will tell your chief."

"He won't trust you," Pran smirks.

"Won't trust me? Do you know who I am! My name is Hari Pratap Singh."

Pran looks at him in disbelief, then turns apologetic and says repeatedly that he will not repeat it ever in his life.

"Forget it. Would you like to have a bath?" Harry asks casually as he looks at the water of the pond.

Pran turns his head towards the pond and a moment later, a puzzling smirk develops on his lips, which he wipes off before turning towards Harry to say, "Let's go for a dip."

Harry jumps into the water, but Pran does not follow him. He takes his crowbar, sits on the land at the brink of the pond and calls Harry in a worrying tone. When Harry swims back to him, his feet on sludge, Pran points his finger towards the other side of the pond and asks, "Who're they?"

Harry turns his head to scour the other side where he sees, across the shimmering water, nothing but green trees, slabs of stones and a pillar-like structure standing out like a monument of the past that people have long forgotten. The next moment, he feels something very heavy hitting his head; in tremendous shock, light goes off from his eyes and the world slips away, felling him like a tree while his heart stops forever.

Pran looks on at his sinking body and at the last bubbles in the water that has turned light reddish, while muttering to himself, "Chief will come to know? Chief will only know that you have died in an accident, crushing your head against a stone, while bathing."

23

Glimpses of the Future (1999–2000)

AS SUNDER Besra sees Lillian coming through the muddy path that has turned slippery after a shower, he turns edgy as he does not know how to broach the topic before her. He did not know, until this morning, that Karma had married her, though without any witness or formality, and they have a son who is being raised by one Agnes and her husband. But now that he knows it, he feels a bit worried.

Is she a happy woman, he wonders as he sees her pink face and fair hands, one of which is holding a big black umbrella and the other the front part of her sari to protect it from being sullied. Within a few minutes from now, she will definitely be crestfallen as she will come to know that Karma desires to die not in this room, but out there, either under the shadow of a thick tree in the jungle, or by the side of the River Koel, or somewhere in a distant valley.

She went out in the morning after she had come to know that one of those two Harijans arrested from nearby area for stealing a cycle was killed in the night in police custody. She went to the town to mobilize concerned people. "This Yadav officer-in-charge is worse than the upper caste officers," she told Sunder before leaving. He closes his eyes and tries to hear her footsteps, wondering whether in states like Bihar a concerned citizens' forum will develop someday, as it has developed in Andhra to see things neither from the Naxalite's nor from the state's point of view, but from humanitarian angle. It has come to his mind only today, after realizing how Lillian is fighting for the rights of the people.

He looks back at the cottage where Karma waits for him, by now ready to leave. Then he reclines against a tree and waits as he is sure that the erstwhile Sister will stop by him. Today, for hours he has deliberated with Karma on so many issues, without knowing that things would take such a complicated turn.

"Why are you standing here?" Lillian asks him as she comes close.

He opens his eyes. "To cool my head."

"Oh God! Why?"

He looks at her, and realizes she has deep green eyes. "You will also lose your cool if I tell you," he mutters as he wonders about her age. 45? 50? 55? Anything is possible.

She turns serious and asks, "What happened?"

He feels satisfied, for he has created an impression of graveness, thus enabling him to be on the point. "He wants to leave," Sunder reveals, pointing his finger to the cottage.

Lillian looks at him curiously, turns her head to look at the cottage, and again turns at him. "Who?" she asks in disbelief, and then utters carefully, as though the words are difficult to pronounce, "Do you mean Karma?"

He nods helplessly, and the sentiment he betrays is genuine. "I tried to convince him that this is sheer madness… but he insists." He lowers his eyes, waits for Lillian to say something, but as he hears nothing from her, he adds, as though to fill the gloomy, uncanny void, "I think I shouldn't have come here."

He waits, his eyes on the ground where an ant is trying to carry home an insect much bigger than its size, but is not finding a way through the puddles; it calls to his mind his own life, his own deeds, his endless endeavour to reach a country of happiness that is eluding him since his childhood. He waits, expecting Lillian to say something so that the conversation can follow, but when even after a long pause she does not utter a single word, he looks up to see her face. He finds her staring blankly between two trees, one against which he was reclining minutes back and the other at a little distance. He waits, his eyes to the other side, and only when he feels that silence is building a wall between them, he says, "I have failed to convince him. Now you see whether you can."

She flinches, and turns at him. "Where does he want to go?"

"We have decided to set out to find Comrade Mahendra."

"Comrade Mahendra! But… is he alive?"

"We don't know," he confesses. "Probably not. But how can we leave him like that? If the father of a family goes missing… don't the sons and daughters try to find him out? If an organization doesn't make attempt to find the lost father of it… then the whole movement is doomed."

Lillian looks at him with wonder in her sad eyes, and nods.

"Comrade Karma, at least, made attempts to rectify some mistakes," Sunder says again. "When he saw that police officer had left his job to join a TB centre… "

"I know. He now runs it which was established by his late wife Dr Rani."

"Yes. Then Karma took up the issue and compelled the leaders to exonerate Comrade Mahendra's name. Then he spoke to Comrade Shankar. Finally, his statue was installed at Puraina by MCO boys. They did it to show that Comrade Mahendra was their man. He was not. Still, as a gesture that was great. But we have to make efforts to know what has happened to him."

"That's great," Lillian mutters vaguely.

"While trying to know about him, we may work for establishing people's right over the jungles. Comrade Karma feels we should work to prepare ground for a future mass movement. Something like what one man, Dhananjoy Basu Mallik. is planning to launch…"

"I know," Lillian cuts him short. "A people's movement to protect the jungle and its inhabitants, including the aborigines. But where will be your base?"

"Not settled yet," Sunder shakes his head. "It will depend on the exact nature of our work. But we will try to be close, so that either you can visit us or we can come to you."

She smiles sadly, but does not say anything.

The minutes pass; a gaggle of geese go by them silently like a group of monks; a sparrow flits about them, as though to entice them to talk. Sunder looks down as he remembers the ant again, and finds it dragging its feet through the water without giving up the load. It has reached a point from where, if it goes straight a few inches, it will reach the trunk of the tree. He looks on at it, as he has nothing else to do. He does not dare to speak, for the wall of silence between them has turned too thick. But when the ant finally reaches the trunk, liberated from its woes, he turns to her.

She too looks up and mumbles, "Let's go."

Sunder does not move, but says something in a way as though he is bound to put forward further explanations, "He says he is scared of nights now. This is strange. All through our life we have moved during the night only."

"He told you?" Lillian sounds resigned.

"Yes. He feels it means his soul is dying fast. And he has this bizarre idea that if he goes out then his soul will be rejuvenated and… when he will die his soul will be alive in me if I work along with him. I don't know what it means."

"I know," Lillian smiles a rather sad but poignant smile as her face betrays her emotion. "The world is ruled by magic, and nothing is impossible."

Sunder looks at her curiously and a glow appears in his dark face. He asks, "You believe in that?"

"We know very little," Lillian replies seriously, trying to overcome her initial shock. "But we don't know that we know so little." She stops suddenly and her face betrays her concern as she looks again at the cottage. "Will he be able to live outside?"

"I don't know; but he insists. He says he wants to die in the fields, if not with a bullet in his chest, at least with fresh air."

"When are you leaving?"

"He insists today."

"For where?" Lillian seems to have regained herself.

"If you allow," Sunder says uncertainly, "I will first take him to Mathaburu where the hills are worshipped on the first day of our new year, which is the first day of the month of Magha, in the middle of January. A thousand feet and you are on the roof of the hill. Mostly we, the Santhals, sacrifice there pigeons, hens, and goats, and we dance when the blood of the sacrifices flows down the hill…"

Lillian feels shocked as she hears the last few words; but soon a chord deep within her heart starts playing to a tune of life that has flown down to the modern age without losing its root hidden in thousands of years of past, from a time when civilizations were yet to be born, when the tribes and the nature ruled the world and mankind vented its animal energy only against the animals, not against cohabitants. The man standing next to her, she tells herself, represents that age, though in modern times, he has turned into a rebel, not without reason. They have lost their jungles, their hunts, their hearth and home, their primordial pleasure, their tradition, even the abodes of their gods as civilization has felled the 'sacred' trees. She rebukes herself for her disgust, and asks, "Any particular reason for taking him there?"

Sunder shakes his head. "We should not have faith in what people say… that you get a new lease of life if you offer a sacrifice there. But the place itself is lively."

Lillian nods as she realizes the tribal comrade of her husband is hoping against hope, exposing shades of his mind before her. "Where is that place?" she asks and folds the umbrella.

"You go down from Dalma hills… eastward and you reach there. Once my father took us there. I was five or six-year old. Soon after that, my father went missing and I started hawking in the trains. I went there twice in those days. Then I was in the movement and after that in jail for years."

Lillian stands still in a way as though she was turning into a statue, her jaws tightened and her teeth biting her lower lip.

"He wants to die while working," Sunder adds uncertainly, looking at the ground from where the ant passed through, and his eyes catch a maimed grasshopper at a distance trying to fly, though it cannot stand in balance.

Suddenly, she starts smiling as she remembers what she told Nidhi, the young woman who came to meet Karma, just last afternoon while explaining her relation with Karma—'love is the most powerful magic the world knows of'. When she will come again to collect material on the story of a Naxalite and a nun, she will tell her that the statement has to be amended slightly.

"Why are you smiling, Lillian*ji*?" Sunder asks nervously.

Lillian looks at him and asks, without wiping the smile, "You believe in magic?"

Sunder feels intrigued, and just manages to wave his hand through the air to make a gesture that shows the positive uncertainty of his mind.

"You know the most powerful magic the world knows is that of love," she says, her tone normal though her eyes are shining with droplets of tears that cannot be noticed. "It is the force that has driven the world. God's love for man. Man and woman's love. Love between a mother and a child. But the strongest is an individual's love for the mankind." For a moment, she turns towards the hut, and then looks straight at Sunder to say, "I have never supported your means, for guns can turn against anyone and even the oppressed may turn into an oppressor. We have seen it in Russia, in China. But you would not join parliamentary democracy to fight in a meaningful way…"

Suddenly, Sunder interrupts her in a way as though he has been compelled to come out of his shell after being hurt unnecessarily, "Sister, neither the gun nor the Parliament is an end by itself. Those are means to serve the people, to uplift the poor and the depressed. Your parliament is a failure and that is why even after five decades of independence, the country is ruled by money and mafia, with no concern for the common man, for poverty, hunger, diseases, deaths." As Lillian looks on, her eyebrows slightly furrowed, Sunder continues, "There is no guarantee that guns will abolish those. True. But all the means can be tried, even your rotten parliamentary democracy, to further the cause of the downtrodden, to serve the majority, not from the up to down, but from the bottom, from the runt up to the lower middle class."

When Sunder stops after his sudden outburst, Lillian nods rather uncertainly. Sunder is one who reserves the right to criticize his own organization, but will not tolerate it if it comes from an outsider, she understands. "Maybe," she tells him, "I, however, feel that you are walking towards apocalypse, though the fault does not lie entirely with you. It will be a never-ending war… Whatever, I was going to tell you something different. I was going to tell you that though I am sceptical of your means, I have always respected your cause. Today that respect has grown many more times." Her voice almost chokes, and her eyes turn wet, though she tries very hard to overcome her emotion. She starts walking towards the cottage using the umbrella as a sort of a walking stick, her steps heavy and slow.

Sunder follows her without making any attempt to console her, for he knows it is futile, and even frivolous; but as they reach the doorstep of the cottage, he conveys his last words, "I will leave after a couple of hours from now. He wants to come with me. Would you not try to persuade him to…"

"Take him along," she cuts him short and with her left hand holds one of the bamboo pillars that support the tiled roof. "He must die the way he wants to," she mumbles in a way as though she will never be able to vent her feelings in words again, and hides her face against her arm.

AS THE afternoon sun follows its dharma and provides him heat and light, Shyamlal sits quietly on a slab, facing the hill of the spirits, and wonders about Comrade Mahendra. He feels repentant for he never showed respect to that man when he was active in Kalipura as a Maoist; he was reluctant at the beginning, for he failed to share the dream, and then he turned indifferent to the man as he realized he was having illicit relation with Bijuriya, his wife. But the day the police surrounded the village and he saw the Naxalites preparing to fight them, he was overwhelmed by the courage of conviction of the man and his followers. He still remembers the night vividly even after almost two decades; he remembers asking Comrade Sunder whether Mahendra would not surrender, and his answer, "He will fight. He will die. He told me to surrender."

A dog comes running down from the village and darts towards the hill of the spirits, leaving Shyamlal to wonder whether it has noticed a jackal, who once took over this Kalipura. "But the dogs will not let them enter again," Shyamlal tells himself and looks back at the village with immense satisfaction. Then he again thinks about the past and ruminates over the days he spent with Mahendra when he could not even remember who he was and said strange things.

"You will create a new world. A world where everybody is equal, where love rules and hate has no place."

Shyamlal nods, sitting alone on the slab, and mutters, "*Jakhni samay aabe, takhni samay hame batabe.* (Whenever time comes, one understands.)"

When he came back to Kalipura, as directed by Mahendra and found Bijuriya, he realized that it was time for doing new things and he conveyed to Bijuriya what Mahendra had told him. "He told me to strive for creating a new world, but I don't know what it means."

Bijuriya heaved a deep sigh and said, "Our world was Kalipura. We were so poor. Still it was safe, good and beautiful. But it was destroyed."

Shyamlal heard her in rapt attention and then drew his conclusion, "Our world was Kalipura. Right. So, we can create a new world by rebuilding it. We can make it a world where everybody will be equal, where love will rule."

Shyamlal gets up and looking towards the road through which an overloaded heavy truck is passing slowly, he mutters to himself, "How happy the Comrade would have been had he seen this new Kalipura."

He walks a few steps towards the road, and sees a jeep appearing from the left, a police jeep that slows down in the middle and then stops, and alighting from it, a constable starts walking towards the village. Without any reaction, Shyamlal looks on at the man as he covers half a kilometre, the distance between the road and where Shyamlal is standing. He is not scared of the police anymore, for he knows that even the policemen, like ghosts and demons, turn powerless against righteous men, who are not scared.

Standing still, he rather wonders that if the village has to expand further, it should go towards the road; but the question is how to clear the grovels and sand that heat up so much in summer that even insects do not live there. "Do we have any right to force the government to help us in reclaiming this land," he wonders seriously.

When the constable comes closer, Shyamlal realizes that it is Ratneshwar, a Backward Kurmi from a nearby village.

Since Shyamlal has rebuilt Kalipura, the constables talk to him with respect, for he has become a name in the whole area, a name that signifies man's capability. The constable comes closer, and after exchange of initial pleasantries, tells him, "Our officers have sent me to talk to you and I have got you here alone; that's good."

Shyamlal keeps looking at Ratneshwar, feigning he has no clue and compelling the constable to reveal further details, "The department has suddenly started a search for Comrade Mahendra Chamar. One big shot called Harry Singh has gone missing. He went missing three years back... but it has suddenly come up. God knows why. They told me that 18 years ago, Mahendra Chamar was arrested from this village. Is it true?"

"True. At that time that road was being built," Shyamlal points his finger to the road. "The police came through that. Then they took ten more years to complete the road."

"You knew him?"

"Yes."

"Can you tell me what happened afterwards?" the constable sees a ray of hope. "They say he was taken out from a jail and then became active again."

Shyamlal smiles wryly. "They know up to that. I know more. He left the Maoists to see through the stones…"

"See through stones?" the constable seems terribly confused. "How could one see through a stone?"

"I believe he wanted to see through his destiny… or through the essential truth of life that should not be seen, known or contemplated even," Shyamlal says thoughtfully, his eyes contorted. "It turned his brain and he went mad. But all through his life, he knew a mantra… you have right to work, but no right to its outcome… and that mantra helped him overcome even his imbecility, his amnesia, all his miseries and turned him into a god."

"What mantra?" the constable asks suddenly, as though to get a clue of some tantra thesis that the locals believe can overcome even death.

"I told you. If you can do your work without expectation, then you too will become a god like him."

"I don't understand," the constable utters helplessly.

"Neither do I," Shyamlal says while looking at the shadow of the constable that is long and faint. "Otherwise, I too would have become a god."

The constable looks askance at him, takes off his cap and scratches his head, and then nods for unknown reasons. "They say he was a dangerous man," he says in a lighter tone, without understanding why he says so.

Shyamlal does not utter anything, and for a while, both of them look at the road as the sun moves down the horizon and the birds begin to fly back to their nests. A raven starts cawing from a tree, a dog comes and sits near them, and the cloudlets floating through the sky turn reddish, as though to remind the world that colours pervade a meaningful existence only at the beginning and at the end.

After a while, the constable asks, "Do you know whether he is alive or dead?"

Shyamlal thinks for a while, shakes his head and whispers, "I told you he has turned into a god. Gods never die."

The constable again looks askance at him, and then nods slowly, for reasons best known to him.